Alberix the Celt

Book 2

Hear Again the Lark

The dim night is quiet and its darkness covers all Gallia; the sun in the bed of the sea, and the moon silvering the crests. But the willow, whose harp hung silent in the winter, now gives forth its melody. Hush! Listen! The world is alive again.
Bardic epigram

Albert Noyer

Books by Albert Noyer

The Saint's Day Deaths (2000)
The Secundus Papyrus (2003)
The Cybelene Conspiracy (2005)
The Ghosts of Glorieta / A Fr. Jake Mystery (2011)
One for the Money, Two for the Sluice / A Fr. Jake Mystery (2013)
Death at Pergamum (2013) Kindle
Unholy Sepulcher (2014) Kindle
Alberix the Celt, Book 1: Weep the Long Sorrow (2014)
The Kashat Deception (2015) Kindle

Alberix the Celt

Book 2: *Hear Again the Lark*

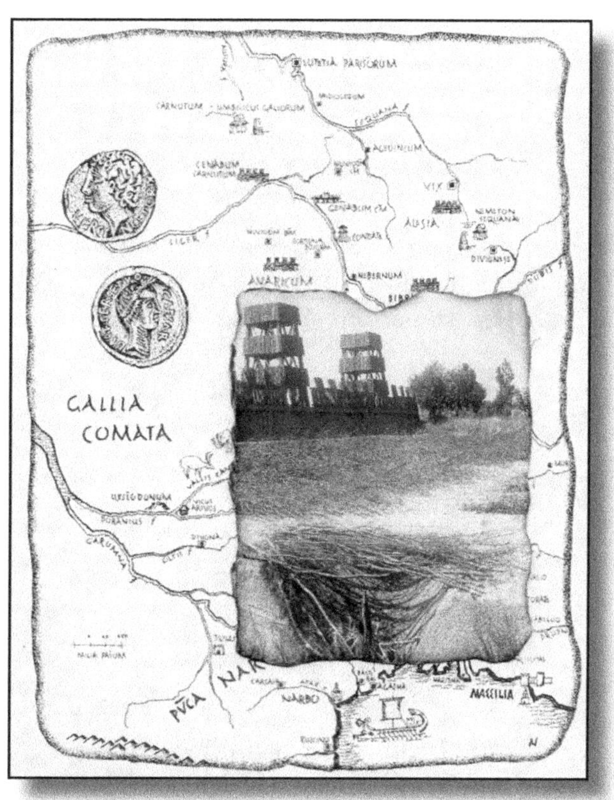

Albert Noyer

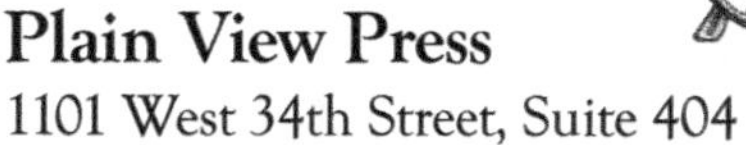

Plain View Press
1101 West 34th Street, Suite 404

http://plainviewpress.net
Austin, TX 78705

ISBN: 978-1-63210-011-5
Library of Congress Control Number: 2015933849

Cover art: Photograph of Caesar's defenses at Alesia (Archeodome, France); map of central Gaul; druidic calendar medallion by Albert Noyer.
Cover Layout by Pam Knight

We Find Healing In Existing Reality
Plain View Press is a 36-year-old issue-based literary publishing house. Our books result from artistic collaboration between writers, artists, and editors. Over the years we have become a far-flung community of activists whose energies bring humanitarian enlightenment and hope to individuals and communities grappling with the major issues of our time—peace, justice, the environment, education and gender. This is a humane and highly creative group of people committed to art and social change. The poems, stories, essays, non-fiction explorations of major issues are significant evidence that despite the relentless violence of our time, there is hope and there is art to show the human face of it.

With gratitude to our critique group:
Jennifer, Carolyn, Roy
and the close collaboration of
John Zarro

BRITAÑIA IÆ
TRISESIS f
CANTUCI
BIBROCI
DUROVERNA
FRETUM CATICUM
GESORIACUM ITIUS PORTUS
NEMETOCENIS
SCALDIS f
SAMAROBRIVA
SAMRA f
OCEANUS BRITAÑICUS
ROTOMAGUS
GAL
DUROCOR
MATRNA
OCCINA f
SEQUANA f
LUTETIA PARISIORUM
METIOSEDUM
CASTRA ROSCI
CARNUTUM NEMETUM
ACEDINCUM
OCENABUM
VIA
SEQUANA f
LIGER f
NOVIODÚM
ALESIA NEMETO SEQUA
CONDEVNUM
SALIMIS
VIGERNA f
CARIS f
AVARICUM
NOVIODÚM ADD
BIBR
DECETIA
VENETICÆ IÚS
MA
OCEANUS ATLANTICUS
CARANTONIUS f
GERGOVIA
VIERIUI f
ELAVER f
MON
UXELLODÚM
DURANIUS f
ULTIS f
CESENA
GARUMNA f
PROVINCIA
NEMA
TOLOSA
NARBO
CARCASO
SI GA
PYRENÆI MONTES
HISPANIÆ
PARS
BARCINO

Ηψπεφβυφεα
Celtic Europe / 58 B.C.E
RHENUS
PONS CAESARIS
ARDUINA SILVA
GERMANIA PARS
HERCYNIA SILVA
LIA
TOKUM
DIVIONE
VESUNTIO
CABILONUM
RHENUS
IURA MONS
AVENTIA
ALPES MONTES
AQUILEIA
OCTODURUS
GALLIA
MARE ADRIATICUM
VIENADRM
CISALPINA
PADUS
RAVENA
NARBONENSIS
APENINUS MONTES
ARELAT
AQUAE SEXTAE
SINUS LIGUSTICUS
ARNUS
ITALIA
MASSILIA
NUS
LLICUS
MARE INTERNUM
ROMA
OSTIA
Author Reconstruction

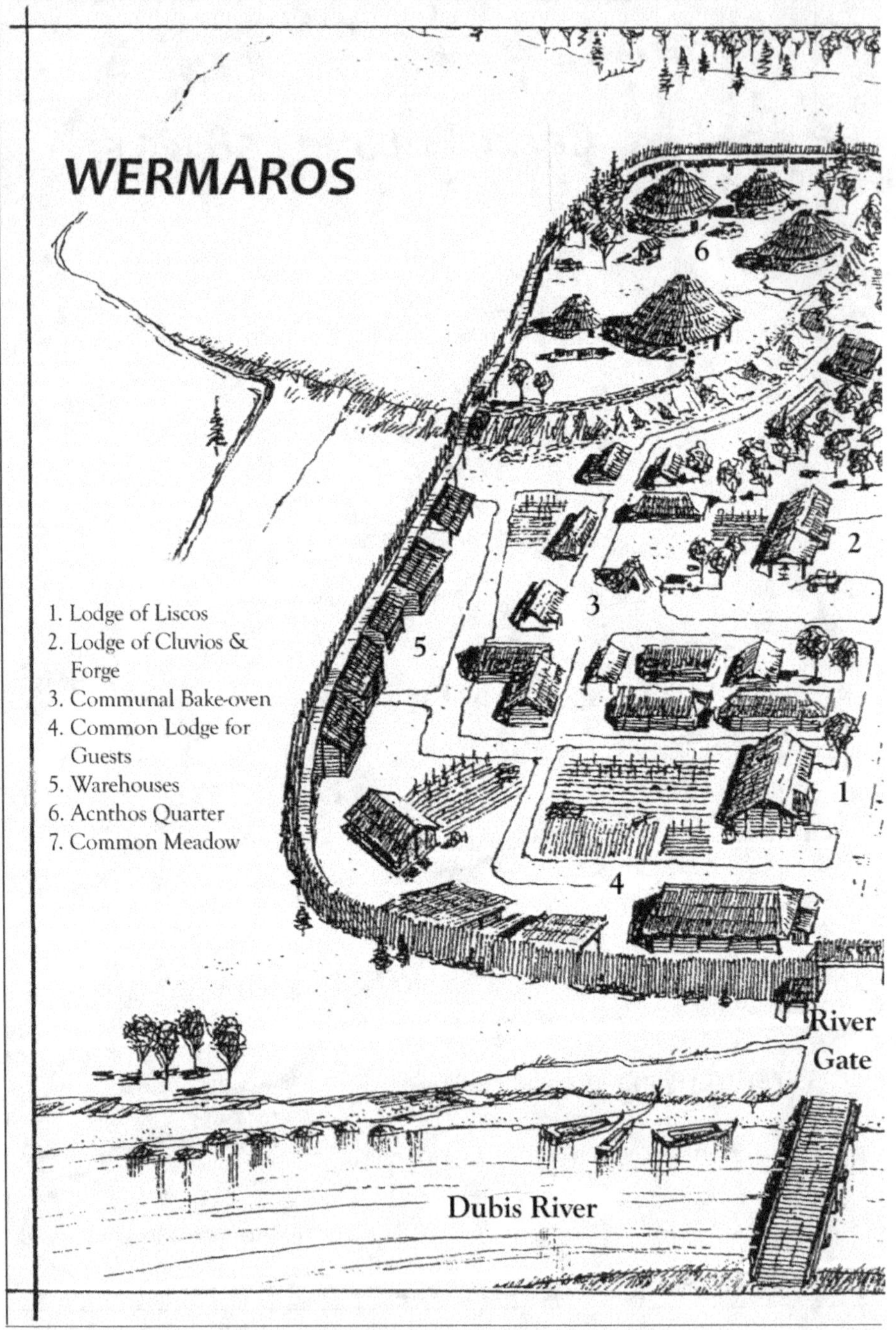

1. Lodge of Liscos
2. Lodge of Cluvios &
   Forge
3. Communal Bake-oven
4. Common Lodge for
   Guests
5. Warehouses
6. Acnthos Quarter
7. Common Meadow

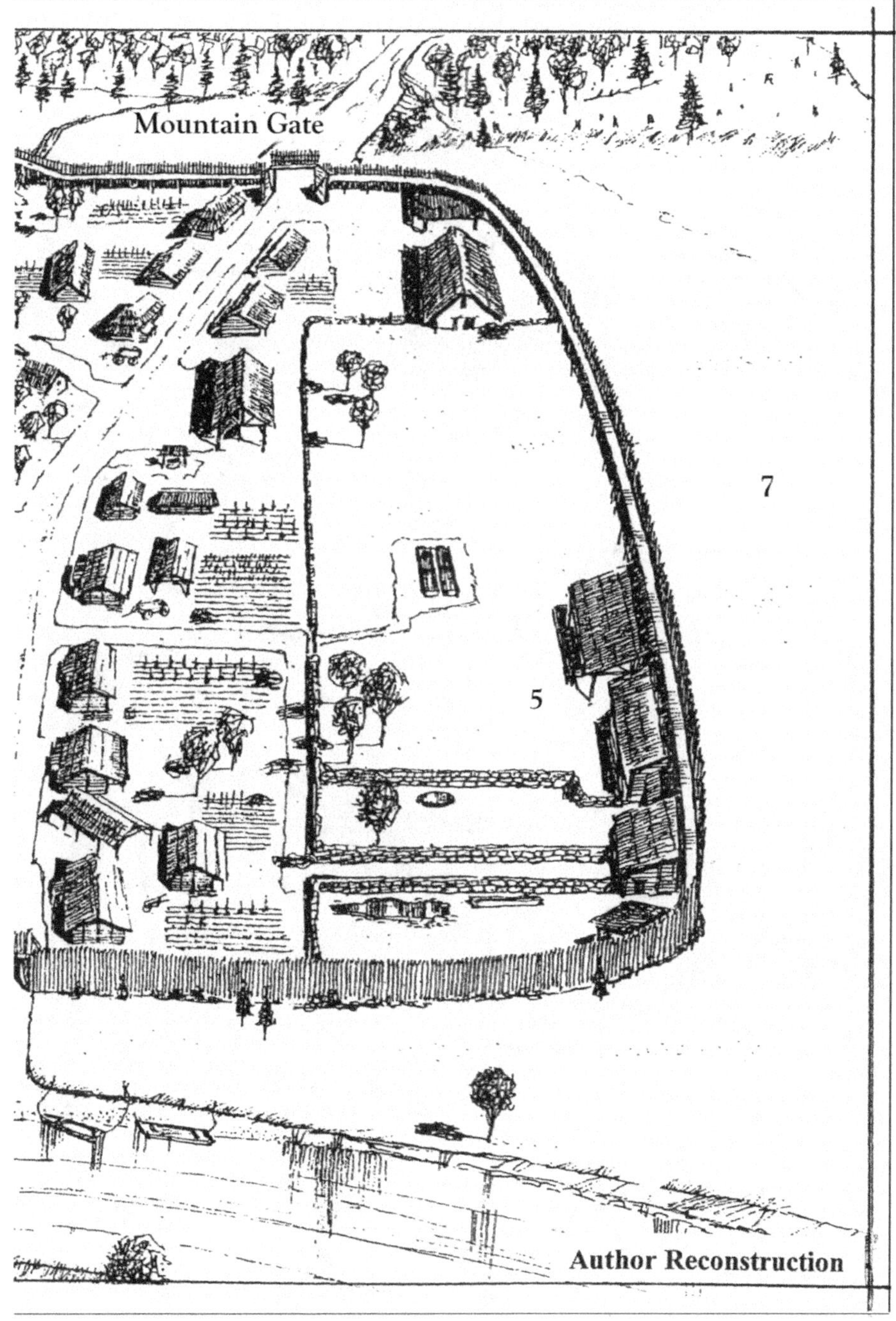

Mountain Gate
7
5
Author Reconstruction

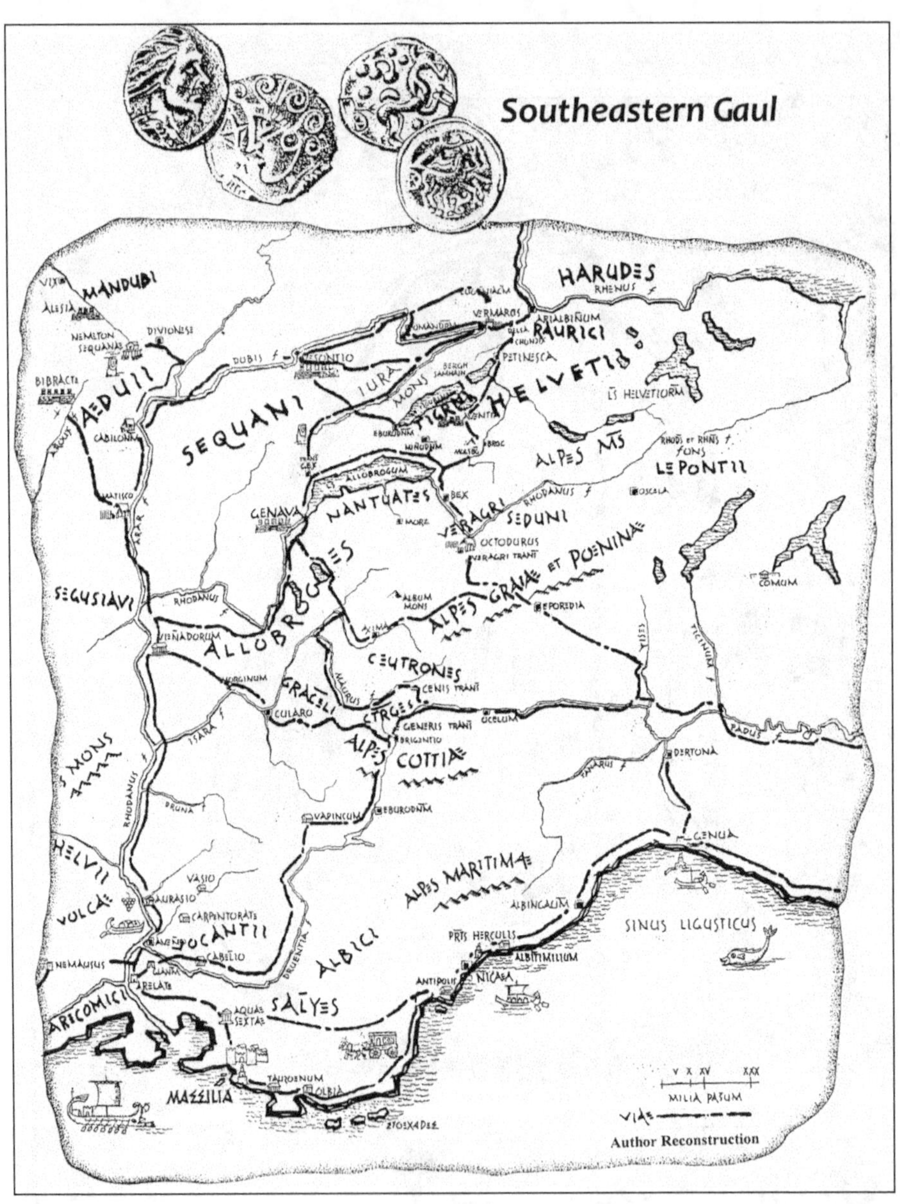

Southeastern Gaul
HARUDES
RHENUS
MANDUBI
VIX
ALESIA
NEMETON
SEQUANAS
DIVIONESE
RAURICI
ARIALBINUM
VESONTIO
VERMAROS
AUGUSTA
CHUNOS
PETINESCA
DUBIS f
BIBRACTA
AEDUI
SEQUANI
IURA MONS
TIGRIS
HELVETIB
LS HELVETIORM
BERGH
SAMMAIN
EBURODNM
MINODNM
CABILONM
AUGINTO
KRAIB BROC
ALPES MTS
RHODS et RHNS f
FONS
LE PONTII
MATISCO
TRANS
GEN
ALLOBROGUM
GENAVA
NANTUATES
BEX
RHODANUS f
VERAGRI
SEDUNI
OSCALA
MORE
OCTODURUS
VERAGRI TRANT
ALBUM
MONS
ALPES GRAIAE et POENINA
EPOREDIA
COMUM
SEGUSIAVI
RHODANUS
VIENADORUM
ALLOBROGES
AXIMA
VISUS
TICINUM
CEUTRONES
NAURUS f
GRAECELI
OGINUM
STRGES
CENIS TRANT
OCELUM
PADUS
CULARO
ISARA f
GENERIS TRANT
ALPES COTTIAE
BRIGANTIO
MONS
RHODANUS f
DERTONA
TINARUS f
DRUNA
VAPINCUM
EBURODNM
GENUA
HELVII
VASIO
ALPES MARITIMAE
VOLCAE
AURASIO
ALBINCAIM
SINUS LIGUSTICUS
CARPENTORATE
VOCANTII
CABELIO
PRTS HERCULIS
ALBITIMILIUM
GLANUM
NEMAUSUS
DRUENTIA f
ALBICI
ANTIPOLIS
NICASA
ARELATE
ARECOMICI
AQUAS
SEXTAE
SALYES
V X XV   XXX
MILIA PASUM
TAUROENUM
MASSILIA
OLBIA
STOIXADES
VIAE
Author Reconstruction

Central Gaul
LUTETIA PARISORUM
CARNUTUM · UMBILICUS GALLORUM
MEDIOSEDUM
SEQUANA
AGEDINCUM
CENABUM CARNUTUM
NOVIODM SM
VIX
GENABUM CTM
NEMETON SEQUANAS
ALESIA
NOVIODM BM
CONDATE
LIGER f
CORTONA BOIORM
DIVIONESE
NEBERNUM
AVARICUM
BIBRACTE
GALLIA COMATA
CABILONM
CAMPUS TUMULORUM
ELAVER f
MATESCO
ARAR f
DUBIS f
ARA D DUMIAS
GERGOVIA
VIENNA
MOR
VALLIS CAVERNARUM
VESARIUS f
RHODANUS
ISARA f
UXELODUNUM
ARGENTIOS
VICUS ARIVOS
DRUNA
DURANIUS f
DIVONA
GARUMNA
OLTIS f
VACIO
CEBENNA MONS
ARARO CARPENTORATE
TRANS
AVENNO
TARNIS f
ALBA
CABELLIO
MILIA PASUM
ALBICA
NEMAUSUS
GLANM
DRUEN
TOLOSA
ARELATE
NARBONENSIS
LUTEVA
AE SEXTAS
CARCASS
ARAT
MARITIMA
PVCA
NARBO
AGATHA
MASSILIA
RUSCINO
Author Reconstruction
VERCINGETORIX
DICT PERPETVO CAESAR

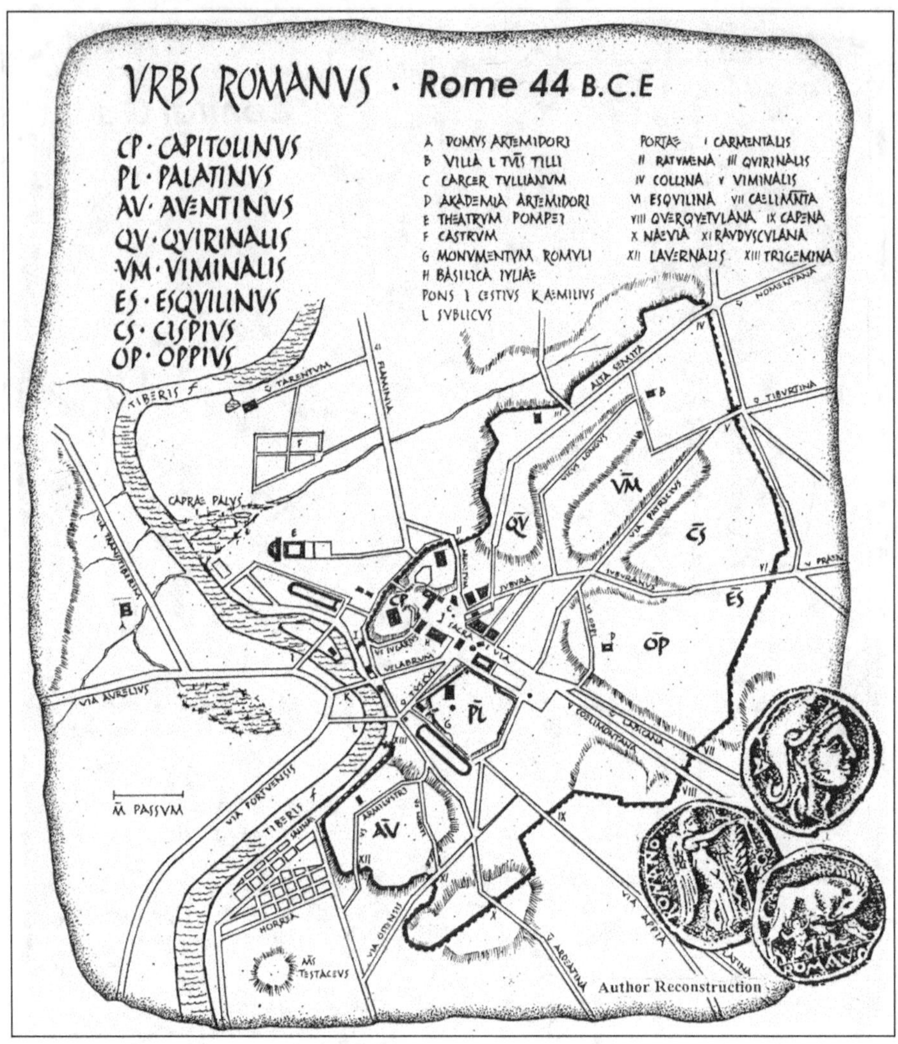
VRBS ROMANVS · Rome 44 B.C.E
CP · CAPITOLINVS
PL · PALATINVS
AV · AVENTINVS
QV · QVIRINALIS
VM · VIMINALIS
ES · ESQVILINVS
CS · CISPIVS
OP · OPPIVS
A DOMVS ARTEMIDORI
B VILLA L TVLLI TILLI
C CARCER TVLLIANVM
D AKADEMIA ARTEMIDORI
E THEATRVM POMPEI
F CASTRVM
G MONVMENTVM ROMVLI
H BASILICA IVLIAE
PONS I CESTIVS K AEMILIVS
L SVBLICVS
PORTAE I CARMENTALIS
II RATVMENA III QVIRINALIS
IV COLLINA V VIMINALIS
VI ESQVILINA VII CAELIMANTA
VIII QVERQVETVLANA IX CAPENA
X NAEVIA XI RAVDVSCVLANA
XII LAVERNALIS XIII TRIGEMINA
TIBERIS
TARENTVM
FLAMINIA
ALTA SEMITA
NOMENTANA
TIBVRTINA
CAPRAE PALVS
VIA LONGVS
VM
VIA PATRICVS
CS
QV
PRAENESTINA
IVERRA
ES
VIA AVRELIVS
OP
VIA COLLINONTANA
PL
VIA FORTVENSIS
TIBERIS
AV
VIA ARDEATINA
VIA APPIA
LATINA
M PASSVM
HORREA
VIA OSTIENSIS
AES TESTACEVS
Author Reconstruction

PROLOGUE

Julius Caesar's political successes at Rome earn him the governorship of two provinces and three legions. Although absent for five years in Gaul, he has effectively run the government with Pompey and Crassus. After Caesar's Helvetian victory, he remained in Gaul to defeat Ariovistus, a German king encroaching on Celtic lands. Yet as Gallic tribes resent the continued presence of Roman legions, talk of rebellion flares and culminates in a massacre of Roman merchants.

A leader emerges in the person of Vercingetorix. With ten legions now under his command, Caesar has established a string of camps, pacified a few Gallic tribes and defeated others, but an attack on Vercingetorix's stronghold at Gergovia fails. Rather than follow up his victory, the king retreats to the fortress of Alesia. Caesar surrounds the stronghold with deadly ground obstacles and twin defensive walls. When a huge Gallic relief army arrives, Romans narrowly defeat the massed warriors. Vercingetorix surrenders and is sent to Rome for execution.

Despite Caesar's victories, much of the Senate is hostile to his reforms and declares him a public enemy. Entering Italy to attack Pompey, Caesar wins a devastating four-year civil war, but is assassinated in 44 B.C.E. Gaul rapidly recovers and prospers under a Pax Romana.

Historical Persons

CELTS

Ambiorix – Chieftain of the Belgic Senone tribe
Brennos – Celtic leader whose warriors occupied Rome in 390 BCE
Casticos – Overchief of the Sequani tribe
Cingetorix – Treveri leader loyal to Rome
Cotuatos – Leader of Carnutes
Critognatos – Arvernian nobleman
Diviciacos – Pro-Roman Aeduan, brother of Dumnorix
Divico – Leader of Tigurini who defeated a Roman army in 105BCE
Dumnorix – Anti-Roman Aeduan, co-conspirator with Casticos and
              Dumnorix
Gobinnatio – Uncle of Vercingetorix
Lucterios – Cadurcan conspirator with Vercingetorix
Nammeios – Helvetian noble
Orgetorix – Helvetian noble, co-conspirator with Casticos and Dumnorix
Vercingetorix – Arvernian noble, leader of the revolt of 52BCE

GERMAN

Ariovistos – king who crossed the Rhine River to settle his tribe in Sequani
           territory

ROMAN

Gaius Julius Caesar – Commander of all Roman legions
Licinius Crassus – Officer under Caesar
Marcus Antonius – Legate under Caesar
Munatius Plancus – Legate under Caesar
Titus Labienus – Legate under Caesar

Main Characters in Order of Appearance

Alberix	22. Helvetian in Roman auxiliary unit.
Triccos	34. Druid associate of Ollam Fodla
Ollam Fodla	46. Druid from Inisfail (Ireland)
Sabia	28. Fodla's druidess, twin to Moira
*Vercingetorix	20. Arverni chieftain elected to lead the revolt of 52 BCE
*Lucterios	30 Cadurci leader who joins Vercingetorix
Simonides	31. Friend of Alberix, secretary to Caesar
Briga	37. Mother of Alberix
Apsa	24. Wife of Alberix
Cluvios	42. Crafter uncle of Alberix
Arvos	36. Foreman of the charcoal makers
Dirona	37. Twin sisiter of Briga
Liscos	61. Sequani husband of Dirona
*Gaius Julius Caesar	47. Commander of Roman legions in Gaul
Lucius Velcanius	42. First Centurion, Legio X Gemina
Marcus Marius	31. Roman engineer of Optio rank
Moira	28. Fodla's druidess, twin to Sabia
Psen-Ammon	49. Egyptian Chief Surgeon of Legion X
*Gaius Fufius Cita	40. Roman merchant at Cenabum
S. Tullius Tilius	41. Caesar's former Quaestor, now a Senator
Artemidoros	32. Greek friend of Caesar's at Rome
Epanactos	30. Liscos's bodyguard at Wermaros
Natanius	29. Judean adventurer

*Actual Persons

Glossary of Major Places

Present-day Switzerland
Arialbinnum — Basel   Brigantium — Bregenz
Ben Samain — Chasseral   Epomanduorum — Mandeure
Wermaros — fictionalized St. Ursanne in the western Jura Mountains
            on the Doubs River

France
Saumis — Saumur   Masillia — Marseilles
Durocortorum — Reims   Portus Itius — Boulogne
Cenabum — Orléans   Genabum — Gien
Carnutum — Chartres   Vesontio — Besançon
Agedincum — Sens   Cabillonum — Châlon-sur-Saône
Gergovia — Gergovie   Noviodunum — Nevers
Avaricum — Bourges   Viennadunum — Vienne
Bibracte — Mont Beuvray   Alesia — Alise Ste. Reine

Italy
Ravenna — Ravenna   Augusta Rauricorum — Augst
Abellinum — Avellino

Rivers
Renos/Rhenus — Rhine   Rodanos/Rhone — Rhone
Arar — Saône   Elaver — Allier
Veserius — Vézère   Liger — Loire
Dubis — Doubs

September — December / 53 B.C.E.

Cold is the nightfall; the valley freezes, a crop of frost is on the fields,
a white covering like salt. When will we hear the lark again?

CHAPTER I

A low September sun reflected brilliant rays off the Liger River—a golden glare that shone into my eyes. I shifted position on the barge's seat to screen myself in the shadow of wine casks stored at the bow, yet in moments the river's glittering brightness again blinded me. The current of a new waterway had angled the barge away from the Liger's center. Our helmsman cursed another river god as he struggled to steer the prow back into midstream.

I leaned farther behind the casks, inhaling a smell of barrel wood and new wine that mingled with evening cook-fire smoke that blued late afternoon air. After propping my back against a cask, I took out a small statue of Taranis, our Celtic sky god. As I fingered eight spokes on a wheel at the god's side, I recalled the strange images I had dreamed on the road to the legion camp at Durocortorum. *Each spoke represented people in my life. Three were empty then the name of Vercingetorix appeared as an answer to uncle Cluvios's plea for me to find a leader among my own people—*A muffled cough interrupted my musing. I glanced at Triccos, a silent druid who had found me at the camp. *Does Triccos believe this Wheel represents our present and reincarnated lives? Most Celts in legion auxiliary units no longer have faith in our gods. Jupiter replaced Taranis in the minds of warriors who believe that gods give victories—and those of the Romani are more powerful.*

At age twenty-two the light blond hair of Alberix's adolescence had darkened to the color of honey-sweetened beer. A recent moustache was full, yet the growth could not conceal a sensitive mouth. Blue eyes reflected an in-born curiosity about the world and a desire to know things beyond a traditional spoke of his destiny.

"Mithra's Bull! Keep her from drifting star-side!" an oarsman shouted out.

The helmsman glowered at him, yet leaned hard on the rudder to correct the vessel's direction.

Mithra. I wasn't surprised to hear a Celt refer to a Persian god. My engineer friend, Marcus Marius, told me that many legionaries were followers of this foreign deity. Part of the cult's appeal was that any member, including slaves, could advance in rank through seven stages to become head of a local cell.

I sat up when harsh caws from a gathering of ravens protested the barge's passage. Evening air had cooled. Now a fish odor from the river overlaid the sweetness of grassy fields along the shore.

Triccos finally spoke, "We arrive in Saumis at the setting of Belenos."

These were the first wods the druid had spoken since morning. "What will we see?" I asked, but he ignored me to scan the shoreline without explaining.

I knew Triccos from seeing him in my village of Wermaros. The middle-aged druid's intense gray eyes were set under dark eyebrows that cut straight across his forehead. A smear of black moustache angled around a tight mouth that never seemed to relax or smile. He was a pupil of Ollam Fodla, who had been taught by Dividiac, my druid uncle. After Fodla arrived and had been in our village awhile, he convinced the chieftain, Liscos, to join a growing rebellion against Romani. The "Shorthairs," as most Celts called them, had been summoned to help his tribe of Sequani against advances on their territory by Ariovistos, a Germani king. Julius Caesar had defeated him, yet most tribes now opposed the humiliating legion presence in Gallia. Before that, Caesar had defeated a vast migration of Helvetii. Gallic attacks against his legions had been unsuccessful, but an Arvernian king named Vercingetorix was rumored to be uniting the tribes in a common effort to drive out the invaders.

I thought back to Durocortorum. *How did Triccos find me at the legion camp with a message from uncle Cluvios to meet with Ollam Fodla? The request sounded incredible since I knew my uncle was barely tolerant of the druid's harangues. My enlistment in Caesar's auxilia had displeased Cluvios, who wanted me to find a leader among our own people. I had agreed to go with Triccos and meet Vercingetorix.*

I pulled my cloak tightly around my shoulders in a freshening breeze, yet my recollection of hearing about Vercingetorix affected me as much as the wind. *Why does this Arvernian king cling to my mind? He shares the vision of peace that was a goal of my father, yet could he become powerful enough to unite the tribes? My Romani friend, Lucius, talks about a brotherhood of men, but do Celts need strangers to teach this? Must men go through a tempering, like the metals in Cluvios's forge?*

My right leg cramped. I struggled to stand up, holding onto the casks for support. The sun had lowered enough to touch the tops of trees on an island where the river divided. On the left bank, a clearing in the forest revealed a settlement of huts crowded behind a flimsy sapling palisade.

Triccos pointed ashore. "Saumis. The barge will not stop. Prepare to leap off."

The helmsman shouted an order, then leaned hard on the rudder to swing the vessel toward a wharf jutting from the bank. I tucked the figure of Taranis into my belt pouch and followed Triccos to the railing. When oars were pulled in, we leapt onto rotting boards, as the barge glided on toward the mouth of the Liger. In half a moon period wine shipped from Massilia and exchanged for tin ore, would rest in the storerooms of Briton merchants.

On the wharf Triccos kicked at a pair of scavenging hounds. Both slunk back, snarling at him. I looked toward the huts. *Saumis is no fortress, only a palisade that any warrior could kick over with one foot, and that cluster of miserable homes. Is this the hub of a rebellion against Julius Caesar?* "What tribe lives here?" I asked Triccos, as he strode toward an open gate. "Where are the villagers?"

The druid again avoided an answer and followed a weed-overgrown pathway past mud- and-wattle dwellings that bordered either side. Triccos had reached the rear gate when he turned to tell me, "There will be the birth of an equinox child at sunrise."

"I was brought here to see a baby? What about Fodla's message about meeting Vercingetorix?" Triccos ignored me again to open a rusted, iron gate latch.

Outside the palisade a road led into dense woods beyond a clearing. After the druid motioned me onto a smaller side-trail, he noted the sun's position and increased his stride to reach our destination before the orange disc vanished behind trees. As the trail wound through an oak forest, a dank coolness became an uncomfortable chill.

Darkening shadows seemed ominous. I closed a hand over the hilt of my sword and recalled a cave where Fodla had forced Dividiac to bring out my father's preserved head and swear vengeance against Germani who had killed him.

I was unsure about how far we walked, but when I made out points of light glimmering among black tree trunks, it was too dark to see clearly. Three bonfires came into view, whose leaping flames won a contest against the last glow of Belenos's fire. Orange sparks swirled up to mingle with a vast sparkle of white stars overhead. I assumed that people standing around the circles of light and heat were absent villagers.

Beyond the fires a cave-like form with stone sides was roofed over by a massive capstone. In the dimness the structure resembled the overturned hull of a sea-going galley. To lift those immense stones would require a tackle-block beyond any I had seen.

"Who built that?" I whispered to Triccos.

He shrugged ignorance of their origin. "An ancient tribe of giants? What man now alive knows? Dolmens are scattered across the face of Gallia."

"Dolmens? What is their purpose?"

"Many stand free. Others are hidden in the Earth Mother's womb and contain signs of death, not life. Some are within a circle of stone pillars, yet all possess a mystical power…" Triccos pulled at his moustache as if revealing too much. "Remain here until I return for you."

Squatting on the ground to be less noticeable to those around the fires, I tightened my cloak to conserve body heat. I surmised the place was a *nemeton*, a sacred shrine, yet couldn't imagine to which god it was dedicated. As the firelight's orange tint played on the dolmen walls, I began to feel uncomfortably warm. Perspiration glazed my forehead. Triccos had spoken the truth: a mystical force overspread the clearing like a tangible tent of power engulfing the dolmen's stones. No streaks of light remained above a western horizon—colors of day had no place here. The void was a realm of Cernunnos, lord of darkness, given over to half-seen mysteries that were manifest in the fragile interval between dusk and dark. Druids taught it was a tenuous period when spirits in the Other-world could cross over to our Now-world.

❧

I started awake at a touch on my shoulder and had reached for my sword before realizing it was Triccos. I slept and dreamed that a band of giants had trapped me behind Dividiac's equinox *menhir* at Wermaros.

"Follow." The druid was a shadow that spoke.

I struggled up, trying to estimate how long I had been asleep by bonfire embers, now only reddened coals. *I must have slept through half the night.* Smoke-laced air was deathly quiet: no buzz of cicadas or chirp of ground insects sounded in the clearing. I looked toward the dolmen. A pale green radiance lighted the interior, yet none spilled out beyond the entrance. Ahead of me, Triccos was silhouetted against the opening. As I followed the druid inside, the force I experienced became oppressive. Although no torches were visible, the interior of a rock chamber was warm and bathed in the colored light. I was aware of a pleasant sweet smell, like a mixture of pine resin and cooking herbs. When I followed Triccos to the rear of the room, I felt mild disorientation: men standing around an altar slab appeared as distorted reflections in a brass mirror.

A nude woman lay on a stone altar, her abdomen swollen in pregnancy. Sculptures of the *Matronae*, our three Mother Goddesses, were on the altar front. A central goddess suckled an infant at her breast. Staring at the woman, I shut out the Now-world beyond this luminous space. A flux permeated my body, seeping in as did molten metal that filled Cluvios's clay molds. My legs were anvil-heavy. Struggling to remain standing, I scarcely heard my name when it was called.

"Alberix, son of Alrix, you honor us."

I looked up and recognized Ollam Fodla. The older druid wore a white tunic bound at the waist with a belt whose silver buckle was the form of a grinning human skull. Silver threads along the hem of his tunic caught the greenish light. A torc of twisted gold wires around his neck gleamed enough to give a slight color to his sallow complexion.

Although disoriented, I noticed a warrior to the druid's right. The man was younger and taller than my army friend, Lucius. He had a Celt's moustache, yet his shorter hair almost made him look Romani. Without realizing why I stammered out his name, "Ver...Vercingetorix!"

Puzzled, he studied me. "Have we met before, Alberix?"

"No, but somehow I knew who you were—" I faltered at further responding.

The pregnant woman on the altar slab abruptly moaned and clutched her abdomen.

Two nearby midwives rushed to help. The oldest crone examined the woman's vagina, and then nervously glanced toward Fodla. "Druid, th...the contractions begin, yet there is no...no sign of a child,"

"Good, it is too soon. The solstice infant must be born when the bright rays of Belenos first appear."

After the midwives stepped away, I recognized the woman as Sabia, one of Fodla's druidesses I had seen at Wermaros.

The dark druid raised his hands to address the assembled warriors. "A sacrificial child will be born of a virgin druidess at a time when night and day are in balance. It is a sign to return all Gallia to harmony. With this sacrifice our war against the Romani cannot fail. Belenos and Caturix will assure victory to our cause."

Through heaviness in my mind, I realized that the druid meant to murder the newborn as an offering to our sun and war gods!

Fodla continued to persuade the warriors. "We have a leader in Vercingetorix. Through him the Romani will be defeated as easily as extinguished cook-fire ashes are scattered to the wind."

I glanced around at a twenty or so of men. They were not villagers as I had thought. All were dressed as high-born nobles, chiefs perhaps. Some wore the colorful checkered clothing of *vergobrets*, Celtic judges. When I recognized Epanactos among them—Liscos's bodyguard—I realized that there had been no message from Cluvios. Fodla wanted to use my father's name and reputation, to enlist Raurici warriors for his rebellion and obtain information from me about the strength of Caesar's legions.

Sabia moaned in pain once again. When Triccos whispered to Fodla, the druid looked toward the dolmen's entrance. Faint light indicated a first flush of dawn. The auspicious moment had arrived.

Fodla stood in front of Sabia with one hand held over her abdomen, then motioned Triccos to a tripod table with the other. He began a druidic chant that called on the Three Divine Mothers and other of our goddesses to assist in the birth—Sequana, Epona and Morrigan. At its ending, Fodla swayed as in a trance, his body rigid, eyes staring at Sabia. He stretched out his hands to touch her forehead and abdomen. When his thin fingers made contact, he uttered a short, shrill command. My neck chilled into a rash of gooseflesh at the supernatural cry.

Incredibly, Sabia's rigid body slowly rose from the altar until it was two hand-spans above the stone slab. Fodla's preternatural power held the woman suspended in space!

Warriors instinctively grasped for sword hilts, but froze in motion: an occult force that an iron blade could not harm confronted the superstitious men.

Fodla intoned in a voice without emotion, "Let the birth occur."

The midwives watched for contractions while examining Sabia's abdomen. Practiced fingers gently probed for the infant's position in the birth canal.

A younger *obstetrix* turned to Fodla. "The woman is unready. Her waters have not broken out."

Triccos!" he screamed. "The birth must begin!"

White-faced, the younger druid selected a clay vial from the table and tried to slip a potion between Sabia's lips.

A crone muttered, "He tries to force the child."

"Old woman, " Triccos hissed, "massage her stomach with vinegar and *hammelis*. It will go badly with you if the child is not born at the moment Belenos appears."

Sabia hovered over the altar as the two druids watched the midwife anoint her body with the astringents, then Triccos handed the younger *obstetrix* a thin-bladed knife.

"Release her waters!"

Trembling, she gestured for a companion to ease Sabia's thighs further apart.

I looked away, gagging at a sour smell of vinegar and suppressing an urge to vomit. I was aware of the midwives bending over Sabia, trying to induce labor, then a pungent odor brought me to full consciousness.

When the fetal membrane ruptured; both midwives frantically tried to stop a flow of blood with linen towels. I slipped down to the base of the wall, felt its rough stone on my back, yet what chilled me to the marrow was Sabia's final scream of anguish.

When I looked up again, a shaft of weak sunlight illuminated the underside of the stone roof. I slowly rose up to see the warriors standing rigid, as if bewitched. When the light reached the altar, Sabia again lay on the stone slab, where a pool of gore spread around her upper legs. The druidess's lifeless eyes stared at a rosy ceiling, her lips still parted as if again mouthing her now-silent death-scream.

Outside, Belenos cleared the top of a neighboring granite equinox *menhir*. A shaft of blinding brightness pierced the entrance to the dolmen and threw light on the body of a stillborn infant that Ollam Fodla held up to the blessing of an uncaring sun god.

❧

That afternoon Fodla called an assembly of the shaken noblemen. He told them that the inauspicious beginning of the revolt was Sabia's fault. The druidess had lied to him. She betrayed his trust and not been a virgin. He assured the men that once the legionaries of Caesar fell to the long-swords of Vercingetorix's Gallic army, there would be hundreds of victory sacrifices to Belenos.

Epanactos avoided me, but Vercingetorix had caught my interest. I watched the king move among the other warriors with a self-confidence that reminded me of Caesar. I saw no alternations of flattery and threats in the Arvernian's manner. How many of our people's leaders were like him? The gathering of Gallic nobles in the dolmen had been impressive and their resolve for war irreversible. *I've seen men in the auxiliae who joined only to loot enemies after a battle. They seem so distant now—those legions, Caesar, even Lucius, who spoke of a brotherhood of men. Am I his brother? Caesar's? That of slaves or even Germani? And yet if Vercingetorix unites our tribes, I would be another enemy sword against Lucius and Caesar—no longer their brother.*

I knew a decision that I hoped might be avoided might face me as soon as the next new moon of Cantios. I would be forced to choose between my Celtic tribe and an alien nation among which I had made good friends.

Triccos interrupted my troubled thoughts. "Young warrior you look distressed. Is it the birth? The child is happy in the Land of the Eternally Young."

"Without knowing what this world is like?"

He ignored my hostility to ask, "You will join us then?"

I grasped his sleeve. "Triccos, what really happened in there?"

"You saw a ritual for tribal chieftains who will lead us against Caesar."

"I mean the illusions. Dividiac administered herbs to cure the body, not to distort a mind. What *hallucinari* did Ollam Fodla use?"

Triccos pulled his arm away to snarl, "Our cause justifies it to mold the rebellion!"

"Where is Fodla now?"

His expression brightened. "The Master prepares to join Vercingetorix as advisor to the revolt. After our victory, he will be appointed arch-druid at Carnutum."

I felt disgusted at this senseless death of an infant. "So the eagle asks the advice of a ferret?" I held up my figure of Taranis. "Triccos, if your rebellion is a true spoke on the Wheel of Life, it will succeed without your dark master."

"Well said!" a voice behind me approved. "We need warriors who understand the ways of our gods."

Triccos stammered his name, "Luc...Lucterios. This is Alberix from a Raurici clan."

"Yes. His father's deeds at Arialbinnum are known even among my Cadurci. Are you with us, young warrior?"

"You should know that my father became a man of peace."

Lucterios countered, "Yet would he have kept swords sheathed against Romani? To keep Gallia free, we need the collaboration of all the tribes."

I quoted a crafter's cynical maxim, "Can an anvil hang by a thread?"

He half-smiled in admitting, "Your tongue indeed is silver. True, Celtic tribes fight each other and weaken alliances, but they had no common over-chief. Now they have a leader in Vercingetorix."

"Lucterios, what did Vercingetorix think happened in there? Or you, for that matter?"

When the Cadurcan did not reply, I told both men, "I'm going back. Deceit and illusion are not a way to begin such an undertaking."

The nobleman's parting remark lost its friendly tone. "Return to inform Caesar about Vercingetorix and the tribal leaders you saw. Tell him that his legionaries soon will wear their winter capes as burial shrouds!"

⊷⊶

That night I slept wrapped in my cloak in woods outside Saumis. No one came to challenge my decision to leave—those warrior-chieftains surely were drinking heavily to celebrate future victories.

By mid-morning I was able to hail and board an upstream barge loaded with sacks of wheat for Cenabum. During the slow river voyage, I again took out my statue of Taranis. After pondering the Wheel of Destiny at the god's side, I felt certain that one of the spokes once again would lead me to Vercingetorix.

CHAPTER II

After I returned to Cenabum I reported the bizarre birth ritual to a tribune at Lucius Roscius's praetorian tent in the camp of Legio XIV. The officer dismissed the incident as another barbarian superstition, and told me I would not receive winter leave. On orders from Roscius I was to report to the house of a Gaius Fufius Cita, one of the merchants in Cenabum who sold supplies to the legions. This unexpected assignment disappointed me. I wanted to return to the familiar slopes of my Jurassos Mountains for the winter, to purge my spirit of the horror I saw in the dolmen and again be with Apsa and my mother.

Cenabum, I was to learn, is a stronghold of the Carnutes, a tribe that holds special honor among Celts. Carnutum, one of the most sacred *nemetons*, is in their lands. Druids call this shrine "The Navel of Gallia." Each summer an arch-druid presides over an Assembly of Men of the Oak, who arrive from all over the country. Inside a temple set in the midst of a vast grove of sacred oak trees, the wooden image of a Virgin-about-to-give-birth watches over a deep well. Votive offerings bubble down to gods in its dark water. As at the shrine of Sequana, these deities cure sickness, receive petitions, and divine the future through oracles that shrine druids interpret.

The next day, Antiochus, a somewhat arrogant middle-aged Greek slave, came to take me to Fufius Cita's residence. As he led the way up a street that climbed away from riverfront wharves, I noticed only a few oldsters sunning themselves in front of lodges. Had all the younger men gone off to join the rebellion? I had been told that Cita was a friend of Julius Caesar's, who gave him contracts to supply *quaestors* with rations and merchandise that our field legions needed.

A lower town congested with barges and wagons bringing supplies to the northern tribes from lands to the south, gradually gave way to larger log-and-thatch lodges crowded together along the hillside's slope. I felt uneasy seeing so many older residents. Scarred and maimed former-warriors who survived battles now herded pigs rooting under their pens. Suspicious crones with dried-apple faces sat on benches and squinted at us as we passed. Antiochus ignored them all to stride ahead.

Abruptly, lodges gave way to an open quarter set aside for foreign merchants. Most windows were shuttered, but I recalled that Romani ate an early afternoon supper.

Antiochus increased his stride and brought me to a good-sized lodge at the end of a street near the town's north wall. Freshly cut logs squared into beams were stacked near the front entrance. Sawhorses and wood chips indicated carpentry, yet no workers were there. I wondered if this was one of the days that Romani considered *Nefasti*—unlucky—and did not work? One lodge alteration was complete: hinged doors with temple-like columns on each side had replaced the simple entryway to Celtic lodges.

At the entrance Antiochus rapped on a bronze lion's head knocker, then called out in Greek. A dusky, almond-eyed woman opened the door. Neither one spoke. I was left waiting in a common room being re-modeled into what Lucius had described as an atrium in a villa. A rectangular opening in the roof was centered above a square basin cemented to act as a pool. A tile band of sea creature images decorated the rim.

Fumbling at curtains toward the far end of the atrium alerted me. A sleek dog of hunting breed slipped through the opening and bounded at me. The animal seemed friendly, yet my hand went to my belt knife handle.

As suddenly, a bland-faced man with black-dyed, lusterless hair appeared and called to the dog. "*Desine*, Pllyn! Stay!"

Fufius Cita squinted at me a moment with small eyes set under an expanse of brow. He seemed to wonder if he remembered my name, then extended a hand. "Alberix, isn't it? You came from the camp of Roscius."

"Yes, Sir, the Legate sent me."

"Of course..." He waved a hand at the unfinished room. "Excuse the work, but my wife must have her atrium. If she can't go to Roma just now, then Roma must come to her." Cita put a fatherly arm around my shoulder and led me past the empty pool. "Son, I suppose it was a surprise for you to be asked here. Of course it was, but I have still another for you." He smiled when pulling back the curtain to a room where meals were served. "I think you know this young historian."

"Simonides!" I exclaimed.

My Greek friend stood from the table to grasp my arm. "*Salutatio*, Alberix! When did we last see each other?"

I was pleased yet concerned to find him rather gaunt-looking and unwell. "At Wermaros, remember? I left you right after I heard about the ambush of Legio Fourteen."

"I had brought Caesar to your village so he could work on his manuscript about the Gallic war." I recalled how Simonides had criticized Caesars' exaggerated reports of victories to the authorities at Roma. "Are you getting along any better with the commander?"

Nervous, Cita parried my question. "Talk about that later. You must try some of my new wine. I planted Falernian vines in the south near Aurasio and they've begun to bear. Alberix, sit at the table with us to dine. I'm Equestrian class and we don't recline like some Patricians."

Antiochus brought a tray with flagons of wine and water, then mixed portions in three cups. Simonides and I nodded approval. Sunny slopes in the Rodanos valley had given a full body to his vintage.

Simonides put down his cup. "Alberix, if you're wondering why I'm here—"

Again Cita cut him short. "His father, Nikomaxos, is a friend of mine. A quarter of the goods sold in Gallia have Niko's signet on them."

"And druids object to that," Simonides pointed out. "You and my father are changing a way of life for many Gallic tribes."

"Surely, son, not by adding to their chieftain's profits?" Cita retorted, then looked at me. "Did you know that this young 'Herodotus' went to Carnutum to observe the arch-druid's equinox rites? Got himself roughed up by guards. Alberix, you're also here because of another friend. Do you recall Junius Balbus?"

I was surprised to hear the merchant's name. "I do. Years ago I escaped from the Sugumbri with his help. How do you know him?"

"Merchants may seem like ants, each concerned with his own kernel of wheat, but we do work together—"

The curtain opened; a woman entered the dining room, smiling. "Gaius, I see our Celtic guest is here."

"Indeed, my dear." Cita rose to escort her to a chair across from us. "Alberix, this is my wife, Cosnia."

"Cosnia Fabia Albina Cita." she reminded him.

Her husband laughed. "Alberix, You may have noted that we Romans have several names. The custom seems to amuse barbarians...and even more than a few of us."

Barbarians like us? I had not seen a Romani woman who was not a camp follower and stood to return her greeting. Cosnia was sharp-featured, with dark hair parted in the center. Two side braids pulled into a knot at the back gave her a Germanic look. Her woolen tunic was belted at the waist. She had chosen gold earrings, bracelets, and finger rings as ornaments.

Cosnia clapped her hands. "Antiochus has the first course ready."

When the Greek slave brought in stuffed squid garnished with boiled eggs and rissole balls, Simonides noted, "*Kalamarakia!*"

"Indeed," Cita boasted. "The delicacy is brought upriver from the Great Ocean."

Antiochus cut a portion of squid, spooned a spicy sauce over it, and placed the seafood on his master's plate. After tasting a bite, Cita beamed, "Excellent! Fine creamy sauce. Tell Seriane it's perfect."

Cosnia nodded at Antiochus. "You may serve us. Alberix, if you have not eaten squid, this is filled with calf brains cooked in a caraway sauce. The fried rissoles are minced porpoise seasoned with mint."

What is minced por-puse? I wondered while trying one of the rissoles. *Fish, oily, and the mint stronger than I expected.* The calf-brain stuffing was seasoned more heavily than I liked.

Simonides had been studying my reaction to the food. "Romans can't seem to leave food in its natural state. Everything is drenched in honey, vinegar, cumin. For example, try that *garum.*"

"A quite salty fish sauce," Cita explained, tossed Pllyn a rissole, then settled back in his chair. He picked at his food until he questioned me in an agitated voice, "My Gallic atrium workers left a few days ago. Were...were things quiet downriver?"

I stalled by glancing at Simonides. "It's all right to talk, Alberix. Fufius is in partnership with Caesar and you might remember something profitable he can use."

Cita masked his annoyance. "Don't mind him. He's been as snappish as Cerberus ever since the commander dismissed him as secretary."

I hadn't heard this. "You're no longer with Caesar? What happened *this* time?"

Simonides finished a portion of rissole before admitting, "Seems he didn't like my criticism of a few exaggerations he was telling Senators. I know that legates try to make themselves shine like parade shields in their reports, but what Caesar writes can make him enemies at Roma. Envy was not the least of the ills that Pandora left us."

"Envy?" Cita repeated as a reprimand. "Now that Aulus Hurtius plies his stylus at your old field desk, isn't there more than a touch of that vice in you?"

Simonides remained defiant. "I admit to it, but now Hurtius will allow Caesar to believe that Gallia is his pet rooster."

Even Cita chuckled at the pun on Gallia; that name and Latin for rooster—*gallus*—were almost identical. He turned to me, "Alberix, in all seriousness, I would like to know how loud this rooster might crow. You came from Saumis. What did you see there?"

How much should I tell him? "Sir, a druid I knew at Wermaros, arranged an equinox birth ritual to persuade a group of tribal chiefs to join his...his rumored sedition."

"Gallic chiefs?" Concerned now, Cita pushed away his plate. "Did you hear names?"

"Lucterios was one, and Vercingetorix, a king I had heard about."

"Yes, the Arvernian, but he's not a king. Was anyone there from the Carnutes, our local tribe?"

"Sir, I don't know. I left that same day."

Cita threw a final rissole to the hound, then wiped his fingers on a napkin. "We needn't concern ourselves about Vercingetorix. He's had a falling out with his uncle and by now may have been banished from Gergovia. We do have a pair of troublemakers here at Cenabum. Gutuater and Conetodumnus—"

Cosnia corrected him. "Con<u>con</u>netodumnus, dear."

He thanked her and shook his head. "Jupiter, what barbarian names! Those two tried to stir up the warehouse freedmen against us."

Simonides took out his wax tablet and stylus. "Alberix, what was this birth ritual you mentioned?"

"A child was born to Sabia, one of Ollam Fodla's twin druidesses. You may remember her."

"Yes, I saw Sabia at Wermaros. Go on."

"Fodla tried to force the infant to come with the equinox sunrise, but it was still-born. Sabia died."

Cita put down his wine goblet to scoff, "Not a good omen for their sedition!"

When Antiochus appeared at the doorway with a next course, Cosnia motioned him away. "We're not quite ready. I shall clap for you." She turned to me. "That poor woman. I have heard that some druids still offer human sacrifices to their gods."

"Fodla would have killed the child. As it was, he offered the dead infant for a blessing from Belenos."

Cita asked, "This was at Saumis you say?"

"A small settlement downriver from here."

"I know the place and it's not fit for pigs to piss in!" Cita touched his wife's arm. "Sorry, my dear, but these Galli have me in a state. If they start trouble there's no telling when your atrium may be finished."

"Fufius, that really isn't important. If this is their way of preparing for war, then perhaps we should think of going back to Aurasio."

Cita toyed with his meat knife without responding. An awkward silence continued until Cosnia clapped for Antiochus to serve the second course.

When he brought a platter of fish to the table, she explained, "Seriane grilled these river trout, but I told her to baste the fish with a sweet-sour plum sauce. There's also mallard ducks braised in a date-mustard sauce. Cucumbers and boiled turnips—"

Impatient, Cita grumbled, "My dear, may we eat? Everything will be delicious."

With the food the merchant lost his sulkiness. As the meal progressed and the Narbonnese wine took effect, even Simonides lost his resentment at being dismissed for insisting that Caesar's reports be accurate. He goaded Cita by detailing the punishment of Acco, a Senone chieftain. The commander had ordered him beheaded as if he were administering Justice in his own province. Ignoring the incident, the merchant described Caesar's traditional mercy to enemies, pointing out that the Greek's own goddess, Athena, meted out terrible punishments when it suited her purpose.

During the duck course, conversation turned to Julius Caesar's family. The Julii claimed to be descended from Venus-Aphrodite and thus blessed by a divinity.

"Blessed?" Simonides scoffed. "Aeschulus says that the gods give a touch of madness to those they love. I've seen Caesar undergo *epilepsia* seizures in his tent. If that's being blessed—"

"Son," Cita advised, "stay with your histories and not medical matters. The moon is responsible for the Sacred Disease. That crystal globe draws moisture to the brain and the commander obviously spent too much time campaigning in the open."

"That's old wives gossip, not a physician's opinion."

Cita threw down his napkin. "Now, Simonides, you're expert at diagnosing illness?"

Under her breath, Cosnia murmured, "Husband, you need a bit of sweetening," then told Antiochus, "We're ready for the dessert course," When a plate of small cakes set on fresh laurel leaves were brought in, she said, "Alberix, these are *mustei*, made with honeyed wine."

The one I tried tasted of cumin, yet it went well with more wine that Cita splashed into my cup. He ate a cake, then wiped his mouth. "Friends, let's put away talk about gods and moons. I need information about this sedition and we're two days away from the nearest legion help. Hades! I feel like a gladiator flat on my back, looking up at a sword pointed at my throat. I'd like to know which way the crowd's thumb will point."

Simonides clapped applause. "Well put, Fufius!"

"This isn't arena amusement!" Cita commented, then took several cakes off the plate and arranged them on the table. "Alberix, let's say Cenabum is here...with Agedincum and six legions over there." He laid a staggered line of four cakes below Cenabum and named them. "Down here is Gergovia, Avaricum, Bibracte, and Alesia. Antiochus!" he shouted. "My dice box."

As we waited, I asked, "Sir, why those four places?"

"Gallic strongholds." Cita raised eyebrows to signal his wife. "Cosnia, my dear..."

She understood his hint for privacy and stood from the table. "I'll supervise washing and storing dishes. Alberix, make our house yours. *Felix somnia*, Simonides."

He thanked her in Greek, "*Efharisto.*" After she left, Simonides touched each of the cakes in turn, then confronted his host. "Fufius, you old rogue! I believe that now you're going to let us in on the real purpose for bringing Alberix here."

Cita filled his wine cup again before answering, "Caesar is not sure how much support an uprising would have and I need information about this Vercingetorix. The Imperator trusts you, Alberix, and only a Celt can move freely in the countryside. With your knowledge of crafting you could easily pass as an artisan." He sipped wine as Antiochus brought in a leather box and two bone cubes.

Simonides remarked in mock drunkenness, "Ah, we'll let Fortuna desh-ide our mutual desh-tinies."

Cita ignored him to show me numerals engraved on each face of one die. "Let's say that each number represents a cake, an *oppidum*, a fortress. So, *unus*, is Cenabum. *Duo* Agedincum, with *tres* the Gergovia of Vercingetorix. *Quattor* is Avaricum. *Quinque*, Bibracte, and let *sex* be Alesia of the Mandubi."

Puzzled, I looked toward Simonides. A knowing grin hovered on his face.

The merchant went on, "I shall disregard one and two. Cenabum and Agedincum are in the north and it's central Gallia that interests me..." He pushed a die toward my hand. "Alberix, if you throw those two numbers, cast again." Splashing a libation onto floor planks, he muttered, "May Mercurius guide your hand."

I felt uneasy, caught in my host's net, yet the wine had served his purpose. I shrugged, tossed the die in the box, and rattled it. Cita licked his lips, staring at the cube as it bounced on the table and rolled to a stop.

"*Tres*, my *Kelt* friend!" Simonides exclaimed. He stood up, tottering, and pushed that cake toward me. "Fortuna sent you to Gergovia of the Arverni. Cita, I'll show Alberix the cot set up for him in my quarters. Bring 'Gergovia' with you to eat," he jested to me.

I thanked Cita and left with Simonides. In his room I put the cake on a table and lay back on a legionary cot. My brain was spinning from the wine as I heard him remark, "Well my *Keltic* duckling, now you know how those mallards we ate felt."

"Trapped, you mean? I suppose your Aesopos has a fable about them?"

"Probably, but I'm too drunk to remember it."

"Can't someone make those dice fall on whatever number they want?"

"Surely, only the gods," he mocked. "Alberix, look on this as a chance to put another spoke on that wheel you always talk about." He handed me a folded vellum sheet. "Here's your travel authorization signed by the camp *praefect*."

I sat up to take it. "Already?"

"Surprise! It's to Gergovia."

"Then Cita knew all along..." My voice trailed off at having been duped.

"Don't worry, *amicus*, I'm going with you."

"You? I thought you were *persona non grata*. Isn't that your Latin for an outcast?"

"By Zeus you are becoming Romanized! Friend, Fufius Cita has decided to get rid of me and you may need the help of a quick-witted *Graecus*. Especially, one who knows something about throwing dice!"

I returned his good-natured taunt. "One Romanized, but perhaps not enough? I...I admit that Vercingetorix has me interested. In a way he reminds me of Caesar."

As he lay back, Simonides scowled disapproval. "So you're thinking of joining him?" When I didn't answer, he said, "Alberix, my people are from a country the Romans conquered and then looted of everything moveable, yet I'm not plotting sedition based on a throw of dice. I don't want to *make* history, just write about it." He turned on his side and faced the wall to end the conversation. "We're both tired and happily drunk. Go to sleep but don't snore too loudly."

❧❦

I awoke at dawn, shivering from cold and an unsettling nightmare. I dreamed that the wooden statue of my clan god, Alar, lay in the forest at Wermaros with its head broken by a falling branch. My skull felt swollen from Cita's wine and I couldn't think clearly enough to understand the dream's meaning. Yet, I realized it could foretell a deadly future for my Alarian clan and the village where I had settled, seven years earlier.

CHAPTER III

Three days before the full moon of the Celtic month of Cantios, a sudden sleet storm at Wermaros stripped trees of their gaudy autumn leaves and sealed the foliage under a slushy rind of white ice granules. Only the black Dubis River, surging around its bend, still displayed autumn leaves in its swirling eddies.

On the morning after the storm, Belenos's veiled rays shown feebly as Briga and Apsa aired out winter furs they had taken from storage chests. Briga's face revealed the strain of caring for Cluvios: small lines had deepened on her forehead and around her mouth. Her lake-blue eyes were in dark-ringed hollows from sleepless vigils at her husband's side. She realized that he would stay inside the lodge during the cold time and dreaded fielding frequent angry confrontations caused by his illness.

Apsa, too, was concerned about Cluvios, but the darkness around her eyes had lessened, as was a stomach-wrenching fear. Her son, Ger, at two-and-a-half years was old enough to be a small companion. She looked forward to the games they played together. Her frail face had filled out to a delicate beauty that made men in the village stare and regret that the woman was a slave from an alien tribe.

Thoughts of Alberix occupied the minds of both women. Briga also looked back on her love-night with Lucius Velcanius, the legion centurion assigned to watch towers that had been negotiated with Licos, the village chieftain. Almost a year ago she had succumbed to frustration and loneliness—Cluvios was too ill to lie with her—and the image of Lucius's lovemaking remained vivid in her mind. It had been soon after the time of her moon-bleeding, so she had not conceived, yet Briga now remembered Lucius with the same sense of separation that she felt for her son, Alberix.

Apsa could ignore most village men but was a victim of awkward attentions by Arvos, the foreman of the charring ovens that provided Wermaros with charcoal. Too often he came to talk with Cluvios about the work—and lick his lips while staring her way with unconcealed lust.

The one consolation that encouraged the two women was that Alberix and Lucius would return from their legions in Gallia and spend the cold season at Wermaros.

Late that morning Arvos loped around a corner of Cluvios's lodge, where the two women were gathering in their furs. He looked at Apsa and muttered an awkward greeting to Briga. A smell of charred wood was strong on the stumpy foreman. The once-bright colors of his checkered trousers were grimy with charcoal dust. Streaks of black remained on his face—he had washed in a hurry that morning.

"Woman, I come to see Cluvios," he told Briga, while glancing around the forge area. "He's not workin' today?"

"My husband is ill and hasn't been at the forge for a twenty of days. May I tell him something for you?"

While Briga replied, Arvos had stared at Apsa like a fox eyeing quail, but turned back to complain, "It's the charrers. They won't cut any more trees after these cloaking's are burned."

"What makes them not wish to do that?"

"Villagers say the forest goddess, Arduinna, is angry because too many trees are bein' felled. They accuse us of destroyin' her forest."

"Yet they want charcoal for cooking fires and implements from my husband's forge."

"*Patrona*, Cluvios should talk to 'em," Arvos mumbled.

Briga balked at his request. "That worry would make my husband feel worse. I shall speak to the men. Apsa will go with me."

"You? Two women?" Arvos eyed them with a scornful smirk. "That would be like a pitcher tryin' to break a stone."

Briga retorted, "Charrer, there is another saying, 'Women are like hornets in their wrath.' Forget not that you are contracted to Cluvios and thus to me as his law-wife."

Arvos paused to reconsider. He had no wish to be stung again—the village girls did that enough with contempt for his short stature, grimy occupation, and their mocking name of *Dubadzo*, "Blackstick'." Realizing that Briga would inherit the forge, when Cluvios died, he doffed his cap and bowed. "As you wish, *patrona*. I'll tell the men you're comin'."

Apsa shuddered as she watched the charrer tramp away toward the mountain gate. "He...he frightens me. "

Briga hugged the young woman's shoulder. "Arvos sees with the eyes of the lonely. Tell Anvalos to bring the cart after our mid-day meal. We'll go up and listen to the men's complaint at that time."

❧❦❧

In a yet-overcast afternoon sky, gray clouds mated with surrounding mountains to obscure both their crests and a weak autumnal sun. As soon as the cart rounded the eastern bend of the Dubis road, patches of bare forest surrounding the charring ovens came into sight. No gray smoke threaded from most of the cone-shaped clay piles, so remnants of the previous day's sleet still mottled the oven mouths. As the cart jostled up the path to the nearest worker huts, Apsa knew that Arduinna was correct: charring could not be an occupation in which Celtic gods took pride. Laborious and grimy, the making of charcoal rendered charrers' faces and lungs a sooty gray that became a permanent dye.

Briga learned about the process when Cluvios had taken her out to watch a burn. In the first step, a circle of horizontal branches was arranged around a central vent hole. Then vertical sticks were placed upright out to the edge. The layers were alternated until a cone-shaped heap slightly more than a man's height was built up. A clay coating applied next "cloaked" the pile and held combustion to a minimum. This assured the production of properly charred sticks, instead of only gray ashes.

In the worker's jargon the process of smearing on the clay was called, "Cloaking the pile." After the clay hardened, the cone was lighted from the top, with the rate of burning controlled by air vents cut into the cloak, and a wicker screen placed on the windward side. As the sticks charred their clay covering collapsed. Workers raked the hot, smoking mass on the ground to assure an even charring of the remaining sticks.

Since the collapse was unpredictable, workers had to be in constant attendance at the cone. After the burned sticks were cooled, broken, and sifted, the charcoal was sacked and carted to the village. Since workers came to resemble an extension of their scorched cargoes, their sooty appearance and forest isolation prompted mocking ridicule among farmers and herders.

Because charcoal was used in cook-fire pits with ease and efficiency, Liscos urged greater production of the fuel, and this had led to the present quarrel. The charring piles rapidly used up trees, and stump-filled clearings extended out more widely with each seasonal cutting. After it became too far to haul back split logs, a new location was found for the ovens. As game disappeared, resentful hunters complained in the village that Arduinna was displeased.

In a half-circle of worker huts, smoke streaked the air from the few lighted cones adjacent to the dwellings. Deer haunches hung from tree branches or were suspended on tripods over oven vent holes, to smoke the venison. A few men tending the cones constantly coughed. When workers sitting in front of their huts saw a cart with two women arrive, they stopped conversing and stood up.

Briga stepped down first. Arvos, a square of damp linen covering his mouth, hurried over. "I explained to the men—"

"Explained why hens come to them instead of cockerels?"

The foreman scowled, but only turned to motion a worker over. The man doffed his hat, mumbling, "Peace to you, Mistress."

Briga quietly rebuked him, "Charrer, you are a free man. What is your name?"

"Me? I'm called Brenn…'Raven'."

Arvos laughed at the apt name, but Briga asked him, "What complaints have you, Brenn? Is it about the cutting of too many forest trees?"

Brenn glanced at the ground and shuffled his feet. "Mistress, they…they say that Arduinna will put a curse on our lodges."

"Villagers believe that?"

"They gossip that your husband is bewitched by Gobann, the forge god."

"Bewitched?" Briga held in her anger at the accusation. "Have villagers forgotten my husband's images of their gods, through which they obtain favors? The iron cauldrons and wheel rims they need. Tools to raise crops? How can these things be evil?"

Brenn hesitated at her reasoning. Arvos glanced at the ground. Neither had experience in reconciling contradictory arguments, each of which made sense in itself.

Briga motioned for Apsa to come and look around at what years of cutting had done to the forest. After a moment, she advised, "The wood could be taken with less scarring to the slopes. The men could begin with dead trees."

Briga agreed and returned to face Arvos. "You will first cut dead trees even if they must be brought from further off. For every tree taken a new seedling must be planted to once again clothe the Earth Mother. Liscos will increase the men's pay and they must alternate between cutting and tending the cones."

Arvos ranted, "Liscos will never consent!"

"Your chieftain *will* agree once I tell him this will fatten his money chest."

Apsa said, "I will set up a shrine to Arduinna at those nearby rocks. Brenn, will you see that fresh boughs decorate her altar each morning?"

"I…I'm only a charrer."

Briga told him, "And important to everyone in Wermaros. You must resume work."

"I will, Mistress."

Briga heard excited babble from the men behind her and knew the crisis was over. Arvos glanced at the workers, then gave grudging approval to Briga's plan. Handled differently, the charrers would have abandoned the ovens: a Celt could not be coerced to do anything he felt displeased any of his many gods.

❧❧

In the days following the arbitration, Arvos brooded in his hut more often than usual. Unmarried, resented as an outsider who had authority over village men, and shunned by girls and women, the foreman withdrew into imaginative erotic relationships that penetrated his mind the way soot soiled his clothing. Apsa and Cluvios dominated his fantasy-life, although the comely face and slim body of the young slave woman easily came first. He realized that Cluvios was dying, the victim of a forge god's displeasure. Might not the deity's wrath extend to a man who supervised the making of charcoal for the forge? Arvos had seen a statue of Gobann at Arialbinnum—a scowling, bearded god who held aloft the tools of his craft. At Ocelum there was a small temple dedicated to Vulcan, the Roman forge god. Celts there offered incense on Vulcan's altar, believing they also honored their own craft-deity in the ritual.

As the charrer nursed his fantasies over too many cups of *cervisa*, he began to ponder how he could please both Gobann and the sky god Taranis with a single bold act.

❧❧

Fifteen nights before the Celtic New Year festival of Samain, Arvos formed a plan. He knew that when Cluvios died the forge would revert to his wife. At Delsa, after the Harude raid, he watched Briga remit the contractual obligations of her husband's *vassos*. She might do the same for him. Freed from indenture, he could leave Wermaros, buy wagons and mules, then hire others to do hauling work for him. He would become a *patronus* himself!

His second burning fantasy was that he could persuade Apsa to go with him.

❧❧

Just before Samain, when winter snow soon would halt charring work, Arvos ordered his men to prepare the final seasonal cloakings. Afterward, he went to Cluvios's lodge at a time that he knew Briga and Apsa would be away at the bake-ovens.

Approaching the lodge, Arvos noticed the outside forge area screened from the weather by wattle panels. He entered the anteroom and saw Cluvios slumped in a chair by the cook-fire, swathed in fur coverings in the dim area.

Startled, the crafter greeted him in a weak voice. "Arvos... What...what brings you from the charrings?"

Shocked at the crafter's ashen face, lusterless eyes, and frail body huddled inside furs, Arvos picked up a bronze figure that had fallen aside. "The god, "Teutates?"

Cluvios nodded and took the figure in thin hands. "There are few images of our most powerful god." After a pause, he rasped, "Why do you come, Arvos?"

"It...it's the charrers again, *patronus*. They aren't pleased."

"I agreed with Briga's decision about the cutting. She said they were satisfied."

"That's mostly the reason. They don't like a woman havin' authority over them. *Patronus, if you* talked to them, we could go without her knowin' about it."

"When? Briga is...is always here."

Arvos licked lips that were pink in a grimy face. "At Samain. That's when most of the men keep to their huts because they're afraid of bein' visited by spirits of the dead."

"Samain..." After a fit of coughing, in which he spit bloody froth, Cluvios recalled, "Dividiac hoped to cross to the Other-World on that night."

"Bein' sick," Arvos probed, "will you go to the bonfires?"

Cluvios shook his head. "No. Briga and Apsa can join the family of Liscos for Samain's eve on the Pillar. Triccos will perform the rituals."

"*Patronus,* I'll bring a cart for you then. We'll come back before they return at dawn." Arvos bent to put a hand on Cluvios's shoulder and whisper, "No need to tell the women. Hurt their pride."

Cluvios stammered in a voice hardly louder than the hearth fire's crackle, "No need...to...hurt...Briga."

❦

The afternoon of Samain eve merged into a clear and cold dusk, where white stars in an indigo sky quickly overwhelmed the pale red of sunset. Orange bonfires were lighted on the Pillar, a near vertical crag above Wermaros on which the villagers gathered. Triccos would perform sacrificial New Year rites to insure that the delicate balance between the realms of the living and dead would remain un-breached.

On a trail that led to the charring ovens, Cluvios, dressed in a woolen tunic-shirt, trousers, and a bearskin cape that Cabirios had given to Alberix, sat unsteadily in a cart with Arvos. No rouge still tinted the western horizon when the two men reached the first burning cones. Red cubes of light shone through vents cut in the clay cloaks. By their faint glow Cluvios saw that the last sticks of wood were stacked into several cone-shaped cores, ready to be set alight. He noted an absence of workers.

"Where are the oven tenders?"

Arvos replied in a hoarse voice, "Remember, *patronus*, it...it's Samain eve. There's hardly a wind. No need for them to adjust vents."

"Will you cloak the final piles after the festival?"

Arvos did not reply as he drove on toward the furthest hut, which was his. He stopped at the edge of a path to help Cluvios down from the cart. "Men who stayed here are inside my hut. You walk first, *patronus*."

Cluvios slowly stumbled ahead, guided by pale light that shone through a sheepskin membrane covering the hut's single window. He was tired. Despite the cold air his head ached. Even so, he had not worked the forge since the autumn solstice and began to feel slightly better. Although a metallic taste still coated his mouth, the pain in his stomach was less. He did not vomit as often. *If I give up the forge, as Briga wants, I could lease cattle. When Alberix returns we could move from Wermaros and build a lodge in one of the meadows along the Vesontio road. I've been an empty husband to Briga. It's far past time that I showed more consideration for her. Perhaps after I–*

Cluvios would never complete his thought.

Arvos reached for an elm branch he had leaned against a tree near the path and swung it in a savage arc at the crafter's head. The blow caught Cluvios at the base of the skull and crushed his topmost vertebrae. Breathing in gasps, the foreman smashed again and again at his patron's head, then dragged his limp, blood-spattered body to a nearby pyramid of sticks, one that would be cloaked with mud after Samain had passed. He pulled aside a section of split logs, propped Cluvios in the center, leaned the bloody branch next to his limp body, then replaced the wood until the crafter was hidden inside.

Arvos was unconcerned about bones that might be uncovered when the men raked through the smoking mass: sick animals often crawled into the stacks to die. Besides, black bone fragments would hardly be noticed among the gray ashes, or, better, could be hidden under his cot.

When he was sure he had rebuilt the pile the way it had been stacked, Arvos groped his way back to his hut.

Throughout the night, the charrer drank all the beer he had, then urinated in a corner of the room rather than venture outside and into a supernatural flux of Other-world spirits of the dead. Lying on his filthy bed, Arvos's mind reeled with images of the bloody head of Cluvios and his emaciated body. He forced his dark thoughts away, toward the bright face of Apsa. So far, the first part of his plan had succeeded. After Briga freed his indenture, he would persuade Apsa to share a new life with him far away from Wermaros and its mocking villagers.

❧❦

Shortly after first light, Arvos awoke to a rustling sound outside his door. His head ached, yet he crawled along the dirt floor of the cold room. He was near panic when he stood to open the portal and lurched through it in time to see the tail of a predator disappear into the underbrush. *Demon spirits can shape-shift into animals.* The unreasoned fear his mind had conjured up lessened, yet he realized that when planning Cluvios's murder, he had not taken scavengers into account. He would have to keep watch over the cone each night, until the cloaking was dry enough for the cone to be set alight.

❧❦

Briga and Apsa returned to the lodge with Ger and Ersa before the mid-sun of Samain day. The hearth was cold and Cluvios gone. A bronze figure of Teutates on the floor could have told the women about Arvos's deadly visit, but the most powerful of tribal gods remained mute.

After Triccos heard that Cluvios had disappeared on the eve of Samain, the druid told villagers that Cernunnos had shape-shifted that night and taken the crafter to the Other-World. Briga noticed that her son's bearskin cape was missing; why would the god have her husband take a winter garment to the sunny Land of the Eternally Young? She also doubted the druid's story. Triccos was not to be trusted any more than his mentor, Ollam Fodla. Yet where was Cluvios?

❧❦

During Arvos's nightly watches over the drying clay, his obsession with Apsa made thoughts about Cluvios being discovered fade in his mind. Even though he returned from his vigils numb with fatigue, he spied on the young woman each day that she rode her horse to gather plants in nearby forest clearings. Since only a light snow had fallen since the New Year, Apsa was taking advantage of the weather to collect plants—precious ilex and mistletoe were easier to gather. She also began building her shrine to Arduinna in a niche on the cliff.

During the new moon of Samon, a month the Celtic calendar designated as *Mat*—"Good"—Arvos decided to confront Apsa. He would tell of his love for her, offer his protection, and manumit her from slave-servant to his law-wife. She would be grateful enough to accept.

❧❦

A few days later, Apsa felt she had cut enough holm-oak boughs from trees near the base of the rock outcropping. She knelt to secure her bag of plants with a leather tie, again thinking of both Alberix and the unexplained absence of Cluvios. *Alberix will soon return from Gallia, so together we can search for his uncle and–* The next word froze in her mind; Arvos abruptly had appeared from behind a fir tree.

Apsa uttered a scream at the sooty apparition and dropped her silver ritual knife. After realizing the figure was not a shape-shifted forest god, she picked up the thin blade and slid it into her belt sheath.

Arvos stammered, "I...I saw Derka, your horse. Did...did I frighten you, Apsa?"

She did not reply—the charrer renewed a sense of the terror she had felt with Silanus, her first centurion owner.

"I...I don't see village girls much..." Arvos attempted a nervous laugh and fumbled for a piece of smoked venison in his shoulder pouch. "Are you hungry?"

She shook her head. "I have enough plants. I'm returning to my lodge."

"Wait!" Arvos shouted the word, but panicked at his boldness. "Can... can I talk to you?"

"Talk?" She tried to sound resolute through her fright. "Talk about what?"

He stepped closer to confide, "I...I may leave Wermaros."

"Oh..." Apsa's sense of relief was short. Repelled by stale beer and urine smells on his clothing, she backed away against the rock ledge behind her.

Arvos followed. "I have money. Cluvios promised me a share of the forge profits."

"Cluvios?" She shivered at a thought that entered her mind. "Wh...what do you know about the disappearance of Briga's husband? When did he tell you that?"

Alarmed, he evaded a direct answer. "Villagers say that Cernunnos took the crafter to the Land of the Young."

"They also say that Gobann was angry with Cluvios. Why would another god reward him?"

Arvos whimpered, "Briga owes me for work I done. I could buy wagons, be my own *patronus* and leave this pig-turd village." After he pulled coins from his purse and thrust them at Apsa from a smudged palm, his other hand reached out to clutch her left wrist. "Here! Come off with me! I can give y' anything y' want."

Apsa struggled to pull away. "Alberix is my man, not...not you!"

"Alberix?" Arvos chuckled and tightened his grip on her wrist "Alberix will lay with the stinkin' dead when the Shorthairs are driven out!"

Apsa attempted to wrench free, but the charrer held her firmly in his hold. In his eyes she again saw the stare of lust in Silanus. Limp from fear, she sagged against the lime-stone wall behind her. Arvos breathed in gasps now, his rehearsed plan of offering the woman a share of his life forgotten. Jerking back the hood of Apsa's lynx-fur jacket with his free hand, he buried his face in her hair and musky smell of the fur.

Apsa struggled against his embrace, gagging at the smell of his clothing, but   managed to push the man back,. Her eyes tearing, she pleaded, "No. Don't... don't. Please, no—"

His face florid with frustration, Arvos stepped back. His spittle sprayed Apsa as he ranted, "You're like the other village sluts! How often did y' laugh and call me 'Blackstick'? You and the others...always in heat for those young studs. I seen 'em ruttin' in the forest like animals, wrapped around each other."

She frantically shook her head to deny that she ever insulted him, but Arvos was incoherent. His mind stripped the girl to an imagined milk-white body, softly curving breasts, and the amber pubic hair that he fantasized, lying on his cot, nursing an erection.

Lunging forward, he tore at the lacings of Apsa's fur jacket. Struggling to control paralyzing panic, she envisioned a haze of bright light around herself—and recalled her silver plant knife. She fumbled for the blade, but Arvos slipped her weapon from its sheath and used it to cut leather thongs securing the front of her jacket. As his knee pressed into Apsa's inner thigh, hurting her despite the thickness of an elk-skin skirt, she tried to blot out his attack, hoping that unconsciousness would make it seem to be only another recurring nightmare.

Arvos dropped the knife after he opened her jacket front. When he pushed his face into her breasts, she staggered back from the rasp of his beard stubble, tripped and fell. His knees held her pressed against the ground as he half-straightened to undo his trouser lacings. He cursed the leather thongs when the knots would not come loose.

"ARDUINNA!"

At Apsa's scream of supplication to the goddess, Arvos dropped the knife to look behind him. The youngest wife of Liscos bore the same name. Had *she* discovered them? Seeing no one, he turned back to strike the woman's mouth. But in her attacker's brief hesitation, Apsa had recovered the blade near her head. She grasped the weapon and brought it up in front of her, to an exposed narrow strip of white belly. The charrer gurgled a scream more of surprise than pain, as weight carried his flabby paunch down onto the slim point. Apsa had grasped the blade below the handle and felt a sear of pain across her palm and fingers as the silver length sheathed itself in her attacker's abdomen. Arvos's blood spattered her skirt. Eyes glazing over, he groped for the knife hilt, then stared vacantly away, as someone looking into the Other-world might, and then fell heavily to one side.

Later, Apsa would not recall how she had wrenched herself from under the dead man's body weight, or why she had not gone to where Derka was tethered. She only remembered running, terrorized, through the woods and back to the village. She had not even paused for two gate sentries, and did not stop until she was clasped tightly in Briga's arms.

After hearing the young woman's breathless account of Arvos's probable death, Briga clenched her fists in desperation. "Your knife is in the brute and Derka is tethered close by. Sentries and undoubtedly villagers saw you running here from the forest. There's blood on your clothing—"

In tears, Apsa asked, "Wh...what else could I do?"

"Let me treat your hand wound first, and then we'll...I'll think rationally."

Briga washed the lacerations with a steep of mullein leaves and wrapped Apsa's hand in linen strips. She recalled that under Celtic clan law, kinfolk were responsible for a crime committed by any of its members. Although neither Arvos nor Apsa were direct family relatives, the charrer was an indentured client, the woman a household slave. Any *vergobret* or druid sitting in arbitration would rule that a slave had killed a freeman, one to whom his patron had vowed protection. The penalty would be death either by burning, drowning, or hanging.

Ersa brought Apsa a hot drink of sweet rubus and mint. Briga stroked her hair until she became relatively calm. "We will have to inform Liscos and Triccos. There will be a *breth*, a trial. With Fodla gone, Triccos will act as judge."

"What will happen to me?"

Briga patted her cheek in hopeful reassurance. "Arduinna saved you today and we shall pray that the goddess again will do so. Rest now."

After Triccos listened to Apsa's account of the attack in which Arvos was killed, he told her a judgment would be made at the site where the death took place. It would be during the following month of Dumann, on the day of the winter solstice. The bright half of the moon would be in its third night.

Yet all knew that the Celtic month of Dumann was *Anamat*— an unlucky one.

CHAPTER IV

Kalendae Novembris. To my sister Thuccydia from her brother Simonides. Home of Arivos in the Valley of the Veserius River, Gallia Comata.

Although I am not sure these letters are getting to Massilia, I shall continue writing, my dear sister, and always pour out a libation to Hermes when I entrust them to the dispatcher. I address this to you for two reasons. Father probably is busy with his accounts and I want you to pursue an interest in history that you told me about. After all, you do have the same name as our great historian of the Peloponnesian War.

Let me tell you how it happens that I am in a remote Gallic village whose name I do not even know. It all began because of Father's merchant friend, Fufius Cita. When I tried to visit the great shrine of Druids at Carnutum, the one called 'The Navel of Gallia,' I was not received too cordially. I knew Cita was nearby at Cenabum, so I went to his home. Not long afterward, Alberix arrived, summoned by Cita for information about a rumored sedition among Gallic tribes. With the cunning that only a merchant could master, Cita tricked Alberix into scouting Gergovia, the great oppidum of the Arvernians. Do you think I would miss an opportunity to accompany him? Cita generously offered us one of his barges for the river journey to Gergovia—he happened to be shipping salted fish and lead south—but before we arrived I ordered the helmsman to put us ashore a distance west of the fortress. I had heard about a strange region of mounds and heated lakes nearby and convinced Alberix that we should deviate from his mission to explore it. Yet it was with no little trepidation that after we entered the land we saw an altar with an inscription in our Greek language. It was dedicated to Lugos, a powerful god of the Keltoi and read: "May Lugos grant you life and power. Help me magical art to cross safely over the Plain of the Mounds." Not being magicians, we felt we could use reason to travel safely and thus set out.

I wished I had my copy of Aristotle with me to get some sense of what the cone-shaped mounds, black stones and hot springs meant, then it struck me! I saw a wall painting of the cone of Aetne belching flame and surrounded by puffs of steam. The mounds were extinct volcanoes, yet underground heat warms surface waters in the area. We climbed one mound to prove it. It was quite smoothly rounded and had a crude trail leading to the summit. I found pumex stone, yet the hill itself seemed to be solid rock, not lava, and there was no caldera depression at the top. We found an altar there to Dumias, a Kelt god that Alberix did not know. The view was breathtaking!

Row upon row of cones, some with round lakes in their bowls and a white vapor of hot springs as far as one could see. Alberix admitted that he experienced a force on that height as some less benevolent aspect of his Earth Mother. I confess it also affected me. For some reason these lines from Homer came to mind: "How have you dared come to Hades, where the dead dwell senseless, the phantoms of mortals who are worn out." Alberix recalled an epigram his druid uncle had taught him.

Black Mountain: haunt of wolves, cragged and dark,

The wind mourns around its summit; wolves howl in its gullies;

The fierce black boar hides in its thickets;

The eagle screams over its crags.

I was surprised. The words fit the site even better than my quote, yet I know Keltoi have bards who recite poems from memory, as did Homer. We were ready to wash off the feel of the place and went back down for a soak in one of the springs.

Except for the sulphurous stench, I could have been in a caldarium. Our spartan supper was crushed barley grains boiled with pork and very hard army biscuit. Alberix jested that I should imagine it as Cita's roast duck.

The next day proved more exciting. We happened upon a wandering pack mule and soon found its owner cornered in a pool by a sow bear. The animal had killed a boar that injured its cub and was not going to let the man leave the water. Alberix was reluctant to kill "Artos the Honey-eater," a powerful animal totem that was sacred to the nation of Helvetii, yet used his crossbow to save the man. Arivos, our host from whose home I write, was feverish from his ordeal, so we boiled snakewort and washed him with the cooled liquid to reduce inflammation. He recovered in a few days, yet volunteered little information about himself. He comes to the Plain to collect pumex stone, which is valued for its magical quality of floating on water, and also blackish glass scattered around the volcanoes. I questioned him about the origins of these mounds and he told a legend about a race of gods who came down from the skyto settle the land. I listened, but since I want truth, not fables, I won't bother to record his story here. When I asked Arivos about caves to the west, where animals were said to have been impressed into the stone walls, he said he lived near the site and had seen the images. Once he noted my interest, he invited us to return with him.

Poor Alberix again agreed to postpone his visit to Gergovia.

Arivos's village-of-no-name is on a ledge. Limestone bluffs line the river at this point and many cave openings are visible all along its length. When he led us into one of them, it looked quite ordinary, yet about seventy paces inside I made out the imageof an aurochon! Arivos said no one could remember seeing one alive in the vicinity, and the only ones I know of are across the Rhenus in Germania. Soon after, I encountered the image of a boar-like animal with two horns on its snout, yet it would have been the size of a cow! Even by dim oil lamp light, I saw horses, deer, wolves, and, yes, hairy elephants! I felt as if I were in the primal womb of Gaea, where our legendary earth goddess conceived all her creatures. When Arivos showed us a rather obscene statuette of a female with enlarged breasts and vulva, I thought a child had fashioned it of clay, but it was made of limestone! I wanted to stay longer, but Alberix suddenly felt uncomfortable in the closeness of the cave and we left.

Arivos has no explanation for the images, but pointed out that they cannot be recent, since a thin layer of translucent stone coats all of them. It would take aeons for that to happen. He has also found oyster shells with the remains of coloring material inside, crude lamps, carvings, skeletons and many stone arrow and lance points. Nothing was made of metal. Could there have been an Age of Stone that preceded those of Iron, Bronze, Silver, and Gold, of which our legends speak? I was able to visit other caves upriver, where crude human images are scratched on the walls. At Samain we witnessed a night ritual performed by tribal members. No animals were sacrificed—only spoken incantations that commemorated the spirits of dead clan members who now reside in the Other-World.

Alberix insists that we move on to Gergovia tomorrow, so I shall write again from there. My deepest affection to you, my sister, and to Father and Mother.

The letter was sent to Nikomaxos's villa at Massilia by one of the few cargo barges whose owner was willing to gamble the chance for profits against disaster in a sudden winter storm. Both arrived safely on the *Eidus* of December.

An excited Thuccydia read her brother's letter to her parents. "Simonides is in the valley of the Veserius River now! Where is that?"

"Veserius?" Her father grumbled his answer, "That's in Gallic land far to the west, beyond the Cesena Mountains. He's *there* with half the merchants *here* wanting him to work on their accounts!"

"Father, at least he doesn't say anything about being dismissed by Caesar."

"Fufius Cita's letter made it clear that he was. Perhaps now he'll come back to an honest occupation among his own people."

"Niko," his wife, Ismene, chided. "Fufius Cita is not a Greek."

"Yes, we Greeks wear actor's masks with the Romans, yet no Hellene will forget what Lucius Mummius did in destroying Corinth."

While, Father, your gods watched and did nothing? Thuccydia again read aloud, "'I encountered the drawing of a boar-like animal with two horns on its snout, yet it would have been the size of a cow. Even by lamp light I could see images of horses, deer, oxen, wolves, even elephants in that cave—'"

Nikomaxos scoffed, "His pictorial zoology garden puts no soup in the pot."

"Father, I think it's exciting."

Ismene wondered, "Does he say anything about returning to Massilia?"

"They're going to Gergovia—"

"Gergovia? That *oppidum* is the capital of Arvernian territory. What business do they have there? He's need here!"

Ismene touched his arm to say quietly, "Niko, when you let our son go with Troucillus you did it because you thought it might help your business. Let Simonides follow his own road in Gallia."

"Zeus! How can it help my business if he's made an enemy of Julius Caesar?" The merchant bolted up. "Enough! I *may* want to hear the rest later on."

As her father stalked from the room, Thuccydia called after him, "My brother says that he'll write from Gergovia." She finished reading the letter to her mother, then slipped a cape over her tunic. "I'm going to the *biblioteka* to read. Mother, one day I hope to write about far off events, just as does my brother!"

❧

Gergovia of the Arverni on the Elaver River

My dear Thuccydia, I had hoped to have time to write in greater detail, but Alberix fears that our ruse has been uncovered and that we are in danger of being detained. The ruse is that to get the information Fufius Cita wants, Alberix poses as an itinerant crafter and I as his slave. This humble status was hurriedly conferred on me at the oppidum gate—actually a brilliant improvisation on my friend's part, since it helps explain my swarthy features and dark beard. Gergovia lies amid a progression of rolling hills on a height that is flat as the sea. Its fortress walls are a fine example of the dry stonework that impresses even Caesar's engineers who see it. However, the buildings are constructed of a blackish stone that gives the town a somber, forbidding character. We saw a camp of many tents pitched around the walls, but no signs of war mustering. We were met by Abidos, a young noble, who was sure Alberix could find crafter work, then taken to Gobinnatio's lodge. He is a vergobret—judge—and uncle to Vercingetorix. A council was in progress. Abidos let us listen from a distance, to emphasize Gobinnatio's leadership skills.

Abidos whispered to Alberix that the speaker was Gobinnatio. "...And when Fabius Maximus defeated our grandfathers and the Ruteni, over three-twenties of years ago, his Senate pardoned us and did not annex our lands to the Narbonensis."

Vercingetorix retorted, "Because the Romani were too weak! Now they return under this Caesar to take all our lands in Gallia."

Lucterios pounded a fist on the table in agreement. Seeing other chieftains stir in uncertainty, Gobinnatio continued his protest at a rebellion. "Nephew, to resist the Romani would bring clouds of blood on all our tribes. Where are the Nervii, the Eubones, now? Helvetii are vanquished. Arverni have no quarrel with this Caesar."

"Nor have we a treaty with him!" a scarred chieftain called out.

"Then, Calidios, you must see the danger. The Aedui have a pledge of friendship with us. Shall we fight them, too?"

Lucterios boasted, "We have agents at Roma who tell us the city is in chaos. Mobs loyal to Caesar fight Pompeius, his rival. I tell you it is civil war there!"

"You make a sound of cackling hens." Gobinnatio gestured toward his druid advisor. "Durnacios there has found no disasters for the Romani in his auguries."

After an interval of silence, one of the chieftains ventured, "Where are the legions of this Caesar now?"

"I'll answer," Vercingetorix told him. "Six are in the lands of the Senones, two with the Lingones, and two among the Treveri."

"Warriors without count!" Calidios exclaimed. "With which legion is Caesar?"

"That is exactly our point," Lucterios said. "He is not in Gallia but in his *Cisalpina* province sitting judgment in the courts. We must strike before he returns in the spring, and certainly by Beltaine."

Cotuatos, one of the conspirators about whom Cita had been warned, stood up. "Chieftains, I am a warrior of the Carnutes, guardians of the sacred *nemeton* at Carnutum. The Romani have merchants at Cenabum who greatly profit from our people. They make our women lust for their mirrors and sweet oils...for useless trinkets. It was not so in the days of my father."

Gobinnatio was criticial. "Your words miss their target."

Cotuatos flushed. "Then I will throw them straight. The Romani must be driven out of Gallia. I swear by my tribe's god that the rebellion will start at

Cenabum. We shall kill foreign merchants there as a signal for all the tribes to join us!"

"But, the Romani legions..." a chieftain protested.

The Carnute laughed. "Without their Caesar the Romani are like lame children."

"His sub-chief, Titus Labienus, is no cripple," Gobinnatio disagreed.

Cotuatos drew out a belt knife, and cut a line on his forearm. "We will bleed the Romani as my arm bleeds. If my entire body must succumb, then so be it!" He turned to taunt Durnacios, "Druid, do you not teach that death is the center of a new life?"

Silenced by the dramatic gesture, the council members watched Cotuatos wrap his arm with a woolen strip.

Durnacios whispered to Gobinnatio, then rose to speak. "Brothers, the resolution of our doubts must lie with the gods." The old druid pointed at two albino ravens perched on the support rod of a curtain. "By those sacred birds shall the gods show their decision!"

Lucterios and Cotuatos protested, but the druid called for servants to bring two platters and a slice of the honey cake served earlier. Placing the dishes on the edge of a bench near the hearth, Durnacios crumbled the cake, divided the pieces between Gobinnatio and Vercingetorix, then ordered the two men, "Each place your offering on one of the platters and return to the council table."

Gobinnatio spread his portion evenly around the dish. Vercingetorix, impatient, lumped morsels in the center. As the men returned to their seats, the albino birds eyed the food, cawed softly, and flapped their wings in anticipation.

Durnacios raised a hand over each of the two men to recite ritual words. "I call upon the gods of your clan to act through their sacred birds. The man whose offering the ravens eat shall be declared in the right."

I stretched forward to watch more clearly. "The fate of Gallia is to be determined by twin carrion birds?"

Simonides held me back to warn, "And possibly ours."

Both albino birds swooped down to the floor. After circling the bench in suspicion, one raven hopped onto its far end. Its mate followed. Approaching the dishes, the first raven attacked Vercingetorix's cake, scattering the pieces to the floor, then began pecking at morsels in the other dish. The other raven joined in gulping down the cake bits that ringed Gobinnatio's platter.

Vercingetorix's supporters sat in silence, but the *vergobret*'s men murmured approval. Durnacios signaled for quiet. The seer's voice trembled, yet his words reached the furthest corners of the lodge. "The gods' will is known. Vercingetorix, son of Celtillos, I banish you from Gergovia, charged with sedition against our tribe. May the setting of Belenos not find you inside this *oppidum*."

Gobinnatio stood up. "All who would join him have safe passage until moonrise. Nephew, do nothing more to risk suffering the fate of your father."

Flushed with anger, Vercingetorix bolted up. His hand slid to the hilt of his belt dagger, but he restrained himself and strode toward the door. Lucterios and Cotuatos followed. If the chieftain recognized me as he passed, he gave no indication. When the three men pulled open the massive portals, a rush of cold wind scattered the rushes on the floor and sent the albino arbiters of the gods flapping back to their high perch.

Simonides continued in his letter.

> *When I told Alberix that Vercingetorix was not the leader he should follow, he did not reply. After the council disbanded, I was banished to the kitchen with the other slaves. Alberix was summoned to the room of a noblewoman who had watched the proceedings from a side balcony above the men. She questioned him about news from outside the area. Although he was able to parry her inquisitiveness about his reason for being in Gergovia, he told me he slipped up once or twice and feared he had given us away. At the audience with Gobinnatio, the vergobret made it clear that he was against a war with the Romani. Yet the druid, Durnacios, somehow knew that Dividiac had been the uncle of Alberix. Certain remarks of Gobinnatio indicated that he knew more about us than he let on, thus this hasty letter. I found a wine merchant who is returning to the Provincia and entrusted this letter to him. I have paid half of his fee of two denarii, please remit the balance to him when this is in your hands. We leave at the change of the midday watch, when there is confusion in the camp and at the gate. With affection, my Sister, and to Father and Mother. Simonides.*

My Greek friend and I left in a cold rain, which churned the road into a sticky ooze that hampered our horses' footing and tired the animals. Early darkness forced us to ask for shelter at the first village we entered. I was directed to a crude inn near the center of a cluster of small wattle-and-mud huts. The owner, a scarred, burly man with a limp, showed us where to stable our mounts. After feeding and watering the animals, we came into the relative warmth and dryness of a common room. A fire blazed in a central fire-pit, around which a boy maneuvered an assortment of wooden buckets that caught rainwater leaking into the room. Ten curtained compartments held straw-filled bunks.

"What place is this?" I asked the innkeeper, in paying for a compartment and food.

"Gerziacum." The man had answered without elaborating, yet no doubt noticed that I did not speak with a local accent.

A thin serving girl motioned us to a low table at the far end of the room. Nearby a group of villagers sat drinking.

Before we reached them, Simonides whispered to me, "Those rustics began guzzling when the rain started and won't go to wherever they sleep until that roof stops leaking."

I told him we had no choice but to shelter here.

The girl indicated stools and returned with a ceramic pitcher of wine, two bowls of thick barley porridge, and a platter of smoked pork and bread. I gave her a *sestercius*.

Simonides placed a slice of pork on bread, took a bite, and glanced around again. "I always want new places to write about, yet this porcine sty leaves me quite wordless."

"Friend, we were fortunate to find this 'sty.' Gobinnatio will have us watched after he finds we're gone. Hopefully, this rain may turn his men back."

One of the drinkers called the girl over to examine the money I gave her. When he glanced toward me and scowled, I realized my error: I had paid with a Romani coin. Urged on by his drunken companions, the man lurched up from the table and staggered toward me.

"You Aedui or Sequani?" he demanded, wavering unsteadily.

I wondered if he was as drunk as he acted—of all the local tribes, those were the two most likely to have Romani coins. I decided to tell him the truth. If the man wanted trouble he would make it no matter what I said. "I'm Raurici, a clan of the Helvetii."

"Helvetii?" The man loudly echoed my reply as mock surprise. "I thought they had nothin' left to give!" He grinned back at his friends, who joined in laughing at his insult.

I flushed, knowing I had to give a calm reply, yet he taunted me again.

"'Goat-tender, you're here for what?"

"For one thing, to keep to my own business." Simonides tensed at my insolent reply and put down his half-eaten bread.

"You're spyin' for the Romani..." Balancing unsteadily, the man cursed and bent forward to grapple with me, but I anticipated his move. I rolled away from the table, reached back to grab one of the water buckets, then swung it an arc that caught him on the back of his head. The pail shattered as the man fell, and splashed water over his startled companions.

At a not unexpected confrontation, the innkeeper grasped a long meat knife in one hand and limped away from the fire pit. When the bucket smashed my opponent's head, a nervous Simonides had risen.

The man ignored us.

"Enough!" he shouted at the sodden drinkers, then nudged the unconscious brawler on the floor with a boot. "Clear out and take this wild ox with you!"

Muttering drunken threats, the men tottered up from the table. Two of them dragged their mate up the ramp and into the mud outside.

"Tempers are forge-hot," the innkeeper commented as he went back to the spit. "The roads are thick with warriors who come to see if Gobinnatio or Vercingetorix will be *vergobret*."

Still shaking, Simonides ventured, "Th...that...should be good business for you."

The innkeeper scoffed, "'Peasants and warriors make poor guests, as we say. Those were men from this village and won't return tonight, but y' best be on your way early."

Simonides acknowledged the warning and motioned me back to the table. "And we best rapidly finish this meal. You sleep. I'll keep the second watch."

I nodded, hoping I had not injured the man too badly. "I know my countrymen. After they've slept off the *cervisa*, they'll come looking for us to avenge my insult and the man's injury."

"But that drunken imbecile started the brawl."

"*Carantos*...friend...you couldn't get a single one of your philosophers to win a dispute with a Celt who felt insulted."

⁂

Dawn light had not yet crept through the gable ventilation when I was awakened by the curses of the innkeeper. I parted the curtains: roof leaks were intermittent drips, but the boy had not emptied the buckets; the earthen floor was awash in muddy, trampled straw.

Simonides bolted upright at the shouting. "Great Zeus, I slept through my watch!"

"Yes, '*carantos*.' If you *were* my slave you could be strangled for risking my life."

"Slave? I do admit I was angry about your ruse at Gergovia. Pride I suppose, yet it's not often one can enter and leave a destiny so easily."

"Our present destiny is to leave here as quickly as possible!"

While the sniffling apprentice sloshed through mud emptying pails, we hurriedly breakfasted on bread and hard cheese. The innkeeper packed meat, bread, and a skin of wine for our journey.

We mounted our horses outside under a weak, late autumn sun that sparkled off the wetness on tree limbs and ochre grasses, yet did nothing to warm the air. Still, we were glad to be out of the rancid stench and hazy smoke inside the inn.

After passing through the sodden village unchallenged by a few wood gatherers who were awake, we made the descent into the valley of the Elaver River. I told Simonides that once we reached the waterway I would return to Cenabum. He could continue on south to his home at Massilia.

※

Around mid-morning, I remarked that there were more ravens than usual roosting in bare trees, and admitted that I felt uneasy at these symbols of death. Simonides explained that rain had washed away the covering of snow and now the birds could scavenge dead animals more easily. If their presence bothered him, he did not say, but we were pleased that the muddy roadway limited travelers: We encountered only a few sodden warriors going toward Gergovia. None challenged us.

I called a halt when the sun had lowered to a hand span above the horizon. The buffeting of the wind had been tiring, and darkness would descend quickly. Our mounts needed forage and rest as well. I had noticed a nearby stream that would provide water. Following the rivulet away from the muddy road, we dismounted in a grove of pines that offered a measure of concealment.

While Simonides attempted to light a small fire with damp wood, I led the horses into cold stream water. I washed mud off our mounts' flanks and let them drink. I had straightened after rinsing my hands, when a line of six horsemen appeared at the edge of the woods. Their lances were lowered in charge position. Nervous, Simonides stood up next to the smoldering moss of his unlit fire. I took the riders to be either brigands or Gobinnatio's men. Both of my guesses were wrong.

The leader of the group trotted his horse forward to call out, "You are detained in the name of Vercingetorix of the Arverni. Mount your horses, both of you."

I asked where we would be taken.

"Does the hen question the fox?" the man mocked, amid appreciative chuckles by his companions. "Mount!" he ordered more forcefully.

His other warriors moved to surround our horses and prevent escape. Not that we or our mounts had enough energy left to attempt a getaway.

59

JANUARY — SEPTEMBER, 52 B.C. E.

My heart is heavy as a grave marker. They are gone: earth's human crop.
Generation by generation they melt away to Cernunnos.

CHAPTER V

As the winter solstice neared at Wermaros, Briga worried about the forthcoming trial of Apsa, the unsolved disappearance of Cluvios, and a lack of news from Alberix.

Shortly before dawn on the morning of a new moon of Dumann—Lucius had called it December—Briga awakened when she heard Apsa leave the lodge and go outside. Quickly dressing, she followed the young woman through the village to the river gate.

Apsa had stopped midway along the bridge to lean on the rail and look down at swirling eddies in the black water.

Alarmed, Briga ran along the span, calling her name. "Apsa! Apsa! Please don't!"

Although startled, the woman immediately understood Briga's fear—in desperation she once had tried to hang herself in the stable of a legion camp. Apsa assured her, "I'm well, Briga. I just came to look at the setting moon. Our druids teach that Dumann is *Anamat...* unlucky...yet the Earth Mother is so beautiful in winter."

Briga looked up at a lunar crescent that grasped the faint outline of the old moon in its hold. A bright morning star glittered low on the horizon. She eased an arm around Apsa. "You must not believe that the druid's judgment will be *Anamat.*"

"I don't know why I called on Arduinna that day. I no longer much pray to gods."

"You distracted Arvos and saved your life."

"Yet ended his," she said. "Now 'justice' demands that my life balances his death."

"No! My sister is wife to Liscos. Triccos would not dare voice a verdict of death."

"I'm a slave. I own nothing to give as compensation."

Briga reminded her, "Under our laws the household pays a restitution price. You are of our family."

Unsure that would happen, Apsa shook her head. "With Fodla gone, Triccos will assert his own authority."

"Sequani do not offer human sacrifices."

"What of that old hunter Alberix found hung in the woods? And Liscos has his long arm after Cluvios's forge."

The claim surprised Briga. "Who...who told you this, Apsa?"

"His son at Epomanduorum wants to own it."

"Cluvios helped him set up his own forge."

Apsa insisted, "Liscos dislikes your husband because he doesn't fear him, and Alberix because he's friendly with Romani. The chieftain is obsessed with talk of a rebellion. If Liscos thought it might succeed, he would embrace it."

Briga fell silent as she watched the horizon expand into a fiery crimson that consumed both the moon-crescent and morning star into its fire. After a moment, she roused herself to face a freshening wind sweeping in from the north. A few white flakes swirled in the air. "There will be heavy snow by mid-sun," she predicted. "We should help Anvalos bring in more firewood."

"Briga, at least *he* has stayed with us. Since Cluvios disappeared I've not seen any apprentices."

"No, the others fear displeasing Gobann by coming near the forge."

"Was the god their paymaster?" Apsa lashed out bitterly. "How long will men be unthinking slaves to what they believe are the works of gods?"

Briga shrugged. "Perhaps one day a new 'Great Over-god' will come to free them of these superstitions."

Laughing at the absurd thought, the two women returned arm-in-arm to the end of the bridge. Briga received a curt nod of acknowledgement from the gate sentries: her husband was gone, thus support from the villagers was cooling like autumn weather for this Raurici woman who still was an outsider.

❧

Briga saw her prediction of snow fulfilled. White flakes began to collect on thatched roofs and fallow garden plots, and then continued to fall in as the shortened days passed. Villagers repeated a common adage: "A north wind brings icy storms and thieving Germani," yet were confident that raids from across the Renos posed less danger than impassable drifts that could maroon the village. On the day set for Apsa's trial, the Jurassos slopes were sheathed in a depth of snow that reached to a herder's knees. Nevertheless, Triccos was resolute: the trial would not be postponed.

❧

On the morning of the solstice, dawn arrived with a cerulean-blue sky. The sun's weak rays set ice crystals on western crests glittering in sparkling facets of brightness. Anvalos hitched Derka to a sleigh, and then led a procession of witnesses to the forest location of the charrer's death. Triccos rode with Liscos. The druidess, Moira, sat across from the two men, holding a covered wicker cage. In another sleigh, Dirona, as Briga's sister and kin to the family, insisted on being present. Apsa, alongside Briga, noticed Epanactos riding a horse at the rear. She leaned over to whisper, "Liscos's bodyguard has returned."

Briga glanced back. "An evil omen. You once accused him of harassing you. Now, Epanactos will attempt revenge by witnessing against your innocence."

"Triccos saw him do so in his lodge. Moira was there attending Sabia."

Briga did not respond. Even Dividiac had admitted that some druids—like their gods—were not always impartial in judgments.

Briga told Anvalos to stop when the sleigh reached a point where they could walk up to the death site. Triccos ordered Derka unhitched and brought along: the animal had been nearby when the murder happened and could be useful in a divination rite.

The trudge through forest snow drifts was difficult, yet when Apsa arrived at the clearing she was astonished at the transformation made by the snowfall. As if to expunge the crime, the ground was unrecognizable under an innocent white covering.

Triccos appeared nervous as he motioned the group into a semi-circle that faced the rock outcropping where Arvos died. Moira stood nearby with the cage at her side. Epanactos had brushed snow away from a log and crouched on his haunches.

Apsa shivered when she noticed spiky green leaves and red berries of ilex plants pushing through the snow; the shrub was a vivid reminder of the attack. Triccos went to slip off the cage cover and open the door to take out a black and white rabbit. It was Apsa's breeder, her only pet.

The druid held the animal by its ears and held Apsa's silver knife in his other hand to announce, "Let the judgment of the accused slave woman proceed according to a Law of the Common Good."

When she saw her knife, Apsa shuddered, but shook off Briga's arm as she tried to comfort her.

Triccos intoned, "We begin with a sacrifice." With a deft motion, he severed the rabbit's spinal cord at the neck, then slashed open the creature's belly. As a stain of red spread over snow crusts, he bent down to examine the rabbit's teaming entrails and then stood up with a perplexed look. "The...the entrails are undiseased. Whole!"

Briga grasped Apsa's hand. "We begin with a good omen!"

Numbed by the sacrifice, she only stared at the quivering body of her pet.

Triccos recovered from surprise to announce, "The blade of the accused has favorably inaugurated a trial. Taranis, Esus, and Teutates are pleased!"

Briga was angered. The druid had twisted a sign of innocence into one of approval by three gods for proceeding with a trial.

"Let the slave woman, Apsa, come forward," Triccos ordered. "She will retell of her crime."

Apsa moved out a short distance from the semi-circle and related the events of that day in a voice as hushed as spills of snow from fir tree branches.

"I searched for ilex and mistletoe when the charrer...Arvos...appeared. He said he would leave the village and wished me to go with him. He became angry after I...I told him that I loved Alberix. It was then that he tried to...to—"

Triccos interrupted her testimony. "You did not attempt escape? Surely, a woman young as you could outrun a stocky person like the charrer. No. Instead, you thrust your knife into him."

"I couldn't run," Apsa insisted. "Arvos held me down. He...he fell on my blade."

"Woman," Triccos demanded, "were you not with child when you came to Wermaros?"

Briga started to dispute the accusation, but Liscos raised a hand to silence her.

The druid continued, "What was the name of your husband?"

"I...I had no husband. I was the slave of a Romani warrior."

"A harlot!" Epanactos shouted.

Triccos looked toward him as if on cue. "Are there other accusers of the slave woman?"

"I charge her!" Epanactos stepped forward, smirking. "Just as the harlot did with Arvos, she tried to entice me."

Apsa reddened. "False! Triccos...Moira...you were there. You both saw Epanactos insult me."

Moira looked down to pick at the cage wicker. The druid stared in silence at the rabbit's cooling entrails.

Hatred replaced Epanactos's smirk. "The harlot is a murderess and under Celtic law must die. A life given for a life!"

Triccos supported his claim. "The woman's guilt is revealed through her own mouth. She admits to killing the charrer, yet if any would speak in her defense, be heard now."

Briga called to him, "I will pay the fine for Arvos's death. As my son's slave, Apsa is of our family."

"A fine?" Triccos scoffed. "Even a slave's life is not payment for murdering a freeman. Arvos had no kinfolk. To whom will the money be paid?" He paused, having recalled another statute of the law. "Slave woman, your horse,

Derka, was present at the murder. Do you wish judgment of your innocence by a trial of food?"

"Food? How?"

"An apple in your dish, another in one belonging to Arvos. Whichever the animal eats *might* indicate a sign of innocence."

Apsa shook her head in refusal, even able to laugh at the absurd proposal. Any horse faced with such a choice would eat both apples!

Dirona pushed Liscos's arm, pleading, "Husband, do something! Speak for the girl's innocence!"

With a glance at Triccos, he warned her, "Sheath your tongue! Druids have authority even above that of clan chieftains."

Triccos confidently licked his lips. "I call again on anyone who wishes to testify about the woman's innocence. Let them come now and swear by the god by whom their tribe swears."

Only the harsh cry of a jay softened by distance, answered the druid. No name of a comforting god came to Apsa's mind as had that of Arduinna on the fateful afternoon.

Liscos looked away and offered nothing. As chieftain and kin of the accused's family, he could have called for a judgment from the druid High Assembly at Carnutum in the following summer, but refused to do so.

As Triccos was about to announce the death sentence, a voice sounded from behind one side of the rock face where Arvos was killed. "I shall speak for the innocence of the slave woman."

For an instant Apsa thought of Arduinna, then realized it was a man's voice. She sucked in breath when she recognized Marcus Marius trudge through snow from behind the outcropping. The charrer named Brenn accompanied him.

Epanactos was first to recover from surprise and demand, "Shorthair, why are you here? This is a Celtic affair."

Marius raised a hand in answering, "Warrior, peace to you. I am in Wermaros by treaty, as your own chieftain will affirm." He gestured toward Triccos. "I did not hear this priest put restrictions on who could testify."

The druid paled to the blandness of snow. "Roman, wha...what have you to tell us?"

Marius motioned Brenn forward. "This man, one of yours, will show his evidence."

As the charrer unwrapped a square of leather, Triccos and Epanactos came up to examine his packet.

Marius explained, "When I went to the ovens to negotiate for the garrison's charcoal supply, Brenn came to me with those bones he found under Arvos's cot."

After poking at the blackened bits with his dagger, Epanactos looked up. "Shorthair, what have a few charred bones and teeth to do with this murder-judgment?"

"Brenn believes they are those of Cluvios."

"My husband? No!" At Briga's anguished exclamation, Apsa clutched her arm.

Triccos sneered his opinion. "An animal crawled into an oven to die. Charrer, have you not seen this happen?"

Before Brenn could answer, Marius asked, "Why would Arvos save animal bones? And these are human teeth...human remains."

Epanactos countered, "It does not make them those of Cluvios,"

"Perhaps, but Brenn also found this..." Marius pulled a scorched neck torc from his belt pouch and held it up.

Briga went to examine the neckpiece, then wiped her eyes in affirming, "It is my husband's torc, thus a life *has* been given for a life. Come, Apsa, bring your horse to the sleigh." Before walking back, Briga turned to Marius. "*Gratias*, I believe you say. Visit us in the village."

"I will, *Domina*."

Drained of the will to protest, Triccos watched the two women return.

Moira ran to them before they reached the road. "Mistress, take me with you!" she blurted to Briga. "I...I no longer wish to stay with Fodla or Triccos. My...my twin sister was sacrificed to their rites."

Briga muffled the druidess's sobs in her cloak as she helped her down the slope. Anvalos hitched Derka to the sleigh for their return to the village.

❧❧

On the following morning, Marius rode from *Castor* to accept Briga's invitation and visit her lodge. Perhaps he could learn more about the nascent rebellion of Gallic tribes. As the legionary approached Wermaros, along the Dubis road, he mused on his service in Gallia and the present situation.

Our two watchtowers have been useless. That Sequani traitor, Casticos, already had conspired with the Helvetii to take over all of Gallia. The tribe planned to move south, out of Genava. Now Liscos calls our towers 'warts on the face of his land,' after negotiating for them and accepting lease payments. The old drunkard sees himself in Vesontio as Over-chief. Mars help us! No Gallic chieftain thought Caesar would move so rapidly to counter their sedition. It's only right that Fortuna gave them a swift kick in the scrotum for trying to make fools of us!

The gate sentries recognized Marius and passed him through. Although it was not an authorized day for a legionary to enter the village, the men knew of his discovery concerning the murder of Cluvios, and his exoneration of the slave woman. As he neared Briga's lodge, Marius was aware that he hoped to see Moira.

Anvalos stopped splitting logs in the yard to take Marius's horse, then motioned him to the entryway. After entering the vestibule he descended the earthen ramp into the common room. A cook-fire glowed with enough light to illuminate Briga as she rose to greet him.

"Welcome, Marius. My hearth is yours."

"*Domina,* it is I who am honored, yet fear my Celtic is poor."

"Marius, you speak our language well."

He quipped, "After almost six years, I should speak like a Celt! How is Apsa?"

"She sleeps, and in time will heal."

Embarrassed, Marius hesitated before asking, "And the...the druid's priestess who came with you?"

Moira's melodious answer came from shadows near the loom. "Roman, I am quite healthy."

Marius watched the woman rise and walk to seat herself near the fire. Despite a fur that covered her body, Moira's movements had a gracefulness that sent a longing through his groin.

"Marius, take mulled wine with us," Briga offered, motioning to Ersa. "It has been long since you last were here."

"Yes, too long." He murmured thanks as Ersa set out three cups and poured hot, sweetened wine into them from a pitcher. The steam smelled of laurel and mastic seed. After a sip, he took a red clay urn from under his cape, decorated in a floral motif, and handed it Briga. "I...I brought you this. We call it a *pyxis* and place ashes of our dead inside for burial."

She fingered the design. "Your friendship with my husband did not freeze. I...I am grateful for this memento."

Marius nodded acknowledgement. "When Cluvios forged ironwork for the towers, we saw each other every day." He sipped wine again and ventured a look toward the druidess. "You...you are called Moira?" At her nod he felt as if he were in a dice game and unsure whether or not to throw again. He committed himself to whatever outcome Fortuna dictated. "Does your name have a Celtic meaning I would understand?"

"It would mean *fatum*. 'Fate' in your language."

"Fate...I see. Ah, have you been a priestess long?"

"Ollam Fodla took Sabia and me when we were children."

When it was clear the woman would not elaborate, to keep her attention Marius babbled, "We...Romans...have priestesses called vestal virgins. They serve for thirty years in a house and temple is at Roma." After an awkward silence, he felt desperate. "Moira, your accent, your...speech...is different than here."

"I came from Inisfail."

Marius brightened at a connection. "That island to the west of Albion. I was with Caesar when we landed among the Britanni. He freed a gang of slaves from your homeland."

Moira did not react but at hearing the commander's name, Briga put the urn aside. "Marius, have you seen Alberix? I hoped you might have been with him."

"No, I came from Durocortorum, and he was with Lucius Roscius."

"Did I hear Alberix's name?" Apsa came out of her compartment, flushed from sleep, pushing back a tumble of amber hair.

Marius half stood, trying not to stare a lithe body outlined under a night tunic.

Apsa sat cross-legged on the floor in front of him. "Marius, a slave has few defenders. I'm grateful for your help."

He glanced at Moira. "Perhaps it was 'fate' that I went to Brenn for the wood."

"About Alberix. Will... will there be more fighting?"

He tried to reassure Apsa—as well as himself. "Caesar thinks not. Ambiorix gave us trouble this summer, but we've chased him and his seditionists back into their swamps."

"Yet our druids rally the tribes," Moira said. "Those who oppose are judged to be traitors."

"In that case what will happen to you? Won't this Triccos consider you a renegade?"

At her shrug, Briga offered, "Moira, you may stay here with us if you wish."

"And when Fodla returns? There is no place in all Gallia where I would be safe."

Marius never remembered what god prompted his outburst. "Then come to the tower with me! You'll be safe there. I...I would see to that."

Incredibly, he heard Briga agree. "The idea has merit. *Vergobrets* would never seek a druidess among Romani."

Marius elaborated, "Moira, you could go to the Narbonensis. Fodla wouldn't follow you into a Roman province."

Moira stared into glowing coals of the fire. *Sabia is dead. Triccos may try to kill me, rather than face Fodla after he finds that I ran away. If I return, he might force me to bear a ritual child by Triccos, as with Sabia.* Without looking at Marius, she agreed. "I will go with the Roman."

Apsa was cautious. "Good, Moira, yet you can't leave through the gates. Triccos will have warned Liscos so his guards will stop you."

Moira said, "There is a hidden door built into the palisade stakes. It is close to our old lodge near the Acantos quarter."

Briga told Marius, "Be by the door at the change of evening sentries. I shall have Moira ready."

He agreed and stood up. "I should leave now. Those sentries reported my visit to Liscos. If I stay too long, he'll think we're plotting against him."

Briga responded with a grim smile. "You understand the mind of my sister's husband all too well."

Marius gestured farewell salute to Apsa and Moira. Briga went with him to the outer vestibule, where she hesitantly touched his sleeve. "Is...is Lucius with your legion?"

"Lucius Velcanius, the *centurio?*"

"Yes."

"That's right, you know him from the tower. No, he's with Titus Labienus. Why do you ask?"

Briga gave a slight shake of her shoulders as if it were of no importance. "Be at the palisade door when Belenos sets. I will disguise Moira as a man."

Timing his return to the village with an early dusk, Marius brought a horse for Moira and picked her up without arousing attention. Muffled in hooded capes, they circled their mounts around and made their way along the river road unchallenged. A party of returning hunters also ignored the two riders.

It was full dark when Marius spotted the glow of *Castor's* watch-fire between crenellations at the top. He pulled the rope to ring a bell that signaled the arrival of visitors. After he identified the day's password, an access ladder was dropped down. He motioned for Moira to climb up while he took their horses into the garrison's animal pen.

The druidess stepped into the barracks room. After putting down a bundle of clothing and throwing back her cloak's hood, Moira received an unexpected reception.

"By Priapus, a woman!" a legionary called out. "Look at the gift Marius brought us."

Gallica," another taunted, "show us th' wool *under* your trousers."

The first man reached for her groin but she slapped him hard enough to feel the sting of his beard stubble on her palm. His companions still laughed when Marius ducked through the low door and realized what was happening.

"Stand easy, all of you!" he ordered, red-faced. "This woman is a Gallic priestess, not a *scorta*."

Moira's sacred connection silenced the jests: even veteran legionaries feared the supernatural power of foreign gods and their priests.

Stammering an apology, Marius led Moira to the walled cubicle that Lucius had occupied. Renewed chuckling outside the wicker partitions indicated that the men's sexual jesting would continue at the engineer's expense.

Marius's explanation was clumsy. "They...the men...have garrison fever. Been without a woman for a long time." After Moira sat on the cot with her bundle of clothing, he wondered if she had eaten. "Are you hungry? I can bring food."

"Roman, I am tired and wish to sleep."

"Of course. Prepare for bed...put on a night tunic. I'll go get this brazier's charcoal lighted." Up close, Marius noticed a thin web of fatigue lines etching the remains of blue dye on Moira's face. *She looks less young than at the clearing where she wore ritual clothing.*

After he left renewed laughter sounded from the common room. Moira's reaction was acrid. *The Roman is promising to tell them what it feels like to mount a priestess. I won't give him much to boast about.*

When Marius returned, Moira lay huddled beneath a coarse gray legion blanket, facing a partition wall. He set down the brazier, babbling, "That was an easy escape from the village. I...we...need to relax with more than a wine ration..." He threw dried leaves on the coals and bent to inhale the smoke.

Moira recognized the smell of kannabis. *Roman, I left behind herbs that would bring you visions of both a Land of the Blessed and the Hades of the Greeks.*

Exhausted, Moira was almost asleep when she heard the mattress cords creak and felt Marius's weight roll against her. She lay still, feeling his stiffness thrusting the back of her thighs. When he pulled her around to face him, she ignored the cold touch of his fingers intruding on her warmth to caress her breasts. His rough hand slid down to fondle a delta of soft hair between her legs and the damp sheath beneath. Foreplay was brief. If his entry was awkward, even painful to the woman, Marius did not notice. His perception was that he thrust into an immense cavern of warm liquid that abruptly surged up out of his own loins and emptied itself in pulsating rhythms into a grotto of long-delayed pleasure.

Moira lay a passive recipient, grateful that the man was not angry-drunk and had not abused her. As an adolescent, she had been harshly violated by Fodla, and any man's hardness still was painful.

After Marius finally rolled off her body, the druidess turned to the wall again, gagging at the smell that came from underneath the blanket. She recalled how much she preferred Sabia's gentle tonguing in their love-play, rather than the harsh thrusts of a male's stiff "sword."

CHAPTER VI

Vercingetorix chose a border village of the Ambivareti, a client tribe of the Arverni, for the location of his recruiting camp. Being outside Arvernian territory would thwart Gobinnatio's efforts to arrest him, and from there he could vaunt the growing number of warriors for the pro-rebellion faction at Bibracte, the Aedui capital.

∾

It was almost full dark when our Arvernian captors returned to the village with Simonides and me. Campfires silhouetting armed warriors blazed in an arc of orange outside the palisade—the barrier looked only a little more defensible than the one I saw at Saumis. As we approached an open gate, the leader of our guards dropped back to ride abreast of me and point to bodies of two men sagging from the portal.

"They been there since the rising of Belenos," he explained. "Vercingetorix doesn't coddle deserters. Those two joined us and then tried to inform Gobinnatio about what went on here."

I didn't answer. The executed warriors appeared to have frozen to death in the brutal weather that followed winter rains.

Simonides glanced at the ragged clothing and makeshift weapons of gate sentries. "A sorry excuse for warriors, Alberix. As a crafter, wouldn't you say they look more like lead than silver?"

I shrugged that I had no opinion, yet my friend's comparison was an apt description for the shabby tribesmen. Was the rebellion as well organized as Vercingetorix would have recruiters believe?

As we approached the front of the largest wattle-and-daub hut, the leader ordered one of his men to take us inside. "You two dismount here. Our king will question you."

In the cramped room three women cut leek and cabbage into a bubbling cauldron set over a hearth-fire. On a darker side of the room, men seated at an eating board looked up to see who entered. Our guard called out, "Found these two near the river, goin' north, probably headin' for Bibracte."

I recognized Vercingetorix when he stood away from the shadows and grinned at the news. "*Dago*...good. We shall find out why."

Lucterios squinted at me. "You're the Raurici crafter. We spoke at Saumis."

Vercingetorix also remembered. "I was with you in the dolmen. "Who is your companion?"

He replied, "Simonides, a native of Massilia," before I could.

"*Were* you going to Bibracte, then?" Lucterios asked.

"I was going there on my way in returning to Massilia."

Vercingetorix was skeptical. "*Graecus*, you take a strange route to the Rodanos delta. Have you come to join us?"

Apparently, the king had not recognized us at Gergovia, or perhaps he trifled with me as his uncle had. I decided to tell what I suspected Vercingetorix already knew. "I'm Alberix, a crafter, but in the Romani *auxiliae* as armorer. Ollam Fodla, must have told you that at Saumis."

Vercingetorix's answer was a suggestion. "Son of Alrix, if you stayed with me a month you would change allegiance back to your own people."

I said, "Many Celts are *auxiliae* I met Romani when they came to Wermaros and built towers."

"I know your story…" Vercingetorix came closer to cajole me. "Join us, Alberix. Warriors arrive, many twenties each day, for a war of liberation from the enemy yoke. These chieftains will leave in the morning and return with men for a Gallic army I shall command."

As the noblemen pounded fists on the table in agreement, Lucterios shouted, "Clouds of blood on the Romani! Vercingetorix is our king!"

The appointed king quieted the outburst with a raised hand. "We have need of armorers, Alberix. Consider yourself an 'honor hostage'." He looked toward Simonides. "You also must stay not to betray us. What are *your* skills?"

"I keep records for my merchant father but prefer to write about events as they happen."

Chieftains at the table laughed at his answer, but chuckling subsided when Vercingetorix told them, "The Massiliote will remain. Celts have bards who sing of great events attained by our people. When they will sing of our victory over the Romani, this merchant's son shall record it for me and for them."

I exchanged glances with Simonides. We both silently agreed that being "honor hostages" was preferable to having our frozen bodies decorate a palisade gate.

❧❦

Throughout the days, warriors from various tribes responded to a rebellion exhorted by druids and chiefs, and trickled into the camp. Yet they were far from the 'many twenties each day' of which the king boasted.

Heavy snow came with the new moon of Dumann. I wondered how mother, Apsa, and Cluvios fared at Wermaros, when I might be able to return. With Simonides, I watched as the circle of campfires extended further around the village. Crude tenting was put up on the slushy fields to protect men against frigid ground and cold nights.

I toured tribal armories to test Gallic long two-edged swords and found many blades that bent as easily as iron weapons captured from the Helvetii. Cluvios taught me forging methods that were like the pattern-welded techniques of Romani, yet even if I wanted to rework these blades there were no supplies to establish a forge.

As the length of each day decreased, the restlessness of idle warriors increased. Simonides recorded our Gallic reputation for violent actions. After several brawls turned deadly, Vercingetorix ordered public punishments that ranged from mutilation to death—stern warnings to malcontents in the over-crowded encampment.

The Ambivareti moved away to avoid unruly warriors. After woods were hunted out of game the feasts of venison that had been one of the camp's attractions ceased. Now that wheat and barley were rationed, slaves went to shake frozen acorns off bare oak trees. I couldn't help but compare the confusion among the makeshift shelters with the disciplined training that legion recruits had received at Viennadunum, when Caesar set out after the Helvetii. I felt it foolish for Vercingetorix to summon warriors in the dead of winter. Fighting did not take place then.

Ever greater numbers of idle men began to desert. I wanted to write Cluvios about my growing uncertainty regarding the success of a rebellion, yet there was no way to get a letter to Wermaros.

⚘

Under an overcast sky on the *Eidus* of December, Simonides recorded incredible news that came to the encampment: A man named Cotos arrived, shouting that Romani merchants at Cenabum had been massacred. Finally, the uprising had commenced!

Vercingetorix heard the commotion and went outside to question the courier. "When did this happen? Where is Cotuatos?"

"Today, before Belenos rose, he led warriors against the Romani. I rode from Condate with the report for you. Words of rebellion are being passed along the river."

Simonides was skeptical. "Have you names for these merchants? How do you know this is not an idle boast of the Carnutes?"

Cotos admitted, "I was not there, but they report that a barge named 'Cosnia' was burned."

I thought of Fufius Cita and his wife. The barge with her name had brought us to the Plain of Mounds.

"Those fools!" a furious Vercingetorix ranted. "We need transports to move supplies. *Cosnia* was the swiftest boat on the Liger."

He calmed himself and motioned us inside his hut. The king's face was gaunt, his hair longer. His moustache had grown, yet he kept himself clean-shaven, perhaps to be easily recognizable in a helmet. His blue eyes reflected a reddish-brown in the glow of the fire as he summarized his plans.

"*Graecus*, it seems that swords are unsheathed. I tell you this so that you may begin the account of how even our children's children will sing of our victory."

"What will you do now?" I asked the king.

"Do, Alberix? I shall attack while this Caesar is foolhardy enough to leave his legions in Gallia without being present. Lucterios will lead his Cadurci south and free Gallia Narbonensis. At the same time I will move my army against legions nearby and collect more warriors the way a reaper gathers grain stalks. It will be as Luernos predicted, 'Clouds of blood will fall on our enemy'." Vercingetorix raised his voice so that sub-chieftains who had come inside would be sure to hear. "From Gesoriacum to the marshes of the Rodanos, we will sweep Gallia free of Romani!"

Shouting approval, the chiefs rushed outside to organize their men into tribal units. Simonides, as stunned as I was at the report, ignored the order to begin writing. Instead, he wanted to return to our tent and talk about what the outbreak of war meant for me.

It was gloomy inside our flimsy shelter, but the joyous warriors—anticipating imminent departure—had thrown their wood reserves onto campfires. The added brightness gave us some warmth and enough light to see. I slumped on my bedding straw. Simonides hunched cross-legged opposite me, his expression grim.

"If...if the report is true, then Cita and Cosnia surely are dead."

"With Antiochus and his wife."

"They would not have been spared, nor anyone who worked for Romani..." He paused and cocked his head. "Hear those boisterous warriors out there? They would attack Roma itself if a talking mule gave the order!"

"You said that this concerns me yet what about you?"

"You're one of the *Keltoi* and must choose on which side to fight. I can make up verses that will make '*Rix Vercin*' look like a demi-god, then depart with my head still attached to my shoulders."

"I did resent Cita's game with me but that doesn't justify his murder."

Simonides batted at straw with his writing board. "Alberix, I also regret it, yet in six campaigns how many *Keltoi* have been slaughtered in the name of the '*Senatus populusque Romanus*'? How many Helvetii alone? I try to escape by writing about events after they happen and then make them into a kind of entertaining story. Hades! In a thousand years what is happening here will be related as a myth, yet Cita and Cosnia were actual flesh and blood. Now both are dead like all the others. That's why I'm so determined to tell the truth."

I looked at animated shadows of the men on the tent's walls before saying, "I killed at Octodurus to save the legion, but the deaths of those merchants is different. They were not warriors..."My look met his. "I understand again why Father wanted a way that would lead to peace. What would you do in my place?"

Simonides hesitated. "I...I'm new at military tactics, but I see this as a two-pronged attack to destroy all the legions here while Caesar is away. On the other hand, the commander has conquered most of Gallia with the superior discipline and tactics of a few thousand men. Alberix"—he reached to grasp my hand—"My friend, you could die on either side, yet your mother hopes that you will follow your father's ideal. Even if Vercingetorix wins a battle or two, how long can he keep his sub-chiefs in line once a reason for their co-operation is gone?"

"You're saying?"

"I'm pointing out that these dice haven't yet been thrown and that you should remember how Cita won over you."

"With false dice."

"Exactly..." Simonides stood to brush straw off his trousers. "I should go back to the king's hut and start a letter to my sister. Maybe begin a *paeon* to him that our Three Fates will eventually complete."

I got up and clasped his arm. "*Grates, amicus.* You...you've helped me think beyond a village palisade."

He returned my grasp to jest, "And you've kept me from pissing into the wind too often! I hope you've learned that lesson for yourself..." Simonides paused as a new round of shouting sounded from outside. "Zeus only knows how you'll sleep with all that, may I say, 'premature celebrating'!"

After he left, I lay back on the straw to ponder what I could do. Later, it was not the noise that kept me awake, but the conflict in my mind about the possibility of a unified Celtic nation, weighed against the reality of our subservience to an alien conqueror.

⚘

A few days later, while preparing to move out of the camp, Vercingetorix was encouraged to learn that Julius Caesar's most important supporter at

Roma had been murdered by a rival faction. The Aeduan who brought the news also reported that Caesar would be too preoccupied with impending civil war to rejoin his legions, even in the spring. The isolation of eight legions in Gallia from their commander—for which Vercingetorix hoped— was to be a reality!

I noticed a smaller man who had come in with the courier. Incredibly, it was Ollam Fodla! I hurried to tell Simonides, but he already knew of the druid's presence.

"Yes, I saw him. I'm not surprised, because druids were behind that massacre at Cenabum."

"Why did Fodla come here? We're preparing to leave this camp."

Simonides made a motion as if throwing dice. "I'll wager any point on the dice that we'll know that by tonight's sunset."

❧

Simonides would have won his throw. Ollam Fodla called together Vercingetorix's clan chieftains and ordered them to bring their most trusted warriors to a nearby oak grove after the afternoon meal.

A red sun lingered above the filigree of black branches as Simonides and I mingled at the edge of warriors who gathered in the clearing. With hoods over our heads, it was easy for us to blend in with many similar men in the assembly.

Fodla's sunken eyes glanced over the ragged groups before calling out to them, "Warrior men of Gallia! I summon the gods by whom your clans swear to witness your oaths. A time for destroying the Romani is here and we have a warrior-king who will lead us to victory." After an outburst of shouting and shield-banging, the dark druid asked, "All who would have Vercingetorix as Over-chief of our common effort, signify in the ancient manner."

Another rhythmic clatter of sword blades against shields sent roosting birds winging out of bare trees and circling the assembly in frantic wheeling.

"*Vox bellorum!*" an excited Simonides exclaimed. "Not even Polybius was privileged to witness such an occasion at first hand!"

I kept silent, recalling the long ago Germani raid on Wermaros that began with similar shouting and ended in disaster for the Suebi attackers.

After a wild clamor of support, Vercingetorix stepped out from the first rank of warriors to quiet them. He realized that if he hoped to hold the men together, he must promise an action that would replace the idleness and uncertainty of the past month.

As the noise subsided, he raised his sword. "I tell you that Lucterios has moved south with his Cadurci to retake the Narbonensis. Luernos has Gergovia and it is Gobinnatio who now is in exile." After renewed cheering, he continued, "The Roman Caesar sits helpless in his *Cisalpina*. The sword of civil war points at his back, and the snows of Gallia block an advance into our lands." Vercingetorix's voice rose in pitch. "Warriors, never have tribes joined together so fruitfully against an enemy as they have today!"

A low sun behind him threw the king into silhouette and surrounded his body with an aura of golden light.

Even Simonides was awed at the supernatural display and turned to grasp my cloak. "A true hero! Alberix, epics have been written about such men! We are present at the creation of a demi-god!"

Vercingetorix again was speaking. "...Caturix, our war god, be witness to my words. With the return of Belenos I shall lead you into the lands of our allies, the Biturges. Our combined warriors will destroy two legions camped among the Lingone tribe."

Further words would have been unheard: jubilant warriors broke forward to clutch at the king's garments, and then hurried to plunder any remaining stocks of *cervisa*. Even the night watches were abandoned as the men drank to the Babd, their bloody patroness of battle. Each boasted of the mounds of booty he would amass when Romani camps were sacked.

Simonides slipped back to his lodge to record the investiture. He told me later that in writing about the day's events he preserved the opening actions of a vast Gallic rebellion. Julius Caesar would not be able to edit or censor the words to suit his own purpose.

I went back to my tent while the sounds of celebration intensified. Until now, I had been able to avoid a firm commitment, but soon Vercingetorix would demand that every Celt declare himself for or against the rebellion.

CHAPTER VII

In the days after Apsa's acquittal for the death of Arvos, the young woman spent much of her free time walking along the banks of the Dubis River. The cold air was cleansing. She felt close to the Earth Mother while following trails of animals that came to drink at the river and then tracked back into the woods. In a silence sundered only by the call of birds, or the sigh of wind through tree branches, Apsa felt caught up in a mystical interplay between the Now and Other-worlds.

Even though her parents sold her as a child, it seemed that unexplained forces always had protected her. Yet druid priests taught that gods were beneficial only to those who made bargains with them and Apsa never owned much to exchange. The concept of an all-pervading entity or force, the Logos that Alberix learned about from Lucius Velcanius, attracted her and yet it seemed another form of the Earth Mother. The goddess, Arduinna, had not physically appeared when Apsa cried out her name, but the distraction saved her from Arvos. Like that of a god, the unexpected appearance of Marius had reversed a druid's death-judgment. If Alberix had not visited the legion stables at the same time she attempted to hang herself, she would not be alive.

A supernatural force working through persons who were not druids was frightening in its implications, yet the divine pattern was there to be unraveled like intertwining Celtic knot work.

❧

On morning of the sixth day after the winter solstice, Apsa felt restless. The unquiet did not subside as afternoon shadows lengthened along the village streets. Leaving Ger with Ersa, she walked across the Dubis bridge. The sky was clear and it would not be dark for another watch period. With a moon rising to balance the winter setting of Belenos, Apsa walked up to a sheltered place where Alberix and Dividiac had recorded the rising of the sun god for the location of an equinox *menhir*.

Shredded by wind, rain, and snow of seven years, the leather panels hung in tatters. Fingering a section of rotted hide, Apsa looked across the valley; the stone marker was invisible among snow-blanketed trees. She brushed cold whiteness from a log where the men had sat for their observations to think of Alberix. He had been gone over a year, yet a letter to Cluvios said that he would return before Samain. Reaching into her belt pouch, Apsa took out a letter in which Alberix had mentioned her.

> *Apsa, I must tell you that I miss you and our outings in the sleigh with Ger.*
>
> *I plan to return to Wermaros in the moon before Samain. Alberix.*

After Cluvios read the sentences to her several times, she memorized the words and was able to recognize letters in Alberix's name, and hers. The message was a fragile reminder of the winter past, yet Apsa had something tangible of Alberix's that she recently acquired. When she went with Briga to bring winter clothing to Moira, Marius gave her the sling-stone that had injured Alberix in Gallia.

Sitting in the tattered shelter, clutching the smooth stone, Apsa closed her eyes to remove her consciousness from the clatter of cook pans at the lodge and Ger's childish chatter. In the solitude a voice of her inner-being might be heard and tapped for a vision of where Alberix could be. She chewed *valerianus* root from her pouch and turned her head to the west, toward Gallia, to envision Alberix's location.

Holding tightly to the sling-stone, Apsa absorbed its power as she spoke aloud about the object's significance in her life and his. "Stone, you injured Alberix yet brought him back to me alive. I helped heal him. Stone, he once saved me from death, thus our debt to each other is in balance. Stone, you traveled throughout Gallia. Help me find Alberix."

Apsa chewed the sedative valerian until tranquility descended. In moments a brightness infused her consciousness until only a blue void, like an expanse of clear sky, remained in her mind. The stone felt weightless, yet, paradoxically, large and heavy as the mountain of Benn Samain. Apsa's finger traced a spiral on its smooth surface while she concentrated on Alberix and tried to discern signs of his location.

With her eyes closed, repeating the words of her incantation to the stone again and again, Apsa's sub-conscious forged a tenuous link with reality: the image of a hare appeared in an aspen grove. Another hare was nearby, caught in a snare.

> *The aspens were in their golden autumn splendor. The dead hare hung limply, but the first animal seemed unharmed, except for a smear of blood on one ear. An eagle swooped from the sky and tore at the flesh of the dead animal, even as the great bird's wings hovered over the first hare. That apparition dissolved. The aspens became the dim outline of a town, larger than she had seen before. In a blue sky one of the letters in Alberix's message was over it—the "A" that she knew as the sound-symbol of her name and his.*

Apsa shivered and the trance broke.

When she opened her eyes the tree skeletons on the western crests combed the last flush of sunset. Breathing deeply, she knew that it always happened that way: the calming sedation was followed by a gradual revealing of her consciousness as a blue void. Then—if they came—the images were in the form of an arcane meaning she must unravel. What did the two hares signify, or the letter 'A' of their names?

After returning to the lodge, Apsa found that Dirona had come to share with Briga part of the mourning period for Cluvios. Apsa's mouth still tingled from the sedative and she ate little. After helping Ersa put away supper dishes and tucking Ger into his bed, she approached the sisters with a plan that had formed as she descended back to the village.

"I...I am going to try and find Alberix."

Surprised, Briga asked, "In Gallia? Impossible."

Dirona differed. "Sister, let Apsa speak. She has reasons for saying this."

"I... I experienced a vision in the forest."

"Go on," Dirona urged. "Describe it, Apsa."

"I was in an aspen grove and saw two hares, one wounded but safe, and another dead, caught in a snare. An eagle appeared from the sky and tore at the flesh of the second animal. It protected the unharmed hare with its wings. Then the aspens turned into the hazy outline of a town. The letter 'A' was in the sky above."

"Could you see familiar landmarks around the town?"

Apsa shook her head. "Dirona, it was greater than any place I've seen, much larger than Octodurus."

"And you saw an 'A' above it?"

"Yes, Cluvios showed me that letter beginning my name."

Now Briga was interested. "Also Alberix, my son."

"That could refer to both of you and a town," Dironia surmised. "How many large settlements in Gallia have names that begin with 'A'?"

"Arialbinnum, for one," Briga recalled. "Aventia is another, but I don't know places farther west."

After a moment, Apsa thought, "Perhaps Moira can help or Marius. He's with her at the watchtower, so I could ask them."

Dirona was cautious. "Be careful. Villagers are not allowed at the towers and you know how irrational Liscos has become."

Briga asked, "He still sees himself as eventual over-chief at Vesontio?"

"Sister, my husband's foolish ambitions increase with his drinking. Cluvios is dead. Ollam Fodla has gone, so whatever restraints they might have had over him no longer exist. After Marius's return, legionaries were banned from buying food in Wermaros. Supplies now are left outside the towers."

Briga listened without commenting, but realized it might be only a short while before Liscos was foolish or drunk enough to attack *Castor*, the nearest tower.

Apsa stood up. "I'd like to sleep now, and I will go speak with Moira in the morning."

❧❧

Liscos's incentive for attacking *Castor* came that evening. A messenger arrived at his lodge with stunning news: fourteen days earlier, Carnute warriors had killed all Romani merchants at Cenabum.

The report was not brought to Briga until dawn. Apsa's decision to find Alberix was increased in urgency—and danger—by the news of rebellion. She also needed to tell Marius about the massacre so he could summon help for the tower garrisons.

When Apsa trotted Derka toward the tower, no guards were at the river gate— celebrations the night before had taken their toll. An early sun warmed the air enough for ground fog to form in forest hollows. Apsa directed her horse through the concealing mists to *Castor*.

Startled at an approaching figure on horseback and not recognizing the rider, sentries suspected a diversion that might precede an attack. They shouted a warning down to men inside.

Apsa threw back the hood of her fur jacket and called up to legionaries at the crenellations, "I wish to see Marius. Tell him Apsa, the friend of Alberix."

One man recognized her. When word was passed to the barracks, a surprised Marius himself opened the doorway to let down a ladder and help her inside

"Apsa? Has...has something happened in the village?"

"I have important news."

Shocked at a look of fear in her eyes, he took her arm. "Come to my quarters." As he led her to his cubicle, legionaries had heard the woman and withheld their usual sexual jesting. Moira was there, huddled in a blanket, coughing, and seated close to the brazier for warmth. "The druidess is feverish," Marius explained. "What have you to tell me?"

"A Sequani came from Vesontio to report that Carnutes murdered all your merchants at Cenabum."

"All killed?" Marius raised a hand to his forehead and shook his head. "Jupiter! That means the Gallic rebellion has matured into violence. Have you heard from Alberix?"

"No, and he was to return here in the moon of Cantios."

"Cantios? That's our October. *Auxiliae* usually *are* back by then."

"Marius, I want to find him. What places in Gallia begin with your Latin letter 'A'?"

"Gallic towns and villages? Why not ask me to name the stars!" Marius laughed, but was serious again at Apsa's intent look. "I don't know. Agedincum... Aduatuca. Avaricum. Why do you ask?"

"I...I've had a vision of where Alberix might be."

"A vision?" Marius fell silent, recalling a sarcastic line from Terentius saying that an oracle could always be cited as an excuse to do or keep from doing something. But the woman's question was hopeless. "How can I help you, especially with this disaster that took place at Cenabum?"

"Go with me into Gallia."

"With you into....?" Marius scoffed disbelief. "Impossible! I'm assigned here. I have my duty,"

"Your towers will need help. How long will wolves let sheep sleep inside their pen?"

"A valid point," he admitted, "yet I don't know Gallia that well."

Moira had been listening. "Roman, I do."

Marius glanced at her, but shook his head. "Out of the question! Apsa, I value your warning, but Alberix might return at any day. You...you should go back to your lodge."

At his refusal, she reluctantly agreed. As Marius stood at the door and watched her descend to mount her horse, he knew his reassurance had not fooled the Celtic woman. Back in his quarters, he poked nervously at the brazier coals.

Moira chided him. "Roman, I know much about visions. Listen to her or your men will be massacred like those merchants at Cenabum. Apsa will seek her man whether you go with her or not."

Marius jammed the poker into the coals in silent anger. He was not used to being counseled by females and resented the fact that these two probably were correct. He wanted to lose his cares in the warmth of Moira's body—despite having realized she was a disciple of the Greek poetess, Sappho of Lesbos. He straightened up to mumble, "I'll be the one who decides what to do."

No, Liscos will decide. Moira watched him stalk out to be with his men.

The druidess was correct—and much more quickly than even she had foreseen.

వావ

Liscos formed his plan by accident—literally. One morning, a few days later, he stood talking with river gate sentries about the rebellion. When a wagon braking down the road opposite snapped a linchpin, the damaged wheel wobbled off its axle, rolled across the bridge, and smashed into a vendor's booth. The wood structure was destroyed and several palisade stakes damaged. Eyeing the results, Liscos envisioned a strategy: if a large enough mill-wheel could be dragged up the slope behind *Castor*, it might be released down to shatter tower stonework. Warriors concealed nearby could enter and capture the garrison. He would regain stature among Gallic chieftains.

Liscos knew that two such huge wheels were available. Located upstream on a bank of the Dubis lay two waterwheel segments that he intended to assemble in the spring and install in a new gristmill.

వావ

The chieftain even stopped drinking to supervise the operation of his plan. Motivated by a handful of coins, the promise of booty—and finally action—six of his idle men roped and dragged the four wooden sections of one wheel into the river. It took half a day to float them to a point just beyond watchtower *Castor*. The next day, as workers pulled the sections to the bank, village slaves began hacking a pathway through forest trees and up the slope. A crude block and tackle helped position the arc-shaped pieces to where they could be assembled with iron plates pegged onto each section.

Marius and the garrison were puzzled by the sound of axes and saws echoing nearby. Their confusion turned to alarm when two men sent out to scout the activity did not return.

By the time Liscos's workers had cleared a down-slope lane behind *Castor*, Marius glimpsed the wheel segments and was able to surmise their purpose. His concern grew as the arcs were pegged together: the tower had not been designed to withstand a ram. A sortie by his few men was not feasible—the Celts would ambush and massacre them one by one among the forest growths.

వావ

On a dank morning that followed a wet snowfall, legionaries of the first watch were stunned to see the heads of their missing companions impaled on spears that faced the tower entrance. After Marius was summoned to witness the grisly trophies, he saw ravens fluttering around them and knew what would follow. While building a Rhenus bridge in the hills of Germania, he and his men had experienced the terror which the unknown could spawn.

In the cramped barracks fear would demoralize his men and turn feelings of helplessness into deadly quarrels.

Inside Wermaros, the topic of bake-oven gossip was Liscos's plan to attack the tower. After Apsa heard the women, she thought that might be another chance to persuade Marius to send for help. Yet with warriors at work near the site, it was impossible to approach *Castor* unseen. It could only be done if an event like a storm forced the men's return to the village. Desperate, she prayed for snow at her forest shrine to Arduinna.

On the same day that clouds had swept in and brought the snow for which Apsa petitioned, news came from Vesontio that Julius Caesar would not be rejoining his Gallic legions. Liscos felt elated enough to resume his drinking.

Watching the thick flakes of white swirl in, Apsa mounted Derka and trotted the horse toward the Dubis road with a second mare in tow. She had told Ersa to put Ger to bed and not tell Briga that she was leaving for the night.

Gate sentries intent on discussing the trouble in Gallia barely looked up as Apsa passed. Further on, she turned Derka up a trail that led below the tower. While it was yet light enough to see, she halted in a protected hollow and ordered both horses to lie down. Wrapping herself in a bearskin pelt, she wedged herself between the animals to absorb their warmth and strength. With a final prayer that the snowfall would be heavy enough to stop work on the millwheels, Apsa prepared to spend a ritual night in the forest.

Snow had continued. Legionaries of the dawn watch were surprised to see two horses and a snow-covered rider emerge from the edge of the forest. This time they recognized Apsa. Marius was summoned and admitted the woman into the barracks. The room was frigid since the brazier and cook-fires were banked low to save fuel.

Fearful of troubling news, he pulled her aside. "Apsa, has something else happened? Why did you come?"

She shook the last snow off her jacket. "I wish to speak with Moira."

"Sh...she's in my quarters."

The druidess was surprised, but the two women sat on Marius's cot and spoke in a Celtic dialect that he did not understand. "Talk in a language I know!" he brusquely ordered.

Apsa told him, "A man named something like Clodos was murdered at Roma. What will this mean?"

"You mean Clodius? Publius Clodius? He's Caesar's friend among Senate tribunes."

"Liscos is joyous at the news."

"I don't wonder. This may keep Caesar in the *Cisalpina* for our summer campaigns."

"And help for you here." Moira proposed, "I could lead you out to warn the nearest legion."

Marius looked toward Apsa. "And find Alberix? Is that what you two were conspiring about?"

Moira ignored his cynicism. "In a few days the millwheels will be assembled. Even if they do not breach your tower stones, Liscos's men will vote to starve you out."

Marius exhaled in frustration and slumped down on a stool. "How can we summon help? Or find Alberix? Where will we even go in Gallia?"

Moira replied with assurance. "There will be signs. I am a druidess and Gallic warriors are known for their boasting."

Apsa untied a bundle she had brought inside. "Marius, I have clothing of our people for you to wear."

"Clothing?" He went to bring a small parchment from his desk and half-smiled. "Ladies, you win the throw. This message already tells the men of *Pollux* tower to come here. How can I get it to Marcellus?"

"Anvalos will take the note."

"Fine. Apsa, come to my table." Marius unrolled one of the scrolls on which Simonides had drawn the eastern area of Gaul. "Where shall we start looking?"

"My vision was of a town and the letter 'A'."

"So you said." The engineer took out a divider and placed one leg on the main Roman winter camp. "Our *hibernia* is here at Agedincum. That's an 'A.' If I swing the other divider leg...let's see...one day, two days' march, then Avaricum and Alesia are the only two places that seem practical."

Moira studied the chart. "Both are on the road to Carnutum. The way is through Cabillonum and Decetia. At Decetia is where we shall find out about Alberix."

"Decetia does not begin with an 'A'..." Marius said and waited for an elaboration.

Moira repeated, "That is where we will *learn* about Alberix."

Marius felt better as he rolled the papyrus. *The certainty of this half-savage priestess defies questioning, yet I feel fairly confident for the first time.* He held up a pair of checkered trousers that Apsa had brought him, to quip, "Lead on then, servants of *Fortuna*...as soon as your Gallic companion puts on his trousers!"

❧

Apsa was correct in anticipating that the storm would force Liscos's men to stay in Wermaros, unable to complete their work. Inside the village the workers waited for slaves to start clearing a forest pathway through snow to the millwheel. Apsa left the mare she had brought for Moira at the tower, then returned to tell Briga of her journey and ask Anvalos to deliver the message to *Pollux*. She met Marius and Moira on a back trail that led west.

❧

Liscos awoke in a fury as deep as the recently fallen snow drifts. His head ached from tempering his frustration at the storm's delay by drinking himself insensible the night before. His elder wives, Trauna and Dirona, tried to calm him, but he stalked out into the blinding glare of whiteness. Trudging to his workers' lodges, the chieftain shamed a few into coming with him to inspect the wheels. He feared that in his absence the tower garrison had destroyed them.

Liscos forced his horse to wallow through snowdrifts up to the site, and his men's mounts followed in the rough pathway the animal made. The chieftain's anger abated when he brushed snow away from the cradling and saw the huge segments still in place.

"The Romani...couldn't...get to you," he panted, stroking the wood. "Now we'll see if...if they're so strong." Liscos paused to catch his breath and decide how best to release the first millwheel.

A man cautioned, "We need more warriors if we're to fight the garrison."

"Then...go back...to the village. Bring them here."

"Now, with this deep snow?"

The chieftain glared at him. "If *you* question the time, will not the Romani be unprepared? In the name of Caturix, go for more men!"

Liscos was not an engineer and had argued with the carpenters over cradling that held the wheel upright while the sections were assembled. His good arm had aligned imaginary props to solve a problem that none of his workers encountered before— holding the four wheel segments upright to be pegged together. Liscos's solution was to angle tree trunk braces into the ground, and wedge them against the lower vanes of the millwheel. The bracing held while the segments were assembled.

As Liscos's breathing eased, his patience evaporated. Abruptly, he stood and shouted for the few warriors present to hammer away the twin supports. Raging again, when he discovered they had not brought hammers, he screamed

89

for them to hack away at the trunks with swords. When their iron blades bent after a few strokes, the chieftain pushed the men away and used his own damask steel weapon—a treaty gift of the Romani—to finish cutting a V-shaped notch in each trunk. Sweating from exertion, he threw off his fur jacket and ordered two men to bring rocks and pound at the wood until the supports gave way.

It took time to find proper-size stones under deep snow, but wood fibers splintered at their hammering. The wheel shifted slightly, yet held in place.

Liscos's face glistened with perspiration. Still nauseous from over-drinking, when glare off the snow blinded his eyes, he moved into the shadow of the wheel to curse, "Cernunnos take the Romani! I'll have their heads on the palisade by nightfall."

A warrior voiced what others were thinking. "Liscos, there are not enough of us to take on the Shorthairs. Wait for more men to come."

Their chieftain stood, raised his sword, and shouted a supreme Celtic insult. "Shame on your beards, you pack of lap dogs! When I lost my arm, it took three Leuci warriors to do so, and all died in the taking!" To demonstrate, he hacked furiously at the props, then kicked the supporting struts with his left foot.

A shrill, snapping sound echoed in the forest as the bracing gave way. Liscos was pitched forward by the momentum of his blow—at the same instant that the wheel, now free of restraints, rolled downward. Immobilized by horror, none of his men sprang forward to pull their chieftain from danger.

Liscos fell hard, rolling on his back. Frantic, he tried to lever himself out from the path of the wheel's gathering momentum, but his good arm slipped on snow. The shadow of the huge disc blocked out the sun and fell across his terror-filled eyes—a precursor of the eternal void that in moments overtook him. The paddleboards crushing his chest muffled the chieftain's screams. A final gasp was unheard above the rumbling of the millwheel as it crashed through the underbrush.

Wobbling down a path hacked through the firs, the wheel struck an outcropping of rock that angled it toward a corner of *Castor*. The impact tore out a section of stonework, but left the tower undamaged. Continuing its roll, the massive disc came to a stop in the center of the Dubis River, still upright.

❧

When Liscos's shattered body was brought into his lodge and the circumstances of the accident told to his wives, Briga recalled an old prediction made by Dividiac. "One day Liscos will be crushed by the wheel of his ambitions." If the prophecy was intended as a bard's poetic speech, it had been fulfilled by the Sequani chief's ill-advised attack on legionaries of Gaius Julius Caesar. At that moment the commander was at Ravenna in his *Cisalpina* Province, with no plans for soon returning to Gallia.

CHAPTER VIII

Located along a northeast curve on the Adriatic side of the Italian peninsula, the port of Ravenna was Caesar's winter headquarters, where he attended to business that aides presented to him as governor.

Secured by the sea and a ring of marshes on the land side, Ravenna had attracted strategic interest because of a naval base at Classis, two miles to the south. During a civil war, Metellus, one of Sulla's legates, had disembarked there thirty years earlier and noted the area's potential as a harbor for the Roman Adriatic fleet.

Although Ravenna itself was only the size of a two-legion army camp, the town boasted an amphitheater and circus, as well as a capitol building, temple to Apollo and a basilica where the governor and his magistrates adjudicated legal cases. Caesar had recognized the site's advantages and commissioned architect-engineer, Marcus Vitruvius Pollo, to undertake the enlargement of port facilities.

❧

The weather was sunny, yet cooled by an off-sea breeze from the Adriatic that brought First Centurion Lucius Velcanius a scent of salt air inside the arena. He mused that Ravenna was a pleasant post for winter duty, similar to Aquileia, and idyllic compared to the camp of Legio X in Gallia, near an ice-blocked Rhenus River.

Velcanius had been detached from that legion to direct the formation of an elite unit of bodyguards for Julius Caesar. The initiative for such a guard had come from Adherbal, a Numidian prince. Like most Romans, he shared a loathing for sea travel, and decided not to risk a winter passage back to his North African country. Instead, he retained eight of his cavalrymen as an escort and brought them back from Gallia to Ravenna for training in dismounted battle tactics. After Lucius heard reports about a trio of gladiators performing in nearby towns, he hired them for the month of Januarius as trainers to the dark-skinned Numidians.

The idea of a personal guard intrigued Caesar, so he welcomed Adherbal's men as a nucleus. A corps of dusky retainers would be a sensation at Roma and the prince's father, an African king at Thabraca, would be more loyally bound to the Republic—and to Caesar.

As Lucius leaned against a training post on the warm sand, he closed his eyes to catch sun on his face. Training would resume after a mid-day rest. He reflected on Briga, the Celtic woman at Wermaros who never was far from his mind. *It's hard to believe that I haven't seen her for a year...seems like an aeon. After twenty-six years of service, I've reached a top rank in the legions, yet have only loneliness for a bedmate. I hardly understand this longing for her. Had not my readings in Stoicism put me above such earthly passions?*

"Lu-cius not happy?" Adherbal's dark brow wrinkled with concern for his friend. "Wish be other place?"

Lucius opened his eyes at the question. "Eh? True, I was thinking about another time."

"You think of mother of Al-brix? Yes?"

Lucius avoided answering. "Do you remember who will train your men in the afternoon session?"

"Woman warrior. What her name again?"

"The *gladiatrix*? Maronea...'The Thracian Tigress'."

"Why she man-fighter, Lu-cius? Why woman not talk?"

"Maronea is a mute. I suppose she was forced into the arena as a slave, but she's a freedwoman now and probably earned her manumission by surviving the games. She and the two men make a living by putting on gladiatorial exhibitions in the provinces. I doubt they've ever seen Roma."

"Ce-sar like idea of Adher-bal to have Numidae for guard?"

Lucius chuckled. The prince could ask questions with the swiftness of a sword thrust. "Well, here you are here at Ravenna instead of Africa."

Adherbal affected a shiver. "Ra-venn' too cold!"

Lucius noticed movement at the area's shadowed archway. "Maronea is coming in with her partners. Get your men onto the sand."

As the prince went to bring in his Numidians, Lucius went over to meet the woman. *Graceful walk, not too much like a man's. I imagine Maronea stayed alive by being more agile than some of the brutes she's fought. Being a mute probably helped. Gladiators are superstitious and might believe she had been touched by a god.*

Lean and muscular, the woman had put on the fighting weapons of a *retiari*—a rope net and blunted practice trident. Her protection was bronze leg greaves, with leather shoulder and stomach protectors above a short skirt. Cup-shaped silver pods enclosed small breasts.

"*Salus gladiatrix!*" Lucius called out, noting that white scars disfigured her arms and upper chest.

Maronea nodded toward him without smiling, held up a net and trident in her right hand, then signed to a partner with the other.

"*Centurio,*" he said, "I'm Atrax. Our other gladiator there is Hellenikos. Maronea wants to give those dark-skinned men experience with *a retiarus* opponent. Most guards think they only need a sword. Also, that weapon would be heavier and a disadvantage to a shorter woman."

"I'm glad her...her breasts are protected."

Atrax chuckled. "*Centurio*, you'll see how she uses those silver cups to find an opening in her adversary's defense."

Adherbal joined them in the center of the arena with his men. Atrax stood by to interpret the woman's signs. Hellenikos watched from the arena's shaded side.

Atrax said, "Maronea signed asking about what practice weapons the Numidians will choose. They're cavalry with short swords, round shields, and lances."

"Try padded lances," Lucius suggested. "Horsemen think they're pretty good with that weapon."

"*Lancae*," he told Maronea.

She nodded and let her net unfold to the ground, then provocatively flicked it at the nearest opponent.

Those Numidians who understood Latin laughed: the spears were over twice as tall as the woman. After a short discussion in Berber, one of the men tied a turban over the point of his lance, then stepped forward, confidently juggling the lengthy weapon.

Adherbal grinned. "Good, Juba. You fight but not hurt woman."

"Take a shield, too," Atrax called in a sarcastic coax. "Isn't that part of your equipment?"

Juba looked at Adherbal, who repeated the request in Berber. The Numidian shook his head in refusal and motioned his companions out of the way.

While Adherbal was talking, Maronea had maneuvered herself around so that the afternoon sun was at her back. She would feel out this Juba, let him think himself superior, and thus become careless. There was time for to ease toward the sun and let reflections from her silver breast-guards blind his eyes. Juba faced her, crouched, with his lance at the ready. Maronea kicked her net behind her—novices intent on out-maneuvering her usually forgot that the entangling web was there.

Bending forward to make as small a target as possible, the *gladiatrix* kept her trident leveled at Juba's throat and waited for him to engage with a first thrust. The Numidian tried to circle out of the sun's rays, but the woman's trident feints at his head kept him in place. Frustrated, angered at a female opponent, Juba abruptly thrust out at her with his lance. Maronea nimbly sidestepped, caught the wooden shaft between the prongs of her trident, and forced it into the sand. The Numidian easily pulled his spear out amid approving shouts from his mates. He repeated the thrusting maneuver, but the *gladiatrix* always deflected his spear away from herself.

Juba's companions began to taunt in Berber what Lucius imagined were allusions to his inability to shaft a woman, sexually or otherwise. He realized that Maronea's tactics were to goad her opponent into a reckless move; she easily could have slid the trident's tip up the shaft and into the man's arm or chest.

Juba tried a different strategy. Feigning another thrust, he swung the lance shaft sideways. The blow struck Maronea on the left shoulder, just below the *galerus*, her curved metal shoulder guard. Even though he failed to follow through with a feigned kill, Juba had staggered his opponent around to face the sun's position.

While he grinned at his success Maronea's face remained expressionless. She watched his eyes. The sun still was where she could use it: a reflecting glare from her silver breast-guards would blind her opponent. She intended to keep it there.

As Maronea deftly moved her upper body, spots of brilliant light danced across the Numidian's face. Juba squinted and tried to step out of the brightness, but the glare followed him. Frustrated, he repeated his previous success. As the lance flailed to the left again, Maronea's trident caught the handle and pushed it away from her head. At the same instant her left hand swung the net out around her opponent's legs and deftly jerked the mesh toward her. Juba tumbled to the sand, his legs entangled in the rope web. Before his startled look could change to indignation, the trident was at his throat. Maronea feigned a kill and stepped back from the stunned African.

Most Numidians applauded the woman. Lucius noted those who did not; he wanted Caesar's guard to be men who respected the skill of an opponent, not those who underestimated enemies and became vulnerable.

Adherbal, smiling, stepped forward. "*Bonum!* Good! You, glad-tor woman, now show more your tricks."

Lucius held up a hand. "Not yet, let's first learn from this. You can translate into Berber what your men don't understand, but thrusting is a common lance tactic and Juba did the normal thing. Maybe he felt overconfident because his opponent was a woman." He paused to let Adherbal explain, noting that Maronea made no move to massage a visible swelling on her shoulder. *Admirable self-control.* At the prince's nod Lucius continued, "What Juba forgot is that his adversary carried a net. Also as important is that Maronea has fought in the arena many times."

"That mean we never be too...too—" A Latin adjective eluded Adherbal.

"*Securior*...too confident. Remember that any opponent you meet has survived up to that point. Never let your guard down, physical or mental."

When Juba stood up, Maronea took his shield off the ground nearby and made an upward movement at his throat with it.

Atrax explained, "Maronea is showing that when she stepped up to him, had he used a shield he might have broken her jaw. A quick upward thrust would have done it."

Lucius recalled that he had used the maneuver on Epanactos when the Sequani had goaded him into fight at Wermaros. "Yes, we're here to learn what gladiators can teach us. Juba, grasp her arm. No bad feelings."

The Numidian lightly gripped Maronea's arm in a reluctant conciliation.

"We here to learn," Adherbal warned his men. "If you not listen to man and *woman*, you fight me!"

After the net and trident demonstration, Atrax and Hellinikos showed the Numidians new methods of defense that used wresting moves if they were attacked on foot by two assailants.

❧

Around the ninth hour shadows had lengthened past the center of the amphitheater. Aemilius Domitinus, *praetor* at Ravenna, came through the entrance accompanied by a ragged, limping companion in a worn, dirty cape.

"*Centurio*," he told Lucius. "This courier just arrived from Roma saying he has an urgent message for Julius Caesar."

"My thanks, *Praetor*. What is your name, man?"

"F...Fufius Trebonius. Trib...Tribune at—" He coughed violently, unable to finish the sentence.

Lucius realized he had seen the man in the Tigurini action. "Tribune, you're in no condition to travel." He called to Adherbal, "That will be enough for today, dismiss your men. Gladiators, be here again tomorrow at the fourth hour. Tribune, I'm *Primipilus* Lucius Velcanius, Tenth Legion. What is your message?"

"For...for Caesar alone." Trebonius sneezed and cursed his journey. "Pluto take this winter weather! At Spoletium the wind could have frozen wine rations. I...I ache everywhere."

"I'll order a hot bath for you at the hostelry."

"I accept, *Centurio*, yet...yet must see Caesar first."

"The Imperator may be hearing legal cases. Take that bath and hot mulled wine while I tell him you've arrived."

Lucius took the tribune to a villa on the Via Hercules that provided lodgings for travelers on state business.

At the basilica, Lucius was told that Caesar had returned to his villa. He made his way toward the *Porta Aurea* quarter, pondering the commander's rising career. *The man is forty-eight now. Another campaign season and he'll have all of Gallia under his shield, as well as the Senatus. He governs three provinces and Roma along with Gnaeus Pompeius. I wonder if the message concerns that officer? Pompeius could undercut Caesar while he's at Ravenna.*

At Caesar's residence in the old quarter, a Gallic servant admitted Lucius and directed him to a second floor study.

"Lucius!" Caesar smiled when he saw his centurion friend and held up a papyrus scroll. "I was just reviewing a case of Cicero's that's quite similar to mine. Sit down a moment. Wine in that amphora. Help yourself."

Lucius mixed himself a watered Falernian, then sat in a folding campaign chair.

Caesar had gone back to reading, absorbed in Cicero's arguments while absently brushing forward strands of thinning hair. "What logic," he marveled, pushing the scroll to one side of the desk. He looked tired. Loose skin at his neck and deep creases alongside his mouth had aged his face. "*Centurio,* about that matter you came to see me?"

"Sir, a Tribune arrived from the capital with a message for you."

"What is it?"

"He wouldn't tell me, wants to talk with you personally."

"It could be that Pompeius is feeling ignored by Senators again. Since Julia is...is dead...our friendship has cooled."

Lucius murmured a condolence, recalling that the commander's daughter was Pompeius's wife and recently died giving birth to an infant that also did not live.

Caesar asked, "Who is this tribune? Do I know him?"

"Fufius Trebonius. He was in your command during the Helvetii campaign, an *auxilia* posting. As soon as the man thaws out in a tub, I'll bring him here."

"Trebonius...Trebonius... I don't really recall him." Caesar shuffled through other scrolls on his desk and pulled one out. "Here's a new commentary by Vitruvius on harbors. Look it over, and then go rouse that tribune. Pour out a splash of your wine to Mercurius, that the news be good."

࿐

Trebonius's message concerned the murder of Publius Clodius by agents of Pompeius, an act by a Triumvirate partner that Caesar had not authorized.

Tullius Tilius, Caesar's *quaestor* in Gallia, now a supporter, had ordered Trebonius to deliver the message. Tilius also made sure that the commander knew which side he was on.

⊷⊶

Caesar penned a conciliatory note to Pompeius, reminding him of their mutual dependence as surviving members of the Triumvirate. The next day he was further disturbed to be brought a report of the Carnute sedition at Cenabum. Fearing that the rebellious action might encourage further hostile actions, he summoned Lucius back to his villa.

After securing the door to his study, Caesar unrolled a papyrus onto a side table. "*Centurio*, smooth out this map of Gallia." Lucius laid a Celtic dagger given him by Liscos on one side; Caesar held the other in place with a bronze statue of Fortuna, then leaned over the chart. "Again, where is this Cenabum?"

Lucius's finger hovered over the papyrus, then pointed to west-cental Gallia and a bend in the Liger River. "Here, Imperator."

"And my legions?"

"Six at Agedincum, there, about fifty miles directly east of Cenabum. Two more are further south in Lingone territory."

"I recall now. Titus Labienus is too far north to be of much help and dare not leave the Treveri unwatched. What date is today?"

"Imperator, six days before the *Eidus* of Januarius."

Caesar smacked his fist into the palm of a hand. "This rebellion coming at the same time as the trouble at Roma is a disaster.! Those Galli hope it will keep me holed up in Ravenna..." He frowned as his finger traced possible routes that relief legions could take, then was interrupted by the rapping on the door. Lucius went to open the portal.

An officer of the Imperator's guard stood outside with a message from the *praefect* at Narbo."

"Narbo?" Caesar pointed to a port on the southwestern coast of Gaul. "That's in my Narbonensis Province and far to the south of Cenabum. What sort of trouble could... Read it, Lucius."

"The *praefect*," he paraphrased, "says that a chieftain named Lucterios has moved his men into Ruteni lands and taken hostages from two Gallic tribes, the Nitiobriges and Gabaldi. That action protected Lucterios's flanks and allowed his warriors to raid Tolosa. The *praefect* fears that Narbo is to be attacked next."

"What insolence!" Caesar strode to a window and gazed at an azure line of sea visible beyond a lush pine forest that bordered the shoreline. "These rebel Galli are mistaken if they think I'll be an anvil to their hammer," he muttered, coming back to the map. After an interval of thought, Caesar turned to Lucius. "*Centurio*, we go to the Narbonensis. Have my new *Cisalpina* legion ready to move out on the Eidus."

Unprepared for the bold move, Lucius questioned, "Supplies, sir? How much will we take with us and for how long?"

Seeming not to hear the questions, Caesar snatched up his statue of Fortuna. "She's flirting with me again, Lucius. Imagine. Would the 'Bald Adulterer' not take up a woman's challenge? I tell you, the goddess has taken a liking to me!"

"Ah...about those supplies, Imperator?"

"Supplies?" He deftly tossed the statue to Lucius. "Take only Fortuna. She will see to it that Gallic allies provide whatever my legionaries need!"

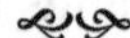

Nevertheless, to supplement Fortuna's often fickle bounty, Lucius ordered field equipment packed in wagons and on mules. The following day, Caesar summoned an Etruscan soothsayer to the temple of Apollo and ordered him to foretell the success of his expedition. The old priest pronounced the liver of a sacrificial rooster undiseased, a good omen, and then intoned cryptic verses that Lucius wrote down.

> *Gallia's pride will be ramped in rain,*
>
> *Yet let Roman swords beware of twins.*
>
> *When Gorgon's stony look dulls the keen,*
>
> *Persist the double-ditch 'til Roma wins.*
>
> *Yet, after the rooster is caught and tamed,*
>
> *Rather than praise, the hunter is blamed.*

The words were a jumble of references to mythological beings, unnamed sites, symbols, and double meanings that Caesar had neither the patience nor time to unravel. Lucius wondered if they would prove prophetic.

At mid-Januarius Caesar left for Narbo with his legion to counter the Gallic threat.

The bubbling political cauldron at Rome cooled more quickly than anticipated. In the emergency, Gnaeus Pompeius assumed the consulship and proved loyal in his friendship with Julius Caesar. The Senate authorized new levies for the army and ordered all men of military age to be drafted for the Gallic war.

❧❧

Julius Caesar's swift and unexpected arrival with reinforcements checked the momentum of Lucterios's invasion in the Narbonensis; he returned to his own territory without challenging the legions. At Gergovia Vercingetorix also was taken by surprise by Caesar's swift reaction to the Cenabum massacre.

Soon after, the situation worsened for the rebellion. A report reached Gergovia that Caesar had re-enlisted retired legion veterans around Narbo. Digging through snow at a pass of the Helvii that led over the Cesena Mountains, the men opened a travel barrier that Arvernians had considered secure until spring. Even more incredible, by the *Nones* of Februarius, Caesar had marched north along the Rhodanus to Viennadunum, then moved up the Arar and rejoined his legions at Agedincum. In just twenty-two days, Vercingetorix's two-pronged attack strategy had been blunted.

Shortly after confirming the truth of Caesar's return, the Arvernian king moved back to his territory and joined his army with men who had come back with Lucterios. Another strategy would have to be formed.

❧❧

Simonides was able to salvage enough papyrus to write to his father and ask Thuccydia to keep the letter as part of his manuscripts about the Gallic war. He found delivering letters to Massilia no longer a problem. After Caesar's return to his legions, many of Vercingetorix's recruits defected to their tribes. The historian had only to find one willing to take the packet and receive thirty *sesterces* from Nikomaxos. The letter which Thuccydia would read to him was written over a period of three months, the last one dated three days before the *Kalendae Aprilis*.

> *My father Nikomaxos.*
>
> *You undoubtedly will be displeased by my latest foolishness, yet like the tortoise in Aisopos's tale who asked an eagle to teach it to fly, I seem to want to accomplish things that are out of my nature. However, I hope to avoid the tortoise's fate! You know by now that a rebellion that had been smoldering has burst into flame. Unhappily, the conflagration claimed Fufius Cita and Cosnia, the couple who sheltered me after I left Caesar. At Cita's urging Alberix went to Gergovia to assess the intentions of the Arvernians and I accompanied him. On leaving the oppidum, we were captured by Vercingetorix's men. Since then I am able to witness Gallic preparations for war from inside their camp. After Caesar's unexpected return to join his legions in Februarius, the sedition almost faltered, yet a strong presence of Vercingetorix and support by the druidic priesthood once again rallied the tribes.*

XIII d. a. Kalendae Martius

Once the Galli received news of Caesar's return they decided to attack the Boii oppidum of Cortona. This remnant of the Helvetii tribe had been installed by Caesar as a client of the Aedui. Thus, Vercingetorix presented his opponent with a dilemma: if the commander kept his legions in camps until warmer weather made campaigning easier, he risked alienating tribes with whom he had treaties. Yet if he moved now to defend Cortona, the problem of transporting supplies for twenty-four thousand men in winter might invite a more immediate disaster. Trusting Fortuna, Caesar decided to aid the Boii.

On reaching Vellaunodunum a rebel Senone stronghold along the route, the legions laid a circumvallation around the town, forced the garrison's surrender by the fourth afternoon and took six hundred hostages to prevent further sedition. Then Caesar moved south toward a bridge across the Liger at Genabum, a frontier town of the Carnutes. In retaliation for the December massacre of merchants at their capital of Cenabum, the Romans destroyed the town. Most of those living there were captured and their lodges burned with a particular fury, because Carnutes were first to oppose Caesar. Afterward, Vercingetorix began a strategy of burning villages and farms located along Caesar's route of march, thus denying him supplies and forage. Since the alternate was the legions' looting of undefended or surrendered territories, and selling of women and children into slavery, the proposal was accepted. As an example, the next day over twenty Biturge settlements were torched.

X d.a. K Aprilis Avaricum of the Biturges.

It has been raining steadily for several days, the kind of warm spring drizzles that precede our dry season at Massilia and sets arid slopes around Glanum bright with wildflowers. The legions have been investing Avaricum for almost a month now, constructing an enormous earthen ramp that reaches up to the walls. Twin towers are at the head of this ramp. Vercingetorix's camp where I am is sixteen miles northeast of Avaricum, protected by marshes and thick woods, yet I go out almost every day to watch the progress of Roman siege operations.

VI d. a. K Aprilis.

We were almost attacked by the legions today as the king set up a temporary camp closer to Avaricum and helped replenish his forage supply. The lack of victuals caused by his burned earth policy is becoming critical to the Galli themselves. Caesar realized that the rain-swollen marshes would hamper his men and went back to Avaricum after a few hours of mutual insult-exchanging. Would that wars were fought so harmlessly, with the only injuries being to each other's pride!

Vercingetorix returned after hearing of the sortie, only to be accused of treason by chieftains he left in charge. They thought he was in collusion with Caesar to legitimize his kingship and had left the camp to give the Romans an opportunity to attack. Vercingetorix told them how weak the enemy was in supplies and broughta few emaciated men he said were legion deserters, but they looked like camp servants to me.

III d. a. K Aprilis

Thus far the Gallic defenders have countered all efforts by the legions to breach the walls of Avaricum. They raised their own counter-towers on the ramparts, filled in underground tunnels that legionaries were digging toward the wall foundations, and harassed the besiegers with raids that even set one of the siege towers on fire. Yet, as I do, Vercingetorix must sense that a climax is nearing in the struggle. Alberix is with me, under confinement. I fear he will soon be forced to choose sides.

❧

In the Gallic camp, Simonides rubbed his eyes and put down his writing materials. Even though it only was past the fifth hour of the day, he felt too nervous and restless to write any longer. A similar disquiet pervaded the entire encampment. Constant month-long rains and the prolonged Roman siege of Avaricum, with Vercingetorix doing nothing to help his allies, had demoralized many once-eager recruits.

Warrior defections made the king impatient during councils. Not a few clan chiefs had become callous toward their men. Breaches of discipline that would have brought a flogging in Januarius now might end with death for the offender. Rumors persisted—despite angry denials—that Vercingetorix had made a secret agreement with Caesar to abandon Avaricum in exchange for being appointed king of an Arvernian province allied with Rome.

❧

Simonides had permission to move freely in the camp. I stayed in a guarded area where men not yet committed to the sedition were confined. One afternoon he bribed sentries with food to visit me. The compound where we stayed was muddy from the rains and littered with rotting food scraps and even human feces.

I sat on a boulder at the farthest edge of the area, looking over the misty landscape of greening hills, when I heard my friend's greeting behind me and turned.

"First the clamor and now the stink of war," Simonides complained, his expression grim. "How have you been, my Keltic friend? You look like a Lucanian peasant in a Roman manure joke!"

"I feel just as filthy!" I knew my hair was a mass of dirty ochre that merged with the bristles of an untrimmed beard, but managed a smile. "What has been going on outside this pig sty?"

"Unless Vercingetorix can bring in a relief army Avaricum will go the way of Genabum, except the Romans will burn the town in order to panic uncommitted tribes to their side. Move over, Alberix, so I can sit next to you."

After I shifted, Simonides asked if I had decided on which side to support, Roma or rebellion. I asked him, "You've said your philosophers try to make a connection between cause and effect. Suppose Vercingetorix *is* victorious?"

He thought about my question before replying. "As I see it, once Vercingetorix dies the old infighting between the tribes will start up again. With the legions out of the way, Germanic tribes will be tempted to again encroach into Gallia, as did Ariovistos."

"The Rhenus tribes?"

"Not only those but Germani farther to the east. What was that chieftain's name again? Ogerth?"

He referred to a time when I had been abducted to a remote village east of the Rhenus. The chieftain's daughter planned an escape for both of us, but I left without her. "Yes, Ogerth. I saw his holdings. Everything was more primitive than our villages."

"Exactly, thus if Germani overrun these lands, they'll drag Gallia back to that primitive level. You'll see the end of much of your people's present way of life."

I kept quiet while Simonides stood up to study the cloudy sky. I knew it would soon rain, but also that he wasn't finished talking. As I thought, he continued.

"Alberix, I think I understand Romans fairly well. On the whole they respect the culture of foreign peoples. They may try to bring them up to their level, yet value stability and orderliness above all else—"

A commotion at the entrance to the camp distracted him. We both looked around to see Vercingetorix walking in our direction with two bodyguards and a druid. Even though a gentle drizzle began, other prisoners in the compound had seen the king and came out of make-shift shelters to find out what was happening. The non-committed warriors in my compound were mud-spattered, their once-bright woolens dirty and torn. All were bearded with coarse hair: the meticulous grooming of Gallic tribesmen was an incidental casualty of war.

When we both recognized Ollam Fodla, Simonides whispered, "Alberix, the swords are drawn and won't be sheathed again until these other tribesmen...and you ...have sworn allegiance to Vercingetorix."

As their guards herded prisoners to one side of the compound at spear point, Fodla searched among them. When he came closer and recognized me, his mouth twisted into a gloating smile.

"Ah, here is the son of Alrix, who never listened to my counsels. Now his ears will be unblocked." Fodla turned to the others to scream, "Listen, all of you! You shall enter the Other-world of the doomed if you do not show loyalty to your king. Kneel! Kneel before your king! May shame fall upon your beards!"

Vercingetorix raised a hand to silence the harangue but as few warriors dropped to the ground in submission, without warning one of the prisoners shouted a curse of defiance and sprinted for a sapling fence. Before he could vault over the flimsy barrier a guard's spear pinned him to the withes. Blood diluted by rainwater soaked through the defector's woolen shirt as he slowly slid into the muck.

A few defiant warriors, Simonides, and I were the only persons standing upright as everyone stared at the dead man. My friend pushed down on my shoulder muttering, "Alberix, only children and fools play with sharp knives. Understand my meaning? Kneel down with me."

Simonides pulled me to the ground with him. Icy slime soaked my trouser knees, but Vercingetorix called to him, "Not you, *Graecus*. Stand! You will keep writing of this war for the sake of our children and their children."

The king motioned for guards to lift him away from me. Before I could react I heard a dull clink of metal against my torc, then felt a sword blade rest against my neck.

I glanced up and saw Vercingetorix through a blur of rain. With his blade threatening my life, I had little but resentment to counter a death that seemed certain. *My father, even Romani, would have allowed me a trial. This execution is the will of one man acting against mine, with not even a vergobret to judge what is right.* I pictured Apsa in my mind. Whatever fear I experienced was replaced by regret that I would never be able to express my love for her. Tell her I understood the trauma she had felt at the hands of Silanus, and I wanted to help her overcome the pain. I realized that I had been too concerned with myself. A further regret was that I would not be able to make Father's vision of peace a reality.

Absorbed in these dark thoughts, I had not heard Vercingetorix questioning me. A sudden sear of pain shocked me into awareness: the king had flicked his sword away from my neck and severed part of an earlobe.

Through the pain I heard Fodla's warning, "Thus it shall be to those who will not listen. They have no use for ears. I expel from this camp Alberix and all others who will not listen! Let Romani waste their grain in feeding them!"

Hands gripped my underarms. I felt myself being pulled to my feet, dragged through the mire to the gate, and pushed outside. My wound stung as I rolled onto muddy ground and I felt for my torc. The silver band that Cluvios had made for me was in place. Half in relief, I clutched the sacred ring. *Your magic saved my life. You encircle a neck that still is attached to a body!*

Along with other maimed warriors I realized I had to get away from the camp before Vercingetorix changed his mind, or one of his sub-chief's decided our punishment was too lenient. I stumbled up and ran along the ruts of a trail leading away from the gate, then turned into nearby woods. I needed to find a hiding place where I could treat my bloody wound.

At a safe distance I found a sumac bush thicket. After I slumped on wet ground to pick a cluster of reddish seeds, I folded them into my cloak hem and pressed the poultice against my ear to lessen bleeding. Dividiac had shown that sumac was a styptic to staunched blood flow. A drizzle diluted the gore into a pale crimson that stained my shirt, but I eventually fell asleep with my head cushioned against the seeds.

❧

The sky was overcast when I awoke, cold and dazed, yet able to reason that it was the following day. My cape had clotted to my wound, so I kept it in place and started out again. By keeping to the woods that paralleled the trail, I hoped I could circle around to the place where rumors had Caesar's camp located at Decetia.

❧

Simonides finished the letter to his father, wondering if he would ever grasp the hand of his Keltic friend again.

> *This afternoon the king confronted Alberix and other undecided Keltoi and ordered them to declare allegiance to his cause. Father, I decided to stay with Vercingetorix, not as a warrior, of course, but to complete at first hand the history of this war. I believe that it will be either the high-water mark of Romans or the beginning of their domination of the entire world. Senatorial decrees may soon be enforced from Albion to the Parthian deserts. Alberix chose to return to Caesar. The Arvernian severed his earlobe for 'refusing to listen,' then expelled him and the others toward legion camps so they might cost the enemy precious food. Otherwise, I believe they all would have been killed. I had no time to even bid Alberix farewell. If the siege remains*

unbroken Caesar may be content to keep what he has of Gallia, if not as a province, then as a federated state for a buffer against the Germani. That the tone of this letter is more personal than usual is due to the nature of my emotions at at the moment. Dear parents and sisters, I shall resume this narrative tomorrow.

❧

Simonides was to be wrong in both cases. Julius Caesar was confident that Fortuna would never jilt him for a barbarian, even a kingly one, and that all of Gallia would be his. When the defenders at Avaricum thought the enemy all had taken shelter during a blinding rainstorm, the town was captured shortly afterward in a surprise assault.

Vercingetorix, stung by the loss of a fourth stronghold in as many months, yet with his army intact, planned to move south along the left bank of the Elaver River. He would continue the war by luring the enemy into the Arvernian highlands that he knew so well.

On that same day, I stumbled into the hospital tent of Psen-Ammon the Egyptian chief surgeon of Legio X. I was feverish from my wound and numb with exhaustion after slogging over muddy fields for over sixteen miles. I believed it to be an illusion of my mind when I saw Apsa tending a wounded legionary on straw covering the medical tent's floor!

CHAPTER IX

Kalendae Aprilis Castrum Vercingetorixi

Simonides greets you, Alberix.

A deserter from your auxiliae told me where you were. You may be surprised to receive a letter this soon, yet it is now easy to pay a Kelt to deliver messages since communication between Vercingetorix's men and your Gallic auxilia units is quite common. Old friend, don't expect any military secrets! I intend to remain neutral in this struggle and report events factually as possible. I hope you keep a record of what happens on your side, so I can include them in my account. Until there are more heroic deeds for me to write about, I am relegated to helping women who prepare meals for the king's advisors!

After the Romani attack succeeded in breaching the walls of Avaricum, many of the defeated warriors slipped away, discouraged over the failure to relieve the town, yet Vercingetorix's position among the tribes is stronger than before, Can you imagine even Titus Labienus coming out of such a defeat and being pelted with laurels rather than lime-stones?

On the morning after the disaster, Vercingetorix called a war council. Fodla was present, claiming to represent all druids. Just as the king began to speak, a shaft of sunshine shone on him as if a blessing from Belenos. He repeated his strategy of destruction and pointed out the foolhardiness of trying to defend Avaricum. He praised the courage of his warriors and told them that when Gallia is united the entire cosmos itself would not be able to oppose them—a boost to the men's morale.

V d. p. Eidus Aprillis

I write on a scrap of papyrus that I save for these letters to remind you to take note of what is happening on your side of the Elaver, yet that isn't quite right anymore, is it? While Caesar moved south along the river's right bank, Vercingetorix shadowed him on the left side and destroyed bridges. Caesar's ruse of pretending to move on with all the legions then fording the waterway was brilliant. We have been on a forced march since the king will not risk his men in battle until joined by more tribes. I have not asked about your injured ear, but if Psen-Ammon is still with Legio X, he can heal you without Sequana's help. Grow your hair longer unless you want the scar to be a wound of honor! I've heard tell of Gallic tribesmen who paint their naked bodies red before battle, so their opponents cannot see where they bleed.

We expect to reach Gergovia in two days. Since the legions crossed to our side of the river, many tribal warriors have deserted. I should have no trouble getting this to you by paying one of them.

I read my friend's letter in a halting translation to Apsa as we sat on a ridge about an hour's walk south of Gergovia. The height gave us a broad view of both the Arvernian fortress and two nearby legion encampments being rushed to completion. Caesar's main palisade covers the slope and crests of a lightly wooded hill and is large enough to protect four legions. A lesser camp to the left is spread over a high spur of white calcite and encloses the tents of two more legions. Along a depression between the two, a cohort of men struggles to dig a double line of ditches and connect the two strongpoints.

When I finished reading, Apsa touched my ear. "Still no pain? That Egyptian surgeon surely kept evil from entering the wound."

"Psen-Ammon? Yes, it's been almost a full moon since the injury."

"At least you chose a lucky phase for your folly."

"My folly?" I grasped Apsa's fingers. "Should I have gone with Vercingetorix? If I had, where would *we* be now?"

"When I saw you come into that tent, I knew I wanted always to be at your side."

"Again tell me the unbelievable part about how you found me."

Apsa repeated her vision of a town, Liscos's decision to attack the *Castor* tower, and her appeal to Marius and Moira for help in finding where I was. She reached into her purse and took out the sling-stone that injured me. "I kept this because it brought us together once before."

I hefted the oval gray shape. "This isn't a stone, it's lead. Metal."

"From the body of the Earth Mother, then."

I gave her back the stone. "I can't explain it, but I'm glad your vision came true."

"Moira was of great help."

"Fodla's druidess?"

"She convinced Marius to disguise himself as a Celt and help find you."

"And you did, Apsa..." I leaned over to pull her close enough to nestle against me.

"It seems so peaceful here," she murmured. "When *will* this war end?"

I helped her up, and pointed toward hillocks surrounding Gergovia. "See those moving specks of brightness? Those are reflections off the spears and helmets of Vercingetorix's warriors. This rebellion is far from over."

"Alberix, why *didn't* you join him? Cluvios hoped you would follow a Celtic leader."

I didn't reply but after I moved a few steps away to watch battle preparations on both sides, I turned back to her. "Apsa, those tribes over there haven't changed because they have a king. Warriors whose pride had been pinched deserted Vercingetorix's camp every day. Punishments became more vicious. Even some clan chieftains resented his leadership and left the camp."

"If Cluvios had lived, do you think he might have advised you differently about a Celtic leader?"

My eyes were tearing when I replied, "Whether or not the evil in his metals twisted his judgment I can't say, but I will never work a forge again."

"What, then, Alberix? I once called you a lark among falcons. Fighting is not in your nature, so you can't stay in the legions. Your mother also knows that."

"Dividiac once predicted that death was the future of our people. I believe it's all this inter-tribal fighting that should die. Apsa, I...may not have had a chance to tell you this, but I see a rebuilt town on the site of Noviodubno, my father's destroyed settlement. Since Caesar hinted that he would offer me a leadership position in Roman Gallia, perhaps I can convince him that the Renos would be a good location for resettling legion veterans."

"That's on Raurici land, isn't it?"

After I nodded, she stood on tiptoe to kiss my cheek. "I want to be there to help you. It's almost high sun and I promised Psen-Ammon that I would gather healing plants for him. You can help me."

I led our mount along the southern flank of the ridge, away from the camps to search the fields and stands of pine forest for plants. At a lush meadow, I tethered the horse to a sapling. Apsa knelt down to lever up a shoot of broad green leaves with the beginnings of seed stalks, and held up the plant. "The Earth Mother shows us the uses of her gifts by their shapes or tastes," she explained. "This 'Lance of Lugos' is spear-shaped, so its leaves stop bleeding when spread on a wound."

"I know. Dividiac and I hunted plants in the fields above Wermaros. Here look..." I plucked a stalk with serrated leaves whose blue blossoms had already closed. "Germani call this plant 'Waywatcher.' It's said to be an enchanted girl who always looks for the return of her lover."

Apsa laughed. "I know another story about that plant. The flower once was a girl with whom the sun god fell in love. Belenos wanted to marry her, but she was so proud of her beauty that she felt herself too good for him. The god became angry, changed her into a flower the color of her blue eyes, and forced her to look at him from sunup to sundown."

"Sounds cruel that a god would do that..." I moved closer to kiss Apsa's neck.

She dodged away to finish the legend. "The girl called on her sorceress mother for help. Yet even magic couldn't shape-shift her daughter back into human form, but it did weaken Belenos's power enough to close the girl's eyes at mid-sun." Apsa fingered the chicory stalk, recalling an earlier life. "Magha used the root for stomach pain and fever."

We stuffed the plants into a net bag and resumed our search. I wandered off toward a fallen tree trunk and called to Apsa, "Over here...honeyroot. Dividiac wore a circlet of the leaves to keep his eyes strong."

"I make a salve from them for wounds."

"And here are Westflowers." I broke off the blossomless stalk of a plant whose narrow blue-green leaves always twisted west to face a setting sun.

We climbed higher among the slopes and found clusters of *sorrel*, a plant whose tart-tasting leaves were sucked by legionaries to relieve thirst, and prevented evil from entering a wound. Apsa picked *arctium*, a potent remedy for fever and skin rash, and found *artemesia*, which she said Magha used as an aid to childbirth and to relieve cramps. Psen-Ammon used a decoction of the leaves as a mild sedative.

No knowledge of the *scientia* that Simonides boasted his Greek forebears had discovered guided our search. Generations of druids or women healers, such as Magha, passed the stories and traditions along from sources none had known first-hand.

We filled two bags with the plants and herbs and rested a while in the shade. I was feeding Apsa wild blackberries when a rumble of distant thunder sounded.

She eyed a horizon of dark storm clouds. "We should start back."

Apsa swung up on the horse behind me and leaned against my back as the animal picked its way down the ridge. We arrived at our starting point just as the first cold raindrops swept in. When I led our nervous mount to shelter in a stand of pines, Gergovia had misted into a gray blur that matched its surrounding hills. I helped Apsa down and ran with her to the shelter of a low-branched tree. We ducked beneath its overhang to sit on a bed of ochre needles and lean against the trunk. With Apsa huddled against me, I buried my face into hair smelling the spice-fragrance of Moondaisies she had tucked above one ear.

Her voice was only slightly louder than a sigh of the wind when she said, "Taranis calls to tell the Earth Mother that his wetness flows down to make her fertile."

I held her more tightly, thinking it would be good to imitate the sky god, yet only pressed my face into her damp hair.

Now Gergovia was entirely hidden behind a gray veil. Field colors darkened and the smell of cooler air changed from a grassy scent to a stagnant odor similar to backwater river pools. Swaying tree limbs above us scattered rain in random splashes on our tunics. I pulled my cape over our heads to shelter Apsa: in the shell of relative dryness, my hand slipped up to cup one of her breasts. Rather than pulling away, she placed her hand over mine.

Despite the thunder, we slept. Wind swept over the drenched land in lingering gusts that set the forest sighing like a woman in a gentle climax. With a faint distant rumble, the storm passed.

When Apsa stirred loose from my hold, a low sun had returned to sparkle on run-off water and blades of wet field grasses. Gergovia reappeared, glistening in the fresh rays of light. Below the ridge, mud-spattered legionaries continued widening the ditch-works; they had labored through the storm to strengthen their fortifications.

Apsa stood and watched the sunlight dance on the far off reflections, then turned to ask, "What will happen here? Will it be like at Avaricum?"

I shrugged uncertainty. "With four legions away with Labienus, Caesar doesn't have enough men to keep Gergovia under siege."

While the greening earth soaked up the sky-god's seed we lingered on the slope, reluctant to end a day we both knew would not soon be repeated. When I finally guided our mount through the gate of the main camp, it was not fully dark, but the fires of the first night watch blazed in yellow-orange light. I was puzzled by baggage preparations being made along the streets. These indicated that legionaries would be moving out.

I went to the medical tent to find Psen-Ammon and ask if Caesar would attack Gergovia. The surgeon surveyed me over the rim of a silver cup from which he sipped a mild narcotic. "It seems, White King, that one of Roma's *loyal* Aedui brought news that the *vergobret* of that tribe was bribed to divert his *auxiliae* to the Arvernian king. The Imperator is taking four legions to oppose him."

"Now? Where are these renegade Aedui?"

"White King, I was only told to prepare for wounded."

"Stay here," I told Apsa. "I'll try to find Lucius and see what is happening."

When I located the centurion he was too occupied organizing his men to talk. Nearby, Marius was with several engineers setting up a row of *scorpiones* along the raised palisade walkway. He saw me and anticipated my question about Caesar's intentions.

"*Fabri*...engineers...aren't going," he said, bending to pluck the torsion strands of his catapult and estimate the weapon's range. These machines will keep attackers from over-running the palisade."

I persisted, "What is this about the Aedui defecting?"

Marius paused to wipe his brow. "Even though Caesar supported their *vergobret* in his election, it seems the man sold out to Vercingetorix. Caesar thinks he can convince warriors that the *vergobret* lied in accusing us of killing two of their nobles. To prove they're alive, Viridomaros and Eporedorix are going with Caesar."

I asked if the camps would be safe from attack. Marius said, "From informers in our *auxiliae* the Aedui know Caesar is leaving. Yet a forced march without trouble could get our men back late tomorrow. By trusting Fortuna, Caesar believes they will."

જ⁊ઝ

Either Marius's talent as an *augur* was unsuspected, or the statue of Fortuna that Caesar carried favored the engineer—both his predictions were accurate. On the evening of the next day the commander returned from successfully resolving the Aeduan problem. In the interval, our catapults repulsed attacks by a band of Vercingetorix's restless warriors. Wondering if the goddess might turn fickle next time, Caesar made plans to abandon Gergovia and march north to link up with Labienus. This would protect his Aeduan flank against a recurrence of the previous treason. He even half-jested to his officers that owning half of the "Gallic rooster" was better than none at all.

જ⁊ઝ

Lucius Velcanius continued observing Gergovia's defenses from the small camp.

Shortly after Legio X returned from the march, he called for me to join him. I squinted at a plateau I had seen some five months earlier with Simonides. Ochre grasses and patches of white snow had given way to green spring growths and yellow dots of sunblossom flowers. Lucius asked me how much I recalled about the outlying areas and a smaller flat area below the main walls.

"Not much," I admitted. "There were a few tents set up around the *oppidum*."

"They're protected by a lower wall. By now there must be thousands of warriors camped behind that barrier."

We stood on a watchtower built at the crest of a steep hill after Gallic forces were driven off in a surprise night attack by men of Legio XIII. When voices sounded from below, Lucius glanced down. Titus Sextius, commander of the Thirteenth, had arrived with Julius Caesar and an escort of other officers.

"...Splendid view of Gergovia," Sextius remarked. "Imperator, you were fortunate to notice that this crest was lightly defended."

Caesar patted the statue of Fortuna under his cloak. "Credit my goddess. On that night she distracted the Galli... Ah, there are *Centurio* Velcanius and Alberix. You both know Titus Sextius. Gaius Fabius is commander of the Eighth. These other men are two of his centurions, Lucius Fabius and Marcus Petronius."

Velcanius saluted the legates and nodded to the centurions, then turned to Caesar. "Imperator, welcome to *Argus*."

Caesar seemed amused. "That's right, the men named this camp after a mythical monster. Alberix, do you know the story?"

"I...no sir," I stammered. "I'm not sure."

"Velcanius, will you explain?"

"Sir, in the Greek myth Argus had a hundred eyes—"

Caesar shortened his story. "And so this camp keeps vigil over Gergovia. My main camp is named after *Cerberus*, the three-headed hound that guards Hades's kingdom."

Sextius added, "Greeks bury a honey-cake with their dead as a sop to the beast."

"We'll not let Gallic honey distract us." Caesar fell silent as he surveyed the panorama, then motioned me alongside him. "Fufius Cita sent you here last winter."

"Yes, I came in Samon...November. He wanted to know the situation in the south."

"I ordered him to send you, yet we misjudged the Carnutes. Where did you enter Gergovia?"

"There, through the east gate..." I pointed to where the height angled down toward a lightly wooded terrace. "There's room for a legion, even two, on that smaller plateau."

"Yes, I've noticed." Caesar restudied the level area ahead. "There's no activity in the Gallic encampment behind a lower wall."

Centurion Lucius Fabius overheard. "Imperator, the *brachatae* are out ditchin' the western approach to their *oppidum*."

"Wisely, too, Fabius. It would be a strategic location for us to erect a ramp similar to the one we put at Avaricum."

Sextius held up a papyrus map. "Imperator, according to deserters, the Arvernians expect us to attack at that point."

"Repeat that again, Titus."

"Sir, the west is a vulnerable position for Vercingetorix and he realizes that."

Caesar pounded the watchtower rail with a fist. "Another of Fortuna's taunts! The goddess has more tricks than a Cretan harlot!"

"Sir?"

"Don't you see, Titus? While the Galli are digging over there, we could sweep through their tents here and with enough luck possibly breach the gate." Caesar looked toward the other men for their opinion. "What do you centurions think?"

Fabius volunteered, "I'm for followin' up our victory at Avaricum before the *brachatae* get many tribes joinin' them. That's the way my men see it."

Petronius added support, "And mine, Imperator. Hades, we could castrate this rebellion right here! Make the *brachatae* think we're going in where they are now, then storm both that camp and Gergovia's main gate."

Caesar moved to one side of the platform to review his position aloud. "Labienus is far to the north leading four legions against the Parisii and Senones. The Aedui have become disappointing allies. Vercingetorix exploited their instability and almost took my camp when I went to settle the matter of their *vergobret*'s treason." He turned back to the officers. "I had decided to move north, consolidate with Labienus, yet Fortuna may have placed the Gallic rooster in front of me for the plucking! Let's test the old girl."

Sextius wondered, "How do you propose to do that?"

Caesar grinned. "Bring me a rooster."

"Imperator?"

"*Gallus*. A rooster, Titus. Centurions, who has one here?"

After a pause, Petronius volunteered, "My Eighth has Hector, a mascot. But, sir—"

"*Centurio*, I won't sacrifice your pet, only watch how it eats grain. If the auspices are good, let's do exactly what the Galli expect, but make it work for us. Take a look here at Sextius's map." With his officers gathered around the chart, Caesar pointed to the low area where the enemy dug a trench obstacle. "At the beginning of the third watch, order a cavalry wing in that direction. Have the men make plenty of noise to make sure the Galli are alerted. At dawn order teamsters to bring out horses and mules without pack saddles, so they can ride. Have the men wear helmets and deploy along that ridge behind us, where they can be seen from Gergovia."

As the plan became clear Gaius Fabius nodded understanding. "From that distance the Galli won't be able to tell if they are legion regulars or muleteers."

Petronius exclaimed, "A brilliant diversion that draws enemy warriors to the west!"

"Exactly." Caesar grinned. "Then we storm their camps!"

"Sir," Centurion Fabius ventured, "It's not my place to ask, but could the Eighth lead an assault?"

Caesar glanced at the legion commander. "Gaius?"

"Imperator, I would be honored. Most of the men have been with you since Genava."

"Good! Legio Eight will attack the camps and the east gate. Have the men cover their helmets with sacking so they won't be detected as they advance. Even if they don't breach the *oppidum* walls they can destroy supplies and burn tents. That should demoralize any new men Vercingetorix recruited."

Velcanius asked, "What of Legio Ten, sir?

"In reserve, *centurio*, against a possible flank attack once the Arvernians realize what is happening. We'll put Aeduan cavalry on the far right and bring them in as a surprise. Let them redeem themselves after that nasty business with Convictovitalis. Sextius, if you keep watch here with your legion, you'll be first to see an enemy counterattack and where." Caesar looked at his officers' intent faces. "Questions?"

Sextius needed clarification. "Is that *tonight's* third watch?"

"Tonight, Legate! I'll have that raw Narbonensis legion go with the muleteers. Keep the men out of direct action, yet be sure they're seen from Gergovia."

Gaius Fabius asked, "What hour tomorrow will the attack begin?"

Caesar paused to consider. "Legate, we'll let the valiant Hector decide that, but you'll have orders and a password before dawn. By Mars, we'll have a victory! Dismissed!"

As Caesar led the way back to *Cerberus* along the double trench, Lucius felt pleased to be able to speak with me. There had not been much time along the Elaver River or while the camps were under construction. He recalled my uncle's death.

"Alberix, I was sorry to hear about Cluvios. What will happen with Briga?

"As long as Dirona can control Liscos's drinking, she'll be well. Did Apsa tell you about his plan to attack *Castor*?"

"Yes, and it's maddening not to know if the attack succeeded. How are Apsa and that druidess who came with Marius?"

"Moira helps at the medical tent. I believe Apsa is almost over her trauma. A few days ago we gathered plants together. Lucius, I...I love her deeply."

"Marry the woman then! Caesar was Pontifex at one time and could perform a Roman ceremony."

"Apsa is still a slave, but I plan to free her at Beltaine."

"Just as well, there's hardly time now and you heard Caesar's orders." Lucius looked toward the dark bulk of Gergovia. "Alberix, you know how I feel about Briga. Do you think now she would marry me?"

"Our Celtic traditions are as binding as your Roman ones, Lucius. Why don't you ask *her?*"

"Yes, well, I'd better get word about the attack to my legion tribunes…" He tightened his helmet strap. "You stay with Psen-Ammon and help with the wounded."

❧

Although Hector had not pecked at the sacred wheat kernels with any particular zest—having gorged all day on earthworms that wriggled from dirt clods being turned over by enlarging the palisade ditch—Caesar sent out orders for the attack plan. Yet the rooster's moderate prediction made him alter the action to only destroying the outer camps, not direct assaults on Gergovia itself.

❧

Centurion Lucius Fabius crouched near the edge of woods at the head of his legionaries, cursing the fact that their numbers were down from about a hundred to less than fifty. He inhaled humid air that smelled of spring earth and heard surrounding trills of insect-hunting thrushes. Beyond the shade, a morning sun heated the greening fields ahead. Squinting into the brightness, Fabius tried to find the best pathway to reach a black stone wall halfway up the slope. With Gallic tribesmen digging to the west, there would be no trumpet signal for the advance—the order would be passed along by word from the lead maniple. After the last rank of legionaries moved out, he would order his men forward.

Fabius wiped sweat away with a corner of his soiled neckerchief. *Attis's Balls it's hot this early! Got to forget what I dreamed last night. Hades, we're takin' the brachatae by surprise. Sweep through their camps and regroup on the road back to Cerebrus. Those work parties will come back to nothing.* He shifted position to relieve a painful leg cramp and recalled Avaricum. *Questors haven't finished an inventory of all that loot, but I should get me an extra year's pay. Finish this furcin' rebellion and retire with enough money to buy me a farm—*

"*Vadete! Vadete! Vadete!* The command for the lead century to advance rippled through the ranks like wheat stalks in an autumn breeze.

The order snapped Fabius out of his musing. When legionaries ahead started out at a trot, their abrupt appearance and jangling armor silenced the birds. Fabius sprang forward, shouting for his men to follow, but his cramped leg buckled. He stumbled a few steps, then regained his footing. Around him running men bawled out battle cries, even though they had been ordered to be silent on the uphill run and not alert enemy guards.

Glancing back, Fabius saw his men following in staggered ranks. A few slumped down, nursing ankles twisted by sharp rock outcroppings hidden by grass. The sun broiled his iron *lorica*. A woolen tunic underneath was damp with sweat. As he picked his way among the treacherous rocks, brambles scratched his bare legs. A hare scurried up the slope in advance of the line of shouting men. He watched it zig-zag into a clump of thorny bushes, heard the hoarse breathing of legionaries nearest him, and pulled air into his lungs by gasps as he neared the wall. The barrier of stonework was the height of a man—no hindrance to legionaries trained to climb such obstacles.

Just before reaching the wall, Fabius turned to signal with his baton and call out an order. "*Gradus Conformtio!*"

The command to form a step was echoed down the line of legionaries. Men I, III, V and VII, in the first eight-man unit to reach the wall, paired off and held their shields at knee level. II, IV, VI and VIII jumped on and were sprung to the top of the stonework. After the first of his legionaries scaled the barrier, Fabius heaved himself onto the wall.

Steadying himself at the point of greatest danger, he thought of his dream. *I was on high wall made of gold stonework, looking down on a deserted town. All the buildings and temples were rich with silver trim, ready to be looted. But I was alone with no safe way down and no one to help me reach the treasure—* "Attis's Balls, I was braggin' about bein' the first into Gergovia, like I was at Avaricum." Fabius flexed his legs and jumped down into a Gallic camp of tents pitched almost to the wall.

Men of the lead century deftly had ransacked the shelters and torched them. Others still foraged through supply wagons. Fabius spotted a tent where a grouping of totems indicated a chieftain's rank. He slashed through the leather and saw a tall, blond-haired man, bare-chested, who had been asleep. He bolted for the opposite entrance, followed by a slave.

Hampered by a clutter of chests on the floor, Fabius chased after the two.

As the Celt mounted a horse, Fabius shouted, "Stop that furcin' chieftain!'

The dark-haired slave dropped to his knees, arms extended for mercy. A legionary in the path of the horse jumped aside to hurl his javelin. The iron head grazed the mount's haunch, but the rider brought it under control and headed toward the one gate that led into Gergovia.

Fabius grabbed the slave by his hair. "Who was that *bracatus?*" The man shook his head, not understanding Latin. "*Vlatos?*" he asked in Celtic—the rider owned a horse and might be a chieftain.

The slave stammered, "*Rix Teu*...Teutomates. Nitiobriges..."

"A furcin' king! I could of got a share of his ransom." Fabius swung his sword at the slave's head in savage arc, severing his skull along the jaw line. He saw a bronze ring circling the neck stump. *The man wore a torc and could of been a hostage, not a slave.* He wrenched off the occult band, then ran through a haze of smoke toward the base of Gergovia's ramparts. A few bodyguards of Gallic nobles fought back, yet the sweep through enemy tents had been an easy legion success.

Women appeared at the top of the massive walls. Many stripped off their tunics, baring white breasts, and stretching out hands to wail for mercy. Some threw down jewelry, furs, and decorated clothing, hoping the Romani would scramble to pick up the loot and spare their lives.

"What now, *Centurio*? We pretty much cleaned out that camp?" The question came from one of Fabius's men with a sack slung over his lorica.

Another legionary pointed toward the women. "This was like stickin' frogs. I'd like t' stick one of them Gallic does!"

Fabius reminded both, "Orders are to destroy the camp, then regroup down th' road."

"Shit!" the first exclaimed. "Let *auxiliae* finsh up here. I'm for climbin' up after those '*gallinae*'!"

Fabius hesitated at a chance for personal glory. Some of his men were on the right flank, near the main gate to Gergovia. He saw Marcus Petronius leading a group of legionaries toward the doors. They hammered on the portal with javelin handles or used sword blades to pry out leather hinge straps.

Scanning the Roman camps, the centurion saw men of the two legions assigned to attack the Gallic center still fighting. Flames and dark smoke engulfed burning tents.

Fabius made his decision. *Forget that furcin' dream!* Sheathing his sword, he clamped the dead slave's torc on a brawny forearm and yelled, "I swore to be first on that wall. Anyone wants women follow me! Longus! Live up to your name and boost me up. You, Sestius. Give him a hand!"

Fabius skinned a knee as the men pushed him up on a shield. After he found a toehold in the blocks he crawled up to the parapet. When the women saw his head appear, they screamed and ran. Clawing his way over the edge, he leaned back down to extend a hand to the next man. "Come on, th' furcin' town is ours for th' takin'. Petronius will have th' gate open by now."

From the height Fabius heard a distant brassy blare of trumpets—Caesar's signal for his attacking legions to halt and regroup.

He ignored the order.

Waiting on the left of the assault cohorts, Lucius Velcanius heard the trumpet signal and alerted his men in Legio X. Smoke swirling from behind the stone wall indicated that setting fire to the tents had been successful. He shouted orders to his men, "We'll hold here for a time before assembling along the road. Sublius, climb that tree and see if the attack *is* breaking off."

A few moments later the man called down," Somethin' wrong. Parts of the Eighth and Thirteenth still are movin' up that hill. Maybe they didn't hear the signal."

"You're probably right, there's an east wind. Come down." Lucius called to his formation, "First Maniple, follow me. We'll verbally take the recall order to the others."

Lucius had guessed correctly: Because of a rising wind and the ravine between Legio X and the assault cohorts, men had not heard the signal. Their Tribunes, who knew the attack plan, had little success in recalling them—most legionaries continued looting the three enemy camps. Spurred on by the examples of Fabius and Petronius, other legionaries tried to scale the rampart or helped batter down the massive gates.

Lucius Velcanius jogged up to the lower wall with his men and climbed the black stones to assess action farther up the slope. Shouting and the sound of horses to the left of smoldering tent remains alerted him that enemy warriors had discovered the assault and rallied for a counterattack. A furious Gallic charge almost pushed back the left flank of Legio V into its own center.

Some of Lucius's men jumped down to the wall's inner side. As the centurion was about to order relief for the endangered legions, a small contingent of horsemen came in from the side and rode close to the stonework. By the animal totems on their helmets, Lucius recognized a chieftain and his retainers.

"*Attendo!*" he shouted. "Attack coming from the left. Lock shields."

Before his legionaries could complete the defensive maneuver, the Celts were on them in a flurry of flashing swords and horses' hooves, shouting their battle cries to unnerve the enemy. Lucius was aware of the wall stones trembling, a smell of horse sweat, and sparks from the mounts' iron shoes striking stone. Most of his legionaries were jammed against the rough stonework, jabbing out with short swords and holding up their shields as a flimsy defense against the momentum of the enemy riders.

Sublius screamed as his shield was caught in the forelegs of a horse and his body snatched away from the wall. He tumbled beneath the animal like a straw doll. His shield splintered under the mount's hooves and sent horse and rider into a deadly somersault.

After the cavalrymen veered away, toward Gergovia, Lucius jumped down to rally his stunned men. "Mostly bruises, except for Sublius. Is he dead?"

After inspecting his broken body, a legionary nodded. "Th' *brachatus*, too. Want me to slash his horse's throat?"

Lucius nodded; the beast thrashed in pain from a shattered front leg. "Centuries Two and Three continue on to call back the men. First Century with me on flank defense."

On the ramparts of Gergovia women had ceased pleading after they saw their warriors arrive. Now they held up children and called down for their men to kill Romani.

Lucius noticed distant legionaries silhouetted at the top of the fortress wall, but could not identify them individually. "Men of the Eighth...fools for glory! We're likely to be surrounded if we don't regroup on the road."

The legionaries looked back in dread as they watched their companions on the wall slashed down by Vercingetorix's warriors. Several fought a death struggle on the narrow stone ledge. Lucius ordered his men to move at quickstep. When he glanced back, legionaries on the rampart had been replaced by wildly gesturing warriors of the Arvernian king. He considered returning to help, but his orders were not to support the assault by Legio VIII, only ease their withdrawal. *Where in Hades's Name is Titus Sextius? His Thirteenth is supposed to cover our right flank.*

Even as Lucius cursed the legate's absence, a fresh wave of warriors ran down the slope and slashed into men who had climbed atop the lower wall. He saw a centurion go down as the Roman line wavered and fell back under the cleaving broad-swords of frenzied Celts.

"Form up! Lock shields!" Lucius shouted the order as he led the way to his confused legionaries. "Marcus! Junius! Valerius! *Caco*...shit...where are the other centurions? Hold positions! The Thirteenth will be moving in to help."

When Lucius reached the front rank, which had managed to form a ragged line, he recognized Junius as the dead centurion. *And Valerius was killed at Avaricum. Do something! The Senatus and people of Roma expect you to set an example. Caesar demands it of you. The slope of this black hill is a shitty place to meet Pluto.*

The centurion's moment of uncertainty was resolved when a legionary in front of him stumbled backward, his skull slashed open. Lucius found himself faced with a blond, blue-painted warrior. Teeth clenched in hate, the Celt raised his broadsword above his head for a second kill.

With all his strength Lucius jammed his shield upward and into his opponent's throat. He heard the rim thud on jaw and simultaneously felt the slide of his short sword entering soft abdominal flesh. As the warrior fell forward, Lucius almost stumbled onto his thrashing body. He regained his balance and battered another attacker's chest with the shield's iron boss. The old wound in his left arm throbbed with pain. His sword hand felt damp with sweat inside a glove, but its leather gripped the bone sword hilt. Without slipping he stabbed forward at a mass of oncoming warriors.

Inspired by their First Centurion's frenzied counter-thrusts, legionaries closed their ranks, shields held high to deflect deadly broad-swords. As Roman sword tactics cut into the Celtic line, surviving warriors wavered, broke, and turned to run toward Gergovia.

"Hold...there," Lucius gasped. "Don't follow...them."

Someone shouted, "There's Titus Sextius's Thirteenth, jogging in at quick-step."

While his exhausted men cheered, Lucius rubbed sweat off his face with his sword arm, then told Marcus, "*Centurio*, we'll hold the flank as ordered. Move your men down to the road."

"There's still fighting at the gate."

"Order the *cornuae* to keep sounding recall until they've been heard."

The situation at the gate became disastrous. When Aeduan cavalry swept around in support of the assault legion, they were mistaken for Vercingetorix's horsemen because of a similarity in clothing. Confused legionaries panicked and were driven away with heavy losses. Marcus Petronius lay dead in a bloody tangle of Roman and Celtic corpses in front of the un-breached entrance portals. Realizing too late the folly of his attack, the centurion had ordered his men to fall back while he held off the Arvernians alone.

Lucius Fabius's body lay beneath the *oppidum* wall, next to that of Longus. Both men had been stripped of their swords, armor, and helmets by exuberant warriors now running through Gergovia's streets to show enemy trophies. Sestius's body fell to the base of the wall, along with those comrades who reached the parapet and been slashed off

The men in Legio VI and XI finally heard the recall signal and dropped back from the ruined camps to regroup at a base of the hill. Lucius's flank centuries harassed any warriors who tried to turn the retreat into a rout. The survivors of Legio VII eventually reached the safety of the road.

On the following morning an angry Caesar reprimanded his decimated legions, yet whether his irritation was actual or rhetorical was never revealed with certainty. After burial parties had finished their grim tally of the dead, the Imperator assembled his legions in camp *Cerberus*. As Caesar addressed the men in a grim voice, a beard he would grow as a sign of mourning already shadowed his face.

"Yesterday, legionaries, the waters of Lake Avernus opened to admit almost seven hundred of your comrades and more than forty centurions. I must in honesty say that their own rashness...and yours...brought them to the underworld of Pluto.

"Foolish actions are not to be confused with courage. None of you lack bravery but that quality alone is not enough to blunt iron swords, as many Galli discovered. Granted that most of you did not hear the *cornuae* signal, yet your officers tell me that you disobeyed orders...*my orders*...to break off when it was evident that Vercingetorix was in a position to drive you from the walls of Gergovia. You ignored them, and then succumbed to the god of Panic after Aedui cavalry appeared. You should have noticed their bared shoulders as allies, yet your inattention identified them as enemies." Caesar paused to let his words recall the event and penetrate his men's consciousness.

Psen-Ammon listened with Apsa and me. "Finally the wasps themselves have been stung."

Apsa was puzzled by the surgeon's criticism. "What do you mean?"

"The Romani entered Gallia like wasps nesting in a new lodge. Now the householder comes to burn them out."

Before I could protest, I heard Caesar continue, "Even though Vercingetorix was absent at Avaricum, I did not attack his Gallic camp. Swamps gave defenders advantage." He glance swept the men. "No Roman ever will die from my recklessness."

After a few legionaries applauded, Caesar raised a hand for silence. "Your heroic assault on the encampments was accomplished under an opportunity that Fortuna revealed to me, yet we must not tempt the goddess. Men of the legions, if mourning for our dead is justified, we need not be discouraged. It was not your lack of courage, but unwarranted *hubris* that brought us failure, *if it was such.*" He emphasized the last four words. "I do not believe we failed. I intended to leave here and link up with Labienus, and that plan has not changed. We will stay at Gergovia a day or two longer, to not let the Galli believe we are slinking away in shame."

Caesar's voice had steadily risen in pitch to a dramatic ending, as he had learned to do at the school of Apollonios. "Only in the eyes of Vercingetorix has there been a Roman defeat. Our legions are intact. Supply wagons are full. Aedui allies once again are firm. If the Arvernians think us beaten, so much the better, for they will become careless. Warriors will return to their homes for spring planting. The rebellion shall wither as weeds cut in the sun of Quintilis. Let us move to final victory in the name of the Senatus and People of Roma!"

The legionaries responded with cheers of support, then dispersed to work details or guard assignments. I returned to the *auxilia* encampment. Apsa went with Psen-Ammon to the medical area.

That evening no smoke rose from funeral pyres such as Homer had described for the fallen heroes at Troy: only twin mounds of black volcanic stones marked graves at Gergovia and Caesar's camp: Roman and Gallic dead lay together, waiting for a fearful glimpse of three-headed *Cerberus* at Avernus, or a new turn on the Wheel of their Destiny.

≈

The disaster at Gergovia rallied uncommitted Gallic tribes to join the rebellion. Even the Aedui, our most loyal allies, arranged a meeting of rebel over-chiefs with Vercingetorix at their oppidum of Bibracte. Several Aedui defected to inform Caesar that the king had been appointed Over-chief of all the tribes. This rankled Aedui who felt the leadership should have been theirs.

Rather than being discouraged, Caesar won skirmishes with enemy cavalry, then ordered my legion and five others on a forced march to joint up with Labienus's three legions in the territory of the Lingones, a friendly tribe.

Afterward, Vercingetorix lost an opportunity to defeat Caesar. By withholding foot warriors in a cavalry action, Germani horsemen won the day. With his cavalry routed, the king took his army to Alesia, a Mandubi fortress and cult center. Druids considered the site almost as important as Carnutum. Although stung by the defeat of their cavalry, warriors rallied around him and encamped both on the gentle slope of a broad plateau, bisected by a river, and inside the high fortress itself: A rumored eighty thousand Gallic warriors waited for Caesar to make the next move.

When Aedui captives reported the mile-long stronghold to be impregnable, Caesar decided not to repeat a direct attack, as at Gergovia, and ordered a blockade of Alesia in our month of Elembiv, the Roman Sextilis. I could see Lucius there. Apsa and Moira would work with Pse-Ammon in the medical tents.

CHAPTER X

It was almost evening, yet torrid late summer air stifled the *oppidum* of Alesia. A breeze had not come off the surrounding hills to relieve the heat and stench in the Gallic stronghold and its supporting camps. As Vercingetorix watched his sub-chiefs assemble in the long shadow of a shrine to Taranis, his face shared the gaunt look of other men, a result of limited rations and sleepless nights. The king's head ached, even though he had allowed himself an extra water ration to speak to his sub-chiefs. *Despite setbacks, they are proud men. Our grain is gone except what Mandubi manage to hide. All cattle and most horses have been slaughtered for food. We're into the month of Edrin and the relief army I expected still has not been sighted–*

"*Rix...*" Critognatos's voice broke into the king's thoughts. "Hunger surrenders a man to his enemies. Time is ripe for a decision."

"So I am warned." Vercingetorix looked toward the sky god's shrine. "Are the druids here? We need their support."

"I have an Arch-druid and Fodla." Critognatos lowered his voice, "Perhaps I should make your proposal. Counsel coming from a king seems a command."

"Well spoken. I shall be at the south wall. Inform me when the assembly is ready." Vercingetorix made his way between abandoned lodges, where straw thatching had been stripped off to feed the last of the horses. He greeted a ragged gathering of warriors at a cross street. The men sat around cook-fires with fuel from dismantled roof beams, boiling whatever rodents or lizards they caught that day.

One man stirring a cook pot grinned. "Snake meat."

Vercingetorix returned his laugh and looked away, touched by the faith of warriors who had been told that an army of Gallic tribesmen arriving at Alesia would break Caesar's blockade. At a wall on the edge of the plateau he greeted white-haired sentries: older men now took guard assignments that allowed rest for younger warriors who tried to storm Romani defenses.

The Arvernian gazed down at a panorama of enemy siege works, wondering again if he had been wise in coming to Alesia and attempting to lure his enemy into a disastrous attack as at Gergovia. Caesar had not taken the bait. Instead, the men of his legions diverted river water into a double moat that fronted deadly obstacles: fields sown with iron barbs, sharpened stakes concealed in pits, tree branch barriers, and twelve-foot-high walls, protected every twenty paces by three-story towers. Eleven miles of inner fortifications that isolated the Mandubii stronghold had thwarted attempts to break out. Assuming the arrival of a relief army, Caesar's legionaries feverishly labored to construct an identical fifteen mile barrier as protection against outside attacks.

To the west Vercingetorix saw smoke rising from an enemy cavalry camp lying in the valley. Eastward, the same bluish haze hung above countless rows of legionary tents. The king imagined that he smelled roasting meat above the stink of his own lower camps and comforted himself with a distant hope. *The enemy is free to forage supplies...cattle ...yet that will end after my relief contingents arrive.*

A series of dull thumps sounded in the distance.

"Catapults starting again," an oldster remarked. "They stone our camps in the evening so we won't get too close to their stockade. And," he jested, "from sleeping too much!"

The barrage of heavy stones was a strategy that drove Gallic camps further up the slope and kept them from a source of water—legionaries had fouled a stretch of the diverted river channel with manure.

As he did several times a day Vercingetorix strained to look in the direction from which more warriors should appear. None had arrived. Alesia's food supply almost had run out. In the solitude he tried to understand the misfortune that had plagued his men since their victory at Gergovia. *My cavalry shadowed his legions as Caesar marched to secure his flank with the Sequani and force loyalty from the Allobroges. A charge by my mounted warriors was broken by hired Germani cavalry eager to share in the loot of a conquered Gallia. I lost three of my chieftains and most of their horse-warriors in that rout. The legions are intact and Ubii cavalry roam the countryside to murder stragglers or terrorize villagers. Druids are with us, so why have the gods not granted victory? It is a year since Fodla's ritual at Saumis, yet Romani are on the cusp of another win.* As Vercingetorix turned to go back, Critognatos approached with Luernos and Abdios.

Critognatos called out, "*Rix*, the council is assembled, but the druid, Fodla, seems in a trance since coming from Taranis's temple."

"He looked so at Gergovia," Luernos recalled. "Perhaps the god has spoken of another victory."

Vercingetorix was cautious. "First let me see the druid. Birds are snared by their feet. Men by their ears."

When the three entered the temple enclosure, the sun had slipped behind a line of distant hills. A moon was in its dark phase, yet Vercingetorix recalled that Edrin was *Mat*, a lucky month: perhaps the two would balance each other.

Under the temple portico, Fodla sat rigidly in a chair. Moira crouched near him. The druidess's tangled hair and soiled tunic mirrored her wild look and restless hands.

Simonides watched from temple shadows, stylus ready to take notes on the council.

Fodla's sallow complexion contrasted with the ruddy faces of the chieftains. As the druid mumbled incoherent words, Arch-druid Calidos noticed Vercingetorix approach.

"What is the druid's babbling?" the king demanded. "Tell me the arcane meaning in his words."

Calidos evaded a direct response. "Great King, it is Taranis who directs Fodla's mind and tongue. The meaning will be clear in time."

"Time?" Vercingetorix snapped. "My cup is drained of time! May the words of Taranis be stronger than the 'swords' those lesser gods forged for me thus far."

After the Arch-druid stiffened in ager at the rebuke, Critognatos went to soothe him. "The king is disappointed that our gods have not granted another victory."

Calidos warned, "The balance of the gods is not that of men. Speak your words to the warriors until the will of Taranis is revealed."

Credit the Arch-druid with nerve! The Arvernian nobleman faced chieftains lined up along three low walls. "Brothers, you may sit down in listening to my counsel."

The men glanced toward Vercingetorix, feeling they should stand out of respect.

One criticized him. "We'll not squat in front of our king like old women selling leeks."

Vercingetorix half-laughed at his rebuke. "Amniarix, legs carry the belly. Rest your legs and wish there were leeks to buy."

Chuckling at the jest, the chieftains eased themselves atop an enclosing wall.

"Men of Gallia," Critognatos exhorted, "I come not to counsel those who wait until the Romani break *in* and make them slaves. I speak to those who vote to break *out* of Alesia."

"Break out?" a chieftain jeered. "How? On the backs of finches?"

Those who applauded the insult were Mandubii: their fortress was under siege and now risked the fate of Avaricum.

Critognatos scowled and raised his voice, "You fear the wooden walls of Caesar, yet his ditches and towers should give you hope." Joined by other chieftains, the Mandubii contingent laughed at a contradiction. "Hear me out!" he pleaded. "If those fortifications have kept us from receiving news of the army we expect to come, Romani know it is so and are afraid. Fear keeps them working on their ditches. Fear of Gallic warriors who will appear numerous as swarms of bees."

"Are we the hive, then?" a Mandubii demanded. "A sealed hive is of no use. In a single moon your rebellion has turned our great fortress into the realm of Cernunnos."

"Were villages burned to frighten the mice?" a bearded warrior called out about the scorched earth policy. "Now hordes of mice have *us* prisoner and eat our grain."

A chieftain raised his sword and shouted, "To die in Romani ditches is not courage, but foolishness! I vote to wait for kinsmen-tribes to arrive!"

Loud murmurs about the desperate situation suggested that Critognatos was losing chieftains to the dissenters.

Before others could join protesters, the hoarse voice of Ollam Fodla was heard. "Taranis...would...speak...with Critognatos."

The dark druid stood and extended a thin hand to guide the Arvernian into the temple. Puzzled, Vercingetorix watched his comrade enter. Had Taranis sanctioned a change of leadership?

While the two were inside, an uneasy quiet settled over the warriors. Simonides prepared to record the outcome, sensing that Fodla/Taranis would sanction an atoning sacrifice equal to the gravity of the hour.

When Critognatos reappeared at the entrance he looked pale. His hands trembled as he cleared his throat in nervousness. "Brothers. The god reminded me what our ancestors did when the Cimbri and Teutones threatened them with starvation, as Caesar does. Rather than surrender they kept alive by eating the flesh of those too old or too young to fight—"

"No! Dishonor!" Those who knew the horrendous story shouted protests. "A shame on their beards!"

"Silence!" Vercingetorix raised a hand and stepped next to the nobleman. "Listen to Critognatos! Through him the god's will is revealed."

Calm again, he continued," Even without our ancestor's action a human sacrifice is a suitable offering. Our descendants would sing of it in remembering this struggle."

With sarcasm, Amniarix called out, "Who will choose sacrifice victims? Will they volunteer for the honor of having their name sung in a bard's verses?"

Despite Critognatos's attempt to speak again, objections against the genocide grew louder. No one noticed Ollam Fodla until he shouted, "Chieftains, if men can show mercy, why not a god?" After the chiefs turned toward him, the druid continued, "Taranis proposes that if you offer ten of your sick and dying, there will be no need to imitate our ancestors—"

"NO!" Moira screamed as she scrambled up to attack Fodla with the ferocity of a wildcat. "You forced Triccos on Sabia and killed my sisiter!"

Critognatos grasped the druidess by the waist and flung her off the porch. Moira clambered up and limped off behind the temple.

Unaffected by the incident, Fodla repeated, "Taranis orders that you exile your old and useless to the Romani! Let our enemies use up *their* grain in feeding them."

The desperate compromise resulted in scattered approval. A few swords clattered on shield rims in support of the action. Relieved at the alternate plan, none of the warriors thought to ask why Taranis still wanted a human sacrifice.

"Choose victims by lot," Fodla ordered. "I swear by the god that the relief army will arrive during tomorrow's sun!"

Vercingetorix unsheathed his sword. "All who agree raise weapons!"

Even a few Mandubii joined in sanctioning the sacrifice and deadly exile: they had not heard Fodla whisper to the king that the god had ordered that all women and children be sent out with the oldsters.

☙ ❧

While warriors searched lodges for sacrificial victims, toward evening Calidos led Fodla to the eastern end of the Alesia plateau. Pastureland there separated a triangular wooded and a series of healing springs and small sanctuaries from the town. The pool of a local god, Moritgasus, was reported effective for treating eye diseases.

Ollam Fodla squinted into near darkness. "Where is the wicker cage?"

Calidos pointed, "Near the god's shrine."

"Wood?"

"Close by. Come..."

Fodla entered the glen and saw brushwood and split logs stacked beneath a tripod of rough timbers. Next to it, a square cage of interlaced willow branches stood taller than the height of several men.

Stroking the willows as he might a woman's body, the druid watched intermittent flashes of lightning between distant trees. "Taranis shall light the flames. One of the god's fire bolts will show his pleasure at our offering..." Fodla clutched the arch-druid's tunic. "I tell you Calidos, tomorrow many twenties of warriors will blacken the hills. At the setting of Belenos, Caesar and his legions will be no more. The Narbonensis retaken and Celtic lands from the White Mountains to Inisfail will be ours!"

Calidos pulled free, troubled that the druid had influenced him to allow human sacrifice in the crisis. "This sanctuary has always been one of healing. Women wash their breasts in the pool of Damona to insure milk—"

Wild-eyed, Fodla screamed, "Prepare the drug for our victims! Let them sleep and dream of their welcoming in the Land of the Eternally Young!"

❧❧

It was pitch dark when I sat outside the hospital tent with Apsa, Psen-Ammon, and Moira, watching far-off lightning that flared on the horizon. Below them, at the western bend of the fortifications, a steady thump-thump of catapults sent stone volleys smashing into Gallic encampments.

During the watch Marius had spotted Moira half-limping toward the palisade's main gate and ordered her admitted. The druidess acted confused, agitated, and refused to explain her absence. He had not pressed her for reasons.

Moira shivered in fright. "Taranis's anger flashes out. I...I feel blood in the air."

"The ants gather for the kill," Psen Ammon remarked. "Their vast numbers can destroy even wasps."

Apsa said, "Deserters from Alesia tell us their food is gone and people starve. How...how terrible for them."

I remained silent. Twenty nights had passed since remnants of Alesia's Gallic cavalry had escaped through gaps in the unfinished fortification walls. Since Caesar feared they would recruit followers to relieve Vercingetorix, he ordered a second line of fortifications that faced outward. In the larger view, I thought it might be us who were trapped. To which "ants" did the Egyptian surgeon refer?

By firelight I noticed Lucius Velcanius approaching and stood to greet him.

He returned my clasp and nodded to Apsa and Psen-Ammon. "I'm posting the second watch. Anything unusual to report here?"

I told him, "Catapults have started, but it's like throwing dice time after time. No side is winning or losing."

Apsa asked, "Lucius, what of that rumored Gallic army?"

"There's truth to it. We're prepared, yet there are factions at Roma who hope Caesar will lose everything here."

Psen-Ammon sneered, "Many fondle the hand they wish cut off."

"True," Lucius agreed. "Luculus is backing Pompeius as dictator... Jupiter! I don't have time to discuss politics! These ditches, walls, and watchtowers could be the only defense between us and crossing the Styx!"

Above the wreckage of the lower Gallic camps, Apsa noticed a flare of light grow brighter on the heights of Alesia. "Lucius, is that a signal up there?"

Psen-Ammon mocked, "Do the besieged notice that friendly ants have arrived?"

"It's Fodla!"—Moira's terrorized outburst chilled us—"He will offer a human sacrifice to Taranis by burning!"

Lucius misunderstood. "What do you mean? I have heard that druids burn victims alive, but–"

"It is so! If Taranis is pleased your ditches will overflow with legion blood!"

The druidess's gestures were as wild and unsettling as her warning. Apsa moved to calm her, but Moira went back toward her tent.

Lucius was cautious. "It could be an attack signal. Alberix, get two horses. We'll report this to Caesar at the main camp."

As the two men guided their mounts between scattered supplies, cook-fires, and wagons, nothing seemed alarming to legionaries that crowded a space between the double fortifications. Men off duty ignored the thumps to sleep in their tents.

At the *praetorium*, Aulus Hirtius, Caesar's secretary, told Lucius that the commander was asleep and refused to awaken him for such a vague report.

⁓ೞ⳹⁓

The surrounding mountains were dark shapes, but the first rays of a morning sun had brightened the sky when fourth watch sentries reported movement at Alesia's main gate. They shouted a warning to the garrison.

I had slept in the *praetorium* compound and heard the noise. When I climbed to the palisade catwalk, groups of people left Alesia on foot and walked down a dirt path toward where it ended at our palisade defenses.

"Don't look like warriors," a legionary in the nearest tower reported. "They're not armed, yellin' or runnin'."

While the dispatch went to Caesar and his tribunes, I climbed to the second level of a tower for a better view. On the pathway, warriors prodded stragglers along with spears, but the exiles seemed to be oldsters and women with children.

Caesar came up a walkway ladder with Gaius Canininus Rebilus, commander of Legio XV. The refugees trudged toward his sector of wall, yet the officers seemed unconcerned about an attack.

I heard Rebilus say, "Those refugees are here, then."

Caesar agreed. "Mandubii deserters last night were truthful. Vercingetorix will conserve food by sending us his useless outcasts."

When the exiles reached a stream a few hundred paces from the defense field, several younger mothers waded the shallow water. Some held up infants, others tore apart the bodice of tunics to expose their breasts in supplication. After crossing, the women and a few oldsters started toward the wall ditches, unaware of deadly obstacles scattered in front of the moat. A woman stepped on an iron barb and screamed. Others cried out after falling through brush that covered pits studded with sharpened stakes at the bottom. Those few who avoided the traps paused at a dense branch barrier that extended ten paces in front of the first moat. Centurions along the wall looked at the two officers for instructions.

Rebilus winced when more women fell shrieking into pits. He glanced at Caesar, unsure of his commander's hesitation. "Orders, Imperator?"

I looked down at Caesar's bearded face, more deeply lined than before. His mouth was set in a grim line. "Legate, we have no spare rations. Keep the exiles out and get someone who speaks Celtic to warn them away from our traps."

I heard and called down, "Sir, I'll tell them!"

Before I could do so, a warrior guarding the group hacked his way through branches, then threw his sword aside at the moat's edge. "*Ego Mandubii!* Arverni banish us from town," he shouted in poor Latin. "In name of *Matrones* give us food! Take us as slaves, but give children bread to eat!"

As a warning javelin arced down from the wall and slid into water in front of the man, I shouted for him to go back. Other refugees heard my warning, yet started forward, their arms extended for mercy. More panicked mothers and oldsters fell into pits, screaming as the pointed stakes tore into legs and thighs.

Immobilized with horror, legionaries watching from the parapet walkway were unable to respond to an order to keep the refugees away with javelin throws.

"Keep away from the pits!" I warned in Celtic. "Go back to Alesia!"

Several warriors escorting the group bypassed the traps, slashed their way through the branch barrier, and waded across the moats to attempt scaling the wall.

Tears blurred my vision. *This is madness! Those people are being slaughtered just as snared birds are clubbed in a net. Justice is balanced on the end of a spear. How can Lucius explain it?* Through my anger I made out a lone man near the branches. He waved a square of wood at legionaries that defended a section of wall, then I recognized the person's slight body and bearded features.

"Simonides!" I slid down the ladder to tell Caesar. "Imperator! Your Greek secretary is over the barricade!" That was not quite true, but I despaired for his safety.

The commander looked toward me, but turned back to Rebilus.

Desperate, I pulled myself to the top of the wicker-work palisade, balanced a moment, then shielded my face with both arms as I dropped into defensive branches on the rampart's sloping face. Dried limbs jabbed my body as I crashed through and struck the bottom with a tooth-jarring jolt. Bruised, but unhurt, I slid into the greenish mud of the inner trench. After wading through knee-deep slime, I clawed at loose dirt on the opposite bank, then tumbled over into water of the outer moat. Mired with sludge and breathing hard, I expected to hear the thud of a javelin or whistle of an arrow. I made several attempts to boost myself up and finally crawled onto the edge. While kneeling on the inner side of five rows of tangled branches, I saw Simonides halfway through, stumbling toward me.

Legionaries on the wall now paused with javelins at the ready and looked toward Rebilus and Caesar. Both officers spoke with a centurion, their backs to the palisade.

"Imperator," another centurion called to Caesar. "One of ours is outside the wall. I believe he's your friend."

Caesar and Rebilius came to look. Legionaries clenched their javelins, estimating the trajectory to the two men and awaiting an order to hurl weapons. The commander watched them—Simonides had reached Alberix and embraced him—then gave his decision in a voice so low that Rebilus repeated it more loudly. "Hold javelins. Help those two fools back inside."

A centurion ordered a ladder lowered to us. I leaned it into the ditch, then against the palisade. When we were helped over the crenellations, wet and mud-splattered, Julius Caesar turned away without troubling to greet his former secretary.

❧

Whether or not the charred remains of Ollam Fodla's ten human victims influenced Taranis, on the next day legion foragers sighted a Gallic relief army. That afternoon the bellow of *carynx* trumpets, resounding from Alesia, signaled that the fortress's garrison also had seen their long-awaited compatriots!

❧

As darkness came on, I stood on the parapet with Apsa and an unsteady Simonides. We watched distant campfires that arriving warriors kindled to the southwest of Alesia.

"They seem numerous as stars!" Apsa exclaimed. "How many men *have* come?"

Simonides replied, "Armies have been known to light additional campfires to fool an opponent, but I recorded the number of men that Vercingetorix requisitioned from each tribe. That should interest my...my former employer."

I hoped, "That could be way to get back into Caesar's friendship."

"Alberix, I can't fault him for allowing you to save me. Who acts as his secretary?"

"A man called Hurtos or some name like that..." I noticed Apsa shivering. "Let's all go back to the *praetorium* area. There's a fire outside the tent."

I hadn't yet asked my Greek friend about his captivity in Alesia and watched him poke the embers. I had eased an army blanket around Apsa's shoulders when Caesar and two companions left the praetorian tent.

I warned Simonides, "I think the Imperator is coming over to us."

"Sh...shades of Pluto..." he stuttered nervously.

When we stood up Caesar casually asked Simonides about his health.

"A few bowls of army porridge...if you can spare them...and I'll be fine." He reached out a hesitant hand. "I...I'm grateful, Commander."

Caesar lightly returned his grasp to admonish, "'Experience is the teacher of fools.' Not deep philosophy but said by one of your own Greeks." He turned to men with him. "My friend, Titus Labienus, Legate of Legio Ten. Aulus Hurtius, here for a sample of military life while recording my campaigns."

After I brought three camp stools, the men seated themselves. Caesar reprimanded Simonides as he added kindling to the fire. "Wood is scarce. There's enough light to talk."

Hirtius noted, "Judging from their campfires, the Galli have enough fuel."

"They celebrate with all they have left, "Labienus ventured, then asked Simonides, "In Alesia did you learn the make-up of this relief army?"

He looked at a graying Roman officer who was almost as much of a mythical leader as Caesar. "Sir, I wrote down the tribes and the numbers Vercingetorix requested."

"And?"

"Some forty-six tribes and two hundred ninety-thousand foot warriors—"

Hirtius promptly refuted him. "They'll never raise even half that many!"

"Probably more than one-half," Simonides estimated. "The king sent false 'deserters' down to frighten Caesar with exaggerated numbers."

Labienus leaned forward. "Cavalry?"

"I recall...some eight thousand."

The legate looked at Caesar with a grim smile. "We've badly hurt them in horse, the only units capable of mounting a disciplined attack."

"Again, how many are foot warriors?" Caesar's question was hesitant, as if he did not wish to hear the number.

"If Hirtius is correct, almost as many as in fifty-eight full-strength legions,"

Labienus was stunned. "Fifty-eight legions? We...we could garrison Albion, Gallia, all of Africa, Germania, *and* Parthia with that number!"

"And with perhaps another nine or ten legions inside Alesia," Caesar estimated.

"Imperator, is it insane to even speak of tactics?" Labienus made a sweep with one hand at the fragile barrier of walls. "We have only these to protect our legions."

Caesar clasped his shoulder. "Vercingetorix will have trouble holding Gallic tribes together, so he must act quickly. It's reported that new warriors are filling in our forward moat, alert our Ubii cavalry to attack them."

"Clever, Imperator," Labienus said with relief. "Throw Germani on their flanks."

"We must break up coordinated actions on Vercingetorix's part." Caesar abruptly stood to leave. "Better to 'lay the straw' early, Titus. Tomorrow will seem aeons-long. Alberix, check with camp surgeons. Be sure they are prepared when wounded start coming in."

I said I would do so. Before Hirtius left, Simonides tried to wheedle a supply of a papyrus from him. Taken aback, the secretary remarked, "So you're the *Graecus* who kept Caesar's notes."

"Not always to his liking, I'm afraid."

"Yes, I've read reports you wrote at the time of that nasty business with the...the Usipetes and Tencteri was it? You were quite objective."

"The commander didn't exactly praise me for it."

"Perhaps not, yet Caesar kept everything you wrote."

"So that future generations can read a half-true, half-mythical account of his campaigns?"

Hirtius's reply was diplomatic. "Come now, give the Imperator credit. I've read the beginning of what he calls *De Bello Gallico*. Simonides, the style is stark and efficient as a legion camp."

"I was thinking of content, not style," he criticized. "About that papyrus?"

"I'll send a servant over. *Fortuna tecum.*"

"And to you, Hirtius, with your manuscript."

Once the others left, Apsa stayed outside with me. She looked toward enemy campfires awhile before asking, "How many men in a legion?"

"With *auxiliae*, about four, five thousand, although we're far short of that number."

"And Vercingetorix has many times that?"

"We have twelve legions and cavalry here. I had figured four or five of his warriors against each legionary."

Apsa rested her head on my shoulder. Despite short water rations to bathe, her hair retained the smell of a flower blossom circlet she wore. "Alberix, what will happen?"

"You have a sense of the mystical. This war began with an unfortunate event, the death of Sabia and her child. Vercingetorix's advisors have little idea about how to control their men in a siege. Those campfires you see over there are divided into clan groups, where warriors will follow his chieftain or even leave him, if he feels like it."

Apsa abruptly sat up. "I don't want to sleep in a tent. Let's find a glen in the forest on the opposite side of their camps. I've saved oil for a lamp."

I was surprised at her dangerous proposal yet consented. We walked past *auxiliae* tents to the east gate. Sentries gave us a tile with the lettered password.

A narrow band of red-orange silhouetted gentle hills around us as we hiked up a trail where trees for building the palisade had been dragged down to our camps. When we turned off along a path that led to the highest point of the woods, both of us viewed Alesia and the relief encampments that were about four miles distant. Dots of light flickered at both locations.

The wind had freshened when Apsa sat on a stone ledge that retained some of the day's heat. She looked at the stars overhead. "The fires of men are no match for those of gods."

I sat with her to look up at the sweep of twinkling constellations. "I wonder if they are celebrating anything."

She moved closer to me. "Alberix, like you, those are Celtic warriors over there. How many more will die tomorrow?"

I continued scanning the sky a moment, knowing the stars held no answer, then grasped Apsa's hand and tried to explain my feelings. "Foolish decisions and treachery by Helvetii led us to this place. Perhaps if there had been an assembly of chieftains from all the Gallic tribes, war might have been voted down, or a general law like Romani have that applies to more than individual clan matters. Only Caesar can enforce a peace now."

"Such terrible killing to acquire it."

"Our tribes are too independent. It's amazing that Vercingetorix has done this much to unite them. Unfortunately, druids convinced his warriors that they cannot lose."

"Oh...Moira wasn't in our medical tent. She's disappeared again."

"I'm not surprised. She became more irrational as the situation worsened and believes that fire was a sacrificial burning."

"Didn't Fodla want to revive the practice?"

"True." I recalled the old hunter hanging in that tree on Beltaine after the druid arrived at Wermaros.

Apsa huddled against me. We marveled at the stars again, trying to forget what the next day might bring, until she whispered, "Make...make love to me."

I was surprised and bent to kiss her. I spread my cloak over grasses in a slight hollow and took off my tunic shirt and trousers. Mindful of the brutal Silanus, I kept my touch light when I caressed her body. She responded by nuzzling my chest. I felt Apsa tremble after I slid my hand beneath her tunic, but hushed her fears and gently stroked her throat and breasts. Her nipples hardened under my fingers. She mouthed a faint cry when I entered her. Although my climax came quickly, I felt no similar release in her body.

Afterward, I held Apsa tightly until we both drifted into sleep.

It was still dark when we awoke in a night filled with insect shrills and the shimmer of new stars overhead. Apsa pressed against me to whisper," We...we have a child. I feel a new life inside me."

I was confused. "How...how can you know so soon?"

"I'm as sure of it, Alberix, as I was that I would find you."

I brushed my lips over her eyes. "Then after this war ends we'll go back to Wermaros until the child is born. Remember my plan to rebuild my father's village?"

Apsa did not reply. I think she was remembering our love-making. I had tried to be considerate, but was sure she felt nothing about what village girls tittered, when they gossiped about lying with a man. When I clasped her tightly again, she dozed off without the terror-dreams of the past.

A distant blare of trumpets awakened us as the sun cleared the eastern hills.

"*Cornuae*. Men are reporting to their cohort standards." I cinched the belt on my trousers while Apsa smoothed her tunic. We followed a trail out of the woods until we had a clear view of the valley: the entire plain was speckled with dark hordes of Gallic cavalry. "Let's not get caught up here..." I pulled Apsa toward our palisade by a hand.

The gate was barred, but sentries recognized us and let us in without the password or their usual jests. We passed vacant legionary tents on the way to the medical shed—most of the men were on the western ramparts nervously watching Gallic cavalry deploy.

Inside the shed, the first ward was unoccupied, except for Simonides. He motioned for silence when he saw us and gestured toward the center aisle. Psen-Ammon stood behind a makeshift altar, dressed in a long white tunic, his head freshly shaven. Senior tribunes circled around the Egyptian to watch his ritual. On a side of the altar, the statue of a goddess wearing a headpiece in the form of a golden vulture held the looped end of a cross-shape in one hand. A flowered staff was in her other.

"The goddess, Aset," Simonides whispered. "We call her Isis. She's gotten quite popular with Roman Patricians. That cross she holds is the *ankh*, an Egyptian symbol of enduring life. The surgeon shakes a *sistrum*, believing musical vibrations express a creative force." As Psen-Ammon waved the rod, metal discs clinked softly.

While an offering of herbs and milk sizzled on the coals of a brazier, Psen-Ammon recited similar verses in the Egyptian language that he had used to cure Lucius and Adherbal at Sequana's shrine.

"Divine goddess, one of whose names is Ankhat, 'Giver of Life,' the Caesar whom you know seeks your protection. He asks that your power be directed against his enemies."

The priest tinkled the *sistrum* over the offerings and continued his invocation.

"Saith Ankhat, 'I have come that thine enemy Vercingetorix—I know his name— shall be overthrown. Saith Ankhat, I have come that I may be thy protector. I waft to thee the wind of victory that as thy enemies are fallen, they shall not rise up. Thine enemies will fall under thy feet and thou will be made to triumph, for I am Ankht-Aset, powerful of the gods'.'"

As the herbs curled into ashes, Psen-Ammon briskly shook the musical discs a third time to repeat the final incantation, "'Behold, thou will triumph, for I am Aset-Ankhat, beloved of the gods.'"

After the priest stepped back from the altar, the legion officers—who had not understood his words—waited for a moment, then realized the ritual was over. In leaving, each tribune placed a silver *denarius* offering in front of Isis.

Eyes closed, Psen-Ammon seated himself on a bench. I started toward him, but Simonides pulled me back. "He won't speak or eat until the battle."

Apsa objected, "He's the chief surgeon."

"But first an Egyptian priest. Caesar sent those tribunes here so they would go back and tell their men about Isis. It can't harm to have an exotic goddess on your side."

Apsa's eyes flashed in anger. "He should make offerings to our Celtic gods of healing! Alberix, I'm going to get medications ready for the other surgeons.

Critognatos chortled as he gazed down from the ramparts of Alesia and watched Gallic cavalry assemble on the vast plain of the Brennos River. The entire area teemed with horsemen in motion. On a hill to the left were more foot warriors than he thought lived in all Gallia. Directly below, contingents of Arvernians struggled to fill in the enemy forward moat with brushwood and earth. Others stockpiled wicker screens to throw over the base and assembled ladders to climb the palisade.

He noticed a few expelled oldsters begging food from the enemy. Caesar had not let them inside the palisade as he expected, except for a few mothers with infants—surely to question them about conditions inside Alesia.

Vercingetorix and his advisors came to Critognatos to discuss tactics. The king told him, "Commios wishes to use cavalry at the outset."

"Commios of the Atrabati tribe?"

"I assume so," Vercingetorix replied. "He was a friend of Caesar, but Labienus tried to murder him for sedition and treason."

"If cavalry go out first, I'll join them with my men." Critognatos pointed over the parapet. "Look to the northwest palisade. There is a weak point where walls fail to join because a river passes through. With Caesar expecting an attack from the west, I'm confident we can slip warriors into the gap."

Vercingetorix was more concerned about his cavalry. "In the assault I wanted foot warriors to support horsemen, yet chieftains say their men are too independent. Each will fight as he wishes." He fixed his advisors with a harsh stare to admonish, "Realize that our victory must come with the first battle. If unsuccessful, warriors will return to their villages more quickly than they came. Gallia's destiny will be determined at Alesia!"

When none of the chiefs disputed either of the king's predictions, Critognatos broke an awkward silence. "I will get my men together and signal you from the enemy camp once we are inside." He raised his sword to bellow, "Caturix, grant us victory!"

With his advisors Vercingetorix repeated the invocation to their war god, yet felt the plea should be to Epona, patron goddess of horses: cavalry would play a crucial role in the fighting's outcome.

With his men following, Critognatos trotted his stallion along a western path that led to the shrine of Moritgasus. At the clearing he noticed a woman scrabbling through an ash pile beneath a partially burned tripod of beams. *She resembles Fodla's druidess who fled. How did she enter Alesia again?*

The troupe's horses picked their way down the slope toward the location of a nearby Gallic camp. Head-sized catapult stones strewn among shattered tents and wagons testified to the deadly accuracy of the Romani machines. At the gap where the palisade allowed a river to pass, Critognatos saw that the closest watchtower was deserted. As he expected, legionaries were concentrated along southwest walls that faced the plain.

After fording the stream unchallenged with his men, Critognatos reached the first contingents of relief warriors, just after high sun. He searched for the Arverni horsemen that Vercingetorix requested, but none was among cavalry wings forming around clan totems. He was pleasantly surprised to note a large number of archers among the warriors; a sub-chief told him they would be used to harass enemy *auxiliae* sent to oppose an initial attack. For Celts this would be a new tactic.

Scattered iron spikes had crippled several horses after impatient clan chiefs and their men rode through obstacles laid in front of the moats. An occasional iron bolt from a catapult ripped through a horse or its rider. Noticing a tall warrior holding up the staff of a chieftain, and gesturing to a group of warriors, Critognatos cantered his mount forward to identify himself. "I have brought my men down from Alesia. Who is over-chieftain of tribes that arrived?"

"Commios," the man said. "If you are Arverni, Vercassivellaunos shares command with two Aedui."

Critogrnatos was furious. "Four different commanders trying to control the warriors of over two-twenties of tribes will be impossible! Victory only can be achieved through a unified assault..." He pointed back. "Your foot warriors are still in camp instead of preparing to follow a cavalry charge as ordered—"

An abrupt sound of trumpets alerted the cavalrymen toward three forward Roman camps. The gates had flung open and wings of mounted Hispanic, Numidian, and Gallic auxiliaries deftly picked their way through the obstacles, then spread out to engage the newcomers. Surprised, not formed up in battle order, the Gallic tribesmen galloped their horses back to the line of archers. A deadly flight of arrows met lead ranks of auxiliaries chasing after them. Struck by the shafts, horses tumbled to the ground and entangled any men behind. Riders pitched to earth in a confusion of lances and smashed shields.

Some among the milling horsemen saw the sortie and rushed to counter the assault. Roman allies rallied and drove them back, yet archers kept the cavalrymen from sweeping the plain, and they were unable to press a victory.

Caesar had located his main camp on *Benn Matrona*, highest of the hills surrounding the valley. From this slope the commander and his staff officers watched in frustration as their cavalry failed to rout the Gallic horse.

Desperate, Caesar gave the signal for Ubii cavalry to move out and attack the enemy left flank. Warriors there were forcing a wider gap in the ditch near watchtower XXIII.

Yelling with a furor that alarmed even battle-hardened legionaries the blue-painted Germani swept around the mountain's flank. Ubii foot-warriors followed, eager to exploit the shock of their horsemen's charge. Cleaving swords felled hapless Gallic warriors, whose bodies were looted in a repeat of an action that previously had destroyed Vercingetorix's cavalry and forced him into Alesia.

Critognatos had slashed his way through *auxilia* cavalry, back toward the palisade gap. Most of his warriors had crossed the twin moats and assaulted legion defenders. Alerted by yells from the Ubii, he watched the blue horsemen leap their mounts across the stream towards him. But they veered away from Gallic cavalry and circled around to charge directly at the archers. *They're Germani but some have helmets with Celtic crests...loot taken in their summer raids.* He saw that they held ovoid shields and many of their mounts were draped with protective chain-mail aprons.

Lances held low, the Germani formed into wedge-units. Carried by the momentum of their charge, they broke through the ranks of archers. Arrows that were loosed lodged harmlessly in Ubii shields or shattered against iron mail. Gallic warriors were trampled under the horses' iron-shod hooves;. Others died from lance thrusts. Fallen wounded were stabbed by Ubii foot warriors who followed.

Critognatos realized his raiding party was caught between the *auxilia* and Germani. At a movement to his left, he wheeled his horse around and had only time to see an Ubii's red hair tied in the side knot of his tribe, and a glint of sun on his lance tip, before the shaft tore into his own shield. When the Arvernian spun around from the momentum, his left shoulder joint seemed torn apart. The shield fell from a now useless arm, but he clamped his legs around his mount to not be unseated. As the blue warrior pivoted back toward Critognatos, he saw the cavalryman charging in, swinging a single-edged sword.

Dodging his wild slashes, the nobleman maneuvered his mount against his opponent's right side—his enemy would have to bring his shield around, hampering his swing. Enraged at the injury, his shoulder throbbing, Critognatos clenched his teeth hard enough for one to break. Still, he hacked savagely at the shield, vaguely aware of a red and black design on the wood.

The Ubii made a vicious slash at the neck of his enemy's stallion—at the same instant that Critognato's blade slid off the Germani's shield rim and into his upper arm. Screaming, the Ubii lowered his guard enough for the Arvernian's follow-up blow to split his skull; the dead warrior slid sideways off his horse onto the trampled grass.

In pain, breathing hard from shock and exertion, Critognatos paused with both arms hanging limply at his side. He sucked in gulps of air, wondering how best to move back toward the safety of the slope, where his foot warriors prepared to attack.

An iron *scorpione* bolt lodged in the Arvernian's spine so suddenly that he felt only numbness in his legs when they lost hold on his horse. Critognatos pitched to the ground.

Whether his dying gaze rested on the temple of the Moritgasus above Caesar's camp, or that of Epona on the heights of Alesia, the chieftain never lived to tell anyone in the Now-world of the living.

CHAPTER XI

Two nights later, the field of obstacles in front of the palisade and a timely arrival of legionary reinforcements under Marcus Antonius and Gaius Trebonius repulsed a coordinated Gallic attack. After this failed attempt, Vercassivellaunos led a picked force of warriors on a night march around the western slope of *Benn Matronae.* Unobserved, the men took positions above the main legion camp.

Vercingetorix moved his warriors out of Alesia to attempt breaching the outer ditch—a pre-arranged signal for Vercassivellaunos to assault the outer palisade. This two-pronged attack almost succeeded: only reinforcements at vulnerable points by a constant shuffling of cohorts prevented the garrison from being overwhelmed. The decisive battle occurred when a final sortie of Germanic cavalry routed the Galli. One of four over-chiefs was killed and Vercassivellaunos himself captured.

After hearing of their comrades' failure, discouraged tribes of the relief army retreated toward Bibracte. Finally losing all hope of victory, Vercingetorix offered the forfeit of his life to advisors. Instead, they voted to turn him over to Julius Caesar's mercy.

∞

The day after the *Nones* of October was set as the date of the formal surrender. This was the feast of *Jupiter Fulgur,* "The Hurler of Lightning," a date not lost on Caesar. At the morning sacrifice he reminded his tribunes that the festival celebrated the god's supreme destructive power, and that Roman power destroyed Alesia and forced its capitulation.

During the forenoon, burial parties carried out bodies of Roman and Gallic dead for burial in the twin ditches that surrounded the palisade. Mule teams dragged horse carcasses into adjacent trenches. Senior tribunes ordered Vercingetorix's envoys to send their tribal chieftains in advance of the king's surrender. A torn-down section of palisade allowed a gap through which Gallic prisoners would pass. All weapons were to be thrown into the moats next to the passageway.

Caesar's magistrate's chair was set up on a cleared section of the gap, from which he would receive the conquered Arvernian leader. Some eighty Gallic war standards captured in the ill-fated assault surrounded the chair, a final humiliation for the defeated warriors.

I watched the surrender ceremony with Simonides. Apsa chose to stay with Psen-Ammon and his wounded men.

Drawn up as an honor guard, legionaries from the cohorts of Reginus and Caninus stood along the route that Vercingetorix would follow. Maniple standards—hands, wreaths, discs, and moons—glistened in autumn sunshine, forming an avenue of bright Romani military symbols that mocked the vanquished king.

Lucius, along with senior tribunes of Legio X, went to escort Vercingetorix down to the camp; rumors suggested that the defeated leader might commit a dramatic act of suicide while on his way to submit to the enemy.

Julius Caesar appeared on the rampart walkway nearest the palisade opening, wearing a parade uniform under his scarlet cloak. Titus Labienus stood next to him. Other legion commanders waited a short distance apart. As many legionaries as possible crowded the breastworks for a glimpse of the Gallic king's surrender.

When Caesar noticed Vercingetorix emerge from Alesia's main gateway, he whispered to Labienus, "One more day, Titus, and just as we discussed I would have been forced to lift the siege."

The legate raised an eyebrow. "This is the feast of Jupiter Fulgur. Suppose there's any connection to our victory?"

Caesar chuckled. "I've poured enough wine to the old reprobate to supply a legion! The god owes us this day."

Labienus gestured toward Vercingetorix. "What will you do with him?"

"Send him to Roma as a prisoner until we celebrate our Triumph." Caesar reached over to squeeze his legate's shoulder as a comrade. "Titus, I said *our Triumph* and I want you there. You held these legions together when I was at Ravenna."

"Imperator—"

"I mean it, Titus. Pompeius will shit shields over the size of our victory and that should teach him a little highly needed humility."

Labienus suggested, "Why not make the chieftains treaty hostages rather than war prisoners? That way other Gallic tribes might more quickly be pacified."

"As an incentive?" Caesar nodded approval. "Clever strategy, Titus! I trust I shall never need to hold up a shield against you."

Labienus reacted with shock. "Imperator! Quite...quite unthinkable!"

"Of course, I was jesting with you."

After the king and his escorts reached the stream, Caesar walked down a ladder to seat himself in his magistrate's chair at the near end of the honor guard. Holding a sheathed sword, Vercingetorix walked toward the avenue of cohorts. An aide carried his shield and broken spear. Passing the Roman guard, the king waded through the shallow waterway in silence and reached the clearing where Caesar awaited him.

Vercingetorix threw down his sword and took the shield and spear segments to flung into the moat. He looked up at his conqueror. "The gods of my people witness that I yield to you."

Caesar did not reply. He held the Arvernian's gaze until he turned away and gestured to Lucius. He led the king through the palisade gate to join other prisoners. The emotional surrender ceremony had ended almost literally in the blink of an eye.

I told Simonides, "With that fleeting moment, Gallia passes to the 'Shorthairs'."

He quoted, "'To stretch out our life, shall we yield thus to these profaners of our house'?"

Puzzled, I asked him. "What did you say?"

"One of our playwrights wrote that. The chorus goes on to say that death is more comfortable than tyranny. But then, Aeschylus died a free man."

After Caesar stood up to congratulate his legates and tribunes, the legionaries dispersed back to their duties. As I helped Simonides down the rampart ladder, I commented that Caesar had not said a word to Vercingetorix.

"I predict that others historians not here will have much more to say. Alberix, I...I'm feeling a bit weak...feverish. Think I'll lie down awhile."

"Rest now and I'll bring you food later." Grateful that we had not needed to storm Alesia, I turned back to look at the fortress when I heard Marcus Marius call my name.

"Fortunate that I found you," he said. "I'm going up to check damage from our catapults, so I thought you might like to look inside Alesia."

"I'd be eager to see what's left of the fortress."

We started up the trail Vercingetorix had taken to surrender—ironically, the same path along which he had sent the useless in Alesia to die. Once inside the gate, the scene was one of horrific devastation: only ruined walls or foundations of a number of buildings remained. The last of the wooden roof beams had been burned in bonfires to celebrate the Gallic army's arrival. We covered our mouths with neckerchiefs at a stench of charred wood, excrement, and piles of rotting food scraps. Only one structure was relatively intact: in a littered courtyard, the shrine of Taranis retained its outer walls and slate-covered wooden roof.

Marius recalled, "Moira mentioned Taranis and that's probably one of his temples. Let's look inside."

On entering it took a moment for our eyes to adjust to the dimness. I heard an eerie humming before I made out a crouched figure swaying back and forth at the far end of the sanctuary. It was the only living being in a scene of horror. Ollam Fodla, his throat slashed, lay slumped against a stone destiny-wheel at the base of Taranis's statue. Next to the druid lay the instrument of his death—a golden sickle used in gathering mistletoe.

A nude woman squatted in front of a pool of congealed gore that seeped from the dead druid's neck. The survivor traced Celtic swirl patterns with blood on the paving stones as she turned to stare at us with wild eyes.

Marius recognized her vacant look. "Great Jupiter, that's Moira! She's insane as the Cumaean Sibyl."

I stammered, "Then she…, she murdered Fodla!"

"Alberix, go outside again," Marius told me in a faint voice. "I'll follow you shortly."

"Why?"

This time he shouted, "Get the furc out!"

I turned and went back into the courtyard. Moments later Marius stumbled through the door, white-faced, his blood-reddened sword held in a hand that hung by his side.

"She…Moira…was a beautiful woman, but cold as a marble Aphrodite because of that son of Minos." Marius retched acrid bile, then ran to lean over the courtyard wall and vomit. He returned, wiping his mouth with a neckerchief. "Let's get back to camp. I've had about all of this Stygian horror I can stomach."

❧☙

Later, when I came to bring Simonides a bowl of horse stew, his complexion was flushed with fever. I sat watching my friend barely eat, while trying to sort out events of the past months. I felt anxious about my mother and aunt—both were still at Wermaros—and decided to visit Lucius that evening.

❧☙

"I've been thinking about them too," Lucius admitted when I saw him. "Caesar will winter in Bibracte and appointed me to command a guard escort that takes Vercingetorix with a few high-ranking hostages to Roma. He's given permission for you and Apsa to go with me as interpreters and be presented to the Senatus. We'll need Gallic help to pass land grant proposals that Caesar wants for his veterans."

"How can I...can Apsa...possibly help?"

Lucius replied with more confidence than facts. "I believe Gallia will become the most important province that Roma has in the west and a vast buffer against Germani incursions. Veterans' colonies will help assure peace and implement senatorial decrees."

"On the tip of a sword?" It was a cynical question worthy of my mother.

"Hopefully not, Alberix, since a *Pax Romana* would benefit everyone."

I didn't continue the conversation; after all, that was my father's dream. "Lucius, I should go back to Wermaros first. My mother and aunt are with Ger."

He clasped my arm. "Approved! Take a few of Adherbal's men from Legio Ten and a guide that knows a road to the Dubis from here. Then meet us at Viennadunum on the Rhodanus with the women and your son."

"I should bring both women and Ger?"

I...I've also been concerned about Briga. You can't leave her and her sister alone at Wermaros. My hope is that we can be married and she'd be willing to settle in Italia."

Lucius was correct about the possible danger to my mother and Dirona so I was eager to leave. "If Adherbal is ready, we could go at first light."

"Fine. There are details I must work out for transporting the prisoners. Apsa can stay with me to treat any wounded chiefs that accompany Vercingetorix." Lucius grasped my shoulder. "*Dea Fortuna tecum*, Alberix, until Viennadunum."

∾

I hired an Aedui guide who led the way along a road that ran from the nearby shrine of Sequana to a source of the Dubis River. In cutting eastward, to join the river closer to Wermaros, we came across the trail I had taken to Genava in the spring of the Helvetii migration. Since I knew the way from there, I paid the guide.

On the trail Adherbal's Numidians strung themselves out among trees still colorful with autumn foliage. I thought I was risking my horse to the utmost on the steep way, but the prince's men charged past me several times in their eagerness to reach the village.

As we came closer to a valley southeast of Wermaros we kept our mounts just inside the forest to avoid encountering renegade Gallic warriors. We only saw a few older men and women harvesting scanty crops on parcels of mountain land. Before the bend in the river, Adherbal pointed to the abandoned *Castor* watchtower on the heights. A huge waterwheel rested askew in the black current of the Dubis.

Ahead, in the village I didn't see wisps of cook-fire smoke curling from vent holes under the eaves. Even though the river gate was closed Wermaros seemed deserted.

"Where people?" Adherbal wondered as he brought his mount to a halt at the gate.

My confusion bordered on alarm. "Strange. No guards or hearth fires—"

"Gate shut, but we get in..." Adherbal called out, "Nabdalsa!"

After a discussion Nabdalsa shouted a command in Berber. His Numidians unfastened lengths of rope from saddle pouches and looped them over the tops of palisade stakes. At an order, their horses strained forward until the barricade of saplings fell in an ear-wrenching crunch of rotted wood and dust-haze. The shallow ditch that encircled the palisade was covered with brushwood. While clearing the debris to enter, a Numidian's foot slipped into a trench of sticky, black ooze.

Adherbal sniffed a dark blob the man held up on a branch. "Alb-rix, what this?"

"Pitch, but it doesn't make much of a trap. Let's get inside and find my mother."

While the Numidians fanned out to search the nearest dwellings, Adherbal and I turned our horses up the main road. Since the door of Dirona's lodge had been forced off its hinges, we paused to look inside. No one was there.

My anxiety increased at Mother's lodge—a beam outside barred the portal. Adherbal dismounted with me to remove the barrier. It was almost free when we heard a shout near the Acantos quarter.

On hearing the sound of horsemen, Triccos came running out of his lodge, carrying two lighted pine torches. The druid ran toward the hidden gateway in the palisade and tossed one firebrand onto the straw thatching of the closest shed. One of the Numidian's arrows thudded into a stake a moment after Triccos ducked through the opening. Once outside he sprinted in the direction of the river, touching his remaining torch to brush kindling along the trench. In moments pitch taken from the towers licked into flames to spawn thick black smoke:

Triccos had ringed the village with flammable ooze to make a death trap for anyone left inside!

A northeast breeze quickly spread the shed fire to other warehouses built against the palisade's inner wall. Clutching his bow, Nabdalsa leaped onto the rampart from his horse, but Triccos ran too close to the stakes for a clear shot. I heard the druid screaming above the crackle of flames and caught the words, "sacrifice" and "Taranis." I needed nothing more to realize that he was offering the village as a burnt offering to our sky god!

After Adherbal helped me move the beam from my mother's door, I ran inside.

Briga and Dirona stood at the bottom of the entrance ramp, each brandishing a forge tool. When they saw me enter, both dropped the makeshift weapons with a cry of joy.

The hug of the two women was fierce as tears came to their eyes.

"What happened? Mother, where are the others?"

"Ger is safe in his bed," Briga explained between sobs. "Liscos was killed trying to attack the tower. Trauna went back to her sons at Vesontio and took Arduinna with her."

Dirona continued, "When warrior recruits left to fight, Triccos convinced remaining old men and women that Wermaros was bewitched. After the last family left, the druid barricaded us inside our lodge."

"As sac-ri-fice to gods!" Adherbal's voice was grim.

"Mother, we must leave immediately!"

"I know..." Briga went to a storage chest and brought back a suede pouch. "Alberix, when you were last here I didn't give you this."

I untied the drawstring and slipped out a silver medallion that Dividiac used to determine where we would go after we fled my father's village. The three-headed god was mute, but I fingered the month of Cantios on his lunar calendar and slipped Dividiac's medallion around my neck. "Mother, I—"

"My son, don't say anything. I want you to have what is left of your uncle."

Adherbal broke in, "Alb-rix, we leave now. Large dan-ger."

To underscore his words, strands of black smoke threaded through the doorway and curled into the room. We hurried the two women outside and saw the western palisade a long barrier of flame. Lodges belonging to Liscos and his vassals burned. Nabdalsa tumbled off the rampart, the hem of his cloak ablaze. His companions directed their mounts toward the breach they made at the river gate, a hundred paces away, but snakes of flame blocked the outlet. Although most horses shied away, three Numidians managed to leap their mounts over the fire.

Triccos had run halfway across the Dubis bridge when a trio of arrows sliced into his back. Carried forward by the momentum of his desperate run, the druid stumbled under the railing and fell into the black current. His body drifted toward Vesontio.

Three-fourths of the village was in flames now, the crackling dry wood and thatch seeming to cry out like some haunted creature.

"Adherbal!" I shouted. "Take Dirona and your other men. Ride to the east corner where the barns are. Pull down *that* palisade."

The Numidian helped Dirona onto his mount. Nabdalsa and his men followed the prince. With Mother clutching my waist, I galloped my mount through garden plots and leaped it over a stone wall. Briga later was to tell me that she did not think of danger, only that it was at that wall that Lucius had first proposed marriage to her.

At the intact palisade the Numidians used their ropes to pull at the stakes, but there was more resistance on this sheltered side where wood had less decay. I wondered for one irrational moment if the village *was* enclosing us in a fiery offering to Taranis!

The barrier finally gave way with a nerve-shattering shriek that echoed from the mountains. We urged our mounts through the fallen debris. After the last Numidian led his horse to safety, the ring of flame continued to burn fiercely and roll out clouds of choking smoke. I dismounted and walked with my mother and aunt a short way up the mountain road to watch the village. The place was only a little lower than where I had first sensed my destiny in the wheel-apparition of the circular palisade. I clutched Dividiac's medallion. With Wermaros destroyed, my destiny was no longer to stay in this village and yet it had birthed what my future would become.

As the last shed collapsed in a whirlpool of swirling sparks, I tried to take the women's minds off their near death. "Mother," I told her, "I'm going to Roma. Vercingetorix is defeated and Lucius will command a guard detail that takes him to the city. Caesar has all but promised to rebuild Father's village as a Renos settlement."

Dirona reacted first. "Sister, I told you when you came here that it was Alberix over whom the gods watched. Your son will finish Alrix's work!"

Mother did not reply and continued to stare at the wheel of flames, until she commented, "Gallia...Celtic lands...belong to outsiders now. Our gods have a strange way of working their will."

I brushed soot from her face and hair. "Lucius needs you, Mother. Go to Roma with us. Dirona, you must come too."

My aunt shrugged indifference. "There is nothing for me here. At least I could help forge Alrix's dream."

"Mother?"

When she smiled a wan assent, I grasped her hand. "Good! Can we stay in the charrers' huts for the night?"

"The workers left, so Ersa is in one of them with Ger." Briga looked at me with fright yet in her eyes. "Triccos became crazed after Liscos was killed. He wanted to emulate Fodla and offer human sacrifices—"

"That's over, Mother. If we find the druid's body downstream, Adherbal's men will bury him."

After the Numidians finished inspecting their mounts for burn injuries, we prepared to ride to the charring ovens. Fed by the pitch, the wheel of fire would burn for several days and be visible at night far up the valley. Any remaining farmers or herders who saw it would be too superstitious to approach a bewitched circle of flames.

As I scanned the river's shoreline while leading the way toward the charrings, I saw Triccos's body snagged on a branch. The feathered shafts in his back radiated as a bizarre marker. "Adherbal," I ordered. "Have your men bury the druid on shore."

"Evil man," the prince grunted. "Let carrion birds eat him."

"No, it was Fodla who made him evil. I want Triccos buried."

Adherbal scowled disapproval, yet called out my order in Berber. While two men dismounted to pull the druid's body onto the riverbank, others scooped a rectangular hole in the soft soil with their hands.

I watched the Africans push dirt over Triccos's body and thought back to the time when I had thrown off my Celtic clothing and decided to stay with the Romani. I now understood the meaning of my act: in ordering the druid to be covered over, I buried my last remnant of dependence on our old gods.

On the day after the *Eidus* of October, a barge swung around a curve of the Rhodanus River and Lucius saw the Allobroge stronghold come into view "Apsa, there's Viennadunum," he called to her from the bow.

She went to look. "Is that where Alberix came when he tried to find you?"

"No, that was Genava, but we trained here before the Helvetii campaign."

"I wonder if Alberix is back from Wermaros with the others."

"I doubt it. That journey is twice as far as we've come." Lucius bent to hug Apsa's shoulder. "You shouldn't worry. He will arrive with Ger, so let's get ready to go ashore."

Viennadunum bustled with activity. Simonides had joined the barge convoy in returning to Massilia. He still suffered a fever, yet insisted on taking Apsa to explore the lower town. Roman surveyors and Gallic masons had begun converting the tent streets of legion camps into blocks of houses and shops for artisans and merchants. Because war had stripped the countryside, the residents were in need of everything. With peace would come new profits to the towns-people.

It would take several days to join vessels with supplies for a downriver journey to Massilia. Lucius stayed with his Gallic hostages on a barge anchored in the river. A shackled Vercingetorix and his chieftains huddled inside a cabin to foil rescue attempts by Segusiavi warriors. A detachment of archers, a field catapult, and the white standard of Legio X warned the curious away.

At the *Mare Internum* port of Massilia, Lucius hoped finally to board a galley bound for Roma.

❧❧

Several days later, Lucius glanced ashore and saw Briga and Dirona wave to him from the wharf. Next to them Alberix held up Ger's hand in a signal of their arrival. Adherbal and his Numidians had stayed at Wermaros to clean up after the fire. They would go on to Roma with the group, to continue training as Caesar's bodyguard in his anticipated twenty-day Triumph.

❧❧

That evening we all met for supper at a hostelry in the upper town where Apsa and Simonides lodged. Despite his gaunt, flushed features, a result of his illness, my friend was in a jovial mood. After entering he looked around the smoky room.

"Alberix, doesn't this place remind you of one at Vesontio where that fight between legionaries and *Keltoi* almost broke out."

The trouble involved Apsa's first owner and I didn't want her reminded of him. "This place is much cleaner. Allobroges seem to be prospering."

His reaction was cynical but honest. "At least the war profited to some tribes."

I grasped Apsa's hand and turned to Briga. "Mother, we want to marry as soon as possible. Lucius, you mentioned the possibility of a Romani ceremony."

He parried my request. "Ah...Caesar isn't here. I...I may have spoken too quickly. Apsa is a slave and you're not a citizen of Roma."

"Why not a Gallic marriage?" Dirona suggested. "I'm sure a *vergobret* could draw up a contract of manumission."

"Splendid idea!" Simonides agreed. "I have notes for a book that describes your people's customs. In it I shall immortalize your wedding!"

"I *would* prefer a Celtic ceremony for her," Briga said, without looking at Lucius.

I asked my aunt, "Must Apsa be a freedwoman?"

"Yes, but under our laws the woman chooses a man. The *vergobret* can explain."

When the innkeeper, a battle-scarred Allobroge, came to oversee the meal and was told of the plans, he agreed to arrange a meeting the next day with Rucillos, the town's chief magistrate.

❧

Rucillos drew up a slave manumission document and marriage contract for the couple. Because Lucius wished to continue on to Roma as quickly as possible, the ceremonies would take place that same afternoon.

❧

I stood with Apsa in the common room of the magistrate's lodge, waiting for him to read from a leather scroll. Lucius and Simonides were alongside the two of us. Mother and Dirona acted as witnesses. A few Allobroge officials came to watch—and undoubtedly share any food and drink served after the ceremony.

Rucillos began, "Twenty-fifth day of Cantios. Alberix son of Alrix, having purchased the woman, Apsa, a slave by right of war, from Publius Silanus, deceased *Centurio* of *Legio Romanus Duodecim*, and having shown receipt of the purchase price to witnesses, does manumit the slave, Apsa, into a freedwoman."

The magistrate handed the document to Apsa, then waited while I embraced her before asking, "Shall you both contract marriage now?" At our nod, he told her, "Under our *bret*-laws, it is the woman who must choose the man."

When Lucius and Simonides chuckled at the custom, Briga pushed them in mock annoyance.

Rucillos continued, "If Alberix agrees to become the husband of Apsa, he must pay a sum that in the absence of her male kin I have set as *vergobret*. Apsa must match the amount. Every year at Samain both of you will count your joint property. Any increase will be divided as equal portions to each. If one does not survive the year the other is entitled to only a half share. Under our laws, the goods of the woman are hers, those of the man, his. Any gifts given to the woman are hers alone, yet are to be returned if the marriage is dissolved by divorce or death."

I noticed Rucillos pause and surmised that under the circumstances he would not mention that a virginity price due the woman from me would not be required.

"Apsa," he asked so all could hear, "do you freely choose this man, Alberix, to be your contractual husband, according to the terms contained in this document?"

Apsa's consent was firm and loud. "I *do* choose him."

"Alberix, if you accept wash your hands in the water bowl that Apsa offers you. Then bring forward the amount you will pay for her."

Apsa looked away as I rinsed my hand in the basin—she had no possessions with which to match whatever I might give her.

While I dried my hands, the *vergobret* continued the ceremony. "Alberix, you have washed your hands of your status as an unmarried man and accepted Apsa as your wife. What do you offer for her?"

I held my hand tightly clenched, then passed what I had to the magistrate. Apsa's eyes widened, then welled with tears: a lead ball was cupped in the official's palm. Wiping her eyes, she reached into her purse and matched the projectile with the one that had injured me before Caesar's invasion of Albion.

Puzzled, Lucius turned to Simonides, who shrugged surprise. "Don't blame me. I have no idea how the *vergobret* knew about those projectiles."

Rucillos asked the couple, "We have no druids present, but do either of you have patron gods to whom you wish to make a petition or thank?"

I shook my head. After a moment of thought, Apsa said, "Arduinna of the forest."

Embarrassed at her remembrance, I thought of Simonides. "I...I petition Sequana, the goddess who heals illness."

Rucillos ended the ceremony. "Let this contract of words and actions be molded into you both like a silver image and keep it shining with honor." He placed a hand on each of our heads to pronounce a Celtic maxim.

"'Long is the road and wide is the mountain of your journey,

Yet where love is guide, the way seems always downward.'"

I believed that would always be true.

After the ceremony, Lucius insisted on hosting a marriage feast for us. At the *Hound and Hare*, a name given an inn on the advice of legionary patrons that had similar signs on their *tabernae*, we sat around an eating board. The low table was one concession Tarvos, the innkeeper, had not made to the conquerors. He personally served part of the meal.

A suckling pig that Tarvos swore was raised only on milk, wheat, and oak-corns, roasted on the hearth. An amphora of wine cooled in a vat of water.

By reading the seal, Simonides discovered the vintage was from Massilia. Fish, cheese, and olives were served with millet bread, wheat cakes, and honey. Barely eating, Simonides noted that unlike the inn at Vesontio, this one had Celts and Romans seated together.

Lucius had the same thought. "Judging from the blend of people here, our *Pax Romana* seems already at work."

"Instead of a *Pax Celtica*." Before Lucius reacted, Simonides added, "Let us hope peace continues. Of course, Allobroges long have been 'allies' of Roma."

I changed the topic away from controversy. "Friend, this wine is from your city."

"But without my father's signet and...and that would not...not please him—" Abruptly the room felt oppressive to Simonides. Nauseated, he struggled to stand up.

Dirona went to help. "Briga and I can take you to your room. Lucius, perhaps a camp surgeon could come?"

I walked Simonides to the door, then my mother and aunt assisted him to his lodgings.

When we went back to our table, Apsa recalled that morning. "Simonides insisted on seeing everything at Viennadunum. He didn't eat anything but drank watered wine."

"A...a good sleep and he'll be fine." I felt hopeful if not convinced.

After the sisters returned, Lucius brought out a small papyrus. "I...I'm not much at reading poetry but do have a few verses by Catullus."

Briga urged, "Read them, Lucius."

"They're part of a marriage song. The *quaestor* copied them for me. Here...

> *'And now you go! May Venus give*
> *to each of you a high success.*
> *Walk the road of law,*
> *so that in an honest way,*
> *you, only in the light of day,*
> *obtain whatever it is you need.*
> *Now this happy day is over,*
> *while we call out, Valete!*
> *Live in honor, love and truth*
> *and utilize your healthy youth,*
> *in games forever fairly played'.'"*

The roomful of men and a few women had grown quiet during the reading. Now they applauded and held up cups of wine to toast the newlyweds.

I raised mine in an additional offering. "To peace...finally!"

Apsa summed up my wish. "And our return to the Renos."

Swaying slightly from the wine, Lucius announced, "I've been away from civilization a long time, but I think we're supposed to follow you to your nuptial chamber while making all sorts of noise."

Briga laughed and held him back. "Lucius, leave them alone. Let's walk by the river."

Ersa rose to take Ger to their room. After embracing her son and Apsa again, Briga motioned Lucius outside. A view from the upper town was magnificent. Wooded hills framed a silver sweep of the river as it curved past the town. When western crests were lost in a glare of low sun, Briga watched the lengthening shadows of buildings and river barges. She had not been alone with Lucius for a long while and comented in a nervous voice, "It...it's warm for Cantios."

"Hmm?" he asked absently. "Oh, sorry. I...I was thinking about that barge where Vercingetorix is imprisoned. I'll talk to him in the morning. Let's take that stroll."

Briga held his arm and started down the winding roadway. They walked in silence, admiring the sunset and observing a rectangular layout of the town with its new blocks of houses. Lucius spotted a painted wagon of prostitutes and surmised they would have a brothel set up before roofs went on the shops.

When the couple reached the south corner of the ramparts, Belenos had melted into the hills. Lucius stopped to look at Briga. *The strain of the past few years is reflected in her face, but knowing that Alberix is safe will help ease her worry.* "You never told me what happened at Wermaros."

"Triccos convinced villagers that it was under a *geis*."

"That means a curse?"

"Yes. He intended to kill us after everyone abandoned the village..." She looked into his eyes. "Lucius, while...while I was isolated in our lodge, I realized how much I missed you."

He grasped a hand to kiss her fingers. "Briga, despite your customs, I want us to marry. I still have the duty of taking Vercingetorix to Roma before my legion discharge. After that—"

She shushed his lips with her other hand. "A warrior's wife is no stranger to waiting."

"Jupiter, I've missed you!" He embraced her in a way he hoped was not rough, then rubbed her back, embarrassed at his hardness she must feel against her.

Briga pulled away. "Come to my room."

"What about Dirona?"

"She will sleep with Ersa and Ger."

No one noticed—or cared—as the two climbed the open stairway to second floor rooms. Their lovemaking was short and fierce; afterward, Lucius worried that he had been too intent on his own pleasure.

"No, it was good for me," Briga whispered, stroking his face.

When her fingers touched the white scar on his upper arm, he winced. "I irritated that old wound at Alesia. The arm isn't worth a *sestercius*."

"Romani man," Briga teased, "there is more to you than an arm."

"And, Celtic woman, you have a beautiful body."

Her fingers caressed his face again, then she nestled with her back against him. "Tell me about Roma. Where shall we be married?"

"Not there, *cara*—"

"Carra? Who is she?"

He laughed. "In Latin the word means 'my love.' Have I never called you that?"

"I forget, but it's a stronger word than our *carantos*…'friend.' Go on about our marriage."

"I haven't seen my parents in…in five or six years. They live at Abellinum, only a few days journey from the capital. Would it displease you if we married there?"

"Of course not, but what will they think of your wild Gauless?"

"Probably keep you in a cage!" Lucius let out a mock roar and turned Briga toward him to fondle her body before entering her warmth again. Her gasp of release came just before his own climax.

Afterward both fell into a peaceful sleep they had not known for years. Lucius awakened while it was still dark, kissed Briga's hair, groped for his tunic, then slipped out of the inn, to the barking of watchdogs and the curious stares of slaves readying to serve breakfast.

Alberix and Apsa had lain talking about the new small life in her womb. If the infant was a girl, they would name her *Salia*—willow. After repeating plans for a Renos settlement, they fell asleep without lovemaking.

Lucius sent word to the barge-master that departure would be at the fourth hour.

Simonides was too feeble to walk, so was carried aboard the barge on a stretcher. Apsa tried to make him comfortable in a tent erected near the mast, away from legion veterans crowding the deck. They would be dropped off at villages along the river.

When I arrived, Lucius beckoned to me. "I'm going to check on Vercingetorix and the other chiefs. Come with me."

I jested, "Lucius, are you sure I won't recant my allegiance to Roma?"

He was in no mood for trifling. "Had you stayed, you either would be buried in a ditch at Alesia or a legionary's slave. Each man received one."

I didn't answer him.

A barge-master's cabin at the stern had been cleared of two bunks and furnishings. Straw covered the floor. A slave attendant who brought food waited near a slop pot. Vercingetorix and three of his sub-chiefs were shackled to the wall by a hand, yet low enough to allow the men to sit or lie down. Iron clamps secured their ankles.

Vercingetorix put down a bowl when we entered.

Lucius removed his helmet. "Arvernian, are you well?"

Vercingetorix ignored him and remembered me. "Alberix, it seems you chose wisely. As reward, have you been placed over me?"

Although he was sarcastic, I replied evenly, "I'm not over you. I accompany *Centurio* Lucius Velcanius to Roma as interpreter."

"*Centurio*, your...senators...cannot speak Celtic?"

Lucius ignored his sarcasm. "Are your companions' wounds treated?"

"By a young woman who comes in."

I told him, "Apsa, my wife."

"Wife? Then your victory is complete! May your sons grow to be valiant warriors."

"Arvernian, they will become men of peace."

Lucius told the hostages, "I'm responsible for your welfare and safe arrival. We leave shortly for Massilia."

Vercingetorix imagined his future. "And then to Roma where we will be chained to Caesar's chariot during his Triumph."

Without responding, Lucius replaced his helmet. "*Valere*...be in health."

Outside, dock slaves loosened hawsers from mooring dogs. A helmsman atop the cabin steered the vessel into the river. Running with the Rhodanus current, and guided at night by watch-fires along the banks, the barge would reach Massilia in two days.

✑✑

On the next morning, Apsa helped Simonides to a side railing and watched passing scenery with him. He had come north from Massilia over six years earlier with Valerius Troucillus and was surprised at the area's development. Transport barges loaded with goods came from lands around the *Mare Internum*. Others glided southward with products from Gallic lake districts and eastern regions not affected by the war.

On slopes to either side of the river forests were cleared and planted with grape cuttings from Italia. Workers harvested the clusters or worked gardens alongside the vineyards. All prospered after some fifty years of peace in the area: the Romanization of southern Gaul prompted Cicero in a moment of cynicism to comment that not a *sestercius* changed hands in *Provincia* without a Roman merchant or land speculator profiting from the transaction! Especially in Massilia.

✑✑

Massilia was the largest port in Gallia, protected on three sides by the sea, and with massive landward walls of crenellated stonework. Founded as an Ionian Greek colony some two hundred years after Rome's legendary date, it was a free but allied city, a *civitate foederata*, with territory independent of Narbonensis jurisdiction. Its citizens were tri-lingual, speaking Greek, Latin, and Celtic—although the Hellenic tongue was more likely to be heard in streets than either of the other languages. City magistrates dealt directly with other nations, coined money, and generally ran their affairs without Roman interference. Massiliotes had their own courts and paid no taxes to outsiders; a sole obligation was to provide such military levies as their treaty might stipulate.

Beyond Aurasio, in southern *Provincia*, the Rhodanus delta stretched into a marshy wetland some twenty miles long. None of the four women on the barge had yet seen such an expanse of sea, nor, for that matter, any land as level as tidal flats the barge entered. Dirona, particularly, was fearful of the terrain, a direct contrast to the familiar mountain-enclosed valleys of her Jura. When the flat horizon of the Inner Sea came into view, Briga's sister screamed and turned away—she had reached the perilous edge of a world she had only known. Dirona went to her deck-tent and refused to come outside.

A twenty-five mile run of open sea remained to reach Massilia. The crew raised an auxiliary sail and rowers increased their oar stokes, but a choppy sea made the voyage difficult. More seasick than the others, Dirona lay on a cot, pale and retching, convinced that her life would end on this heaving expanse of alien water where no Celtic gods existed to whom she could petition for help.

Simonides asked to be brought outside. When he sighted the stepped lighthouse at Massilia, he rallied enough to stand and clutch the railing. Eyes misted over, he watched the terra cotta roofs of houses, temples, and public buildings grow larger above the seawall. "There was a time in Gallia I never thought I would see home again," he told me, holding my arm for support. "*Efharisto.* Thanks, Alberix, for saving me at Alesia."

"You'll recover more quickly at your home."

"A little sea air and I'll be fine for the rest of the journey."

"What journey? You're not coming to Roma with us."

He laughed at my absurd reaction. "Friend, you think I would miss a chance to see *Roma Aeterna?* Twelve Titans couldn't keep me away!"

Lucius came to identify galleys moored in the harbor and along the docks. "I'd wager that some of those vessels are going on to Ostia."

"My father will be able to tell you that."

"That's my hope, Simonides. I admit to being nervous with my hostages outside Roman jurisdiction."

I thought it unrealistic to consider an attempt to free them. "Lucius, no one knows they're with us."

"Alberix, I wouldn't count on that. Rumors move swiftly as the west wind."

Our helmsman steered for a docking basin alongside the massive towers of the port's land gate. On shore rows of stalls crowded against the city walls. Slaves unloaded merchandise, while traders haggled over exchanges.

After we moored at the wharf, Dirona rested a while to recover. Simonides insisted that he was well enough to walk the distance to his father's villa. Lucius stayed on board, scheduling a guard contingent for the period they would be in port.

At the entrance of the Greek youth's villa, his mother, Ismene, uttered a cry of despair when she recognized the emaciated, bearded face of her son.

Even his strong-willed sister, Thuccydia, broke into tears. "*Adhelfos...* Brother...what did they do to you in Gallia? Your letters never mentioned an illness."

"I'll be fine," he assured her. "With mother's mullet stew and father's Corinthian wine—"

Ismene insisted, "You're going to the Asklepion tomorrow, but as soon as Cleomenes can be found, I'm bringing the physician here to treat you."

"If that will please you, *Mitera*..." He turned to introduce us. "These are friends. I've written to you about Alberix. Briga is his mother and Dirona her sister."

She nodded recognition without smiling at me, the barbarian *Kelt* who had dragged her son all over Gallia. After he introduced Apsa as my wife, Ersa took Ger to play in a walled garden.

Ismene ordered the cook to reheat a pot of barley pottage, then led us into a dining area. "My husband isn't here. Nikomaxos went to Avennio to supervise his grape harvest. Wait a few days to meet him."

"*Mitera*"–Simonides braced himself for a protest–"I...I'm going on to Roma."

Her response was cold as a *Borealis* wind. "Why is that and when?"

I told her, "Lucius wants to board the next gallery leaving for Ostia."

Simonides explained, "Lucius is a centurion in charge of prisoners–"

"Prisoners?"

"Vercingetorix and several Gallic chieftains are being sent to Roma."

"I forbid you to go!" Ismene exclaimed, then turned to her daughter. "Thuccydia talk sense into your feeble-minded brother."

"*Mitera*," Simonides replied before she did. "I am not going to pass up this chance."

Thuccydia avoided her mother's glare. "I...I would like to see Roma myself,"

"Then take my place," Dirona offered. "I will never sail anywhere again! I'll leave this flat land and travel upriver to where mountains begin."

"Sister, what *will* you really do?" Briga asked.

When Dirona shrugged defiance rather than answer, Simonides proposed, "Stay here with my family. It would repay my debt to your nephew and–"

"Dirona was a chieftain's wife," Briga interrupted.

"Sister, know that all of Epona's horses couldn't drag me onto another galley!"

A servant brought barley soup that ended the argument. Everyone ate in silence, pondering uncertain futures. As the meal ended, Cleomenes arrived and went with Simonides to a bedroom.

After his examination, the physician shook his head. "Much too dry. Gallia has put your humors out of balance. You need sea moisture to bring balance again."

Simonides argued, "Physician, it rained incessantly in the north."

"Nevertheless, I am prescribing barley water and grape extract. No wine, mind you! Excess heat must be flushed from your body."

"No bleeding me?"

"Not when you need fluids." Cleomenes thought a moment. "You say you were in *Gallia Comata?*"

"Yes."

"Allow me to feel your abdomen. Is this area tender?"

"A little."

Cleomenes straightened. "Young man, you risk *Febris Gallicorum*. Stay on my water and juice regimen. Do not get out of that bed until I see you again in two days."

"*Efharisto*. I...I do think I will sleep now."

Cleomenes instructed Isomene about her son's fluid intake. Afterward, she assigned rooms to her guests. Briga told her that Lucius probably would arrive for the evening meal about an hour before sunset.

Apsa and I played with Ger awhile, then everyone rested until the meal.

❧❧

The villa of Nikomaxos was Greek in style, rather than Roman. A cobbled entrance courtyard was where an atrium and pool would have been located. The second floor veranda overlooked this open-air space. Rooms were paved with a pebble-mosaic pattern and the *triclinium*, where meals were eaten, displayed black and white mosaic scenes of *Mare Internum* sea creatures.

Ismene planned a meal of sea mullet, leeks cooked in oil and vinegar, a local soft goat cheese, olives and wheat bread with honey. In order not to alarm his mother, Simonides forced himself to come in and eat, yet went back to his room immediately afterward.

❧❧

During early afternoon, a servant had come to Lucius with the supper invitation. He went to the docks and found several galleys that would take advantage of a light tide and leave in the morning. Using Julius Caesar's authorization, Lucius secured passage for his hostages by dividing them up among two of the vessels. He and his group would accompany Vercingetorix's contingent.

❧❧

After supper, Lucius told of his plans for leaving in the morning. Dirona again refused to go. When Ismene gave her son his barley water, Simonides was told. He came to convince Dirona that she had learned enough about trading from Liscos to be of use to his father in dealing with Celtic tribes.

Thuccydia had taken over her brother's accounting work and promised to help the woman in exchange for lessons in the Celtic language.

⚮

Shortly after sunrise, the prow of a twenty-six oar cargo galley, *Tridens Neptuni,* cut across swells rolling from the sea into Massilia's bay. A fortunate northwest breeze billowed the mainsail to ease our crossing toward Alsium— not Ostia— on the north Italia coast.

I leaned on a rail, listening to monotonous hammer cadences that timed oar strokes and thought of my aunt. *Dirona was first to predict that gods would guide my destiny, but now I don't much believe in any gods. I'm sailing off in hopes of fulfilling my father's dream with the help of an alien people who conquered Celtic lands. "'Fate leads the willing, but drives the stubborn'."*

"Alberix, did you say something?"Apsa asked. I hadn't noticed her come up to me.

"Nothing, really." I shielded my wife in my cloak against a freshening wind. "I only wondered how the Fates happened to put us on board a galley bound for Roma!"

October 52 B.C.E. — August 44 B.C.E.

Man is born and then is laid low: like ashes, the wind blows away
Alexander the Great and Caesar and all who were in their trust.
Grass-grown is Troy. Witness Gergovia, how it is. Alesia also.
and the Romani themselves; perhaps they, too, will pass!

CHAPTER XII

"The Temple of Jupiter Capitolinus!"

Lucius shouted the name after he glimpsed the gilded bronze of the temple's pediment as a bright flash through a saffron haze that veiled part of Roma. On a hill about two miles distant, the god's dwelling pushed above squat roofs and colonnaded porticos that clustered together in a film of afternoon cook-fire smoke.

"Jupiter Capitolinus!" Lucius repeated, as if he disbelieved his eyes, and turned his horse back to the carriage where Briga and Apsa had watched for the city to appear.

Briga felt excited at being close to a center of the Romani world. "You did see that temple?"

"Yes, up ahead, and a good view from this Janiculum hill. I'll halt the guard column here a moment."

Mounted legionary guards trotted their horses past to gawk at a city most had never visited. A few men had been in the Gallic campaigns since the Helvetii rout. Adherbal's men had joined them, but had no concept of the city's vastness.

Briga stepped from the carriage to tease, "Where are those seven hills Dividiac spoke about?"

Lucius poked a finger toward the distance. "There...the Palatinus... Quirinalis. That's...the Viminalis, I think. Hades, I can't recall all their names!"

Briga ran to catch Ger, who had started down the hill. She held him up to see a distant scene known only from her druid uncle's visions—Dividiac never had visited the city. She had imagined a row of verdant knolls, each crowned by a golden temple.

I dismounted and joined the group. "*Roma Aeterna*, Lucius? I expected to see a scene from our Land of the Eternally Young."

"The city *is* enormous!" Apsa exclaimed. "How many Alesia's could fit inside those walls? Lucius, how are all those people kept occupied?"

"Much as villagers were at Wermaros, except there are more here doing the work. Roma has entire streets of leather workers or potters. There's even a district just for booksellers."

Briga shaded her eyes to look toward a lowering sun. "And inns? Lucius, where will we stay tonight?"

"Truthfully, I was too excited to think about that. There's a legion camp on the *Campus Martius*, where I'll take Vercingetorix."

Briga started to protest. "After my horrible week on that filthy gallery and where we stayed overnight in those two ports—"

"Pisae and Cosa. I did expect better accommodations."

"Lucius, I'll *not* sleep in a legion tent! Don't you have guest lodges here?"

"There *are* public inns...*cauponae*...and I have letters of credit against Caesar's advances to the Treasury."

"Gallic plunder," Briga muttered in a bitter aside.

Half in anger, Lucius retorted, "That's how war is! Vercingetorix and those other clan chiefs would have looted Italia in the same way."

"And those who are not warriors pay the price."

"Caesar has been lenient, Briga. He sent back thousands of Aedui and Arverni who would have been sold on the slave market. Only Convivtovitalis was executed."

"Will those chieftains die here to entertain in the games you've told us about?"

"Vercingetorix and the others will remain as hostages until Gallia everywhere is at peace. Hades, Woman! Commios escaped at Alesia. The Cadurci of Lucterios still can raid the Narbonensis—"

Lucius strode off a few paces away to let his irritation subside. Briga came to him a moment later. "I'm sorry if I upset you, but my people are Celts. I know you're worried about the hostages. Is that why we disembarked in that town before Ostia?"

"Alsium. I feared that word about Vercingetorix had gone ahead and wanted to avoid an incident. Thousands of Roman families lost sons in a war the Galli prolonged..." He hugged her shoulder. "Briga, we should enter the city before dark."

Lucius had ordered his Numidians back to the wagons, when a horseman rode in from the direction of the city. A military Tribune reined in his mount to call out, "*Centurio*, you are in charge of a Gallic prisoner detachment?"

"I am. *Primopilus* Lucius Velcanius."

The officer waved a rolled papyrus at him. "I'm Tribune Faustus Luculus, charged with relieving you of your command and taking over the Gallic prisoners. My men wait just beyond the ridge."

Surprised, Lucius demanded, "By whose authority? My orders from Julius Caesar are to conduct these hostages to the Curia and present them to senators."

Luculus again held up his scroll. "I'll take care of it, *Centurio*. My authority is from consul Metellus Scipio."

"Scipio? I thought Gnaeus Pompeius was sole *consul*."

The Tribune laughed. "You've been away among the *brachatae* too long! Pompeius shares the *imperium* with his father-in-law."

Lucius felt uneasy at this unexpected development. "How did you know we took the Via Aurelia at Alsium, rather than landing at Ostia?"

He answered with a demand, "Show me these Gallic chiefs and the barbarian king."

"Trouble here, Loo-chus?" Adherbal's loud question as he approached startled Luculus.

"This Tribune says he has authority to take the hostages from us."

"No!" the Numidian protested. "We take to sen-tus."

Luculus recovered and spat aside. "*Centurio*, you dress your slave well. Why have you not taught him humility?" He glanced at Briga and Apsa, now standing near their wagon. "Those camp followers. What kind of discipline did the 'Adulterer' keep in Gallia?"

Lucius flushed. "Adherbal is a Numidian prince, an ally. He and his men are here to train as Caesar's guard. The women are friends under my protection."

As you say, *Centurio*." Luculus looked back along the line of wagons. "Now, where are these *brachatae* prisoners?"

I had watched the confrontation. Lucius motioned for me to escort the Tribune to wagons in the center of the guard column, then stalked back to his own. Adherbal followed him.

"Who was that?" Apsa wondered. "We couldn't hear everything from here."

"Scipio has authorized that fool to take over the hostages."

"Ski-pio?"

"Evidently a new co-consul, yet Pompeius is behind that order. Caesar was right not to trust the man."

Adherbal's hand went to his sword hilt. "We fight this Pom-pays?"

Lucius laughed at his naïve enthusiasm. "Stand down, you dark Hercules! That wasn't Pompeius, just one of his sandal-lacers. Besides, Caesar sent you here to learn about Roma, not to destroy it."

Briga observed, "I gathered that the officer didn't think much of Caesar?"

"One of his concerns is that Pompeius has had years to turn senators against him. An informer at Alsium must have reported our arrival there."

"*Centurio!*" Luculus shouted back. "Counter to regulations, these prisoner's hands aren't fully shackled."

"They're hostages, not the same status as prisoners. Their legs are in ankle irons."

"Well, they're my responsibility now." The Tribune rode back and handed Lucius the papyrus. "Here's Scipio's receipt for the lot."

"My orders are to quarter the Galli in the *Martius* legionary camp."

Luculus snorted, "They will go to the *Tullianum*."

"That notorious prison? Caesar gave no such order and the Senatus is to decide their place of confinement until the Imperator's Triumph."

Luculus spat out, "If Pompeius had listened he would *be* the Senatus. Instead the fool humored Cato and turned down a dictatorship I proposed!" He swung his horse around and shouted for his men to separate the Galli from other wagons in the column.

"Dictatorship?" Lucius watched two wagons carrying hostages move out. "Pompeius's ambitions were leavened with poor advice."

The troubling confrontation alarmed Briga. "What will happen now?"

Lucius did not answer—the lead hostage wagon had drawn alongside and he signaled for the driver to rein in his mules. The Arvernian king and his cousin were seated on the floor, back to back. Iron rings clasped their ankles. "Vercingetorix, another officer now is now in charge of you and other hostages. You must obey his orders."

Looking out of the wagon, he surveyed the city panorama. "So, *Centurio*, we arrive at the navel of your world. Your eagle has conquered the raven."

"Arvernian, I wish you just treatment."

The defeated king emphasized his captivity by rattling the ankle chains. "Caesar's goddess has triumphed. Caturix was impotent."

"You did for your people what any citizen would have done for Roma. The Senatus will consider that."

"Do you believe so?" Vercingetorix scoffed. "The Wheel of my destiny has led to Roma, as did that of Brennos long ago. You still commemorate how he humbled your city. Surely, a race that celebrates its defeats hardly will notice the death of another 'barbarian'."

"You are treaty hostages, not condemned criminals."

Vercingetorix ignored the distinction. "The Wheel of Destiny does not stop its turning. Now Gallia lies beneath its rim yet I predict that your Caesar also will be crushed, perhaps in a month dedicated to your war god. Is he not called Martius?"

"Yes, and his month has that name."

"Our druids preach that all things return to a balance. Recall, *Centurio*, how Raven is final victor on a battlefield."

Tribune Luculus reined up to see what delayed the wagons. "By Minos, move those prisoners on!"

The driver clucked his mules into motion. Legionaries in the guard detachment watched their departure, then looked toward Lucius for instructions. As he walked toward them, they instinctively straightened up.

"At rest," he ordered quietly. "Men, you have carried out your final duty to the Republic. The hostages now are the responsibility of that Tribune and our Senatus."

Despite being freed of their service, the guards murmured among themselves and awaited new orders. Lucius sensed their disorientation and walked among them, stopping to touch scars.

"Gergovia?" he asked a legionary whose forearm wound was a jagged red welt.

"*Vero*...yes, *centurio*."

"Unit?"

"Legio Thirteen."

Lucius stepped back to raise his voice. "Legionaries. Citizens. Most of you have such wounds, which should remind your senators how much gratitude you are owed. Yet your minds hold terrible memories no senator can see. Images of blood...comrades butchered alongside you. Troubled sleep that left you shaking until you awakened and realized the terror was a nightmare." When he paused, the only sound was a distant rumble of departing wagons and the rustle of the men's cloaks in a late afternoon breeze. "No pension, no grant of land can adequately reward you for those years of service to Roma. You are free now. Free of night watches in sleet or heat. Free of latrine digging. Wet food, wormy food, or no food—even of legionary biscuit!" The men chuckled at a reference to rations edible only when broken into hot water or stew. "Caesar's supporters will propose land grants for veterans. You will get help from tribunes who represent the plebs and can veto legislation that might cheat you of your rights. Now. Dress ranks!" Lucius concealed a smile as the men fumbled to attain a formation. "I have two final orders. First. Report to the *praefect* at the *Campus Martius* for your discharge plaques. Second. Go find your wives, girlfriends, or...or any woman you can, and get drunk as Bacchus tonight! Dismissed!"

Laughter, then applause, filled the ranks before the men dispersed. Watching them, Lucius felt a tug of emptiness.

Briga came to hold his arm. "I could not understand everything you said, but your words, your voice, gave them courage to bear an uncertainty they feel. They respect *you* Lucius."

"They...they're good men."

"Lucius, you're blushing! You are a good man, so that is why I came with you. But I don't look forward to sleeping in a legion camp tonight."

"Nor do I, so let's go back to our wagon. I'll inquire around about a nearby inn."

When Briga asked Apsa about Simonides, she was worried. "He sleeps now yet his fever and rash worsen. He passes blood."

The poor report alarmed Lucius. "We must find a physician to treat the man."

Wait..." Briga recalled. "Didn't Caesar give Simonides the name of a person where we were to stay?"

Lucius smacked a fist to his palm. "Jupiter, I'd forgotten! Also Greek, wasn't he? Alberix, where would Simonides keep the name?"

"With his notes, I imagine."

"Apsa, try to awaken him. There's no use attempting to find an inn if we can locate our host."

A few moments later Apsa looked out of the wagon and shook her head. "His mind is back at Alesia. He only mumbles. Perhaps Simonides told our muleteer?"

"Of course. I'll ask Turpio."

After Lucius spoke to a man who hauled goods between Alsium and Rome, he exaggerated a thoughtful pose. "A friend of Julius Caesar who is *Graecus*? *Centurio*, there's many *Graeci* at Roma."

"True. Alberix, do you remember anything else?"

I told him I thought Simonides said that the man's father was an historian and wanted to meet him. Turpio heard me, nodded, and yet still hesitated.

Lucius tossed him a silver *quinarius*. "A dose of *sesterces* has been known to cure an ailing memory."

Turpio tapped his forehead with the coin. "Ah, the son of Theopompus! Then it's Artemidorus you look for. *Magister*...Teacher...at an academy in the city."

Lucius held up another *quinarius*. "Yours if you take us to his house before sunset."

Turpio beamed, "Plutus smiles on me! As the god would have it, the villa of Artemidorus is little more than a mile from here. Good view of the city and a—"

"Take us there quickly," I told him. "My friend is very ill."

Turpio slipped the coins into his belt purse. "I haul a lot of sick ones come from Gallia. Take 'em right to the temple of Aesclepius on Tiberina island."

Lucius helped Briga back into her wagon. I remounted my horse as Turpio clucked his mules into motion and turned back to Via Transtiberim.

The villa was a half-hundred paces back from a dusty side road lined with poplars and umbrella pines. Farther on, a planting of cypresses marked where the track dipped into a gradual slope, then rose into the forested side of the Janiculum. Below, brick kilns lined a broad bend in the Tiber. Wharves held reddish terra cotta tiles waiting to be ferried downriver to station points along the river.

A grove of gnarled olive trees screened an approach to the villa. A man wearing a straw hat held a small basket as he plucked the fruit.

"There's a garden slave," Lucius noted and hailed him. "*Servus*, is your master here?"

"Master?" The olive picker repeated the word as a question and came to the wagon. "That depends on my weakness. A dish of these olives with goat cheese, fresh bread, and a cup of Falernian have *my* allegiance!" Before Lucius could reprimand his insolence, the man smiled. "*Centurio*, your conclusion was wrong because your grasp of logic is weaker than your understanding of war. 'Slaves pick olives,' you thought. 'That fellow is picking olives.' '*Ergo* he is a slave.' Correct reasoning, L. Velcanius, might lead you to conclude that others could pick olives."

Man, early thirties, intelligent, smooth shaven, strands of white in dark hair... swarthy from the sun, not afraid of manual labor. "You're Artemidorus and you know my name."

He chuckled on being recognized. "True, Lucius Velcanius, First Centurion of Legio Ten. You bring with you several *Keltoi* and a Massiliote."

Still flushed from embarrassment, Lucius introduced me, Briga and Apsa, then said, "Simonides is very ill. He needs a physician."

"The Massiliote has a fever?"

"Since just after the *Eidus*."

"What other symptoms?"

Apsa replied, "Red patches on his skin...hoarse voice."

Her description alarmed the *Magister*. "Blood in his feces?

"A little, yet he hardly eats."

"A diagnosis like a form of the plague. We must isolate him, yet I have medications that may help."

I felt relieved. "Can your slaves move Simonides inside?"

"Slaves?" Artemidorus chortled at the term. "There are no slaves here, Alberix, only men and women who wish to learn. My students realize that it is possible to fill an amphora of the mind with learning. Bring your wagon to the entrance."

As in households at this supper hour, cooking odors permeated the villa. When I followed the others down a short hallway, I noticed a garden on the right. Two young men carried Simonides to a room facing the greenery. Nearby doors closed off similar rooms. We entered an atrium—the open air court that Cita was building for his wife at Cenabum. Artemidorus invited us to sit on stone benches near the central pool. On one side the marble statue of a nude woman held up a fallen tunic, with one foot poised as if she were about to step into the water. On the wall opposite was a series of paintings that depicted maps.

"My 'slaves of learning' will make your friend comfortable, then another student, a *medica*, will examine him."

"*Medica?*" Lucius questioned in surprise. "That would be a woman physician."

"Precisely, Velcanius..." Artemidorus glanced up at the evening sky. "It's still quite pleasant outdoors. I don't much care for indoor living, although my logic has yet to justify my remaining at Roma during the cold season."

Curious, I asked, "What is that wall map?"

"What our *terra firma* looks like. Didymos, a freedman, comes in to work on the charts in exchange for wine and conversation."

Lucius jested, "Alberix is newly married, but I'm interested in that statue of a lady."

Artemidorus laughed when Briga reproached him with a scowl. "*Domina*, that is an Aphrodite by Praxitiles, a copy of excellent workmanship. The goddess reminds me that we aren't always ruled by logic and..." He stopped his explanation when a young woman came from the sickroom. "Here is Vestia. These are friends of the unfortunate Massiliote. *Medica*, may we hear your diagnosis?"

Her reply was terse. "*Magister*, he suffers from Gallic Fever."

"I was correct, then. How will you treat him?"

"A brief sweat in the *caldarium*, then administer *ephreda* and *dichros*. A diffusion of *capsella* will alleviate fever. *Urinaria* to help pass out the plague."

"Excellent! Keep the room darkened, yet allow in fresh air."

As Vestia turned to leave, Apsa asked her, "May I help? I know of medicinal herbs and can tell you what I have used."

Briga joined in. "I also can be of help."

After Vestia looked to Artemidorus for permission, he nodded assent.

"Amazing," Lucius remarked after they left. "*Magister*, I've not seen a woman physician before."

"Vestia is not her given name. Velcanius, everyone who studies here takes on the *nomen* of a patron god or goddess. I find that if students submerge their old identities they learn more rapidly."

Lucius was curious about their arrival at the outskirts of Rome. "How did you know we were coming? What is your connection with Julius Caesar?"

"My father is a long-time friend of the commander's. Caesar sent him a few of his writings on the Gallic war and asked for advice about using a more polished style. Father likes the writing the way it is...terse, stark, and highly detailed."

"On the Aurelia we encountered one of Pompeius's arrogant tribunes. Has the atmosphere turned against Caesar?"

"Perhaps a fable of Aesopos will help answer that question. 'As a lion and a boar at a pool began to quarrel to the death over who would drink first, they stopped upon realizing that vultures waited nearby to devour the loser.' Velcanius, the commander and the consul have an uneasy alliance, thus vultures in our Senatus eagerly await an outcome."

Elpince, the *Magister*'s wife, came in to meet her guests. Dark haired, a woman of about his age wore a simple belted tunic of blue, tied at the shoulders. A thin gold chain around her neck displayed a palmetto-themed pendant. Matching earrings were the same design. Her greeting wasted no words on pleasantries.

"*Centurio*, the *Magister* tells me that you came from Gallia, therefore your report of the war should be authentic. Our forum is filled with fools and opportunists."

"How so, *Domina?*"

"We hear on one side that Caesar will bring every legionary a Gallic slave of his own at no expense. On the other that the price of slaves will rise, because the Imperator will free *Keltoi* to be members of our Senatus." Elpince turned to me. "You are *Kelt*, young man. What is your opinion?"

I recalled Caesar's offer to make me part of new governing councils. "I believe Caesar will appoint loyal *vergobrets* to administer areas. Not 'opportunists' from Roma."

She smiled at either my reply or my innocence. "Indeed, the Roman way is to utilize local men in our conquered provinces. Yet the cost of building new temples to foreign gods that do not have a twin in our pantheon will be enormous—"

"My dear," Artemidoros broke in, "our guests must be quite exhausted. They should wash before we dine, and retire early."

"I'm aware of that, *Magister*. I ordered Cook to prepare a simple meal of fish, leeks, cheese, and olives." Elpince half-bowed to him. "With your Falernian, of course."

Lucius asked, "Artemidorus, may we accompany you into the city tomorrow?"

"Of course. You'll want to visit my *Akademia*."

As Elpince had promised, the meal was simple. We were grateful to be in our beds shortly after dark.

CHAPTER XIII

In the morning while we walked toward the Via Aurelia, Lucius recalled that the view eastward from the Janiculum was the most panoramic one of the city. The Alban Hills, rising out of the Latium plain, were visible from ten miles distant.

Across the Tiber, meandering walls built by Romulus and Servius Tullius embraced the Seven Hills and could be followed in almost their entirety.

As Artemidoros led, I went with Apsa, both of us gawking at a mass of distant buildings and streets we scarcely could believe. Lucius walked behind us with Briga, pointing out important sites he remembered.

When we reached the junction of the Transtiberim and Aurelia, our host stopped to orient us. "We'll take the Aemilius Bridge and pass around the Forum Boarium. There are sites that might interest *Keltoi*."

Lucius asked, "Isn't that the Temple of Fortuna near the bridge?"

"Indeed, and the round temple you Romans admired so much when you saw that style in Hellas."

Apsa wondered, "What are those building on the hill straight ahead?"

"The Palatinus? Villas of the very wealthy. Also a few senators live there. Cicero has two homes. Below the walls are ancient places most sacred to Romans. Shall we enter the city?"

Starting down the Aurelius toward the river, the group was jostled by vegetable carts driven by shopkeepers to the Holitorium markets. On the Aemilian Bridge, Artemidorus led the way around cattle being coaxed toward the slaughterhouse. He turned right at a wide, paved road lined with wharves where animals were unloaded from barges. A strong stench of manure and the lowing of penned beasts mingling with loud calls of auctioneers, marked the closeness of a cattle market.

The *Magister* turned up the Via Tuscus, an avenue that led to a central forum and marked the eastern boundary of the Boarium markets. At the Junction he pointed to a grove of trees near the base of the Palatinus hill. "That fig tree marks the site where Romulus and his brother, Remus, drifted ashore to be suckled by a she-wolf. Perhaps *Keltoi* do not know the story?"

I said, "It's one of the first that Lucius told me."

"Indeed it is twitted by some that Romans behave like wolves because their ancestors were nourished on lupine milk." When Lucius clenched a fist, Artemidorus calmed him, "Of course, the premise cannot be supported by syllogism. Now, above those stairs is the hut where Faustulus *allegedly* raised the twins after rescuing them."

Briga had been quiet, remembering a temple at the *nemeton* of Sequana, the oldest she had seen. "How long ago was this?"

Artemidoros looked toward Lucius. "Tell us, *Centurio*."

Annoyed at being goaded, he counted, "This is the four-hundred and fifty-fifth year of the Republic. About seven hundred years, Briga."

"And the hut is still there?"

"*Domina*, you have a right to be skeptical." Artemidorus continued along the Tuscus to describe walls around the Palatinus said to have been constructed by Romulus himself.

I wondered how many of these legends were accepted as true, even by Lucius. A centurion with his experience could not be as devout, or gullible, as a peasant—or even a visiting Celt!

As the cattle market became further away, savory smells wafted from food shops along the street. Lucius swept a hand toward a broad area that reached to the base of the Capitolinus. "This all was swampland once. We built a sewer to drain it...about here. Correct, *Magister?*"

"Indeed, *Centurio*, yet it was Etruscans that drained the *Velabrum*."

Lucius did not challenge his mild rebuke, but it was not until several temples at the principal forum appeared that he was excited again. "Briga... Apsa, there it is! The center of Roma!"

Briga puckered her forehead in disbelief. "You rule your world from this... this former swamp?"

Lucius ignored her remark. I had noticed that Artemidorus belittled most of the locations as his way of softening the sting of being a Greek in a conqueror's land.

To the left of the first temple was an area where foundation stones were being laid for a row of arches. Lucius kicked at the rubble. "Where's the Sempronia? It *was* next to the temple of Castor and Pollux."

I recalled the names of watchtowers at Wermaros as Artemidorus replied, "Velcanius, it was razed for a new basilica."

"Paid for by?"

"Julius Caesar. The Basilica Julia will commemorate your commander's unfortunate daughter."

"Her husband, Pompeius, is not a contributor?"

"Indirectly. Julia died in childbirth and he impregnated her." Before Lucius could protest the insult, Artemidorus deftly added, "Caesar may not intentionally prick Pompeius, yet this building will be a constant irritation."

He pointed across the way. "*Centurio*, nor are the Curia and Porcia any longer standing. Those ruins across the Via Sacra were a result of Clodius's mob."

Lucius muttered, "I've been away far too long."

Apsa changed subjects. "Sir, do you hold classes here?"

"My *Akademia*, being much more modest, is not among those in the Forum. You will find it up on the slope of the Oppius and away from city distractions. *Domina*, Lucius later can show you other sights. Walk with me now to the Arch of Fabianus."

Lucius bristled at his suggestion. "Why must you take her there?"

"*Centurio*, should we conceal history from those who might be displeased by events? Indeed, the arch commemorates a Roman victory over Arvernian and Allobroge tribes."

I thought of my friend. "Simonides should be here to see this!"

Lucius said, "He would know that Massilia called upon Roma for help when those two tribes raided his city. Allobrox and Arverni warriors opposed our legions under Ahenobarbus and Fabianus. Because Aedui supported us, the invading tribes were beaten back near the Isara and Rhodanus Rivers."

Artemidorus correctly charged, "Senators used the victory to annex the Narbonensis. Your *Provincia*."

At the arch, Lucius examined sculptures with Briga and Apsa: images of legionaries holding up Gallic trophies—ovoid shields, bundles of spears, and clusters of war trumpets—decorated panels on either side of the archway. Winged victory figures filled the arch spandrels. An inscription, "Q F ALLOBROGICVS CON, ran along the lintel.

I looked at the carved figures in silence. Our people celebrated a victory with feasting, and no memorial had been built except to our divinities.

Briga wondered, "This Fabianus was made one of your gods?"

"No, no..." Lucius suppressed a nervous chuckle. "He was consul and hardly divine."

Artemidorus interjected, "Your Caesar claims descent from a goddess, *Ergo*, a.basilica may be dedicated to 'The Divine Julius,' He is said to spring from Venus. Any half-witted Sophist could lay a foundation for doing so."

"Let's move on," Lucius said to avoid another conflict with his host.

I began to see how mocking Romani was common among Greeks, who considered themselves culturally above their conquerors in refinement and taste.

The Sacred Way became crowded with men wearing the white togas that Romani put on. Senators surrounded by a retinue of clients or citizens hurried to hear advocates argue cases in the Basilica Aemilia. Slaves in rough homespun tunics ran errands for their masters or accompanied women as they shopped for the day's needs. A short distance to the east where shops were located, craft and tradesmen opened their booths. Hawkers circulated among the crowd, calling out items to buy at a bargain.

Lucius still felt irritated at Artemidorus's patronizing. "*Magister*, where do senators meet now that the Curia is destroyed?"

"One would think in the temple of Hope. Concordia would do as well yet they chose that of Saturnus, the devourer of his own children." He chuckled at the irony. "It seems your senators have developed a sense of our dramatic Greek tragedy."

Lucius taunted, "Roma swallowed your homeland, but not the Kronos you gave us."

The remark stung Artemidoros, but he was equal to the jibe. "*Gave*, Centurio? "You stole our temples and presented us with legion camps in exchange."

Passersby stopped to stare at our Gallic clothing and anticipated an argument between the *Magister* many recognized, and a centurion they did not.

Artemidorus stifled his emotions. "Velcanius, if the workings of the gods are capricious, those of men need not be. Let us be at peace with the universal Logos." He pointed toward the covered passageway of a marketplace. "There are Stoics at that portico who teach acceptance of one's fate."

"I'm familiar with their philosophy."

"Ah, then, I must get to my *Akademia*. I trust you shall find your way back to my villa for our evening meal?"

"We came all the way from Gallia and found it..." Lucius grasped his sleeve. "I jest, *Magister*. *Gratias* for all you've done."

"Just so..." Artemidorus bowed to the women. "I wish you a pleasant day."

The man disappeared into the crowd.

Tullius Tilius, standing nearby, had been with Lucius at Wermaros and recognized him. Elbowing bystanders, he called, "By the gods, *Centurio* Velcanius, isn't it?"

Lucius turned. "Who...?"

"*Quaestor* Tilius, a senator now. We built watchtowers at that miserable Sequani village."

"I recall." Lucius pointed toward us. "You'll remember Alberix, nephew of Cluvios. This is his wife Apsa, and his mother, the chieftain's sister-in-kin."

"Ah, yes, old Liscos. Killed attacking *Castor* I'm told, and a well-deserved fate." Tilius wondered why the Celts were here and decided not to mention that Epanactos and two companions stayed at his villa. "In any case, all of

Roma is jubilant at the news from Gallia. Caesar's triumph should out-stage any ever presented to the populace. Lucius, what brings you to the Eternal City?"

"We're here on Caesar's orders. I brought Vercingetorix and Gallic chieftains to present to Senators, then one of Pompeius's tribunes took charge of them."

Tilius linked arms with him and walked a short distance away. "It's said that envy and lust are immortal. Despite Caesar's victories, or rather, because of them, Pompeius's heart devours itself in envy. Clodius's gang did not help calm matters. As you know, Lucius, I'm Caesar's man, yet now the real power is with the two consuls."

"The Senatus was to decide Vercingetorix's place of confinement, but he's in the Tullianum prison. I'm going there now to make sure the Arvernian is safe."

"He may be better there than in a villa. Because of this Gallic war, many widows and sonless fathers are bent on revenge."

"The Galli are hostages, not war prisoners. Where is the law?"

"Law? *Centurio*, sift through the Curia ashes for an answer." Tilius beckoned to clients waiting nearby. "I must get to Saturnus's temple, but I'll contact you through Gaius Trebonius. You recall that he commanded the supply *auxiliae*." He paused before saying, "I hear you're staying with Artemidorus?"

"Yes. Senator, we'll need your support for veterans' land grants."

"Work through Trebonius. As a Tribune, he can veto any opposition. *Valete*, then."

"*Valete*." As Lucius led the way toward the prison he reflected, *Tilius pretended not to know why we were here, yet knew we stay with Artemidorus.*

Under arches of the Basilica Aemilia, stall-keepers from barbers to moneychangers had set up tables in the shadowed recesses. Beyond, at a rectangle of charred timbers, slaves listlessly stacked reusable bricks from the Curia ruins, or raked ashes to haul off in two-wheeled carts. The doors of the Temple of Janus were open to indicate that the Roman State was at war somewhere in the world. Lucius did not explain the custom to his friends—the doors rarely closed.

The unadorned hulk of the Tullianum brooded in sharp contrast to the graceful columns of Concordia's temple next to it. Both buildings occupied a triangle where streets angled steeply up the eastern flank of the Capitolinus.

A crowd in front of the prison, jabbering about the Gallic captives and hoping to catch a glimpse of them, made Lucius uneasy. Grasping Briga's hand, he motioned for Apsa and me to follow. At the Tullianum eight legionaries commanded by a centurion were on guard duty.

Lucius identified himself. "L. Velcanius, First Centurion, Legio Ten. I brought the hostages to Roma and wish to speak with Vercingetorix."

"I was told to expect y'," the officer replied, "and y' won't talk to turtle shit! The *brachatae* are isolated. Only Pompeius gets to see 'em."

Lucius held in anger. "Those chieftains are senatorial hostages. Tribune Luculus acted illegally in bringing them here."

"Then get the 'Chickpea' t' plead their case." The centurion winked at his men as they laughed at Cicero's nickname.

Briga realized that Lucius was not accustomed to sarcastic refusals and said, "This crowd frightens me. May we leave and wait for Tilius to help you?"

Lucius ignored her to threaten the centurion. "I'll see your skin on a *furca!*"

When his guards unsheathed swords the onlookers hooted for a confrontation between the two legionaries.

Briga pulled Lucius away. "You didn't come to fight. Show us more of the city."

"This situation isn't what I expected..." He squeezed Briga's hand. "You always handle my anger better than I."

To distract him, I asked, "What is up those stairs?"

"They lead to the Capitolinus summit and a good view of the city." Lucius looked back. The centurion had ordered his men to warn the crowd away from the entrance at sword point. "Let's climb up, then go back to the villa."

♣♣

Since Epanactos, the bodyguard of Liscos at Wermaros, had taken the dead chieftain's place, he was invited to Roma as a Gaul presumably loyal to the Republic. Tullius Tilius slightly knew the Arvernian, but was unaware of his part in the rebellion. The new senator agreed to house him and two companions, Trigvoros and Dunamos.

The three Arvernians quickly became an embarrassment. Tilius had supposed that introducing Epanactos to senators would strengthen support for Julius Caesar, yet he had pleased only those who favored Pompeius. A translator hesitated at voicing the Celt's harangues, which exposed alleged legion atrocities, and at Caesar himself to discredit the commander and force his recall.

After Caesar's incredible victory at Alesia, and the Senate's declaration of a future twenty-two day public thanksgiving, Epanactos's usefulness vanished: wild cheering by crowds at the games of the Flaminus and Maximus celebrations precluded any attempt at censuring the commander. Even

Pompeius realized he could do nothing at this time to counter his rival's popularity.

The fall of Alesia depressed Epanactos. After he heard that Vercingetorix would be sent to Roma, his interest in the king's fate made him avoid all senators but Tilius.

❧❦

Tullius Tilius's recent bride, Valaria Anaria Tilia, avoided her husband's guests as much as possible. Of Celtic ancestry herself, she nevertheless left two house slaves, Cossos and Araurica, to attend to any needs of the men. Epanacatos and his companions rarely ate meals at the villa, preferring to patronize taverns around the Forum Holitorium. Located near the new theater of Pompeius, this district of vegetable stalls included a number of *lupinariae*, which the three patronized. Boatmen at the docks could be paid for information: it was there that Epanactos learned about the arrival of Gallic prisoners and Vercingetorix.

❧❦

On the day of Tilius's chance meeting with Lucius, Epanactos had decided to dine with the senator, hoping to learn about plans regarding Vercingetorix's fate.

Valeria pleaded a fever and absented herself from the dining couch next to her husband. The Arvernian usually stared at her during a meal, which frightened the young woman. She no longer trusted Cossos and Araurica, believing that Epanactos had corrupted them with seditious ideas.

During the meal Tilius kept Cossos nearby if needed as a translator. After gulping a cup of wine and finishing a first course of boiled eggs and asparagus, Epanactos brought up the subject of the Gallic prisoners. He had decided to speak through Cossos, a Tigurini, so Tilius would not know how much Latin he actually understood.

With a wink at his two companions, Epanactos told Cossos, "Ask the senator how many Gallic chieftains were brought here following the setback at Alesia."

After the translation, Tilius snorted, "Setback? Tell him that Vercingetorix was defeated at Alesia and is here along with several of his chief seditionists."

Epanactos probed for details. "Ask what will happen to them."

Tilius dabbed his mouth with a napkin before answering, "They are held as hostages in the *Tullianum* prison to prevent further uprisings." Anxious to change the subject, Tilius had Cossos tell him about meeting Lucius and the others that morning.

The slave repeated, "The senator says today he saw someone you know. A centurion with him at Wermaros. Also Alberix, his mother, and a slave woman who is his wife."

Epanactos was surprised enough to ask in Latin, "The slave was named Apsa?"

"A flaxen-haired and very beautiful woman," Tilius replied. "The *centurio* is Lucius Velcanius. Surely, you must recall him."

Epanactos nodded that he did remember, but kept silent for the rest of the meal.

Afterward, he motioned Trigvoros and Dunamos back to their room. "Shut the door! Did you understand what the senator said? Liscos's sister-in-kin, Briga, is here, and Alberix with that camp slut. They could finger us as seditionists."

Dumnos reacted first. "I'm for going back instead of rotting in prison. Let's head north to Gallia in the morning."

Epanactos flipped his dagger point into a floorboard. "First we have to find out what's happening *in* Gallia. How bad the defeat at Alesia was in terms of what army we have left. Cossos can find that out at the docks."

Trigvoros objected. "With Vercingetorix as good as dead, what's the use?"

Epanactos eased his blade free and looked up. "What did you say/"

"The king. He'll be killed like Acco of the Senones."

A plan flashed into Epanactos's mind quickly as one of Taranis's fire bolts. "How would you *corma*-swiggers like to wet your swords with Romani blood and enter the Land of the Eternally Young with glory? We could be remembered like Brennos of old."

Dunamos frowned. "What're you getting at?"

"Ever hear tell that if you wish to catch a fox, you should know his tricks? I say you also must know his weak points. The Shorthairs have Vercingetorix imprisoned and the last thing they expect is that he'll escape. Would a fox worry about a quail cornered in his den? No, but outsmart that fox and the bird goes free."

Trigvoros failed to understand the imagery, yet was ready to perform any deed that might afford him pleasure in an Other-world. "What do you want from us?"

Epanactos's uneven teeth showed in a mirthless grin. "Get Cossos to find out where those Wermaros women are staying. The three of us are going to outfox a fox!"

Late that afternoon when sunset flooded the city in a golden haze and long shadows angled toward the Tiber, I walked with Apsa along the road back to Artemidorus's villa. Lucius and Briga stayed a few paces behind. All were tired: it had been an incredible day with our minds filled by recollections of Roma's streets, temples, buildings, noises, and smells.

I touched Apsa's abdomen. "How do you feel? Too much walking?"

She smiled at my concern. "The child is only a month along, but I am a little tired"

"Wait until I tell Simonides everything we saw! Fever or no, tomorrow he'll want to go with us."

"Alberix, he's very, very ill."

"I know, Apsa, but I'm excited for him. I...I could hire a carriage like the ones we saw today. A mattress and pillows would make him comfortable."

When we saw Artemidorus waiting for us halfway up the lane, I became alarmed at his grim expression. Had some of Pompeius's ruffians heard his criticism of Roma and threatened him or burned his academy? I ran ahead. "Sir, has something happened?"

"I bring evil news," he replied softly. "Your Greek friend died just after mid-day. My wife...Elpince...was with him."

"Died? Simonides is...is dead?" Stunned, I shouted the opposite. "No! He... he was asleep when we left this morning!"

"While in Gallia a bond between the *atomoi* of his body and spirit was weakened by lack of proper nutrition."

Atomoi? My friend is dead and this Greek babbles philosophy. "What?"

Artemidoros explained, "*Atomoi*, are minute particles that make up our physical world. In the Massiliote's case, they no longer had strength enough to bind together." He looked toward Lucius. "*Centurio*, your own Lucretius Carus wrote a poem that presents the teachings of Epicuros on the theorem."

Impatient at his responses, I demanded, "Where is Simonides?"

"In his room. Elpince and Vestia washed the body."

I pushed past him to the villa and found Simonides on a bed, dressed in a white tunic. Sunken cheeks and eyes made my friend difficult to recognize, yet I retained the image of his wit and ready laugh on the journey from Cenabum to Gergovia. Chrysanthemum and Marigold blossoms surrounded his body. A spicy scent from the flowers filled room—a smell I would never forget.

"There are copper coins on his eyes," I noted. "He...told me about the custom."

Artemidoros explained from the doorway, "To pay the boatman, Charon, for ferrying him across the Styx, yet did your friend believe this myth? Priests conjure up phantoms that make mortals tremble. The fools hurry to offer sacrifices they think will hold back a god's anger or induce one to scatter gracious fortune on their affairs. Knowing nothing of the spirit's nature, a fear of eternal punishment after they die haunts them in life."

"What is the nature of this spirit?" I asked to picture an afterlife for Simonides.

"When the *atomoi* of breath and heat leave a body, its limbs and mind die. Yet these particles constitute the basis of the cosmos and are not destroyed. Thus, death should be nothing to us. After death disrupts the union of body and spirit we shall be nothing, thus nothing can happen to us again. No power may stir our senses again."

Briga rebuked him. "Our people believe that we may eventually return to this world in another body."

"*Domina,* even if the *atomoi* that composed us could be reassembled and brought back to their present state, our chain of identity would be snapped. We would remember nothing."

Apsa asked about a reason for the monuments and memorials she saw today.

The *Magister* stated, "Men wish something of themselves to linger on. The thought of extinction fills them with self-pity, yet to become immortal would be a greater tragedy. Be assured that there is no punishment to fear after death. One who ceases to exist cannot suffer, just as one who has never existed cannot feel. Therefore, if we return to sleep and peace, what reason for grief?"

His reasoning did little to temper the emptiness I felt. "Simonides was the first true friend I had who was not Celtic. We enjoyed many adventures together."

"Thus the *atomoi* of your memory are stirred into activity. They in turn affect your emotions. As in mixing water with wine, the two become one substance."

Artemidoros's words made a kind of sense and Simonides might have agreed with his compatriot. I preferred our Celtic belief, where warriors hoped to meet again and wives and children reunite with husbands and fathers.

He read my thoughts. "*Kelt,* if we admit of rewards, we also must include inflictions. Yet who will be judge? In what shadowy basilica will the case be heard? Who the prosecutor? Defender? I fear that the halls of Minos could not hold those whom *Justica* would confine there. No, the premise is ridiculous! Your friend lies without concern for those matters."

Lucius put an arm around my shoulder. "I'll write to his father. Simonides left a bundle of notes in his travel bag."

We stood in silence for a time, each remembering impressions the youth had made on us. When our host spoke again, his voice held a compassionate tone that his logical explanations had lacked.

"In truth, your friend died of plague, the 'Gallic Fever.' You survivors may thank a Celtic or Roman god that you yourselves did not succumb." He lightly touched my sleeve. "Alberix, it is best to cremate your friend's body now."

Artemidoros led the way to a place beyond his vineyard where students had amassed a pinewood funeral pyre. I helped Lucius carry the shrouded body of my friend outside and lain on the wood. As flames blazed up to brighten the dusk, Lucius walked me a short way to the ridge that overlooked the river and buildings of the Eternal City. Below us watch fires were reflected from the Tiber. Other distant spots of orange formed a bright mosaic within dark buildings.

"Tomorrow," Lucius suggested, "we could go to a potter and buy a *pyx* so his ashes can be returned to his family."

I disagreed. "No, leave him on this hill. If Roma is *not* eternal, he will want to record what happened." I looked into Lucius's face, ruddy from the light of the blazing pyre. "I can't accept that...that 'nothingness' of Artemidoros. Simonides *must* know what is happening here."

Lucius understood. "Simonides sought out the truth. Perhaps the most honest man I've known. Honor him for being faithful to that elusive ideal. Shall we go back?"

"I'll stay here a while longer."

"Fine."

As Lucius went with the others, Apsa broke away to be with me. As he held her back, I heard him say, "Your husband needs solitude now. No woman can share what he now feels."

Lucius was partly wrong. That night Apsa held me tightly while my sorrow found release in a flow of tears.

CHAPTER XIV

The Roman calendar listed the seventh day before the *Eidus* of November as a work day, so the Senate assembled in the Temple of Saturnus. Senator Tilius would be there, so Lucius wanted to attend the session, sure that Pompeius's agents would take every opportunity to undermine Caesar. A priority would be prompt legislation that would allocate land grants to legion veterans.

Rain and chilly weather followed our first visit to the city. Mercurius, a pupil of Artemidoros, drove us to the Forum in a covered carriage. Gilt-work on temples gleamed through a morning drizzle. Flower stalls were speckles of color among dull brick or stucco shops at the first level of apartments near the Palatinus. Only a few chilled vendors huddled in stalls under the arches of the Basilica Aemilia. With gusts of rain soaking merchandise customers were few, but in nearby porticos browsers took advantage of cover to look through bookseller shops.

When Mercurius let us off in front of the temple stairs, Lucius told him, "I don't expect this session to last beyond the sixth hour. Senators will get to the baths and soak off chills."

"*Centurio*, I shall visit bookseller stalls until then."

Lucius wore a new tunic on which he displayed his legion decorations. Three silver discs with images of an eagle, Apollo, and Mars hung from leather straps across his chest. Two neck torcs given him by Caesar from Gallic booty were on a band around his neck.

I had on checkered trousers under a belted tunic. My silver torc gleamed in the soft light. Taking the temple steps two at a time, we found that except for a line of lamps at the far end, the open doors were a source of light inside. In a niche between the lamps, I saw an enormous statue of Saturnus: an old man, well-muscled, holding a scythe. A serpent circled its own tail. The god's right hand held a child. Lucius said the rusting chains draped at the base were dedications from freed slaves.

This assembly of wealthy men held my attention. On either side of open floor space, senators sat on folding chairs or stood along the walls. One of their number spoke from the floor's center.

Lucius whispered, "The hawk-nosed man speaking is Marcus Porcius Cato, and practices the strictest principles of a Stoic. He's even bare-footed on that cold marble. I think he's criticizing Caesar's upcoming festival games."

"...over twenty days of debauchery," Cato ranted, "as if this Caesar was the god of a Saturnalia! Across the Via Sacra, a basilica raised in the Forum by my great-grandfather lies in ashes, all because of this conqueror who hires *sicarii*...thugs...to terrorize our city! We meet here because the riotous agents of the 'Adulterer' likewise destroyed our Curia..." Cato paused to let angry murmurs from his supporters grow louder, then raised a trembling hand for silence. "Yet is it the Porcia that rises again? Do masons lay down bricks for a new Curia? No! A basilica dedicated to Caesar's daughter shall blot out stars above this Forum. And I tell you it is the blood of dead Romans that pays for this shameful monument in the form of spoils from Gallia."

Caesar's clients were on their feet, shouting protests against Catos's attack on the deceased Julia.

Ignoring them, his index finger cut jabs in the air. "Senators, I tell you that it is not the sons of Galli or Britani whom you must fear. No, it is a commander of ten legions. Gaius Julius Caesar!"

Mixed hooting and applause echoed from the temple walls. Lucius leaned toward me. "Marcus Cato is the most honest man here. If he is against Caesar we've not made a good beginning."

As Cato's supporters surrounded him to praise his speech, another senator walked to the center of the floor. I recognized the man we had seen a few days earlier. "There's Tilius."

Lucius moved closer. "Let's see if he can pull Cato's sausage from the fire."

After the legislators quieted down, Tilius pointed to a seat where Cato had returned. "Senators," he began in a tone of mockery, "how can we expect a *swineherd* to understand the compassion of a father for his beloved daughter?"

Caesar's clients applauded a pun on the Cato *nomen*, 'Porcius,' yet the orator was on his feet with an instant rejoinder. "At least swineherds can recognize slops! Let's see what kind our distinguished colleague serves up."

Tilius ignored opposition catcalls. "Cato speaks of 'the spoils of Gallia'? I was there when the Aedui and Sequani invited us to oppose the illegal migration of Helvetii through their lands—"

"And through our *Provincia*," an associate called out on cue.

Tilius let Caesar's faction applaud before continuing, "Romans did not throw the first javelin and the gods of our ancestor rightly blessed the response of the Imperator."

"There is only one Imperator at Rome, Pompeius!" a supporter shouted.

"Hear him out! Let Tilius make his case!" The distinctive voice of Marcus Cicero sounded from gloom near Saturnus's silent statue.

Tilius's appeal changed direction. "Senators, ask the priests of Jupiter, of Juno, or those of the great Saturnus, 'Where are the spoils of Gallia?' They answer that the state treasury is enriched." As he walked along the circuit of men, clapping overcame sarcastic hoots from his opposition. "Others who are not priests, senators or even tribunes, ask about the spoils of war..." Tilius pointed at Lucius. "Ask men like that *centurio*, who risked their lives for the Republic. The only 'loot' they want...and I mock the term...is what they were promised. Land and security! Did we come here to criticize their commander or to honor men like this *centurio*? In serving Caesar, Lucius Velcanius served Roma first!" This time many in Pompeius's faction joined the applause as they faced around to gawk at the legion officer. With momentum built up, Tilius came to the crux of his speech. "I propose that this Senatus immediately draft legislation granting land and authorizing new colonies for our brave legion veterans!"

Even as he returned to his seat amid applause, senators gathered in groups to discuss the proposal. Lucius asked me, "Did you understand everything?"

"Not all of his words, but did Tilius win what he proposed for the men?"

"Hopefully. I noticed some of Pompeius's supporters joining us out of a sense of justice for those veterans. Also the fact that Caesar still commands ten legions that *have* conquered Gallia. Tilius was good, but you should hear L. Tullius Cicero argue a criminal case. How he presents his defense is more important than whether or not his client is guilty." Lucius listened to the senators, hearing words like "*ager*," "*Campania*" and "*Gallicus*" above the murmur of voices. "They're talking about locations for the land grants."

"*Veto!*" Abruptly, a loud voice rose to challenge the senators. A man ran onto center of the assembly shouting, "*Veto!* The proposal is nullified."

Lucius said, "It's Faustus Luculus, that tribune who took charge of the prisoners. He could kill any legislation before it can be enacted into law."

Shoving matches had broken out on the two sides when a scowling, gray-haired man stalked into the quarrel. "Senators, listen to Faustus Luculus!" Cicero pleaded. "Hear the tribune out. Have Romans taken to behaving like barbarians rather than civilizing them?"

At the reprimand only labored breathing was heard from assembly members who had tussled with opponents.

"Senators!" Luculus announced in affected anger, "Gaius Julius Caesar has no authority to order any legislation without first consulting Pompeius! I predict that civil war will result if this proposal passes!"

Stunned silence dominated the room until Cato came forward again. A soft pat from his bare feet sounded on the marble floor, his voice scarcely louder. "Compatriots, I know your thoughts. I had not yet the age for a *toga virilis* when the proscriptions of Lucius Cornelius Sulla decimated this very chamber. Some here hid in cellars as agents of the Dictator searched for you. You heard family members being murdered in rooms above you. Senators, if

Tribune F. Luculus is suggesting a moderate course of action, have patience! How little of that virtue Sulla had and civil war resulted!"

Tilius sagged in his chair, realizing he had lost support for his proposal at that session. Few of the elderly senators and tribunes needed a reminder of the terrible years when two Republican armies opposed each other and almost destroyed the city.

Fufius Trebonius sidled up to Lucius. "*Centurio,* it will take more than a *speech* to pass that land legislation."

"Regretfully, Tribune, but if you're referring to bribes, Caesar has ample funds. They would be well-spent."

Several senators walked over to look at me out of curiosity and ask Lucius for news about friends and relatives in distant legions.

Longinus Cassius, who survived an ill-starred campaign of Crassus into Parthia, inquired about a cousin. "Tribune Spurius Licinius. He was in Rebilius's legion."

Lucius shook his head. "Senator, I...I just don't know. Rebilius held the main camp with Reginus. The Parthian attack was heaviest there."

Tilius intervened, "Cassius, the centurion isn't a *quaestor* as we were and didn't keep records. Besides, I *must* talk to him."

"Of course. *Dea Fortuna tecum, Centurio.*"

Tilius guided us through the crowd. "Cassius belongs to Pompeius's faction and you just saw how working on Caesar's behalf isn't easy. Luculus is an indicator of how the vote will go. I'm afraid you'll have to wait."

"Wait how long?" I demanded, impatient for land to be awarded.

Lucius clutched my sleeve. "Alberix, we'll have to convince senators to support the commander. I'll rent a house. Meanwhile, work on your Latin with a tutor."

Seeing my frown, Tilius forced a smile. "Patience is not a strong point with your tribes. Try to cultivate that virtue."

I ignored him to tell Lucius that I wanted to see the craft work done here, then turned, stalked down the stairs, and headed for the shops beyond the arch of Fabius.

Tilius held Lucius back. "Let him go. There is yet a primitive furor in these Gallic men. Come and meet some agents of Caesar."

⁕

Epananctos, standing with Trigvoros under an arch of the Aemilia, had watched Lucius arrive at the session. Now he saw Alberix run down the stairs and disappear into a nearby street. "Trigvoros, something said must have gotten under his shield, so we must drive that wedge deeper. What do you think of the tribune who talked with Senator Tilius?"

"Trebonius? A weak-willed rooster and the captive of his ambitions."

Epanactos grasped his compatriot's arm. "I saw it too, and we will need the help of an official to free Vercingetorix. Get Cossos to arrange a meeting with Trebonius at some tavern."

"Why would the tribune come?"

"Flatter the rooster. Tell him we need advice. Does not each bird like to hear itself sing?"

Trigvoros said, "I heard that the *Graecus* died. Alberix's friend."

"Excellent! That will make it easier to get to the two women, Briga and Apsa."

❧❧

Two days later I went to visit Artemidoros in his *Akademia* and mentioned that on the way I had seen every male citizen carrying a weapon. He laughed when I asked if he thought that civil war was close, and told me they were going to one of Roma's seven hills called Aventinus. There they celebrated the *Armilustum*, an ancient festival where swords and javelins were brought up to be purified by sacrifices.

❧❧

During the month of November, Celtic body ornaments became wildly popular jewelry items at Rome. Senators' wives followed a lead begun by those of magistrates and wore barbarian combs, arm bracelets, brooches, and shell necklaces. At a theater performance a golden neck torc worn around the throat of an aedile's mistress engendered three more such sightings on the next day.

Merchants hurried to meet veterans returning from Gallia at Ostia, eager to buy any barbarian trinkets they brought back. It soon was apparent that the most sought after gifts this coming Saturnalia would be any item of barbarian gold, silver, or bronze work.

Sculpture workshops along the Tiber were overwhelmed with Patricians' orders for marble copies of a Pergamene "Fallen Galatian Warrior." One hundred and seventy years earlier, Attalus Soter I commissioned the statue for an altar at Pergamum that celebrated his victory over invading Galatians. Almost as popular, although twice as costly, was what Cicero called, "An image of magnificent despair." The sculpture showed a Celt who, rather than face captivity, supported the body of a wife he had killed before thrusting a sword into his own heart.

Even slaves profited from the sudden fad: cloth and leatherwork apprentices smuggled packets of henna dye to daring Roman ladies wishing to color their hair the bright copper shade of barbarian women.

❧

By the end of the month Epanactos had formulated a plan to free the Gallic prisoners from the Tullianum. Because of the sudden popularity of anything Celtic, he found Gaius Trebonius an approachable, even eager, conspirator. Discouraged by the length of time it would take for veteran's land legislation to pass—and by Caesar's deteriorating influence in the capitol—the tribune now avoided Tilius whenever he could. The senator's patronizing attitude rankled Trebonius, even as he eagerly acquired the tastes of a Patrician through association with the lawmaker.

Five days after the *Eidus* of November the wily Cossos arranged a second meeting with Epanactos in the warrior's favorite *taberna*, AD MARTIS ET VENUS. The tavern attracted its drinking clients from ex-legionaries. A number of cubicle-rooms on the second floor hosted patrons who paid for their devotion to the Goddess of Love.

Gaius Trebonius glanced at a painted sign at the entrance that depicted a nude Venus astride Mars, blatantly taking the active role in a sexual act. *An advertisement for prostitutes who work upstairs, yet I've seen similar paintings in the bedrooms of patrician villas. This one only is painted more crudely.*

As he entered, the tribune pulled a hood on his cloak forward, glad it was cold outside; the cowl made him resemble other *pleb* patrons. The crowded common room smelled of stale wine and food overcooked in olive oil. Beyond the entrance counter, Epanactos sat with two other men at a table near the rear stairway. The Arvernian spotted Trebonius, gestured, then started up the stairs with his companions. After glancing around, the Tribune followed.

On the upper floor two hanging oil lamps barely gave light to a narrow corridor whose cheap incense odor failed to overlay a rancid tavern smell below. Muted laughter came from inside nearby rooms. At the first lamp one of the doors abruptly opened. A dark-skinned girl, wearing only a cloth band across her breasts, skipped across to the cubicle opposite. Four rooms past her, Epanactos beckoned to Trebonius from another doorway.

"*Salus,*" he said in Latin: after several weeks of hearing little else and learning new words from Cossos, the Arvenian understood the language fairly well.

"*Salvete...*" Trebonius returned the greeting and glanced around. The cramped space was furnished with the couch of a *Lupenaria*, a wooden table, and two chairs. A wash basin was set next to a soiled towel. The charcoal brazier in a corner gave heat and additional flickering light to an oil lamp on a ceiling chain.

Epanactos closed the door, then motioned Trebonius to a chair and pointed to a barrel-shaped man with the slant of a fractured nose. "That's Contundo,"

The tribune thought he looked vaguely familiar. *His name means "Bruiser." If he's a boxer or wrestler, he's won most of his matches.*

Epanactos slumped into a chair opposite and jerked his thumb toward a slightly-built companion sitting on the couch. "That's Natanius."

Trebonius studied him. *His skin is too swarthy to be entirely by the sun. That isn't a Roman name, only Latinized.*

Natanius noted his puzzlement. "Actually, I'm Natan ben Zesakia, from Yehuda. You Romans call the province 'Judaea'."

Contundo snickered, "They cut a piece off his *priapus* when he was born."

"Women don't seem to mind. Makes me more exotic."

"We didn't come to talk about pricks," Epanactos reminded the men. "Contundo, you tell the tribune about our business with him."

"I was Milo's 'Bruiser...'" He chortled at the pun on his name. "Even if he's in exile, lot of his men are cuttin' up Caesar's followers."

"I...I've heard," Trebonius recalled nervously. "Bodies are found every morning but Pompeius is too preoccupied with his new young bride to much care..." He paused to consider his answer. "Epanactos said you needed an Equestrian in a plan for embarrassing Caesar. I...I'm promising nothing."

"Bruiser" looked at Epanactos with narrowed eyes. "You said y' *had* a man."

"Easy, Contundo..." Natanius stood up. "Tribune, we don't like to deal in threats here yet you heard what happened to Clodius. If Contundo doesn't like someone, his 'health' isn't worth a copper *as*."

Trebonius spluttered, "This...this is nothing...nothing is illegal is it?"

"Illegal?" Natanius chuckled and sat down again. "Let me explain. In my country a few years ago, Pompeius was asked to arbitrate a quarrel about who should rule. He picked Hyrcanus over Aristobulus and set him up as a client king of your Republic. As long as a king doesn't allow his neighbors to threaten Roman interests, the Senatus leaves him alone. Epanactos thinks that an arrangement like that could be made with this captured Arvernian king."

"But Vercingetorix is in the Tullianum as Caesar's prisoner," Trebonius objected. "Pompeius hasn't any authority to do that."

"*He* seems to think he has. Pompeius may have refused the dictatorship, but he's about to accept the title of *Princeps*."

"I've heard. His designation as 'First Citizen' is bound to displease Caesar, a nominal co-equal in the Republic."

Natanius quoted, "It's said that the dead and the absent get farther off each day. I believe that Pompeius and Caesar will go the way of those two rivals in my country, except it will be your god of war who arbitrates between them."

"You mean civil war?"

The Judean shrugged. "Epanactos would settle for Vercingetorix being out of prison. If it came to war, Pompeius could use a few thousand Arvernians on his left flank."

"Then if Pompeius is behind this, why do you need me?"

Natanius ignored his question. "This Aristobulus I mentioned. Pompeius had him arrested and sent to the Tullianum. We helped him escape."

"I...I recall the name now. Aristobulus was one of the Asian kings first displayed at Pompeius's Triumph."

"Exactly, Tribune. I can get Vercingetorix out, but we need a house where we can conceal him until Senators confirm him as a client king of Pompeius. A tribune like you could make the proposal before that. Ah...those of his faction would be very grateful."

"How grateful?" Trebonius asked.

"Say, one hundred thousand *sesterces*."

"For house rent and a few speeches?"

Natanius hesitated—the tribune was not quite the fool Epanactos had implied.

Contundo was blunt. "We need t' get into the Tullianum. You're friends with that *centurio* what came from Gallia and the *brachatus* with him."

"Lucius. Alberix. Yes, I..." Trebonius felt himself perspiring and wiped his brow.

Natanius elaborated, "They both want to see Vercingetorix and make sure the king is doing well. A sick hostage can't be ransomed. We'll get in with them once you work out the arrangement. A...gratuity...they could give the guards."

"When do you plan for this to happen?" Trebonius asked,

Contundo grinned. "At the Saturnalia. Half of Rome will be drunk outside, and the rest inside playin' with Priapus."

Natanius said, "Tribune, as you well know, slaves almost get away with murder at the December festival."

Trebonius dabbed his forehead with a neckerchief. "I...I have less than a month to convince senators and get their support?"

"Time enough for you to approach those who favor Pompeius. Plant a seed in their minds that will sprout once the king is free." Natanius handed him a leather pouch. "For expenses, and also a list of senators who will work with you against Caesar."

CHAPTER XV

Natanius chose the second day after the beginning of the seven-day Saturnalia festival to initiate his plan for entering the Tullianum. December nineteenth was the *Opalia*, a feast celebrating Ops, the wife of Saturnus-Kronos and mother of Jupiter. The Judean adventurer reasoned that a guard detail would be small and especially lax on this double holiday. Many celebrants would be at Saturnus's temple, which was situated directly across from the prison.

Natanius had rehearsed taking Vercingetorix back along a darkened street, the Argentum, then behind the Curia and Porcia ruins to the Vici Subura. An extension of the street led to Trebonius's villa on the Esquilinus.

❧

By the ninth hour of a chilly December twilight, *Opalia* festival bonfires blazed and threw out light and warmth. A few days before, a man called Natanius spoke Latin with a guttural accent and had come to Artemidoros's villa. He understood Greek and told the *Magister* that Vercingetorix wished to speak to the centurion who had brought him to Roma. Natanius promised he could get into the prison. Lucius, eager to examine the king's condition, decided to trust the stranger.

Now Lucius and I, accompanied by Natanius, watched the Tullianum entrance. Only two legionaries were on duty, warming themselves at a fire. One swigged from a wine skin brought out from under his cloak. I was uneasy and guessed Lucius had his own reservations about our venture.

The Judean whispered to Lucius, "There's another guard inside. For the last few nights I've watched the three exchange places on their watch."

Lucius was not convinced. "You believe they will take bribes to let a couple of revelers gawk at a Gallic chieftain?"

In answer Natanius eyed our short tunics and hooded cloaks. "Is the Galatian ready? Both of you unarmed?" I showed my empty dagger sheath. Lucius handed him a money pouch from under his cloak. "Good. Move forward and act like you're a little drunk."

Strolling casually, we crossed the paving stones.

Lucius and I stayed back a short distance as Natanius approached the guard, briefly warmed his hands at his fire, then cajoled, "A few extra *sestercii* might have bought off this shit-duty for you and your companions, eh, friend?" After the man grunted an unintelligible reply, Natanius pointed toward us, showed him the money pouch, and whispered in confidence, "My Patrician friends over there want to gawk at a real Gaul. With all this fuss about the *brachatae* these days I was wondering..." The coins clinked as he tossed the pouch from hand to hand.

The other guard saw Natanius and came to the fire. "Who's he?"

His comrade took him aside to explain. Obviously the more sober of the two, the second guard shook his head and told Natanius, "Orders is not to let anyone in."

"I'm talking about Patricians with influence. You both might like being guards at a senator's villa better than in this cesspool."

"Patricians?" He glanced over at us. "Is that them?"

Natanius leaned close and pressed the pouch into the man's rough hand. "Pissers. They don't have the nerve to ask you, just enough money to pay."

"Sorry. Orders." He rested a hand on the hilt of his sword. "Move off now."

Natanius pulled back the pouch. "Well, friend, your watch is soon over. Perhaps your relief will allow them a quick look."

The guards glanced at each other a moment, then the first one grabbed the pouch. The other motioned us to an arched entrance. "Make it quick. Silo's inside, but I'll take his place."

"Silo is the third guard?"

"He'll take y' down to where the prisoner is."

"Good." Natanius beckoned us forward.

Near the cells Silo sat at a table carving a bone dagger handle into the shape of an eagle's head. He was not surprised at the trio of strangers or their request; other patricians brought friends down to look at barbarian and other prisoners.

On the right a few stairs led down to a dark corridor that followed the outer wall of the building. The doors of a series of cells opposite retreated into darkness.

Silo took a lighted taper from its iron holder and pointed to the distance. "Cella Six, near the Pit. Talk through the bars."

As we entered the corridor, Natanius murmured, "The same cell where they confined Aristobulus. At least the Arvernian isn't *in* the Pit, or you would have to shout down to be heard."

"What is this Pit?"

Lucius explained to me, "An underground cell that gave the prison its name. A *tullus*...jet of water...is inside a cavern that was the original place of confinement. The cell is vaulted now. Executions take place there."

Not a place to linger! We reached a cell door marked with a crude VI. Natanius took out a serrated iron key and fitted the wards into a grid on the latch. Pushing up, he slid back the bolt that secured the door.

Lucius asked, "Where did you get a key?"

"Go inside."

The damp cell stank of mold, urine, and feces. A figure wrapped in a blanket sat up, blinking in the dim light. I was shaken to see the haggard face and matted beard of Vercingetorix. He was said to be little more than twenty years old.

Lucius told him, "This man said you wanted to talk with me."

Seeming confused, the Arvernian tried to recognize his visitor. Then the grating sound of a door opening came from an adjoining cell. Epanactos hurried out, followed by two men. The three quickly had swords at my throat and that of Lucius.

Epanactos spoke rapidly to Vercingetorix. I caught the words "escape" and "client state," but the king seemed not to understand. Hunching down, he explained, "I'm Arverni, here to free you. We know Romani who would make you king in a country allied with Roma." Epanactos stood to extend a hand. "Quickly, we have a rope ladder to an opening in the roof."

Vercingetorix understood enough to ask, "This is a plan of Caesar's?"

"No, no. Senators opposing him will help us smuggle you out of the city."

The king glanced toward Lucius and me, but didn't recognize us in the poor light. Then he told Epanactos, "I cast my sword at the feet of the Roman Caesar as a sign of submission. If I am to die it shall be with honor. I will not run to live after in shame."

Natanius felt trapped in the putrid dankness; it had not occurred to him that this king might not be willing to escape, as Artistobulus had done. "We can't force the man," he hissed. "Get back on the roof, all of you. Soon as that guard finishes dividing up our bribe with Silo, he'll come down here."

With the swords still threatening us, Contundo hesitated. He was used to street brawls, not a cramped cell in an unfamiliar building.

Being inside the cell had kept a furious Epanactos from physically venting rage. As Vercingetorix lay back on the straw, he seethed, "We risked our lives to free you!"

Natanius said, "He's made his decision. We must leave before Silo becomes suspicious."

In the hallway faces appeared at the barred windows of adjoining cells: other imprisoned chieftains had heard talking. When Vercassivellaunos called out his cousin's name, the voice echoed down the corridor.

The Judean pulled Epanactos by the arm. "Arvernian, out!"

The two men with swords looked at Contundo . "What about these two?"

"Slit 'em!" Epanactos growled, pointing to us.

"No!" Natanius warned. "Leave two bodies here and Pompeius will hear about it. Flat blade them—"

A blow to the side of my head knocked me down. Lucius fell, also stunned, but dimly aware of one of the swordsmen bending over him with a knife and slitting open his belt pouch.

Staggering to our feet a few moments later, heads throbbing, we groped the wall for support and inched back to the entrance.

Silo met us halfway. The legionary surmised what had happened and shook his head. "Next time you Patricians go lookin' for somethin' new don't pick a thief for a guide." He looked in Lucius's empty purse and grinned. "Didn't leave you a furcin *as!*"

"My head still is on my neck."

"Get out!"

Outside, Lucius led the way to a fountain near a house of the Vestal priestesses. After we ducked our aching heads in cold water, he touched an angry welt at the side of my face. "How does *your* head feel?"

"Ringing..." I touched the nub of ear that Vercingetorix severed in his camp.

Lucius dried his hair on a cloak hem. "And I feel about as worldly as a Lucanian who shoveled manure all his life. I left both flanks exposed and fell for a trick that got the Judean inside. That was a warrior from Wermaros—"

"Epanactos,"

Lucius recalled, "I had a run-in with him in the village. What in Hades's name is he doing at Roma?"

"Or this Natanius and those others in a plot to free Vercingetorix? What is a client state they mentioned?"

"Provinces governed by rulers accountable to our Senatus. If Pompeius *is* behind this, the battle line is drawn up. It's the Judean who puzzles me. We were a way of getting *him* inside the Tullianum, yet he already had a key to the cell."

"A lump of wax pushed into the lock would make an impression for a mold. I helped Cluvios cast lost keys that way."

"Then he had bribed other guards. We should get a report of this to Caesar."

"Vercingetorix held to his surrender terms, Lucius."

"True, but this throbbing in my head will have to subside before I can think clearly."

Walking slowly back to a house Lucius had rented on the Via Transtiberim, we watched Saturnalia revelers throng the Via Sacra. Both of us accepted a gulp of wine from a drunken youth. The Forum was crowded, although most celebrations took place in homes where masters waited on their slaves. Lucius said this imitated a mythical Golden Age of Saturnus when all men were free. We inhaled an odor of roasting suckling pig, the traditional meat served by street vendors and in taverns.

Lucius mused, "Being so long in Gallia, I'd almost forgotten what the Saturnalia is like. Shops and businesses shut down for a week. Even Artemidoros closed his Academy."

Our house was just below the *Magister's* villa. Walking around the Capitolinus, we took the curve of the Via Jugaria, which circled to a gate in the walls. On the flank of the hill we heard amorous couples among the dark cypresses and pines and caught glimpses of lovers in the gardens. Warmed by passion, they made love despite the chill air.

I felt a rush of desire for Apsa. The hidden sounds also aroused Lucius, who said, "I've had enough of Roma and want to get to Abellinum. Your mother and I will be married there."

"I'm happy for her and you."

"I know I can't replace your father, but I'll try to give her a good life."

I grasped his sleeve. "You will."

At the Carmentalis gate revelers had thinned out. We shrugged off insistent beggars by Lucius showing his empty money pouch. "Let's not take the Cestius Bridge." He pointed beyond the Tiberina Island it spanned. "The ferryman will work tonight and charge plenty, but we'll be closer to our house."

"It's good he knows us. You can pay tomorrow."

It was well past the eleventh hour, but wharf taverns still were crowded and noisy. Most homes across the river were dark since citizens were either in the city or asleep. We found the boatman sober enough to commiserate with our poor fortune at being robbed—common during festivals. Lucius jested that the boatman was like Charon ferrying souls over the Styx to Hade's kingdom. He quipped in return that Death could carry a consul in his boat as easily as a slave. The remark upset Lucius. He hurried me up the dirt lane from the riverbank.

Our house was dark, the gate to the garden open. Whenever Ersa expected us to be late she left a lamp burning in the atrium hallway. None shone. Alarmed, Lucius ran through the garden. The boatman's death-jest came back to me. I called out Apsa's name but heard no response. Our torch abruptly sputtered out, so we felt our way along the wall to the kitchen. Coals still glowed in the stove. Using tongs, I lighted two lamps with an ember.

I followed Lucius as he strode toward our bedrooms, then stumbled over a form on the floor. Bending down, we both were stunned to find the body of Ersa. An irregular pool of blood had seeped from a knife wound in her chest and congealed on the mosaic tiles.

We shouted for Briga and Apsa again, but only heard Ger crying as a response.

In our bedroom the child stood in his crib, sobbing. Neither woman was with him. I held my lamp low and noticed a scrap of papyrus lying on the bed. "Lucius. Come in here!"

He entered muttering, "I don't understand. Nothing is stolen yet the women are gone. Have you found something?"

Just this..." I held out the wrinkled note.

Lucius read a message scrawled on the papyrus in poorly formed letters:

MVLiERiS SPoNSio SVENT aVT MORiBVNT

CHAPTER XVI

Artemidoros held the papyrus we brought to him near a lamp and squinted at the writing. "The two missing women are held *sponsio*, as a guarantee. 'Hostage' is a better word. '*Moribunt*?' The writing is so poor it is hard to determine if the tense is correct."

I asked, "It refers to death?"

After he nodded, Lucius said, "I see it as a threat to kill Briga and Apsa if we don't cooperate."

"With whom and to do what?" I was confused as well as anxious. "Is this connected with that plot to free Vercingetorix?"

Artemidoros put down the papyrus to look at me. "Of what plot do you speak?"

Lucius explained about our visit to the Tullianum, "Evidently, this Natanius was hired both to get into the prison and keep us away from the house. Epanactos had his men cut through a roof to enter the Tullianum."

Artemidoros snorted, "That prison is six centuries old! A child could dismantle its crumbling tufa vaulting."

"Do you know anything of Natanius, a Judean accomplice?"

"Natanius? I only heard of Judeans in the Forum. His people worship an unseen, nameless god with a single temple in Jerusalem, their capital city."

"What would be his interest in helping a defeated Gallic chieftain?"

"He surely was well paid. Did he seem to be one of Clodius's bullies, like the other three you mentioned?"

"No. Epananctos was the leader with a brute he called Contundo. They hardly seemed to know each other."

"Then this Judean is an adventurer. Just as Odysseus, some men are perpetually restless in searching for themselves."

"When I find him..." My angry look completed the sentence.

"Patience," Artemidoros counseled. "Roma is a city of inhabitants numerous as stars. You could search every apartment in each block from now until the next Saturnalia—"

"We don't have time!" Lucius interrupted.

"Exactly, *centurio*, thus it is your mind and not your feet that will find the two women. Go home. Sleep as best you can. The child can stay with us for now." Artemidoros escorted us through the atrium to his entrance.

"Tomorrow, arrange to bury the unfortunate slave woman, then return here at the fourth hour. We shall apply logic to your quest."

ᘏ

I lay on a couch that still held Apsa's scent until daylight. When I finally fell asleep, my dreams were of the murdered Ersa, my wife, and my mother.

Lucius lay trembling with a sense of helplessness and anger until he also slid into an exhausted doze.

Artemidoros lay awake longer than usual. He had trained his mind to accept the flux of a universal *Logos*, but the senseless murder of a slave woman and possible deaths of the *Kelt* youth's wife and mother disturbed his tranquility. If the Arvernian warrior's plot had failed to release Vercingetorix, there was no longer a reason to hold the women. They now were liabilities that needed elimination, lest they identify those responsible.

ᘏ

Lucius called in a man who staged funerals to take Ersa's body to his mortuary. I didn't know if Romani had investigators who solved murders, but Lucius was too preoccupied with finding Briga and Apsa to talk about it.

When we returned to his villa, Artemidoros showed us the message again. "Coarse work, a poor hand. Not the most talented scribe in the Argiletum if this came from there. There's peculiarity to the N and V. Do you see it?"

Lucius shrugged annoyance. "Of what help is that?"

"Could you recognize Alberix's voice in the dark?"

"Of course."

"This writing is just as distinctive..." He handed back the papyrus. "I suggest you find the scribe. Bribe or terrorize him into revealing who commissioned the note."

I asked, "What if the men who have Apsa and my mother find out?"

"And harm them? They know that you search, yet if the plot was aborted, the women yet may be freed."

Lucius was doubtful. "I don't trust Epanactos to do that. At Wermaros I bested him in a challenge so he sees a way to even the balance."

Artemidoros brought a vellum map from his work table and unrolled it. "Reason suggests that those of Pompeius's faction are behind this, wishing to subvert Caesar."

I studied the chart for clues. "Where could two women be hidden?"

He swept a hand over the plan. "Roma is like the labyrinth of Minos. To find them you must tire your mind before wearing out sandals."

Lucius surmised, "If senators were involved they know by now the plan failed."

Artemidoros half-smiled at his reasoning. "Therefore, *centurio?*"

"They'll want to disassociate themselves."

"Excellent! You walk with your mind now!"

I suggested that Senator Tilius might know something of the plot.

"Well said, *Kelt!* Last night you were ready to search Roma apartment by apartment, and now you have reasoned down to a single villa."

Lucius brightened at the prospect of questioning the senator. "*Magister,* where does Tilius live?"

"Ask in the forum. A *sestercius* will buy that information."

We retraced our steps of the previous night and paid the boatman. A litter bearer who knew the way to Tilius's villa overheard and offered to take us. I refused to ride, so Lucius paid him for the information. We briskly walked up the Subura to its junction with the Vicus Longus. That roadway led up a shallow valley toward the senator's villa on the Viminalis.

Tilius greeted us in his reception room. After hearing of the abduction, he admitted trying to enlist the support of the Sequani tribe through Liscos. Epanactos and two warriors had come to report that the chieftain was dead. He acknowledged that his efforts to bolster Caesar's cause had not been successful and that Epanactos and his companions left before the Saturnalia. He knew nothing of a Natanius or Contundo.

Next we went to the Argiletum, where scribes wrote letters for illiterate citizens who could pay for them. Those Lucius questioned said the penman was either unskilled or purposely had been clumsy. Frustrated by a lack of progress, he decided we would visit Adherbal at the *Campus Martius,* and also talk to the *praefect.* Perhaps his men had heard talk of the conspiracy in taverns they patronized.

❧

An extensive, horn-shaped plain between a bend of the Tiber and the northwestern walls of Rome, the "Field of Mars" was bisected by seasonal torrents of the *Petronia.* The stream drained into a marshy delta, the *Caprae Palus,* and then entered the Tiber. Wild animals by which the "Goat Pond" received its name no longer roamed the area.

Long ago, Roman armies had recovered the plain from Etruscans and named the site after Martius, their god of war. Here, the citizen army of

Romulus first assembled. In the *Martius*, horse exhibits and races of the *Equiria* were celebrated twice a year to honor the god. Schoolchildren learned that Romulus left in a storm cloud from these fields and now lived with Jupiter in the sky. When older, the youths heard that disgruntled senators had torn Rome's founder to pieces, and to avoid civil war, a story was circulated of his miraculous divinity.

On the far side of the *Petronia* a legion camp billeted Rome' garrison of two cohorts and served as a training ground for recruits. Levies of men depended on the Republic's foreign policies, but since the Sardinian war, six generations earlier, the camp always had been in use.

Near the Capitolinus, the *Martius* was being developed as a suburb outside of Roma's walls. The paved Via Flaminia reached the Adriatic Sea at Arminium. A circus built for public games, and Pompeius's 17,000-seat theater, attracted citizen to the new area.

The *Tarentum*, a mysterious region at the northern limit of the *Martius*, held ancient hot springs patronized by ill citizens. Foul-smelling sulphurous vapors hung over the bubbling pools, although tongues of fire once said to come through fissures in the ground were gone. These signs of the Underworld gave the region its original name of "Fiery Fields," thus cults of Pluto and Persephone formed around these reminders of infernal regions.

Fifteen priests lived near a basilica, where pilgrims came to be cured. Their yearly duties included supervising the *Ludi Tarenti* games. Constructed over hot springs nearby, separate bathhouses served men and women. Visitors did not wander far from the basilica: caverns reeking of noxious fumes suggested an entrance to the Underworld similar to that of Lake Avernus, west of Neapolis. Stories told of secret cave-dens where legion initiates from the garrison performed rites to a Persian god called Mithras.

☙❧

Two sentries at the legion camp's gate told us that Adherbal's Numidians were visiting Praeneste. The *praefect*, Petronius Cominus, lived in a new brick barracks-headquarters at the camp's center.

As we walked a street to the *Praetorium*, Lucius noted, "Not many tents are up but then the training season won't begin until March. I'm sure that Pompeius built that barracks to house Roma's garrison."

Cyrenius, an aide in the *praetorium* office, asked why Lucius wanted to see Cominus.

"Tell him that *Primipilus* Lucius Velcanius of Legio Ten is here from Gallia." As the man went down a hallway, Lucius muttered, "Probably everyone here is one of Pompeius's men. I'll try to stay neutral."

Halfway down the hall Cyrenius held a door open and called back, "*Centurio*, Petronius Cominus will see you."

When Lucius and I entered his office, a stocky, gray-haired man with weather-creased features stood up to extend a hand. "Gallia, eh, Velcanius? Thank Jupiter my service was in a less barbaric and much warmer part of our Roman world."

Cominus ignored me, probably thinking I was a slave or a servant.

Lucius corrected him. "*Praetor*, this is my friend, Alberix. Armorer in our *Auxiliae* and son of a deceased Gallic clan chieftain."

Cominus nodded to me as he came around the desk. His left arm hung limply at his side; somewhere in his career the muscle and nerve had been severed. He hesitated a moment, then extended his right hand palm up. Surprised, Lucius recognized the Mithraic gesture and returned the ritual greeting.

Cominus identified his rank and den. "*Pater, Mithraeum Geminorum.*"

Lucius responded with his grade. "*Heliodromos*, but I haven't been able to worship lately. Not too many of us are west of the Rhenus,"

The *Praetor* laughed. "And I'm sure this Gallic sedition kept you on your shield. We'll celebrate the birth of Lord Mithras on December twenty-fifth. You're invited, of course. Most of the garrison is on leave so there's plenty of room. Your Gallic comrade can watch."

Lucius thanked him. "*Grates*, sir, we would like that."

The officer seemed friendly enough. Having Lucius as a cult brother might help us get information.

Cominus noticed me looking at objects displayed on shelves along the room. "My 'children' from almost thirty years of campaigning," he chortled, ruffling the mane of a tawny pelt hanging on the wall. "Got this lion with only one javelin throw! That striped hide you're standing on is from a horse-like creature natives call *zebro*."

Almost as if speaking of actual children, Cominus described his leopard skin and Elephant-hide shields, barbed African spears, statues of bizarre gods from Egypt and places I hadn't heard about, Byth-inia and Syr-ia. One relic was the mummified body of a sacred cat.

Cominus turned back to Lucius. "That's enough reminiscing on my part. You came here on business. Take chairs."

Once seated, Lucius leaned forward. "*Praefect*, several men entered the Tullianum last night in a conspiracy to free Vercingetorix."

"What? I've had no report."

"When do guards brag about getting extra wine money?"

"Bribed?" Cominus scowled. "Go on, *Centurio*."

"Sir, I won't go into details just now, but Alberix's wife and a woman I'm to marry have been abducted as hostages. If the escape plot had succeeded, there evidently was more we were to do."

"Didn't you command a guard detachment that brought the Arvernian to Roma?"

"I did, Sir. The conspirators must think I had his confidence because of that."

"But if he's still in prison, the women are useless to the conspirators."

"Exactly!" I broke in. "Where could they hide them?"

The officer spread his hands in helplessness. "There are more people at Roma than in a hundred-fifty full-strength legions. Give Cyrenius this information. *Centurio*, I can order men here to question tavern keepers, but it will be like trying to hit a mile-off target with a single catapult bolt."

"*Praefect*. we're appreciative."

Cominus walked us to the door, where he repeated the Mithraic hand gesture. "Be here on the twenty-fifth, fourth hour. You, too, son. Lord Mithras accepts all men so we could start you off as *Corax*, a Raven."

We saluted the *Praefect*, then Lucius gave Cyrenius the information.

Near the gate, I saw a three-story log traing tower similar to those built at Alesia. "Let's climb to the top. You can show me more sights of Roma from up there."

"Fine. I might be able to point out places I'd almost forgotten."

From the height we had a view of the city to the southeast. Lucius identified the stone theater of Pompeius, which dominated a cluster of buildings around the Holitorium Market. Beyond them, hills and apartments humped up above a bluish hazee.

In the north, white farmhouses dotted ochre fields. To the east of the camp, a swamp glittered with an occasional sparkle of open water set among reeds and grasses. Beyond the marsh a basilica structure stood at the edge of smaller buildings. Steaming vapors appeared to rise from the ground.

I pointed them out to Lucius. "Those look like the hot springs that Simonides and I found near Gergovia."

"Some sort of healing waters…" Impatient, he said, "Let's get back. Artemidoros may have a plan to help us find Briga and Apsa."

We left the camp and returned to the Tiber ferry in silence. Any hope of discovering the women among almost a million inhabitants required a faith that in our own ways we realized could not be based on supernatural help from either his or my Celtic gods.

Despite the efforts of Artemidoros and Cominus's legionaries, the twenty-fifth of December came with no word of the missing women. Discouraged, I decided not to go to the Mithraic rites but Lucius convinced me that I might find usable clues in rumors the men might have heard.

As Mercurius drove us to the camp, I tried to recall what Marius had told me at Wermaros about this cult. "Lucius, what happens there? Marius said he would take me to a den, but not much else."

"What was his rank?"

"He didn't tell me."

"Mithraism is new in Italia except at Ostia and a few other ports. Cominus knows about the Persian cult because of his Asian service. I found out while serving in Bythnia."

I said, "I thought you were what you called a Stoic."

"There's no conflict. Stoicism doesn't have rituals and is too abstract for most legionaries. I joined to be part of the men. As Cominus said, there are no class distinctions among worshipers. Even a slave could become *Pater*, head of a den."

"Tell me about what I'll be seeing."

"The ritual is secret. Mithras is a mediator between men and the highest god that Persians identify with Helios, the sun. Some call the deity 'Truth' or 'Good,' but I'm not much on the cult's theology. For me Mithraism, like Stoicism, is a standard of conduct. Men universally desire what's right…or should…and the cult tries to center them in this."

"Are women admitted?"

"No. That's a limiting decision, yet women have their own secret cults of *Magna Mater* or *Kybele*. They're similar to the 'Earth Mother' you Celts worship."

After we reached the *Praetorium*, Cominus and Cyrenius led a group of legionaries along a wooded path that ended in a hilly region southwest of the Tarentum. Lucius explained to me that other members were at the Mithraeum, dressing for the ceremonies and ritual meal.

About a quarter mile from the hot springs we had seen from the tower, the men entered a villa that concealed an entrance to a natural underground cave, where the cult met. Inside, beyond the atrium, a reception room concealed a flight of stairs that led to a vesting chamber.

I followed the others down to a small anteroom where a white fabric covered the rock walls. An incense-like pine scent filled the air. Bright flames flickered in three tripod oil lamps. As my eyes adjusted to the wavering light, I made out a grotesque sculpted figure in the center of the room. A lion's head with a semi-human face was atop a four-winged, nude human body. An enormous serpent coiled around the torso until its head peered out from atop the lion's mane.

Lucius noted my reaction, the same that startled everyone who first saw the statue. "Kronos symbolizes infinite time. The four wings represent seasons. That serpent is the course of Helios during the year. Kronos holds two keys that open the sky to admit souls at the twin solstices."

I didn't understand everything. Beyond the statue was the red standard of a legion. Centered below the emblem of a green cedar tree, gold letters spelled out LEGIO III CYRIACVS. A sculpture of two male figures filled an opposite niche.

Lucius followed my gaze. "Those are Castor and Pollux, the gods whose temple you saw in the Forum. They symbolize the name of this Mithraeum, *Geminorum*."

As Lucius finished speaking, a group of men came from behind a partition. All wore short white tunics with belts of colored material. Several had put on animal masks. After Cyrenius handed Lucius a similar garment, he went to the vesting area. Left alone, I moved against a back wall of the anteroom to watch.

About thirty worshippers were present. On the right side, those wearing Raven masks assembled near the legion banner. Next to them, other members held an unlighted torch, crown, or lamp. On the left, men wore a curved cap and held jars or sickles. They aligned themselves next to a few participants in lion headpieces, who carried torches or jars. Lucius came out with Cyrenius: both wore gold crowns and held a lighted torch and wooden globe.

When Cominus entered the chamber, the air was heavy with incense fumes. The officer wore a long white tunic and held a golden sickle. Two attendants at his side brought a bowl and towels. After he stood before the Lion-headed statue to intone a prayer, I recalled he said his rank was *Pater* and imagined him as a kind of Arch-druid.

"Divinity," he intoned, "whom men call *Aion, Saeculum, Kronos, and Saturnus*, you create and destroy all things. You are master of the four elements that make up the cosmos, the eternal heat that shapes all things. We ask that you clothe us.

> *Help us put on the Lorica of Righteousness.*
> *The Helmet of Truth.*
> *The Belt of Perseverance.*
> *And the Sandals of Thankfulness.*"

At the next litany the men joined in.

Arm us with the Javelin of Moderation.
The Sword of Devotion.
And the Shield of Wisdom.
Permit Lord Mithras to be our intermediator with the great Sol Invicus. To him and to his servant, Mithras, we dedicate these rites.

The monotonic recital, fluttering lamp flames, and heavy incense smoke made me feel nauseous. My mind spun in dizzying circles. I had not understood all the words and watched as Cominus led the men from the anteroom into the temple. I walked in last.

I estimated the rectangular cave to be about thirty paces long. Lamps burned at intervals along the length. Colored draperies hung over bare walls. Overhead a blue-painted vault, speckled with yellow stars, arched over to stone benches on each side. Cushions were scattered on each bench and hollowed-out bowls gave off incense fumes.

Drowsy, I slumped on the nearest bench.

At the far end of the temple I made out an altar sculpted with the image of a man wearing a cloth cap. Astride a bull, he held a dagger in the act of sacrificing the animal.

After the procession of men formed on two sides, Cominus took a bowl and filled it with water from a well cut in the floor. He motioned for two attendants to accompany him and went to men wearing Raven masks. Cyrenius followed, holding a glass flagon and spoon.

Cominus faced the Ravens. "Initiates, what is your rank and sign?"

"My rank is Corax," the men replied in unison. "The sign is Messenger."

"What is your planet?"

"Mercurius."

After the officer splashed water on the initiate's hands, Cyrenius poured a yellowish liquid from his flagon into the spoon and onto their hands. He intoned, "May the water of *Terra Mater* and the urine of the sacrificial bull, along with purification by blood that you will receive prepare your bodies and minds for an eternal rebirth with Lord Mithras."

As the men dried their hands on towels, I realized that I had understood enough to know that Mithras offered the initiates the same kind of rebirth that druids promised our people. Cominus moved on, asking the same questions of the other members. When he reached the Lions, evidently one of the higher grades, his words changed.

"Leo, since your sign is Fire and unites you with the Unconquered Sun and Lord Mithras, your purification is not with extinguishing water, but with preserving honey."

He took the jar from the attendant and poured a measure of the sticky fluid into the men's palms, saying the preserving quality of the honey would be a cleansing agent. He resumed the ritual with those wearing soft cloth caps.

When the *Pater* came to Lucius, he repeated the water purification rite, then said, "Messenger of Helios, our *Sol Invicus*, whose birth we celebrate today along with the mystical coming of Lord Mithras, I ask you to bring the sacrificial bull to the *Taurobolium*."

I began to feel relaxed from the hallucinogenic smoke. Lucius walked to the altar's right side, then reappeared holding the golden tether of a small white bull.

Two Raven initiates had disrobed. I heard the creaking of iron hinges as a floor grating near the altar was lifted. The initiates descended a stairway inside a pit.

Cyrenius announced, "Ravens Aulus and Atrius will be purified in the blood of Taurus, then join us in the festival meal of bread and wine."

My pupils had dilated just as at our Samain celebrations where druidesses served drugged wine. *Abruptly, the dank cave felt oppressive. Sweat beaded my forehead. Nausea rose in my throat. I struggled to my feet and groped back through the curtain into the anteroom. Kronos leered at me and the serpent writhing around his legs seemed alive. I pushed past the entrance drape and bolted up stairs into the villa's atrium.*

Outdoor mid-day light was muted by clouds releasing a cold drizzle. Dark blotches spattered on paving. I turned my face to the rain and sucked moisture from my mustache. I sat on wet tiles until my nausea passed, then stumbled through the garden and outside. Shivering, glancing around to see where I was, I noticed steam rising from pools in the Tarentum a short distance away. *Warmth. I'll go there.*

At the pools pilgrims waited out the rain under covered pavilions. After a sulphur stench renewed my queasiness, I found a pine tree and sat underneath to chew fresh needles and relieve an impulse to retch. I closed my eyes and immediately dozed, until the shrill sound of a woman's laughter awakened me. A copper-haired girl came from the nearest bathhouse with a man, holding his arm and giggling at something he said. As they walked closer I recognized her companion and blurted his name, "Epanactos!"

Startled, the Arvernian looked toward me, then pushed the woman away and sprinted back to the bath. I tried to stand, but my legs felt numb. After massaging my calves I hobbled after him. From outside the bathhouse door I heard angry shouting. I pushed the twin portals inward to a room opaque with steam. Through the haze I saw men clustered at the far end of a circular pool.

Although I instinctively pulled back from a movement to my right, a blow caught me on the hand I raised: Epanactos had swung a wooden bench at my head. Despite pain, I gripped him around the neck, trying to lock onto my other arm above the wrist and choke him. In struggling to loosen my grip, Epanactos slipped on wet tiles and skidded with me into the pool. My head went under. I felt a warm liquid sucked into my nostrils, but the water was only waist deep. Coughing, I recovered my footing.

Epanactos was on his feet, face florid with rage. He lashed out with a fist and caught me on the mouth. The taste of blood mingled with sulphur-water as I struggled to grasp his long hair and wrench his head back. Then I felt myself pulled off him. Attendants also dragged Epanactos from the pool, but he shook them off and ran outside.

When I waded to the pool's edge to heave myself out and follow, two attendants pushed my head under water and held it there long enough to teach me the wisdom of not resisting any further.

༺༻

After a Tarentum physician bandaged my bruised hand, Sestius, a priest at the healing shrine, questioned me. He was sympathetic, but not much help.

"The Arvernian who attacked you has come here for about two moon phases, but from where I know not. A coarse creature."

I was desperate for information. "That girl with him. What do you know of her?"

"She seems a common *scorta,* a prostitute. Our healing springs attract the wealthy."

"That could be good."

"Good?" Sestius questioned.

"If she's a prostitute then someone here may know where her *lupenaria* is located." I touched my throbbing jaw. "Physician, can you send for my centurion friend at the *Mithraeum* and tell him what just happened?"

After being told of the attack, Lucius interrupted his ritual meal and arrived with Cyrenius. It took only similar answers from pool attendants to determine that the girl went by the name of Calypsa, and that she plied her trade at a tavern named AD MARTIS ET VENVS.

༺༻

That evening, when I went to the tavern with Lucius, slaves already had carried out the woman's body. Calypsa had been strangled with her own crimson breast-band.

⚘

"The Arvernian is no doubt responsible," Artemidoros stated, after he heard me tell of my chance meeting with Epanactos. "Emboldend by Dionysios, he quite likely boasted to the girl of an enormous ransom he would receive for freeing your mother and wife. Calypsa, you say?"

"Yes, that was her name."

"Our unfortunate Calypsa perhaps saw an opportunity to reap a reward by betraying the barbarian, yet he was the more clever of the two."

I said, "We received no ransom demand. Do you think Apsa and my mother are alive?"

"This Epanactos remains in the city...a good sign. If the women were dead he would have no reason to stay. You saw him at the Tarentum pools?"

"Coming from a bathhouse with the girl."

"The healing pools are popular yet I have observed that pilgrims avoid a nearby cavern area. Come"—Artemidoros beckoned me outdoors—"My terrace overlooks the *Martius*."

At a last row of apricot trees along a ridge, we looked down on a distant bend of the Tiber. Steam from the Tarentum pools clearly was visible as billowing white vapors in the cool air.

Artemidoros said, "That ancient 'Field of Fire' is seen as cursed. If Cato teaches that the door of taverns and brothels are entrances into the realm of Hades, many citizens believe that they are actually on the *Campus Martius*."

"You say there are caves there like the *Mithraeum* I saw?"

"A subterranean honeycomb..." He turned to me with a knowing smile. "*Kelt*, your mind has formed an image?" At my nod, he advised, "Do not ask shrine priests for information. Talk to pool attendants. Better yet, find two beggars who sit near the basilica entrance." He chuckled at his own wit. "I give you a *paradoxon*. 'Ask someone who is blind. That person will see what even a hawk might overlook'."

⚘

Two beggars at Tarentum known as *Didymoi*, "Twins," occupied a permanent station beside the basilica's entrance doors. They possibly were not even brothers, much less the twins their Greek nickname implied. The man called Alketos claimed to be blind. If the filmed-over eyes he turned skyward were any indication, he was truthful, yet no one bothered to check the extent of his affliction. His partner, Megakles, was lame. That beggar's only possession was a crudely fashioned crutch with which he supported himself while leaning against a brick wall by the door. The presence of both men embarrassed shrine priests—their afflictions made a poor recommendation for any healing power of the pools—yet the *Didymoi* were tolerated because they were known to be slightly mad and hence touched by a god. Megakles reinforced the illusion by periodically ranting in a gibberish that amused visitors. Alketos supplemented donations by telling fortunes; it was safe to predict that any wealthy Romans who visited the shrine would eventually inherit many more *sesterces*!

❧

Surrounded by a low wall, the Tarentum basilica faced a road along which visitors arrived by boat from the nearby Tiber. I scanned the yellow and red brick building, then walked into an entrance garden. Dry stalks of summer flowers drooped among green Cedars of Lebanon.

Megakles, the lame beggar, spotted me, gestured with his free arm, and called out, "Behold, the golden-haired Apollo comes! All-powerful god of the arts deign to sweeten our distress with your bounty!"

As Alketos rattled his alms cup, I smiled at their partnership and dropped a coin in the blind man's metal container.

He recognized the clink of silver. "A *denarius*! Indeed the generosity of a god. For such a sum, sir, I will predict good fortune for you. Sit in front of me, 'Odysseus of the Golden-Hair'."

I didn't know the person he mentioned, but squatted on the ground.

The blind beggar's fingers examined my head, feeling the skull shape and moving to my face. "Brother," he said to Megakles, "the youth has a noble head, a man born to lead." When he felt my mutilated ear he said, "'Golden hair,' you have known punishment and you are not Roman."

He puzzled me. "Being blind, how can you tell?"

"The scar is wrong for a battle injury and your hair is long." He lowered his voice. "For your generosity I will tell you how I know you are *Kelt*. The shape of your skull proclaims your origin as if written in stone. Brother, are his limbs sound?"

"So it seems, Brother."

"Then"—Alketos rattled the coin I had given him—"his *denarius* seeks more than a caress from my hands."

I said, "You again are correct. My...my wife and mother have been taken hostage. I need help in finding them."

"For ransom and you have not the money?"

"Another reason." I told the brothers about the conspiratorial visit to Vercingetorix, the women's abduction, my search with Lucius, and the discovery of Epanactos at the Tarentum baths.

Alketos was quiet until a group of pilgrims had passed by, then snickered, "Rustics from Neapolis. Their speech would betray them in the halls of Minos." He turned his face toward me. "'Golden-Hair,' three *Keltoi* with Latin accents worse than yours have passed by here for over a month. One was with a girl whose perfume spoke eloquently of her profession."

Excited at his description, I asked, "Did they mention two women named Apsa and Briga? Anything about their abduction?"

Alketos fell silent. His brother looked away. I thought they hesitated in a demand for more coins. "A...a gold *philippi* if I find them. The prostitute's client murdered her last night."

Megakles frowned. "Calypsa's destiny was to sell a healthy body while ours is to market infirmities. Vengeance is for the gods, 'Golden-Hair,' yet were I able to walk and my twin see, we would search caves in the *Martius*."

I was disappointed at his advice. "Caves? There are hundreds here! In what direction should I look?"

Alektos scoffed, "Did your druid uncle not teach you arcane wisdom?"

I was stunned. "How...how would you know Dividiac was a druid?"

The blind beggar gave me no answer. Megakles hopped back to his side of the doorway and cackled, "The caves, young Apollo. Search in the womb of Gaea."

Once Alketos made out the dim form of Alberix stand and walk out of the garden, he said, "Brother, I felt his neck torc. The nameless *Kelt* was a man of rank and I reasoned correctly that a druid priest would be in his family."

"The luck of Odysseus! Now, Brother, prophesy to *me*. Will this barbarian bring us his promised gold piece?"

Before Alketos could reply, Megakles spotted two fashionably dressed, obviously wealthy men, limping up the walk. "Zeus be praised, the Dioscuri approach!" he called out to them. "Hail, mighty Castor and Pollux! Health to the sons of Zeus and Leda!"

I headed back to question pool attendants at the sulphur baths. The *Martius* caves could wait.

The heat stifled breathing and a pervasive stench of sulphur was constant in the near-airless space of a small cavern. Dunamos crouched near an open-saucer oil lamp whose flame sputtered erratically. As the guard whittled birch wood into an animal shape, his recurrent cough echoed off the rock walls. Behind the Arvernian a low passageway led into the cave's mouth, but wooden beams outside sealed off the opening.

Apsa and Briga sat huddled at the far end of the cavern where lamp light barely reached them. Both women had on only the sleep tunics they wore when abducted.

"Ask him again," Apsa whispered. "We still don't know where we are."

"Warrior," Briga called out in Celtic. "What is it you want? Money? Gold?"

Dunamos coughed, spit aside and continued working his wood sculpture.

"He doesn't know," Apsa said, loud enough for him to hear. "His masters only trust him enough to watch over two weak females."

Risking the man's anger, Briga took up the badgering. "Why don't others take turns guarding us? Only a fool sealed here like a salamander would suffer rotten air with us."

"Sheath your tongues!" Dunamos snarled. He needed no further reminder of his low status in the eyes of Epanactos.

Caves had never frightened Apsa—they were the womb of the Earth Mother—yet this chamber of dark, odorous stone was a malevolent ulcer on the goddess's body. She knew that outer timbers blocked the entrance and were pulled aside whenever Epanactos or Trigvoros entered. If she could get past Dunamos while he dozed, there was no way to remove the barrier from inside. Even he had to wait for his companions to return with food, before stepping outside the cave to eat and breathe fresh air.

Apsa turned to count the scratched lines she made each mealtime on a wall next to her. They had been captives for six days.

When a noise at the entrance alerted Dunamos, he hurried to stand up. Faint dusk light entered the passageway with Trigvoros as he crawled into the cave chamber. Epanactos and a man the guard had met followed.

Natanius stood to brush dirt off his tunic and then faced Epanactos. "I tell you again that the garrison is at half strength, yet almost five hundred men could be searching for us. Even Trebonius has left Roma. It's time to free the two women."

"Free them?" Epanactos spat out in anger. "I'll stick the bitches and leave their corpses here to be gnawed by ferrets!"

"Like the fool you are, will you do it in the way you killed Calypsa? If that tavern-keeper who owned her spots you, even the Tullianum would be no protection from his revenge."

"Dunamos complained. "Me, I'm for getting back to Wermaros."

Briga heard and stood up to tell him, "Then you will return to ashes. Triccos set fire to the village and perished in the act."

"Woman, it's burned down?" Still enraged, Epanactos strode to Briga and slapped her face.

Natanius stepped between the two. "Enough! We came here to get Dunamos. I've secured funds and a barge downriver to Ostia. From there you three can make your way north to Gallia."

Red-faced, Epanactos pushed past the Judean. "First, I'll settle unfinished business with the slave bitch."

Natanius grasped the Arvernian's arm to hold him back and called to Trigvoros, "Tell your friends that all your skins together won't be worth a worn *sestercius* after they peel them off a furca."

"The Judean is right," Trigvoros said. "It's almost dark outside. Epanactos, let's get to that barge of his and leave here."

"Not until I gut this doe—"

As Epanactos unsheathed his dagger, Natanius seized the man from behind and swung him around. When both stumbled onto the oil lamp, the clay dish shattered, its flame sputtered out. Only a band of feeble twilight across the floor from outside gave light to the cavern.

Natanius shouted for the two women to lie on the ground at the back of the cave.

Once down, they heard scuffling, then a scream of pain. After sounds of a struggle and grunted oaths, a final scraping noise came from the passageway. One of their captors had escaped.

All was still before Natanius's hard breathing was heard in the dark. "*Dominae*, follow the…wall…on your left. Come around…to… the entrance."

When Briga groped for one of Apsa's hands it felt cold despite the cavern's heat. She eased her way along rough stone wall contours toward the glimmer of bluish light, then felt a dark figure reach for her.

Natanius had caught Briga's sleeve. "You'll have to…crawl out. The cave lowers into… into that passageway. *Mahair*…quickly! Go now!"

A chill wind penetrated Briga's thin tunic, yet she was grateful to be outside. A moment later Apsa and Natanius scrambled from the opening. All three knelt among the scrub growth and dark branches of a stand of pines that concealed the cave's entrance.

"Dunamos got out and escaped." Natanius wiped blood from the thin blade of his knife onto grass. "Walk toward those lights at the Tarentum. None of your captors would go in that direction."

"What of Epanactos and Trigvoros?"

Natanius shrugged his shoulders in uncertainty while he sheathed the knife. "Perhaps not dead, only wounded."

"Are you going back in to make sure?"

"I will not."

Briga stood up, anxious to get away from the cave. Apsa hesitated. "There... there was another man whose nose had been shattered. Will he look for us?"

"Contundo?" Natanius shook his head. "This was a simple assignment for him and he was well paid. I wouldn't be concerned."

Who *are* you?" Briga asked. "We...we owe you our lives."

"*Domina,* at Roma it is never prudent to ask a stranger's name. That arouses suspicion concerning your reason. May your gods protect you both." Natanius stood and disappeared into darkness beyond the trees.

After Briga took Apsa's arm to walk in the direction of the baths, she abruptly realized why the young woman fearfully had asked about their other abductor: both Contundo and Silanus were cast from the same brutal mold.

After the two exhausted women stumbled into the basilica, shrine priests alerted Cominus at the *Martius* camp. Soon after, a runner arrived at the villa of Artemidoros with the favorable news.

CHAPTER XVII

Apsa sat up in bed, insisting that she wanted to prepare breakfast, but I told her to rest a while longer and recover from her week of fear.

She sniffed an arm. "The bath did help. I've almost soaked off the smell of that horrible cave."

We watched Ger play on the floor with a toy wagon filled with acorns. He laughed when I spilled them out and then put them in again, one by one.

Apsa said, "While I was gone, Elpence sent Vestia over to take care of Ger. I'm grateful." She patted her stomach. "And our child I'm carrying also is well."

"Good, but where is this cave where Epanactos kept you and Briga? If he isn't dead, I'll kill him myself."

She seemed disappointed at my anger, as much for its intensity and lack of control. "We're safe, Alberix. If anything, Ersa's murder is a greater hurt than my brief capture."

"Where is this cave?" I persisted.

"So you would murder Epanactos if you could? What of all your talk of Romani justice?"

"This is a Celtic affair."

"Yet you joined Caesar because you thought his way of justice was better than the unending quarrels among our clans. Now you want revenge like any other warrior! I was in that cave with your mother, not you. Don't you agree with us that if Epanactos is alive. a magistrate must punish him?"

Frustrated, I shouted, "I don't know!"

"Lucius could tell us—"

"Lucius! Lucius! Apsa, Roma's cohorts couldn't locate you. It took a blind beggar to tell me where to look."

"Did you find us? No. We owe our lives to a Judean fortune-hunter."

Stung by her response, I muttered, "I...I would have found you. Eventually—"

"After we both were dead? Husband, it's only because of Natanius that I'm alive to argue with you..." At the thought, tears glistened in Apsa's eyes.

I realized how senseless it was that we quarreled. I went to sit next to her on the bed and kiss away tears. In a moment we were both laughing. I said, "Later on, I want the full story of how you and my mother were abducted. Apsa, while you were away I thought about our time in Roma. Let's get out of the city. By now Lucius should be ready to go to his parents' farm. Abellinum, is that what he said?"

"Yes..."Apsa wiped her eyes with the back of a hand. "Certainly, *I'm* ready to leave."

I held her hand against my cheek. "But I don't want to stay at Abellinum on someone else's land. I would like to go back to the Renos *now* and not wait for senators to authorize a colony. Who knows what Germani or renegade Gallic warriors are doing along the river?"

"Didn't the fighting end at Alesia?"

"That would depend on how many men those chiefs who didn't submit to Caesar can recruit. Our campaign season starts next month."

"The thought of you leaving to fight again is frightening. You're an armorer. Can't you serve in another way? Please ask Lucius for advice."

"All right, Apsa. We're going to Artemidoros's villa to celebrate your return with a supper. I'll talk to him there."

❧❧

Artemidorus had invited Antistius to examine the condition of the two abducted women. At the meal the physician prescribed a cathartic to rid their bodies of an overbalance of sulphur, and suggested an interval by the sea to increase the balance of clean Air in their blood.

"*Centurio*, if you're going to Abellinum, also visit Salernum." Antistius turned to tell Apsa, "At least a month by the sea, young woman! The primal elements of Air, Earth, Fire, and Water influence the body's four Humors."

She told Alberix, "I could collect sea shells to take back for crafters at Arialbinnum...if that Raurici town still stands."

I didn't want to postpone scouting to find out, but Antistius continued, "Salernum has a Hellenic influence that is quite stimulating, wouldn't you say, Artemidoros?"

"I agree. Its origin was a Greek colony with nearby Posidonia and settled far before Romulus and Remus crawled about suckling she-wolves."

The Physician chuckled. "As a Roman I might take offense if I didn't admire Greek learning so much. I read in Eristratos that—"

"Physician, the meal is light," Elpence interrupted with a forced smile. "Let us keep conversation that way. Lucius, when are you planning to leave Roma?"

"As soon as I receive the balance of my discharge stipend..." He clasped Briga's hand. "I have an appointment with the *Praetor* on the day after the Januarius *Nones*."

Elpence wondered, "Alberix, will you like farm work? I understand that you were raised as a crafter."

"I'm thinking of going back to the Renos." I noticed Briga's puzzled look and explained, "I've told you I want to visit the site where Father was building his new village."

"What can you do alone?"

Lucius told her, "He may not be alone. I've recommended that site as a location for a veteran's colony."

Antistius cautioned, "*Centurio*, at this time not many senators are willing to legislate anything favorable to Caesar."

"Favorable to the Republic, then? That would be a location fortified by a garrison of veterans keeping vigilant eyes on trans-rhenus Germani marauders."

"Put that way," the physician conceded, "your proposal might convince Senators. No salaries to pay and if you *can* recruit veterans willing to go north, I do have a few influential clients among my patients."

Lucius said, "Cominus could post an announcement at the *Martius* camp, yet it might take a year for arrangements to be completed."

"I'm not waiting a year!" I loudly objected. "Can't you get me assigned as a scout to report on the location and get me there sooner?"

Briga said in a voice of hope, "Alberix, you might like Abellons,"

Lucius corrected her with an indulgent chuckle. "*Cara*, that's Abellinum."

Apsa thought Artemidoros might help. "Sir, perhaps you could ask for Caesar's support with my husband's colony when you write him."

"Indeed, we want no Germanic Brennos attacking Roma this time."

When everyone laughed at the absurd thought of barbarians ever threatening the Eternal City, I wondered what our druids might predict.

By the time I finished Vestia's sweet course of honey cakes and cooked apricots, Apsa had persuaded me to stay at Abellinum until our child was born, sometime before the midsummer solstice. Artemidoros agreed to promote the desirability of settling veterans on the Rhenus frontier to Caesar. The physician offered to muster support from his senatorial clients for land grants to one hundred veterans and their families.

When Lucius received the bulk of his savings and a discharge stipend for twenty-seven years of military service, the combined sums were large enough— over 100,000 *sesterces*—to qualify him for the Equestrian class. Petronius

Cominus congratulated him in a brief ceremony and presented the centurion with a copper plaque engraved with his name, rank and record.

Lucius bought a heavy wagon and two mules to haul our belongings. We left for Abellinum on the *Agonalia*, a festival Lucius said honored Janus, the two-faced god who ushered in a new year by looking at past and present. I thought the occasion symbolic and appropriate.

❦

Abellinum, a veteran's colony established on the Sabatus River by Cornelius Sulla, some thirty years earlier, had prospered. Rich farmland laid out in rectangles around the settlement produced harvests that were sold as far as the coastal towns of Selenium and Surrentum. Dried fruit and wine were carted to Neapolis. The gentle rise of Mons Vesuvius, eighteen miles southwest of the town, served as a guide for peasants taking their produce to Herculaneum, Pompeii, and Neceria.

Since one of Cominus's legionaries would travel to Salernum, Lucius hired him as a teamster. He wanted a stop at Praeneste to visit the sanctuary of Fortuna. Since the goddess had so favored his military career, he left a donation with shrine priests in his name and that of Julius Caesar.

In the morning the families continued on the Via Latina, planning overnight stops at Frusino, Aquinum, Cales and Capua. The latter town had not completely recovered from devastation brought by an ill-advised alliance with Hannibal, a Carthaginian invader.

Leaving Capua on the Via Annia, Lucius pointed to the tile roofs of Abellinum as they appeared in the hazy distance of early evening

Lucomo Velcanius, the father of Lucius, and his mother, Tanaquila, tearfully greeted a son they had not seen in eight years. After hearing reports of the Roman defeat at Gergovia, both had worried they might never see Lucius again. The elderly couple welcomed Apsa, Briga and me with more than polite warmth.

Velcanius ancestors were Etruscan people displaced by Roman expansion. Lucomo recalled stories about the uncertainties of their exile. If he changed his son's given name of "Luceres" to the Latinized "Lucius," he never forgot that his forefathers might once have been kings of Etruria.

❦

During a welcoming meal on the afternoon following their arrival, Lucius gave Briga the gold betrothal ring he bought in Roma. The family served as witnesses. Over Lucomo's vintage Falernian wine, the wedding date was set four days after the Kalends of Februarius. Tanaquila said it was the festival of

Concordia, the patroness of familial harmony. This gave Briga about seventeen days to familiarize herself with her strange new surroundings.

❧❧

In consideration of their differing Roman and Celtic marriage customs, Lucius suggested a modified Roman ceremony. Briga would wear a traditional bridal tunic held around the waist by a knotted cord. Tanaquila offered her a saffron-colored cloak to put on over the tunic. Wisely, Lucius did not have Briga wear a customary metal collar that symbolized her subservient status as a female. She in turn dispensed with pads of artificial hair and arranged hers in the loose tumble that Lucius favored. From her future sister-in-kin Briga received a veil she had worn at her own wedding: the orange silk *flammeus* would be a headpiece and covering for an upper part of the bride's face. A wreath of woven marjoram stems from Tanaquila's garden held the scarf in place.

❧❧

On the day of the ceremony, a priest came from the Temple of Ceres accompanied at Tanaquila's insistence by an aged Etruscan *haruspex*, to determine if the auspices were favorable. The diviner pronounced that all were *Mat*. After Lucius's affirmation as groom, Briga repeated her own marriage vow, using her new Roman name of Briga Quinta Velcania. The couple offered wheat cakes to Ceres.

A nuptial banquet amid many libations to Mercurius and Martius as thanks for Lucius's safe return lasted until evening. Lucomo and Tanaquila proudly presented their son and his wife to their guests. Lucius's mother dedicated a few furtive splashes of wine to the fertility goddess, Prosperpina, daughter to Ceres.

After the meal and drinking guests omitted a customary raucous procession of escorting the bride and groom to their bedchamber. Nor did Lucius honor tradition by lifting Briga over the threshold. He did explain that it forecast poor luck if she should stumble, yet felt it prudent not to tell a Celtic bride that the custom commemorated the forceful taking of Sabine girls during Roma's early history.

Although both were exhausted, the couple made love with a quiet intensity that celebrated their long-postponed union. While her husband slept, Briga lay awake for a longer while. She felt secure in a white stucco farmhouse protected in a countryside that had not known war for two generations. She thought of Alrix's holdings, where her son wanted to go. Surely, the fields had been abandoned. Wars disrupted oral land purchase agreements or destroyed written ones. Whatever ownership documents Dividiac possessed at Wermaros had burned in the fire. Now her son wanted to reclaim land as devastated and lawless as after a clan wars. If he tried to take his inheritance as son of a chieftain, squatters would challenge his right—men who only conceded that the swiftest sword decided tenure. After his child came, could she convince Alberix to settle here?

Toward morning Briga fell asleep, holding tight to Lucius and trying to understand how the Wheel of her destiny had rolled into an alien place named Abellons.

❧❧

After inpecting property in the area around the village, Lucius bought an abandoned villa on the slope of *Mons Virgo*. When Briga objected to owning slaves he hired freedmen to restore the vineyard and cropland, then determined to organize the farm as efficiently as he had his legionaries. Lucius confided to his new wife that he eventually wanted to run for the office of magistrate in the community.

Briga planned to set up a loom and teach village girls how to weave the intricate Celtic patterns that were popular among well-placed Romani women.

Alberix's and Apsa's second child was born four days before the *Eidus* of Junius, a green-eyed girl with a touch of copper-red in her hair. To the disbelief of Ger they called her Salia. He thought it strange that so small a person should be named after the broad expanse of a willow tree. Apsa explained that the *salia* was one of eight Noble Trees sacred to Celts.

Lucius took me to Abellinum's basilica and observed the *duovirii–aediles* and *quaestors* that governed the town with a council of citizens. I would need these governing skills in my plan to rebuild a settlement. Lucius commented that if the local advocates' arguments in legal disputes were not up to the oratorical standards of a Cicero or Cato, they were less cynical and more honest. Justice usually was satisfied in verdicts.

❧❧

Early summer passed while carpenters, masons, and plaster workers renovated Lucius's villa under his supervision. Field hands plowed weed-overgrown land to prepare for next year's plantings. Vines were pruned and manured according to Lucomo's instructions. He took a previous owner's wine-making equipment out of the pressing shed to clean and repair. I estimated work would be done by the Lugnasad, our harvest festival, but failed to foretell the arrival of a legion comrade. Marcus Marius came to the farm on the Kalends of Quintilis, the fifth month of a Roman year. After he rode into Abellinum with a group of merchants from Neapolis, townspeople directed him to the villa of "*The Centurio.*"

"I sooner would have expected Lugos," I jested as we sat under a laurel tree, sipping Falernian. "I last saw you at Alesia."

"And Moira..." In recalling the druidess's gruesome death, Marius glanced away at distant hills. "I...I expected to stay in Gallia all of next winter. Our victory at Alesia didn't end the war and *Provincia* is threatened again." He handed me a rumpled manuscript. "I came from Cenabum to give you this message from Caesar. It also has orders for me."

"Caesar? Let me call Apsa to hear what the commander says. Will you read it so I don't get anything wrong?"

Marius gave me a comradely slap on the back. "Of course."

With my wife settled under the tree nursing Salia, Marius loosened the Imperator's wax seal with his dagger. Caesar writes, 'I dictate this in haste to Hirtius after learning that renegades under Lucterios invaded Narbonensis. Caninus and Fabius tracked them to the *oppidum* of Uxellodorum. I shall join my legates there as soon as I set a punishment for Gutatus the Carnute. My men apprehended him this afternoon'."

"Gutatus?" I recalled the name. "He ordered that massacre of Roman merchants at Cenabum that began the sedition. What happened to him?"

"Punishment was quite ugly. Caesar writes that he was forced to agree when tribunes insisted on flogging and beheading the man."

"Go on with the message."

"'But it is not concerning military matters that I write. I have received Lucius's report about an attempt to free Vercingetorix and endanger my command in Gallia. I would prefer to believe that Pompeius knew nothing of the matter.'

"'The following and a sealed document will interest Alberix. I authorized the formation of a Gallic legion, *Alaudae*...the 'Larks'...with recruits drawn from Arvernian nobility. After the men receive citizenship I shall designate the unit *Legio V Alaudae*. I learned that the crested lark is a popular bird totem on Gallic war standards, yet the word also can mean 'Great.' Why not enlist such a symbol in our service'?"

I remarked, "How would my Dividiac and Cluvios feel about Caesar's decision?"

"I hope they might see it as an honor. Let me continue. 'I find interest in Alberix's plan to scout the former Rhenus territory of his tribe for a veteran's land grant. We spoke of such settlements when I spent a winter in his Jurassos village. Titus Labienus reports the Sequani pacified, thus it would be advantageous to establish colonies on Helvetii land. I approve. Alberix must visit Aventia, or Aventicum, as I am instructing my chart makers to label the old Helvetii capital. Let him report to me on progress the tribe has made in resettling their old lands. I also favor the Lake of the Allobroges for veteran colonies—the sheer beauty of the mountainous countryside invites it. I will name a town there *Julia Equestris* in honor of my beloved daughter, Julia. The enclosed documents will give substance to Alberix's search'."

Marius whistled in surprise after he read the first line on the parchment. "Alberix! Congratulations! Listen to this. 'One. A diploma of Roman citizenship to Alberix, his wife, and heirs. I franchised the entire *Cisalpina*, so why not a single Celt if it benefits the success of his mission and that of Roma'?"

I flushed at news that was as if a new spoke of my Wheel had been put into place.

Marius continued, "He mentions me. 'Two. Authorization for Marcus Marius, *Optio Fabrum*, to accompany Alberix and recruit a *contubernium* of skilled legionaries, metal workers, carpenters, metal drainage experts, et cetera, for preliminary land exploration and surveys'." Marius looked up. "I'm to go with you! How exciting to build up rather than destroy."

"What else does the commander say? There's another section."

"'Three. Authorization for Marcus Marius to deliver a copy of my will at the House of the Vestals for safekeeping. Let the *Pontifex Maximus* witness the seal'." Marius unfolded a final letter with instructions written on the front. "Caesar wants this message delivered to the villa of Artemidoros."

"When we stayed with him he mentioned that Caesar was a friend. What does the commander say?"

"It isn't sealed, so... 'Greetings to Antistius. My *epilepsia* seems better. I shall reach forty-nine years in Quintilis and begin to feel the strain of campaigning. My command ends in a year, yet I intend to run for the consulship'." Marius held up the note. "This last section is for Artemidoros. Let me just skim Caesar's closing paragraph. 'Times such as these...I leave for a campaign in unknown country... long for the quiet of your *Akademia*. When I am again consul I shall call on you for advice, knowing it will be given as honestly as it will be wise. Greeting to Elpenice. G. Julius Caesar.'"

Apsa turned Salia up to burp her against a shoulder. "Lucius will be pleased about your citizenship, Alberix."

"He once wanted to adopt me."

Marius said, "And it seems that I'm off to Roma before joining you. Caesar chose me because I traveled to Vesontio with Labienus and the Ninth and Fifteenth. You'd left with the guard detail taking Vercingetorix to Roma."

"I didn't misunderstand, did I? We *are* going to the Renos?"

Marius waved the parchment. "It's right here. Caesar claims that twelve thousand Sequani fought on the Arvernian side, but that seems far too high. At Vesontio, Labienus called together local chieftains and ordered them to take an oath of loyalty."

I recalled my first dangerous visit with Simonides. "What is Vesontio like now?"

"Doing poorly since trade with the Rhodanus is only a trickle of what it was before."

"Marius, do you remember where the Arar and Rhodanus rivers come together? We camped on that triangle of land while trailing the Helvetii. Wouldn't that be a strategic place to build an *oppidum* and town?"

He chuckled at what he would propose. "That citizenship diploma already has you thinking like a Roman! I'd reached the same conclusion but here we're talking about the Rhenus frontier."

"I know. *Cara*"—I hoped Apsa would agree—"if I left with Marius, I could come back for the winter. You could return to the Renos with us in the spring when Salia is older." When Apsa said nothing, I knew she felt others once again made decisions for her. "Marius, where can you get eight skilled men to return with you? Roma's garrison is loyal to Pompeius."

The engineer thought a moment. "Labienus is with the Fifteenth at Ravenna. I could ask him to send men to meet us at Aventicum."

I noticed Apsa's tense patting of Salia's back and reassured her. "There's little danger in the trip."

Marius told her with scant conviction, "None at all, *Domina*."

Apsa replied, "Salia and Ger will keep me occupied until the snows. Just come back as soon as you can." She stood up to add in a cool tone, "It's time for Salia's nap."

After Apsa was out of hearing, Marius remarked, "It's hard to please a woman, so that's why I never married. About your route. With Caesar's authorization you should easily get a patrol galley from Neapolis up to Genova. The *Cisalpina* wasn't touched by the war and I have a new map of the Genevris Pass and on to Aventicum."

I hardly glanced at his chart; my thoughts were about going back to the Renos and take up my father's unfinished task.

The next morning I ordered a hand copy of my citizenship and authorization scrolls, then Marius and I estimated travel times. He would leave Roma and take the same route to Genova and then Aventicum.

CHAPTER XVIII

With incredible good fortune, Marcus and I arrived at the old Helvetii capital within a few days of each other! A cohort of legion engineers with building and foundry specialists—also Arverni slaves—had begun the construction of a Roman town lower down than the *oppidum* had been. On Caesar's orders, alpine towns were rebuilt without stone ramparts. While material was hauled from destroyed lodges and circling walls, engineers surveyed an urban plan with rectangular street blocks and a central forum. Plans we saw eventually included a theatre, arena, and temple dedicated to the goddess Aventia.

Farmland in the area was under cultivation. Fields reaped by an ingenious Celtic harvesting machine, the mule-powered *vallus*, lay as ochre stubble around rebuilt villages in the north and in the direction of the Allobroge Lake. Former warriors, whose battered shields and iron spears lay rusting in siege-works or hung as trophies in Roman temples, now strung nets in the Tigurini lakes to trap metallic-hued fish. The Gallic defeat at Alesia was not yet a year past: perhaps the underwater silvery flashes recalled the metallic glint of legionary javelins and swords, as these fishermen waited for a catch and pondered the defeat of their native clans.

Following the four-day Lugnasad harvest festival, Marius and I left Aventicum with an eight-man legionary contingent that Titus Labienus sent to join us.

On the way to the Renos I guided the column of legionaries on horseback along a route Cadurcos had shown me seven years earlier. Around the tenth hour that first day, at the pass that marked a fork to the road above Wermaros, Marius ordered a fortified camp built for the night. With the palisade begun, he went with me to the site of the razed Sequani village. I wondered if local herdsmen had rebuilt the lodges. Almost a year earlier I had watched Wermaros burn, but was unprepared for the shock I felt on seeing its ruins. Inside blackened remnants of the palisade, a tangle of grasses and scrub bushes overgrew village paths and gardens. Roof and wall beams had collapsed into rooms of lodges, filling them so completely that I had trouble locating our forge shop.

The bridge over the Dubis stood, and the river road showed usage, but in returning to the Earth Mother Wermaros swarmed with field creatures burrowing into room cavities. Ravens strutted among the ruins, searching out rotting carrion. The black birds cawed protests at our intrusion and flapped off to the forest. I watched their flight, then reined my horse onto the trail that veered toward *Castor*.

Marius followed me to the watchtower. The vacant structure stood, but its high entry door, torn loose, left a gap that Marius said resembled a cyclopean eye staring out. In the river, buffeted by the current, Liscos's millwheel had heeled over. The spokes and rim showing above the water resembled a gigantic pendant of Taranis.

We followed the road that wound westward along the waterway. When I spotted four men setting fish traps and called to them, they scrambled for stacked spears. "Bare your shoulder," I told Marius, then shouted, "We come in peace. I lived at Wermaros."

An oldster recognized me. "It's the crafter's nephew! He went with Romani at the start of the war."

I cantered my horse toward them. "Where are the villagers now? I rescued my mother and aunt after Triccos set fire to their lodge."

"It wasn't the druid," a man scoffed. "Taranis fought the sorcerers and destroyed Wermaros with his sky fire."

"There was no magic. Triccos was responsible," I said, then recognized him. "You're Catuso the carpenter. Where do you live now?"

He pointed upriver. "Near *Benn Belenos*. Not many of us are left here."

Marius understood the Celtic name. "'Mountain of the Sun.' At least it's not called after a war god."

I asked, "May we return with you to tell about the Gallic peace and help you resettle?"

"Caburos can go with you. I must tend a kiddle trap in the river."

A younger man beckoned us along a dirt trail. We walked our mounts and arrived at a settlement of mud-and-wattle huts built there because of a curse they believed lain on Wermaros. I recognized Marulos, one of Lisco's oldest vassals. Now head of the small community, he invited us to eat at his hut with several advisors.

During the meal Marius and I explained how a new peace could bring the prosperity of the Narbonensis to Gallia, including his Jurasassos Mountains. Marulos understood: he had gone to Vesontio with Liscos and seen products shipped north from *Provincia*. When I asked about Arialbinnum, the chieftain's anger surfaced. Germani warriors had taken advantage of the Helvetii migration to encroach on lands southeast of the Renos. A feared mass invasion of warriors had not occured, but Marulos raised an awkward point when he reminded Marius that Germanic cavalry had fought with Caesar against Gallic warriors. They also would want land grants as rewards. At that point I urged the villagers to look beyond the present and cited Caesar's reputation for mercy toward conquered tribes. Titus Labienus had impressed the Sequani by appointing a Gallic over-chief at Vesontio. As before, the tribe was self-governing, yet protected from predatory raids by neighboring clans as happened in the past.

We brought our eight legionaries to *Benn Belenos* and stayed in the village through Samain. Marius explained Romani administration: taxes would be less than former tribute paid to Ariovistos, and local chieftains would collect them. Legions stationed along the northern stretch of the Renos would keep Germani on their side of the river. Tribal territories would be self-governing within a framework of civil and legal codes.

The plan was lofty, with some of it from Marius's imagination, yet the overview pleased the elders. Marulos was amazed that Romani raised a Celtic legion called *Alaudae*—no tribal chieftain would allow former enemies to reassemble under arms!

⁕

After Samain the name of Julius Caesar was coupled with that of Lugos of the Long Hand. Bards revived epic songs of a past Age of Heroes, with hopes that it would return to Gallia.

I declined an invitation to stay the winter, because I was anxious to visit Arialbinnum. Since the site of my settlement was to the east of the town, I wanted see how much devastation had been inflicted on the area. Marius agreed: reporting an unproductive journey would risk the censure of a commander whose passwords were "swiftness" and "surprise." By a throw of dice, four legionaries were to stay and secure this village until spring; the other four came with Marius and me. Caburos, eager for adventure, rather than harsh life in a village, offered to guide us.

⁕

Marius recorded that on the day before the *Nones* of November we left for the Renos. Caburos retook the Delsa road to Arialbinnum, a reversal of the frantic escape our family had made on that long-off night eight years ago, when my father was killed and his village torched.

Delsa was being rebuilt after being burned when villagers joined the ill-fated Helvetii migration. We found Bireg abandoned. That was where Dividiac's divination had set my destiny toward Wermaros. After a group of passing hunters near the Renos told us that a small band of Germani had crossed to the Raurici side of the river, Caburos took a forest trail that circled into the mountains. We found a vacant woodcutter's hut and spent the night without a fire to avoid alerting them.

In the morning our guide pointed out a stream that flowed north and then west, to empty into the Renos at the site of my projected colony. As we rode to explore the waterway, a light snow fell. We tethered our horses and hid behind the crest of a rise that sloped down to the river.

Caburos pointed toward a clearing with several huts and a horse enclosure along the whitened riverbank. "Germani, probably Harudes or Suebi, but they only winter here."

I said, "While waiting for spring to raid up-valley."

"Marulos was correct," Marius recalled. "They'll take what they want of Celtic lands, yet wait until warmer weather to do so."

"I want them out *now*," I insisted—to muffled laughter from our legionaries.

"Now?" Marius questioned. "Alberix, our mission is to report what we observe. Go down there at this time and you'll freeze your scrotum off waiting to be ransomed!"

"You're saying I'd be captured?"

"Assuredly, and I doubt they would even bother with ransom demands. You'd simply be sacrificed to Germani winter gods."

Unconvinced, I said to him, "Marius, you're the engineer. Figure out how to get those squatters to leave."

Caburos said nothing. The Romani muttered about my sanity.

Marius reconsidered. "How...how many do you think there are?"

"That flimsy palisade can't hold more than ten...fifteen...horses."

He sucked in a breath at my estimate. "Men, let's go back to that hut and persuade this lunatic to change his mind. The poor weather will keep Germani inside today and seven of us aren't going to frighten them away."

His remark gave me an idea. "What did you say?"

"We don't have even a *contuburnum* of eight men here."

"No, I mean about frightening away those squatters."

Marius could be sarcastic. "*Amicus*, those are warriors down there, not milk maids."

I turned back to the guide. "Caburos, do you know about those forest demons that villagers mimic at their mid-winter festivals?"

His eyebrows rose at my question. "After bonfires are lighted on the solstice, they costume themselves in evergreen branches and wear animal masks."

"Exactly, and Germani have a reputation for being superstitious. I saw that myself when I was taken to one of their villages."

Caburos grinned. "I'm quite good at making those solstice outfits."

"We'll just frighten them to death?" Marius snorted. "Is that it, Alberix?"

"I don't want the Germani dead, just forced out so they can pass word around that there's a *geis*, a curse, on this place."

By the time we returned to the woodcutter's hut I had persuaded the legionaries that our ruse could be successful. I went out with Marius and two crossbows I had brought along, to bring back the heads of deer and boar.

Caburos showed the men how to cut pine and holly boughs, then fashion them into giant figures twice as tall as a man. Grotesque masks were made of bark and pinecones. After draping the greenery over their mounts, the bulky coverings made the animals unrecognizable as horses.

Marius and I returned in early afternoon with two boar heads and one of a stag. The men skinned the heads, stuffed them with moss, and fixed them atop three of the evergreen horse-monsters.

I was satisfied with the demonic creatures. "Now, Marius, for tactics. I must convince their sentries that I've been attacked by something from their Other-World, a supernatural being. You've just shot animals with a crossbow."

"It's a small hand catapult."

"With a range of about forty paces. Let's quietly lead our horses to the far edge of these woods and find a spot above the squatters."

A legionary asked, "Then what?"

"I'll explain as we go along."

☙ ❧

It was late afternoon after everyone understood the plan and was in place.

From an edge of the forest I watched two sentries at the gate of the horse pen stamp their feet and speak to each other, probably cursing the frigid weather. Snow stopped falling but ground fog formed in the early twilight. Darkness would come quickly.

I looked toward Caburos, hidden under a branch-demon atop his horse. Similarly disguised, Marius and the four legionaries waited near him. Even our two packhorses were fitted with the grotesque body shapes of giant forest demons.

"I'll be down there, talking to those sentries," I repeated to the men. "Marius will circle around with his crossbow to just inside the woods. Your signal is when he drops one of the guards. Ride out shouting what you Romani called our 'Celtic furor'. If that doesn't panic the Germani to their horses, turn back. I'll chances getting away."

"Arduinna be with you," Caburos invoked, evergreens muffling his voice.

I unsheathed my knife to slash at the neck of my tunic and my mutilated ear lobe. The wound was shallow, but blood stained my jacket. I sheathed the blade and began a run down the slope toward the two guards.

Tudros glanced at the foggy edge of the darkening woods and saw a figure stumble out of the line of trees. He shouted to his comrades about a possible attack. Both guards brought up their spears: the tunic and neck of the man staggering toward them was covered in blood. As the stranger fell at their fee, screaming Germanic words, other warriors came out of their huts to see what happened.

Tudros told them, "He speaks in our tongue, yet his mind has fled his body."

I hoped I was correct in assuming that these men were assigned this isolated duty because they were less than the cleverest warriors among their chieftain's tribe. I brought my voice under control and babbled more of what I remembered in their language. "Waldgott!...Teufel...angry! One devil took my head in his jaws...see ear. They can kill by a look!"

Tudros and his companions scanned the forest edge. "What...what do these demons want here?"

"This place is cursed. *Geis!* Did you not see signs of destruction?"

"We found half-burned posts. Used them for the horse pen—"

"Aieeee!" I screamed. You have desecrated their sacred ground!" *I hope my voice is heard by Caburos up the slope. Why hasn't Marius dropped anyone yet?"*

I still cringed on the ground, but at my cry, a knot-haired Harude, taller than the others, came out of the largest hut's door.

"You listen to a fool!" their leader shouted, kicking snow-covered dirt at me. "The only curse here is the cold. Tudros! Drag him inside! Even an empty mind has hands to carry firewood and melt stream ice into water."

In the moment that Tudros bent to force me up, his head burst in a gush of crimson blood. His body pitched forward to redden the trampled slush with gore. I pointed toward the forest and let out my unearthly scream again. "Aieeee! *Waldteufel* come to kill you!"

In the murky light eight massive figures emerged from the forest—darkened silhouettes that loomed twice the size of horses and riders. The forest creatures' eerie bellows sounded as supernatural as their appearance.

The Harude warriors stood immobilized by fear while their leader tried to grasp the nature of the apparitions: one demon was a stag, the totem of Cernunnos, Celtic lord of the dead. Two demons had the heads of Mocchus, their enemy's boar god. The others were Tree Spirits of fir and holly.

My anxiety increased as the apparitions came closer and I thought our ruse would be uncovered. I screamed for the hesitating warriors to escape on their horses then tried to think of something to further panic them. Marius did that for me.

Their skeptical leader gurgled a death rattle as a wound that ripped his chest gushed blood and his lifeless body twisted down to further redden the snow.

The Harude squatters had seen enough. With bawls of terror, they tore at the animal pen's gate latch, scrambled inside, and leaped atop the first horse they found. Outside, the warriors rode their mounts in a frantic effort to reach the Renos. Once there, they forced the animals into the raging current and swim toward Germania. Those not swept past Arialbinnum clambered out over rime ice on their side of the river and disappeared into the vastness of a black forest.

Marius trembled when he ran up to me. "I couldn't get a clear shot until that barbarian bent down. I hadn't much used a crossbow before."

The legionaries laughed as they shook off branches and dismounted. All wanted to hang the two dead Germani on the fencing as a warning, but I ordered the bodies cremated on a funeral pyre made of the rotting palisade stakes.

⚬⚬

That winter a wild story of Celtic sorcerer-gods, who killed with their look, circulated around Harude campfires. Germani clan chiefs ordered that land within a half-day's ride from the river be forbidden as cursed territory. A few warriors doubted the tale and ventured to the river's north bank to gaze across.

Standing in line, eight immense forest demons stared back at them over the swirling water of the Renos and into Germania.

CHAPTER XIX

I later found that by the time we had reached the Renos, a siege of Uxellodunum was successfully completed—a last encounter between remnants of Vercingetorix's warriors and our legions. Lucterios and Drappes were captured. In the north, Labienus pacified the Treveri.

Before entering winter quarters, Julius Caesar ended the campaign season by taking two legions to secure Aquitania. Afterward, he set out for the Narbonensis and distributed rewards to community leaders that supported him during the rebellion.

Legates dispersed their legions among the Belgae, Aedui, Turones, and Lemovices, thus the cold season found virtually all of Gallia garrisoned by Roman legionaries.

Soon after, Commius the Atrebate surrendered to Marcus Antonius, effectively ending Celtic tribal resistance.

෴

At Roma, on the *Eidus* of Januarius, Claudius Marcellus and Lucius Paulus took office as consuls for the coming year. Marcellus opposed Caesar. Paulus accepted a "gift" of 1500 talents, ostensibly to continue work on his Basilica Aemilia. In Februarius, the tribune, Gaius Curio, found his debts conveniently dissolved and as quickly became Caesar's agent in the Senate—just in time to veto legislation that would deprive his patron of the Gallic command. Senators reacted to a Parthian threat against Syria by ordering both Pompeius and Caesar to release one of their legions for Asian service.

Pompeius's counselors advised him to recall Legio I; he had loaned the unit to Caesar after the commander's Fourteenth was lost in an ambush. That legion and one of the commander's own would deprive Julius Caesar of two legions. As happened, instead of being sent to Parthia, the combined force stayed in Italia under Pompeius's command.

Supporters of the Imperator were alarmed when senators refused to extend his Gallic tenure. Further opposition occurred when consuls-elect for the following year were Cornelius Lentulus and a cousin of Marcellus—both implacable enemies of Caesar.

෴

After the festival of Belenos word reached Abellinum that Senators had not acted on the proposal to charter a Renos colony.

Lucius entered his name in the town's magistrate elections, but a summer vote by the entrenched administration defeated him. Bribery and a slandering campaign to discredit the centurion's "Roman-ness"—because he had a Celtic wife—seemed the reason for his failure to win office.

During the last four months of the year, every traveler from Roma spread rumors of the unrest at the capital. A letter of Artemidoros to Lucius detailed its gravity.

> *Roma III d. a. Nonae Januarius*
>
> *Artemidoros greets you, Lucius Velcanius.*
>
> *I several times intended to begin this message to you, but ever since Caesar crossed into Gallia Cispalina last November the situation here has worsened day to day. Now Pompeius is alarmed, the Senatus fearful, and Marcellus and Lentulus call for the commander's skin at every session. Curio's veto and those of his successor, Marcus Antonius, so far saved our friend's position, but the intransigence of tribuni makes a mockery of the power of Senatus and Republic.*
>
> *Aulus Hirtius, now Caesar's emissary, arrived here on the day after the Nones of December to meet with old Scipio, Pompeius's father-in-law. Yet Hirtius left the same night, which Pompeius did not see as an act of reconciliation. A few days later Cicero, met with Pompeius and wrote to me that the proconsul thinks civil war is inevitable. Cicero has broken with Caesar over his attempts to thwart the Senators, as well as over a series of abuses he condoned among his officers.*
>
> *Have reports reached you that the Senatus recently voted Pompeius the command of all legions in Italia? This entire deadly business seems to be unfolding like a drama by Aeschylus, once more proving his contention that it is evil in mankind, not envy of gods, that destroys human relationships.*
>
> *VI dd. A Eidus Januarius*
>
> *Today Roma was as tense as I have seen it. Scipio proposed that Caesar be declared Enemy of the Republic if he fails to relinquish his Gallic command. Antonius and Cassius attempted a veto but were expelled from the Curia. They left for Ravenna disguised as slaves. The tragedy is that Pompeius and Caesar would accept Cicero's compromise: both men could keep their provinces and two legions. Naturalists attribute the status of events to Earth, Air, Fire, and Water and these forces now surface. A thin trickle of Water, the River Rubicon, separates Romans from civil war resulting in Fired cities and Earthen funeral mounds, yet all depend on the same Air to sustain life. Remember me to Briga and Apsa, whose children must be growing like wildflowers in spring meadows.*

❧

On the festival of the Carmentalis, the eleventh day of Januarius, Julius Caesar crossed that thin trickle of the Rubicon, using Legion XIII as a spearhead into Italy. Titus Labienus, who had been with him from the time of the Helvetii migration, and to whom Caesar gave much credit for his Gallic successes, broke ranks over the illegal invasion, then moved his legions south to link up with Pompeius.

Arriving from Gallia, Caesar's legions encountered little resistance down the Adriatic coast: municipalities opened their gates to the legendary conqueror.

❧

Over a year later, no action had been taken on my Renos colony, so I returned to *Benn Belenos* with Apsa and the children. Another letter from Artemidoros summarized the dangerous situation.

Roma Kalendae Decembris AVC DCCIV

Artemidoros of Cnidos to Alberix, son of Alrix.

I trust your village is still at peace; we hear no reports of unrest in Gallia, even though legions are largely withdrawn and serving with Caesar. Perhaps news from Italia is as scarce as the few reports we receive from beyond the Alps, yet surely word of the commander's success in Hispania has reached you. This came after his failure to prevent Pompeius from sailing to Macedonia with thirty thousand men and most of our Senators. Even Cicero was hopeful that the Imperator could detain him and force peace between them. It was not to be.

Caesar visited Roma between Martius and Aprilis just before leaving to rally the Republic's legions in Hispania. I say 'Republic,' yet even Cicero realizes that form of government is dead. The man was in a quandary all spring: he owes his pardon to Pompeius, but since his son-in-law is with Caesar, also wishes to be his friend. Caesar left for Hispania and routed the Pompeiians in a campaign of only forty days. In the elections of Sextius, Publius Servilius and Caesar were voted consuls for the next year. The following month, the commander felt he had enough legions to attack Pompeius and sailed for Macedonia. Yet the Republicans had nearly a year to consolidate their forces, which resulted in a stand-off at the port of Dyrrhachium. The Saturnalia will be subdued this year. Families who were the best of friends avoid each other because their sons serve on opposite sides. Valerius Catallus, my poet friend, anticipated these days when he wrote:

'Men lost, perplexed, in frantic search for the correct road,
The battle of wits, the wars to be foremost,
Eternal strife, night and day,
To climb toward heights of riches and power.'
My greetings and those of my household to you, Apsa, and the children.

The disaster at Dyrrhachium prompted Caesar to turn inland, toward Thessaly. Pompeius followed, then yielded to the demands of senators in his camp and planned an attack. Near Pharsalus, 69,000 legionaries—22.000 of which were Caesar's men—faced each other in the greatest battle yet fought by Roman against Roman. Caesar skillfully directed his smaller force to route Pompeius's inexperienced men. As his camp was stormed, Pompeius escaped to the sea. The following day, 169 republican cohort standards and nine legion Eagles were brought to Caesar.

Pursued by his nemesis, Pompeius saw the cities of Asia turn against him. He sought to find refuge in Egypt with the boy-king, Ptolemy, whose father he once had supported. The king's advisors, fearful that Pompeius might try to usurp Ptolemy's throne, murdered and decapitated the Roman on an Egyptian beach.

Marcus Cicero, disenchanted at the proscriptions of exile or death drawn up for Pompeius's enemies, returned to Italia. Marcus Antonius, appointed Caesar's second-in-command, allowed Cicero to live at Brindisium, but not enter Roma. In a letter, he complained to Artemidoros.

Brindisium Saturnalia   AVC DCCV

My dearest friend Artemidoros, I hasten to send you a personal Saturnalia greeting and ask how I may return to Roma. I would be grateful if you wrote to Caesar on my my behalf. Some think he still craves my support and whatever prestige may yet accrue to me. I believed my actions were for the good of our Republic. I regret the ignominious death of Pompeius Magnus and suppose you have heard of how Egyptian palace eunuchs, a paid dispenser of rhetoric, and an opportunist, decided his fate. Septimus, who once held a centurion's command under Pompeius, performed the actual beheading.

Julius Caesar is Master now, even appointed Dictator II in absentia. I understand he remains at Alexandria, quelling some trouble or other, but please see what you can do to get me out of this Apuelian cesspool, where the stink of fish markets is more than I can bear. M. Tullius Cicero

Julius Caesar defeated Egyptian forces that tried to expel him from the country, then dallied in the company of the twenty-two-year-old Cleopatra until December.

A year later he moved into Africa to rout a republican army at Thapsus. On his return, Caesar commissioned the astronomer Sosigenes of Alexandria to bring the current calendar months into synchronization with the seasonal length of a solar year. When he added eighty days to the end of December, Caesar proclaimed the New Year to begin on the Kalends of Januarius.

In Martius, the commander thwarted a final attempt by republican armies to regroup in Hispania; his eight legions defeated thirteen of the enemy's. Titus Labienus lost his life in *Hispanis Baetica*, along with one of Pompeius's two sons. Caesar returned to Rome in Quintilis, to prepare for the Triumphs that events always had postponed.

Lucius would describe for me the first of three Triumphs that took place that autumn.

Abellinum Kalendae Octoberis

Lucius to Alberix and his family at Benn Belenos.

Caesar's triumphs are a few days past and perhaps Roma will never see the like again. Many are asking how a Roman can celebrate victory over other Romans. Briga refused to come with me, but I had to attend. It was a September morning, somewhat cool, yet quite pleasant. A month earlier agents posted notices for veteran tribuni and centuriones to assemble at Caesar's expense and share a victory banquet on twenty-two thousand dining couches! The first day was for Gallic victories with the procession to assemble at Pompeius's theater. I decided not to march with veterani and found a spot up the Aventinus where I had a good view of the route. The marchers came through the Porta Carmentalis, then along the Via Triumphalis:first the veterani, then slaves carrying Gallic treasure on litters decorated with evergreen garlands. Marchers held signs that listed Caesar's accomplishments for the crowd to cheer, and cheer they did! Thirty major battles. Eight hundred towns taken. Three hundred tribes subdued. Bucina and cornua players helped marchers keep step. In front of Caesar, litters carried Gallic prisoners. I saw Lucterios. Vercingetorix stood above the others, although I would not have recognized him from his bearded face. Actors prancing around the prisoners portrayed the Rhenus and Rhodanus Rivers in captivity—even Oceanus was fettered!

At the procession's end, Caesar in a full-purple imperial toga, drove a chariot with four magnificent white horses. Every person at Roma was a spectator and cheering must have reverberated as far west as Ostia! At the Circus Maximus the veterani turned to enter the Via Sacra. Caesar's Basilica Julia is almost completed and a new forum north of the Subura is under construction at his expense. I did not come down to see a sacrifice at the Temple of Jupiter O.P., but heard that Vercingetorix and the other Gallic prisoners were strangled afterward in the Tullianum.

What I have described, Alberix, must seem quite unfeeling in view of your origins. My intention was to shock you and restore my own equilibrium. I mean this: despite the civil war being almost ended, and with it danger to the Republic, Caesar again was appointed Dictator for the third time. In the past our Senatus occasionally gave one man such power in a term of six months. Caesar abuses the office and most senators do not object. I tell this because of the respect we have for the law. If you worship a goddess again, make her Justicia.

I could not in good conscience remain for the celebration of Caesar's other triumphs over Egypt, where his paramour, Cleopatra, watched from a discreet pavilion with their son Caesarion. Nor over Pontus, and Juba the African, since Caecilius Scipio, lost that latter war. Before Caesar returned there was talk of plots against him. I dismissed that as the gossip of market idlers, yet a few men of quality who sense the Republic will not be restored, might be involved. I visited Artemidoros. Caesar confided to him that one of his legion commanders, Muniatus Plancus, is in line for the governorship of Gallia. The proposed veteran's colony at the Rhodanus-Arar confluence and on the Rhenus, will be his first responsibility! I close that good news with greetings from your mother and my parents. Valete. Vivat Res Publica!

❧❧

Julius Caesars's reform of the calendar gave him an additional eighty days of life, before conspirators acted to end his dictatorship. Artemidoros described the bloody *Eidus* of Martius in a letter to me at *Benn Belenos*.

Roma XVI d. ante K. Aprilis

Artemidoros greets you, Alberix.

By now you have heard of Caesar's murder, yet I know you will want details, even truth. Since you were one of his few honest followers, I relate what transpired. 'The Dictator's goddess finally jilted her lover.' Thus I might say, if I thought deities cared about men. In truth, the gods had nothing to do with it, yet what men believe or pretend to encouraged Caesar's enemies. I understand he had decided not to go to the Curia on the day of his murder because of nightmares related by his wife, Calpurnia. Much of this is the beginnings of legends. Gossip is out concerning the days preceding the death. Citizens now recall strange lights and noises in the heavens. Vultures perching in the Forum. The appearance of men with alarming bodies. Even Caesar's victim of a routine sacrifice is reported to have lacked a heart. I suspect Cassius bribed old Spurinna to predict danger on the Eidus, knowing that Caesar's pride would make him openly ignore her warning. Cassius made sure he was heard scoffing at the poor omens and urging Caesar to do likewise. That very morning, I received confirmation of the conspiracy from a colleague of Marcus Brutus—names, place, everything about the plot. I wrote down information, intending to rush the message to Caesar. Once I learned that he left for the senatorial meeting, I was able to intercept him near the Carmentalis—even press the papyrus into his hand. Yet I was only one of many in the crowd. He took me for another petitioner and never read my warning.

Once inside the Curia that Pompeius rebuilt, petitioners continued to surround Caesar. Brutus Albinus kept Antonius outside the building with a contrived conversation while the conspirators struck. Servilius Casca first stabbed Caesar, then the others in turn to share guilt. Lastly, Marcus Brutus thrust into his "friend" with a sword. All was such confusion that it is said the conspirators even injured themselves. Caesar fell at the base of Pompeius's statue and died there. When Antistius examined the body, my physician recorded twenty-three stab wounds. Brutus attempted to give an oration justifying the deed, but senators panicked and ran out. Soon, shopkeepers on the Holitorium closed shutters. No citizen knew what to expect next, yet the rest of the day passed quietly. Marcus Antonius quickly understood that power lay with the conspirators and gave a speech recommending Brutus and Cassius for provincial governorships. He was in turn praised for averting another civil war. But next day, when Caesar's body was carried into the Forum, Antonius saw how the citizenry reacted to a reading of his will—each man was given LXXV drachmas and Caesar made his new gardens a public refuge—he incited the mob to a fury. They looted Forum shops of furniture to throw on the funeral pyre.

When ablaze, the crowd lighted torches from it and set out to burn the villas of Cassius, Brutus, Casca, and others involved. The conspirators fled Roma. Antonius is in power and seized all of Caesar's correspondence and plans. Young Octavianus, grand-nephew and heir-designate of the Imperator, is on his way here from Apollonia. The boy is not yet nineteen. Is another lamb about to be thrown to the wolves? May it be a false rumor, but the Senatus fears that after Gallic tribes learn that their conqueror is dead, all will revolt. Munitius Plancus, hopefully, is strong enough to quiet any unrest and follow through with the charter for your colony. I am confident that senators now

> *will ratify most of Caesar's proposed legislation.*
>
> *With sadness, my greetings to Apsa and the children.*

❧

I read the letter with disbelief, yet recalled that Vercingetorix had predicted such an event and on that date! The myth of Caesar's invincibility is such that many Celts still hold that Lugos had dipped the man in his magic Cauldron of Immortality. I wanted to keep informed about legislation that affected my colony, and so wrote back to Artemidoros the next day. Before the letter reached Roma, a message from L. Muniatus Plancus came, ordering me to arrive at the site of his new veterans' Renos settlement no later than the *Kalendae Maius*. I still was saddened over Caesar's murder, yet over-celebrated that evening!

Sextius, 44 B.C.E. — Sextius 43 B.C.E.

Those in Gallia-of-the-Long Hair have drunk bravely of death.
Is the icy winter past?
Listen: a lark from the yellow-tufted bough sends forth its call!

CHAPTER XX

Lucius Muniatus Plancus, sweat-stained and tired, jested to his middle-aged companion, Decimus Aelius Agrippa, "I would give half of Gallia, Decimus, for a good soak in a bathhouse *caldarium!*"

The senator barely listened. Agrippa had mused for too long about how his future might depend on a friendship between his nephew, Marcus Vipsanius, and Gaius Octavianus, the nominal heir of the dead Gaius Julius Caesar. Both youths were eighteen years old.

Agrippa ended the speculation. "Do you think this Octavianus will claim his inheritance? Marcus Antonius does have vast military and governing experience."

A weary Plancus shrugged uncertainty. "Marcus Cicero supports Octavianus and so do your fellow senators."

"Governor," Plancus's aide interrupted. "Will you bathe in that stream before supper?"

The water undoubtedly was colder than that of a *frigidarium*, but Plancus saw a chance get away from Agrippa. "I would prefer something warmer, less exposed, but yes. See you at the mess tent, Decimus."

As Agrippa watched the governor stride down the hill to the water, he felt a mixture of jealousy and fear. Under Caesar, Muniatus Plancus had commanded a legion since early in the Gallic war, then been given the Narbonensis Province as a reward. Now he was commissioned to establish three veteran's colonies—one here on the Rhenus, one at the Rhodanus-Arar Confluence, and another on a shore of the Allobroge Lake. Agrippa wanted to live at the Confluence colony in Gallia, yet the best Vispanius had done was the Rhenus colony. Marcus Antonius had had enough audacity to criticize him for not more openly supporting Julius Caesar during the civil war.

The approach of the site engineer and his Gallic assistant cut short Agrippa's brooding. He could not recall either man's name.

"*Salutatio*, Senator," Marcus Marius called out. "Alberix and I have completed marking the wall perimeters."

Agrippa slighted his work. "At least two months late, *Optio*."

Neither Marius nor I responded to his taunt. Caesar's murder had delayed every facet of his legislation.

The senator went on to complain, "By the time we are able to watch Plautus in the theater, his jests will be more sour than the wine here."

Marius remained optimistic. "Senator, by the first snowfall we'll have the main street surveyed and substantial lodges built on about twelve blocks. You can wager that our veterans will make themselves comfortable for the winter."

"What did that man say?" a woman's shrill voice demanded. Agrippa's wife appeared at the opening of a tent next to the *praetorium*. "What did you say?" Faustina Agrippa repeated to Marius.

"*Domina*, we will have log homes for the winter."

Faustina turned to her husband. "Decimus, I will not stay the cold season among these barbarians. We *must* travel back to Roma."

He again impatiently reminded her, "You know I can't risk someone else running for *duovir*. That position is why I'm here. We...we need to save *sesterces*."

I felt uneasy. The senator and his wife had joined us at Viennadunum, and then complained about conditions all the way to the Rhenus. Now he talked about governing the colony.

I nudged Marius to one side. "*Duovir?* What does he mean?"

"You know about municipal government...two magistrates, two aediles—"

"I understand that much, but what is Agrippa going to do?"

"He'll help govern the colony with whoever is elected with him."

"Marius, I want a say in it. I'm the reason we're even here in the first place. What if I talk to Plancus?"

The engineer guided me by the arm into the street, out of hearing. "Alberix, Caesar *was* your patron and he's dead. All you have now is citizenship, yet that gives you the right to be elected as one of the *duoviri*. Agrippa will make every attempt to buy the office."

"Won't men vote for the best candidate?"

"You mean one who promises them the most! The senator knows all the sewer-muck political tricks. He's here and flirting with Octavianus through his nephew..." Marius grasped my shoulders to look me in the eye. "Alberix, I *will* help you run against him."

"*Grates.* This is different from tribal elections and I'll need help." I looked away across the river, toward Germania. "Marius, I've heard that Raurici are rebuilding at Arialbinnum. I'd like to see what's happening there and speak to the *vergobret*."

"Not difficult. Take a few *auxilia* cavalry and go observe for yourself."

"No, I mean alone. I could see more that way."

"Then leave a *Decurion* in charge here. Things are quiet."

I agreed with him. My intention was to see if the over-chief at Arialbinnum might be willing to coordinate defense plans against Germani with those of our colony.

❧

Several days earlier Pupianus, a priest-augur, had sacrificed a pheasant found on the forum site and pronounced its liver healthy. With that favorable omen, the oldest legionary veteran present hitched a white bull and cow to a plow and cut an irregular furrow that marked out the colony's limits. Two understrength centuries totaling about ninety men from Legio VI began erecting a ditch-and-wall fortification around the high ground, where the first blocks of houses and shops would be located. Closer to the Rhenus, veterans still lived in temporary wattle-and-mud huts. Cavalry *auxiliae* members had pitched tents a short distance downriver. A number of older discharged legionaries had braved late winter cold and moved onto the site earlier to choose homesteads and clear land.

Munatius Plancus chose the Junius *Eidus* to call a meeting that ratified land claims and set up voting procedures for electing the colony's council and officers. The date marked important festivals, the *Matralia* honored single or married woman, and the goddess Fortuna, favorite of the governor's former commander, Julius Caesar.

A platform built next to the praetorian tent displayed the *curulis sella*, a magistrate's chair of office. Nearby, a white banner caught the wind. The legion's men decided to name their unit. Apsa embroidered a Wolf-and Twins design above centered letters.

LEGIO VI

FERRATA FIDELIS CONSTANS

Plancus opened the meeting with a speech about Romanizing the area. His *quaestor*, Lucius Baebius, read a roster of citizens whose property qualifications made them eligible for office. Decimus Agrippa topped a list of several candidates. Reminding them that the colony was under military law, until a civil charter was issued, Plancus listed his building priorities—a paved forum, temple to Jupiter, and a basilica and curia that would house government offices.

The governor had decided he could not go as far as his Narbonensis Province for the winter and prepared to leave for Viennadunum. There he would be close to the proposed Gallic administrative center and in a better position to cope with any uprising that Cicero continued to predict after Caesar's murder.

Plancus put Baebius in charge of the colony as acting *Praefect*, and ordered cavalry patrols sent out each day, even authorizing them to cross the Rhenus to harass overly curious Germani and keep the barbarians off balance. Marius thought the provocation foolish.

A day after the *Matralia*, the governor left the nascent settlement he called COLONIA MVNATIA RAVRICORVM. My tribe's name was included with his—or, I should say, "after his."

❧

On the following morning, I rode into Arialbinnum, about eight miles to the west. Many younger Raurici men had been killed in the war, but a few oldsters probably recalled my father and his visionary ideas about tribal co-existence. If some resented that it was a Roman-imposed peace, not a *Pax Celtica*, I would urge them to accept reality and cooperate together against hostile tribes.

❧

On the north bank of the river, Latobrigi, Sugambri and renegade Suebi warriors, looked across to watch the settlement grow. It was land they feared, because forest demons had cursed that stretch of river. They laughed and waited for malevolent *Waldteufel* spirits to destroy the newcomers. Yet the tribesmen saw the magic animal and forest totems burned without harm coming to either Celts or Romani. Their newly planted fields turned lush with what spies reported to be barley and wheat. The Germani observed that men living in huts were gray-haired and wondered about them—even as younger men built a palisade in the legionary manner on a height above the river. Tents a short distance away housed horse-mercenaries that were in the Shorthairs' service.

Reports came to Germania that other Romani far away to the south wasted their warriors fighting against each other, that their roads ran as deep with blood as the streams of Germania. All that winter a rumor about the death of the demi-god, Tiwaz-Caesar, circulated, even in remote forest settlements.

❧

Gurther of the Suebi saw his chance to do what the demons had not done. His wife, Frieda, encouraged him try anything that would kill Romani—and especially *Kelten*.

In the last days of the Roman month of Quintilis, Gurther's warriors reported that the harvest was complete. The gray-haired men joined their slaves to finish gathering crops before autumn rains arrived. Many baskets of grain were stored in huts along the river.

Gurther convinced a hundred warriors that a raid carried out with the speed of Tiwaz's fire bolts would bring a reward of storage pits filled with winter food. The Suebi knew something of the Romani from the time that Ogerth, Frieda's father, had hired a renegade centurion in a failed attempt to train his warriors in the Shorthairs' battle tactics. A *Kelt* hostage who came with the centurion promised to help Frieda leave a dung-village she hated. He had deceived her and escaped alone.

A mile to the east, in Germania, Gurther had rafts built for transporting his horsemen to the Raurici side of the river. He planned to glide them ashore on the night of a full moon, land a bit upstream of the settlement, and in the first light of dawn attack the huts.

❧

As his bobbing craft angled toward the south bank, Gurther inhaled a reassuring smell of earth and grass, mingling with those of the river and his warriors' horses. He glanced at the darkened sky, hoping he correctly judged the speed of the current. He planned for horsemen to land out of sight, and then have foot warriors pole their rafts along the shore until they reached the settlement. They should arrive at the same time that his horse warriors surprised and attacked the Gray-hairs, and moved slaves onto the rafts. He had repeatedly told his men about the need for swiftness; they must be crossing back into Germania before the hilltop garrison was alerted and rallied to oppose them.

Although Frieda had dressed in a man's trousers and jacket, she shivered in dank pre-dawn mist. By moonlight, Gurther noticed her discomfort. Because of the others he did not slip an arm around his wife to solace her. "*Gute,* Frieda. Only a sound of the river," he whispered as the raft swept toward a dark line of trees on shore.

She was intent on the raid and recalled a larger settlement down-stream, where the river turned north from its course. "Will we attack a *Kelten* village at the bend?"

"Arialbinnum? *Nein.* Another time. If this goes well more Latobrigi will join us."

Gurther braced himself as the raft lurched into the bank, then looked back across a dark waterway sparkling with moonbeams. Angling toward shore, ten rafts each transported five horses and riders. Four other craft carried foot warriors and would haul supplies back to the north bank. He felt proud that he had organized his quarrelsome tribesmen into a compact fighting force.

By a setting full moon, warriors quietly led their horses ashore. Gurther thought it almost too bright, yet the light helped him line up men as they had rehearsed. The first group would attack the cavalry camp. Others would follow him and break into the huts, massacre the Gray-hairs, and take slaves and supplies. As important, fifteen archers stationed themselves at the stream below the upper palisade. These bowmen would surprise and repel attempts by the garrison to relieve farmers and herdsmen. By the time the Shorthairs had rallied to mount a counterattack, his warriors would be re-crossing the river, poling their plunder back to Germania.

The raid went as planned. Slashing into tents of the horse *auxiliae*, Suebi warriors killed many who came out and left others entangled in downed leather tent covers. As supply rafts appeared in the growing light, the horse pen was breached and its animals brought out to be herded aboard.

Torched huts blazed as half-awake veterans stumbled outside to be cut down by long-swords. Slaves were beaten toward the river under an orange glare of fires and the first blinding rays of sunrise.

The wild yells of the raiders awakened Lucius Baebius at the same time as his aide rushed into the praetorian tent.

"Sir," he shouted, "a raid on the veterans' huts and *auxiliae*!"

"Raid?" Baebius questioned. "By Gallic renegades?"

"Horse warriors, Sir, from what I can make out."

"Signal the garrison...*cornuae*. For...form them up," Baebius stammered. This was his first command in a battle situation.

Even before the trumpet warning, garrison legionaries grasping short-swords were outside their tents in night tunics and without helmets or shields.

Baebius shouted to Fleginas, one of his tribunes, "Where is the furcing *primopilus*?"

"Sir, there is no First Centurion. These are guards and construction cohorts...mostly engineers."

"Then...then get the men armed and...and down the hill!" he screamed, climbing a ladder to the rampart walkway. "Get them out of the furcing palisade!"

Fleginas rallied several legionaries at a gate to the Via Cardo, but a flight of arrows felled three men among those who burst through the open portals. Their bodies rolled down the bluff into the stream below.

Wild yells sounded from the Germani bowmen. Marius heard the clamor and hurried from his tent to climb the ramparts. In a nearby tent Apsa awakened and ran to join him.

Most of the huts along the shore burned, their smoke drifting eastward to mask the sun. At the river, warriors tried to goad horses and mules onto the rafts. One tipped, sending animals and men thrashing into the water.

Baebius saw Marius. "*Optio*, you...you're a line officer! Wh...what do we do?"

Marius pulled Apsa down behind the stakes before he could answer: a second flight of arrows arced toward the palisade and scattered legionaries attempting to form a battle line outside the gate. A few had thrown javelins but their weapons fell short of the massed archers.

After Marius told Apsa to stay down, he realized his men carried no shields. He yelled for them to go back for them. A few who had anticipated the command held the wood protection up against a new volley from the bowmen.

"Apsa, get back to your hut," Marius ordered. "Barricade the door."

"I'm staying here to help the wounded."

"The furc' you are...down the ladder, woman. Follow my order!"

Marius came down behind her and sprinted toward the gate, shouting, "You men there! Testudo formation to dismantle palisade stakes where the hill isn't as steep. At my order, lock shields and charge the enemy flank."

Below, the archers watched in puzzlement as the barrier was torn down, then shifted nervously as a line of rectangular red shields appeared in the gap. None had yet confronted a legion formation.

Every even-numbered legionary in an eight-man squad held a shield above his head to protect companions that pulled away fencing. A new volley of arrows were harmlessly embedded in curved wood or angled off a shield's bronze *umbo*.

Renewed shouting came from the hilltop: When a line of vertical shields rippled down the slope, a command from the Latobrigi chieftain loosed another hail of arrows. The wooden wall never wavered. A glint of iron javelin points, bobbing above bronze helmets, became visible as the Romani came closer. Behind, a second line of shields formed on the hilltop. The horses of mounted archers reacted to nervous leg pressure and shied in confusion.

The line of shields stopped twelve paces from the Latobrigi. Javelins were aligned, paused a moment, then thrown forward in a glittering arc that tore into human and horse flesh. Mingled screams of pain and panicked neighing reached Marius before the wall moved forward again. After a scattering of arrows opened gaps in the line, a new rank of legionaries moved in to fill the breach. When a second line paused to level javelins, several archers dismounted and sprinted for the river.

Gurther perspired despite a chill morning breeze. Another raft had capsized. Captured horses nervously milled around, panicked by the fires and shouting.

"Leave the animals," he yelled to warriors. "Take supplies and slaves."

When Gurther saw Gray-hairs who survived form a defensive square and swing farm tools or weapons at their attackers, he realized they were former legionaries, not farmers. He noticed his wife viciously stabbing at every fallen enemy she could find.

"Frieda!" he called, running to her. "*Kommen!* Get on a raft." He pulled at her sword arm but she jerked free in rage.

A few mounted archers rode in, yelling as they pointed toward scarlet rectangles bobbing over the ground toward them—more Romani than Gurther had seen before. Realizing his enemy had regrouped, he shouted to the archers, "Break through the Shorthairs with your horses! Scatter them..." Then he paused to listen: the rhythmic sound of men's voices repeated a name.

"Caesar! Caesar! Caesar! Caesar!"

Marius, near the stream, heard the chant. The swelling chorus grew louder until even the Germani recognized the hated name: Shorthair warriors were calling on the ghost of their dead commander. Inhabited by his spirit, they became supernatural beings. Their shields were red, not by dye, but with the blood of slaughtered victims. A frightened Sugambri sub-chief shouted a retreat order to his men, then urged his horse aboard a raft. His bodyguards clattered their mounts on behind him.

"*Nein! Nein!*" Gurther screamed. "Your horses can break through legion formations! *Angriefen!* Attack!"

The legionaries reached the south edge of the burning huts and moved between them toward the river, stabbing at Germani with short swords. Suebi who had dismounted to help carry baskets onto the rafts, faced around without weapons. The lead swordsmen thrust them back into bloodied river shallows.

As Frieda slashed wildly at a shield, she felt the chill slide of a blade through her tunic. The Suebi woman fell back with a fire-like searing pain beneath her right breast. Staring in disbelief at a bloody wound, Frieda felt numbing cold throughout her body, before darkness clouded her consciousness.

Gurther saw his wife fall and ran to hack savagely at the shield-bearer: slivers of wood and metal flew from the edges. The assailant tripped backward. Without pausing, tears blinded Gunther as he chopped at a closing red circle before he was beaten to unconsciousness by the rim of a shield.

With their leader down, the last of his Suebi clambered aboard over-loaded rafts. Some pushed wounded men from other tribes into the river and saved companions. The rafts were poled into a swift current that set them gyrating downriver toward Arialbinnum. Slaves jumped off and swam back to shore. Many were Germani, yet life as a slave among *Kelten* was preferable to a savage existence they remembered in dank holdings inside the dark forests of Germania.

◦◦◦

I returned from Arialbinnum just before high sun that day, shocked at the sight of smoldering ruins and legion burial details lining up corpses beneath trees. Others dug two massive graves in field stubble. After I crossed a pontoon bridge over the stream, three legionary guards stopped me. I knew Scaeva, one of them.

Concerned, I asked him, "What...what happened?"

In answer he unsheathed his sword. "Alberix, *Decurio* of the *Auxilia?*"

"You know me, Scaeva. What went on here?"

"In the name of Lucius Baebius, Acting Commander of *Colonia Munatia Rauricorum,* I place you under arrest."

"Arrest? On what charges?"

His order was brusque. "Dismount, *Decurio*. These two guards will place you in confinement."

CHAPTER XXI

Marius stormed into the praetorian tent. Lucius Baebius and Decimus Agrippa looked up from a papyrus both were studying. "What are the charges against Alberix?" he demanded, realizing he sounded angrier than he should with them.

"Easy, *Optio*," Baebius warned. "Calm your tone or I'll have you tried for insubordination."

Marius took a deep breath. "Sir, I just want to know the accusation against Alberix. He wasn't even here during the raid."

Baebius glanced at the papyrus. "That's one of the indictments. 'Desertion of duty'."

"Desertion? He went to Arialbinnum to see about arranging a mutual defense treaty between the town and our settlement."

"He admits that, yet we believe he also alerted Germani. They attacked the day he returned."

"He was gone less than a month."

"A moot point, *Optio*. They needed time to take advantage of his treachery."

"Alberix is Celtic. What would he gain from doing that?"

Agrippa toyed with a sleeve of his toga. "Perhaps he went to conspire with his Raurici brothers who survived the war."

Marius ignored him. "Again, *Praefect*, what would be his motive for doing so?"

"*Optio*, that will be brought out at trial." Baebius stood to end the session, but added, "Senator Agrippa and I believe that Raurici take advantage of our civil unrest at Roma to sharpen their swords for more sedition. The proceedings will be day after tomorrow."

Marius struggled to hold in rage. "Sir, I'll represent him, but...one day to prepare a defense? I need to talk with Alberix."

"As you wish. He's held in one of the lodges and confined under guard for his own safety. In the Germani raid *veterani* and the legion lost fifteen from their units. The *auxilae* suffered serious casualties..." Baebius let Marius to draw his own conclusions and handed him the papyrus. "You're dismissed."

"But, Sir—"

"Dismissed, *Optio*!"

Apsa waited outside the *praetorium* for the officer to come out and ran to him. "Marius, what is happening? Why is my husband kept under guard?"

He took her arm to respond, "Alberix will be tried before a military tribunal. I'm going to see him now. Come with me. Where are your children?"

"With Alpina."

"Your new Helvetii servant. Good, this shouldn't take long."

At the lodge, Marius explained to guards about his assignment to defend Alberix. Knowing both him and Apsa, they saluted, and moved aside.

It was stifling inside a small room without furnishings. While Marius slid open twin window shutters, I embraced Apsa and sat on the floor with her.

Marius squatted in front of us with the papyrus. "Friend, you're accused of sedition for having a part in that Germani raid."

"Sedition? I see Agrippa's nose in this. I'm opposing him in the elections."

"I've thought of that, but these are charges against *you*. Baebius needs someone to blame about the raid in his report to Plancus."

"Are he and Agrippa working together?"

"Undoubtedly so, yet difficult to prove."

Apsa asked, "What is this military tribe you mentioned?"

"Tribunal. Instead of jurors, Baebius and *tribunii* Metellus and Fleginas will sit in judgment on your husband."

She reached for my hand. "What did Alberix *do?*"

"They claim he went to Arialbunnum to stir up sedition, either with Germani or members of his own tribe."

"That's insane!" I protested. "I have a document pledging the *vergobret*'s help against enemy raids. It took me three weeks to convince him and his advisors."

Marius's expression brightened. "You have a treaty in writing? Where is it?"

"In my saddle pouches. Guards brought me here so quickly that I didn't have time to empty them."

Marius scrambled up, and helped Apsa to her feet. "Get everything out of his pouches, take it to your tent, and stay there. Don't talk to anyone about this treaty."

I stood up to watch my wife leave and told Marius. "That should prove my innocence."

"They could call it a trick, in case you were discovered."

"Who are 'They'?"

"The indictment doesn't have to name anyone, just list charges. A clever lawyer like Agrippa could make your treaty document work against you, so I don't want Apsa mentioning it. I have much planning to do, but I'll come back early tomorrow."

I thanked him and sat back onto the dirt floor. Guards closed the shutters again, dimming indoor light, but I didn't notice. I had planning to do myself.

Marius walked to the south gate, then along a path to the veteran's compound. Slaves still cleared away charred remains of burned huts. Two fresh mounds of earth marked the burial sites: Forty-five Roman dead, including five women and six children, lay under one. Thirty Germani warriors, who would never ride nor wield a sword again in this world, filled the other.

A group of Suebi prisoners linked together with neck chains sat sullenly under a nearby grove of trees. Marius walked to them out of curiosity—it was a long while since he had spoken their language. Most prisoners suffered slash wounds that medical orderlies had bandaged. The engineer walked among them, and paused when he saw that one was a woman; she had cut her hair short and dressed as a man. A blood-soaked bandage covered a wound under her right breast. The curve of her bosom barely was visible beneath a soiled tunic shirt. She breathed in gasps.

"*Frauiz?*" he asked, wondering if he had the correct word for a female. She glanced up at him with a glazed look. "What tribe is she?" Marius asked a blond warrior with a head bandage sitting nearby. The man glowered at him without answering.

A medical orderly crushing herbs in a mortar, laughed. "Barbarians, they don't talk much."

"Probably the first 'Shorthairs' most have seen, yet their strategy with the archers was quite clever."

"Galli learn our tactics fast. Hopefully these Germani won't get that chance again."

"Thank Jupiter." With a final look at the woman, Marius went back to his tent, recalling a story Alberix told him after his disappearance into Germania. *He mentioned a feisty woman who fought like a man. Obviously that's still happening. Marius you have a defense to prepare. You're not a lawyer and are up against a panel of judges who have all to gain by finding Alberix guilty before Munitius Plancus returns.*

A sweating, nervous Lucius Baebius and his two tribunes sat at a rough table set on a raised platform in the center of an incomplete forum. Next to the officials, the Legio VI *vexillum* hung listlessly in the heat of a summer morning. Around the field's perimeter, the colony's garrison and veterans ringed an open space to watch the sedition trial of a Celt in their Gallic auxiliary. By now most knew the accused was a Roman citizen, thus punishment could include beheading. A group of shackled Germani prisoners sat on the ground, brought to witness Roman justice in an effort to influence barbarians about the benefits of ceasing useless resistance.

At Baebius's signal, two guards brought me to one side of the platform, several paces away from my judges. I looked toward Apsa, barely hearing the charges being read.

"...Desertion from duty. Conspiracy with Germani to betray this colony's defenses. Plotting sedition with renegade Galli at Arialbinnum, and incrimination in the deaths of Roman citizens and allies at *Colonia Muniatus Rauricorum*." Baebius rolled up the list of accusations and nodded for his clerk to record the proceedings in writing. "Who will speak against the accused?"

"I shall." Agrippa stepped forward amid a murmur of surprise from spectators.

Baebius intoned, "State your name and qualifications."

"Decimus Aelius Agrippa, member of the *Senatus Romanus*, uncle to Marcus Agrippa, a close associate of Octavianus, the rightful heir to the Divine Caesar."

Marius knew that no special 'qualifications' were necessary. Any citizen could call for a trial. *This is Baebius's strategy to impress tribuni and advertise the senator to the crowd.* He suppressed his laugh by a cough. *Divine Caesar? Am I fighting a kin of the gods, too? Agrippa is currying favor with the judges. He could be Bacchus's uncle and Baebius would have let him testify!*

"Accepted. Who shall be advocate for the accused?"

Marius glanced toward me. "I shall, *Quaestor*."

"Name, quickly."

"Marcus Marius, *Optio* in Legio Ten. Now attached for duty with *Colonia*—"

"Yes, yes, we know all that," Baebius interrupted. "Senator Agrippa, present the evidence against the accused."

Agrippa called witnesses who saw me ride off in the direction of Arialbinnum, then described the surprise raid by the Germani. He testified that my auxiliaries had been leaderless and unprepared. Fifteen were killed. In a rhetorical style honed in the Senate, Agrippa described the gruesome deaths of nineteen veteran legionaries and members of their families who survived the Gallic wars only to die here in a raid I had encouraged.

It was all I could do to avoid lunging at the man.

Sweating, wiping his face with a neckerchief, Agrippa concluded by demanding the death penalty allowed for sedition. Exile would merely send me away to plot further treason against the Roman State.

Marius also perspired as he stepped in front of the judges' table. Having experienced the Celtic reputation for having short tempers, he decided to prevent his client from any foolish action by addressing him first—and appeal to Caesar's friendship with Alberix.

"Sir, I would like the accused to answer my questions."

"So would this tribunal," Baebius chortled. "Proceed *Optio.*"

Facing the spectators, Marius walked slowly around the platform as he spoke. "I could tell you of the services that this son of a Raurici clan chief performed for his adopted country, yet the 'Divine Caesar' did so more eloquently than my words with his diploma of citizenship." He held up the parchment. "How many of you can claim direct citizenship at the hand of your late Imperator?"

Surprised and irritated, Baebius called out, "Question the accused about present charges, rather than reciting his past."

"Yes, sir. Alberix, in Governor Plancus's absence, who was in acting-command of this colony on the day of the raid?"

Agrippa nervously bit at a hangnail.

I was surprised at the question. "His *quaestor*, Lucius Baebius."

"Exactly. Did you name an officer to command the *auxiliae* during your absence?"

"Yes, a *Decurio.* Vindelicos."

"Who survived the raid. If need be we shall talk with him." Marius turned to Tribunes Fleginas and Metellus. "I submit that the appointment of Vindelicos was the extent of the accused's responsibility. I call on *Centurio* Fabius Pedius to testify."

When a scarred, gray-bearded veteran limped onto the platform, Marius went to meet him. "*Centurio, grates.* Your brother was Quintus Pedius, killed in Hispania fighting under Julius Caesar?"

"He was, Sir. *Primus hastatus.*"

"A responsible Roman command for which he died," Marius stated loud enough for the furthermost spectator to hear. "*Centurio*, who were posted as guards on the night of the Germani attack? Do you have names?"

"Sir"—Pedius hesitated to stroke his beard in thought—"Sir, I...I know of no guard detail that night."

Marius feigned astonishment. "No guards? No sentries on duty against a surprise Germani attack?"

"None were ordered...that...that I know of."

"None?" Marius repeated. "Whose responsibility would that have been? To mount a guard, I mean?"

Pedius looked toward the table. "One of the *tribuni*."

"I mean in command above those officers—"

"Just a moment, *Optio*..." A flushed Baebius was on his feet, shaking his indictment scroll at Marius. "I'm not on trial here!"

"No, but in the Governor's absence a guard posting was your responsibility."

Sulking, Baebius slumped down. Murmuring among the onlookers grew louder. Marius turned back to Pedius. "Who ordered the palisade stakes torn down so the men could form up against the archers?"

"Why...you did, Sir." He sounded as if Marius had forgotten.

"And where was the *Quaestor?*"

"You furcing latrine digger!" Baebius stood so violently that his chair fell backward. "I...I'm charging you with insubordination!"

"Sir..." Marius felt nauseous and wished his voice sounded louder. "Sir, we should recess and go into the *praetorium*. I...Alberix, that is... has a document to show you."

Baebius growled assent, relieved to end the questioning. Inside the tent, he lashed out at Marius, "I'll have your balls nailed to a furca!"

Marius held up a parchment case. "Then you'll never benefit from reading this. Alberix—"

I took the case and handed the document inside to Baebius. "Sir, this is an agreement from the *vergobret* at Arialbinnum to help us defend this section of the Renos frontier."

Marius made a writing motion with one finger. "*Quaestor*, it needs your signature and I don't think the Governor would be displeased at what...ah... what *you* were able to accomplish."

Baebius sat to scan the sheet, muttering, "I'm a supply officer, a legion accountant, *Optio*. I didn't ask for this command."

"No sir, so 'misplace' your trial record and release Alberix. We both know Agrippa's motives in pressing false charges. A serious reprimand to him—"

"*Optio*," Baebius warned, "don't push your luck! The senator could have you transferred to the Parthian desert in the wink of an eye."

"Jupiter help me Sir, not without due process."

Baebius ignored his insolence, snatched up a reed pen on his desk, and signed his name to the parchment. "I'm in no mood to argue points of law. I'll send a report to Plancus about the raid with a copy of this treaty. Your Gallic friend is free. Both of you are furcing dismissed!"

Late that day we had a celebratory supper to mark my release and Marius's role in outwitting Lucius Baebius.

"You beat the fox at his tricks!" I clapped Marius on the back. "I can't praise you enough."

"There were three foxshes," he corrected, purposely slurring his last word.

I easily imitated him. "*Two* foxshes."

"Or shall we shay not-too-bright 'geese'?"

I laughed at his retort. We sat at the remains of a meal Apsa and Alpina had cooked and included copious amounts of our military wine ration.

Marius said, "Baebus is an accountant an' usually commands cohorts of numbers. Still...he should know about security..." He held out his cup. Alpina shyly smiled at him in filling it again. "Should be more sober... How many of our people died, an' how many barbarians? I'll wager 'Bulb-ass's report will be key-stoned with excuses that exaggerate Germani strength, but most will be 'bout the treaty an' his part in ordering you to Arial...Arialbinn...that Raurici town to negotiate for it."

Apsa told him, "Marius, that's in the past. I'm just glad my husband is free."

He took a final gulp of wine, then pushed his cup away. "Oh, somethin' unbelievable. A woman was fighting with th' Germani! I saw her among wounded prisoners. Injured badly, too."

Apsa felt concern. "A woman? I'll go down and try to help her."

"*Capsarii* have her ban-aged up. See her tomorrow." Marius changed the subject. "Alberix, what will y' do now?"

"Plancus implied the colony will be under military rule for at least a year. Perhaps they'll hold elections next Elembiu for the year after."

"Elimbu? You better start callin' your month Sextilius, " Marius made an unsteady count on his knuckles. "And y' ll have to file in Quintilis t' be eligible. That gives y' a month t' recruit votes."

Before I could reply, Alpina came in to announce a visitor, but Junius Balbus brushed past her. "Ah, my old friend..." He glanced at Marius and Apsa while grasping my hand. "My search again ends at the edge of Germania!"

I had last seen the merchant about ten years earlier. He had aged, but not lost the excess weight that came with good living. "Balbus, I can't believe you're here. Why were you looking for me?"

"You saved me from a winter of boredom! No matter. Introduce me to your charming friends."

"My wife, Apsa. Marcus Marius, *Optio* in charge of colony construction."

"My dear, you're remarkably beautiful." Balbus bowed to Apsa, then told Marius. "How kindly *Fortuna* smiles upon me. I find both an old friend and a man I would be searching for." I tried to explain that Balbus was a merchant, but he contradicted me. "Alberix, I am now a farmer of taxes."

"*Publicanus?*" Marius had sobered enough to question his occupation.

"Correct, *Optio*, although I yet maintain merchant contacts."

Marius explained, "*Publicani* harvest provincial taxes and keep whatever they can squeeze out above the amount due. Surely, Balbus, you're not here for tax money?"

"No, no. Have you seen a chart of the area? This colony is the hub of a four-spoke wheel...a crossroad to the cardinal directions. Great Jupiter! When I first saw that map, I realized this was the navel of Europa's fruitful body."

"And ready for the rape," Marius mumbled, but Balbus had turned to accept wine.

After a sip, he raised the cup. "Better than that army *posca* we had in Germania, eh, Alberix?" He patted my arm. "This youth preserved me from a winter of weariness. I, of course, *had* saved his life."

I asked, "How long will you stay here?"

"Oh, I'll be back at Roma by the *Armilustrum*." Balbus sat and helped himself to a slice of honey cake. "*Optio*, I'm interested in buying an apartment block near the forum. That is why I need to talk with you."

"We've laid out fifty-five blocks so far, but I don't sell real estate."

"Good, fifty-five blocks. I'll tell you the sort of buildings I want put up on mine. Alberix, I'll need someone to manage my businesses. Interested?"

Before I could answer, Balbus finished his wine and stood. "I must see the *quaestor* about a tent of my own. Daedalus's Bull if I'll share with eight sweaty legionaries! Alberix, consider my offer." He bowed to the women. "Until morning..."

After I returned from going outside with him, Apsa frowned, "I don't like the man."

"Same old Balbus..." My excusing laugh was weak; the merchant came on as strong as a siege engine.

Marius said, "Didn't I meet him at Gesoriacum? *Publicanus!* If citizens complained, Balbus would expect the governor to back up his theft."

Apsa wondered, "Is it true what he said about the colony's location?"

"In that he's correct," Marius agreed. "North on the Rhenus to the Amber Sea. West through Gallia toward Oceanus, and the tin island of Albion. South over the Veragri pass to Italia and Africa. We're definitely the center of Europa."

Alpina returned with Ger and Salia before tucking them in bed.

When Apsa took the girl, Marius held out a pastry. "Ger, tell me how old you are."

"Almost six..." He snatched the morsel and immediately dropped it.

I tossed the crumbs into the hearth. "To bed, now, Ger, and I'll bring you another piece." I kissed Salia, then splashed wine into Marius's cup. "See what you're missing?"

"Hmmm. Alpina *is* quite a beauty. I must figure my years until retirement. *Colonia Raurica* would not be a bad place to settle down."

≈≈

Governor Munatius Plancus, thoroughly alarmed at the costly raid from across the Rhenus frontier, procured reinforcements for the colony through his agents at Roma.

In that October, more veterans and land grant settlers than had been lost to the Germani arrived with their families. Many were artisans that could help in constructing permanent buildings. On Marius's recommendation I was transferred from my auxiliary command to oversee metal workers. Although I had not worked a forge for a long while, the duty was more suited to my temperament and experience. Marius also persuaded Baebius to turn over Latobrigi and Suebi prisoners as slaves for his construction cohorts. The colony's streets and lodges had to be finished before winter snows halted work.

Before long, stone workers set up a brick kiln and marked out a quarry site. A main sewer trench, dug to connect the Forum dwelling blocks with the stream, emptied downriver into the Renos. Bricklayers vaulted the open ditch into a sewer tunnel. By the end of November, clay tiles were stock-piled for roofing the basilica and temple buildings in the spring. Quarriers split limestone slabs to pave the forum and the colony's two primary streets, the Cardo and Decumani.

Remembering Cluvios, I contracted with Raurici at Arialbinnum to haul iron ore from the reopened mines at Chondix. My forge workers soon turned out farm tools, saws, axes, blades and hammers, as well as bronze hinges for doors and storage chests.

Moderate autumn rains kept the colony's streets from deep mud. The winter was mild. Well before the time Celts celebrated Beltaine, and Romans the festival of Jupiter Victor, the rutted lanes had dried to a hard surface. Huts and wooden lodges were dismantled and replaced by brick and stucco structures.

❧❧

On the Eidus of Martius, a sacrifice to Concordia with prayers to avert a new civil war marked the first anniversary of Julius Caesar's murder.

The prospects for peace shortened as the days of the year lengthened. Marcus Antonius left Rome for his *Cisalpina* province, still refusing to recognize Octavianus's claim as Caesar's heir. Aulus Hirtius and Vibius Pansa were installed as consuls on the Kalends of Januarius; both men supported Octavianus and republicans in the Senate. Cicero abandoned a plan to follow Marcus Brutus into Asia and returned home to oppose Antonius. Consequently, he was ordered to leave the *Cisalpina*, which was under the command of Decimus Brutus. When he balked, the combined legions of Hirtius, Pansa and Octavianus attacked Antonius's followers and defeated them, near Mutina. Both consuls died in the action. Despite the victory, the Senate snubbed Octavianus as "a mere boy" and offered the Imperium to Marcus Brutus; Cassius in the East; and to a son of Pompeius at Massilia.

❧❧

Reports of the Mutina defeat and Antonius's escape to *Gallia Transalpina* reached *Colonia Munatia Rauricorum* on the evening after the feast of Jupiter Victor.

Marius and I discussed the dangerous situation while inspecting the forum paving and basilica foundations. He said, "By leaving Roma, Antonius made the same mistake as Pompeius. The Senatus saw in him the same ambition as in Caesar. In the civil war he was the commander's sword hand."

"The man is at his best in a crisis," I recalled. "Remember his skill at Alesia in reinforcing weak points? What will Antonius do now?"

"I imagine try to join Lepidus in the Narbonensis. This means that Governor Plancus will have to choose sides. Let's hope all this turmoil doesn't affect our colony."

"Antonius is a more vengeful person than Caesar."

"True, and he'll issue proscriptions as plentifully as salt rations. Anyone he doesn't like is on the list. Marcus Cicero first."

We had arrived on the height where the northeast side of the basilica was under construction. A torn down section of palisade made room for an extension of the foundation. Through the gap, I saw the stream below bordered by lush growths. Beyond, a light green color hazed the furrows of recently plowed fields, where farmers risked a late frost to push crops toward an early harvest.

Nearby, a work detail of sullen Germani slaves rested in the sun with tunic shirts off.

I noted, "If we exchange those slaves in a treaty, they may have learned something useful to take back to Germania."

The words were hardly out of my mouth when one of the men sprang up, lunged past Marius, and clutched my throat. The unexpected attack threw us both off balance. We rolled down the slope and landed in the stream's sandy bank. My opponent stood up first, breathing in gasps. Scrapes on his bare shoulders oozed blood. As he crouched to attack me again, I recalled wrestling sessions and got up on one knee. When he leaped at me, I tried to put a hammerlock on his head. The man's skin felt gritty as I tried holding him, but he twisted free, bawling Germanic curses when he faced around.

Three legionary guards side-slipped down the hill with swords drawn. The slave ignored them to lunge at me. I managed to catch his head under an arm, but couldn't hold on. He punched my abdomen and spun away. The first guard reached the stream and raised his sword to slash him down.

"Don't...kill him," I gasped. "I...I want to know why he attacked me"

Two guards pinned the man's arms behind his back, yet in his defiant look, I felt a shiver of recognition. After ten years, I remembered he was one of the Suebi warriors who had been with Ogerth. He had beheaded a legionary and been a friend of Frieda.

While the guards awaited orders, Marius picked his way down the slope. "What in Hades's name does that slave think he's doing? Guard, lop his head off right here! Show the others how fortunate they are to keep theirs."

I stepped between them. "Marius, I'm not hurt. The man should have a chance to explain himself."

"We don't give a trial to slaves. This barbarian Spartacus should be sent to meet his sky gods right now!"

"He's Suebi. Confine the man to his hut and I'll talk to him after I clean up."

Marius ordered reluctant compliance. "Guards, put him on half-rations until Alberix arrives."

≈

"Why would he attack *you?*" Apsa asked as she treated my welts with a *saponaria* ointment.

I had hoped she would not bring that up. "Evidently, the man recognized me from the time I was Ogerth's hostage in Germania."

"You've never talked much about that time."

"Silanus was responsible. I didn't think you wanted to be reminded of him." Apsa did not reply and I avoided mention of Frieda. "Ogerth's warriors were Suebi and why this one raided our colony needs explaining. I'll talk to him in the morning."

❧❧

When I entered the dim hut the slave was crouched at a far end, shackled by a leg to one of two posts that supported the roof. I came in with a skin of *cervisa* and plate of bread and sausage. I watched him eat and poured out a cup of beer, while asking, "Why did a Suebi fight with Latobrigi warriors? Your holdings are far to the north." I waited, but he neither answered nor looked up. "You remembered me. There was a woman in your village, Ogerth's daughter. What is your name?"

He looked up to answer in a mixture of Germanic and Celtic. "Gurther, son of Radigan. Frieda became my wife. After you arrived, *Kelt,* she was as a child with a new plaything. Ogerth came to believe that she would help you escape...even go with you. You found a hidden boat before we could search for it."

"Then...that woman with you who was wounded—"

"Frieda. One of your healers told me she died."

"When?"

"Before the cold season rains. I asked that her ashes be thrown in the river she loved, but the man laughed and said she was under earth. When it came to Romani, Frieda nursed the hatred of Tiwaz. And, *Kelt,* also of you."

"I...I'm sorry. What of Ogerth?"

"Killed in an attack on Aduataca."

"Gurther, there will be no charges brought against you. I wish you peace."

In response he gulped a mouthful of beer and spat it me.

Outside, I wiped my face and walked down the slope toward the Rhenus, where huts of new arrivals were located. I looked back: the pale stucco walls of finished apartments at *Insulae* I, II and III, gleamed in the fresh light. A team of surveyors laying foundations for a wall that would encircle the town shouted for me to move. Farther down, I saw an off-duty legionary and asked him where Germani dead were buried. He pointed to gentle loop in the stream and said that only two mounds were visible.

At the site no markers told which dead lay under the weed-overgrown earth, no names of tribes. I chose one area that looked to be recent, picked wild daisies to scatter on the mound, then sat nearby to ponder an unbelievable joining of destinies that rivaled any of Dividiac's myths about our people. I stayed, thinking of Frieda until the white-and yellow blossoms blew off the earth.

That night Apsa seemed receptive to love making, perhaps to soothe my injuries, but I only kissed her face and turned away. During a long night, the faces of Frieda, her husband, and my dead father and uncles disturbed my uneasy dreams.

❧

The graffiti appeared in summer—derogatory or obscene references and puns concerning my parentage, courage, and manliness. Also of other candidates for the six civil magistracies that were open to campaigning in the month of Quintilis.

Marius came with me to look at an inscription scribbled on a wall near the palisade, GALLI INTELLIGENTIA GALLICUS HABENT. He read it, then slapped me on the back. "Laugh, Alberix! It's a tired pun on the Latin word for 'rooster'."

"'We have the intelligence of a rooster' and I'm supposed to laugh?"

"Less insulting than one I saw yesterday, '*Galli fornicati Gallinae*'"

I rubbed out the charcoal letters. "Agrippa's agents?"

"No doubt, but the least of what he'll spend to get elected. I hear that on the *Neptunalia* he'll host a banquet for the colony, hoping diners will believe that's how generous he'll be once in office."

"They can't possibly be fooled that way."

"*Veterani* expect material bonuses. If Agrippa convinces them he's wealthy enough to build a theater and arena, they'll vote him in."

Again, I felt my candidacy futile. "What do I have to offer? Plancus never acted to establish my ownership of Father's lands."

"'Where war trumpets blare, laws are silent' is the saying. Governor Plancus is in no hurry to validate your claim."

"Then what chance do I have? Agrippa and his cronies will bleed the colony dry."

Marius persisted, "My mother used to say, 'Truth and oil rise to the top'—"

I snapped, "Enough stupid sayings, *Optio!*"

He pulled me away from the wall. "Alberix, it only means, 'Be truthful.' Offer the voters good government and honest taxation that will build a theater and arena for them. Show them that a 'rooster' knows more than how to screw chickens."

I had to smile at his imagery and optimism. "Dividiac had his own sayings. I remember this one, 'Fools set out milking pails for the wise to stumble over'."

Marius laughed. "Then get yourself to a bovine barn! I have my own work to do."

◈

Agrippa had considered a public celebration five days after the *Quintilis Nones*, to mark the birth of Julius Caesar, yet at last report the uncertain political situation seemed to favor a restoration of the Republic. Rumors suggested that the month might be renamed Julius in his honor. After Antonius's defeat the idea was dropped.

For celebrating the *Neptunalia* Agrippa asked clients to have their slaves cut tree branches and construct a traditional bower where worshippers prayed that autumnal rains would be abundant, yet not destructive. Wooden tables, benches, and awnings set up in the new forum provided covered dining places. Amphorae of wine and barrels of *cervisa* brewed at Arialbinnum stood in the shadows of a market arcade.

In mid-afternoon, Lucius Baebius presided over a brief ceremony to Neptunus and then feasting began: fish from the Rhenus; roast ox and wild game; loaves of wheat and millet bread, and seasonal vegetables were served. By Roman banquet standards, the food was simple, yet copious and without cost. Baebius and Agrippa sat with a guest of honor, Vitruvius Pollio. The colony's architect had arrived to inspect a year of construction before traveling to Roma for the winter.

Marius had finished his meal and excused himself, an act that did not displease Agrippa since he thought him too friendly with opposition candidates.

When portico shadows extended toward the marketplace wall, Marius brought me and others who ran for office to hear Agrippa's oration, which would close the banquet. As I stood near the basilica, I heard the charge of a candidate, Titus Puleio, a centurion who had served under Pompeius.

"This is only one of Agrippa's bribes," Puleio complained. "He's going t' give out enough *sesterces* between now and th' *Kalendae* t' pay a legion!"

Another candidate grumbled, "I put my pension into farm land an' can't afford to bribe every citizen who votes."

Puleio spat near a column base. "Agrippa will get it back with plenty o' interest."

I asked him, "Most voters were legionaries like you. Won't they support their own?"

"Not when the senator promises 'em a new arena by next year. They all want this place t' look like Roma soon as possible."

"It can be done without bribes. Puleio, you admitted Agrippa will drain the treasury."

"Citizens believe just about anyone tryin' t' get elected will do that sooner t' later. Agrippa's got enough *sesterces* for an arena...even a theater."

The senator stood to the applause of most diners and walked to a rostrum set up in front of the tables. Slaves brought benches. Minucius Sextius, his co-candidate for magistrate, motioned for men campaigning for *aedile* and *quaestor* to sit on them.

"Citizens and friends..." Agrippa held up a pudgy hand in a calculated rebuke at paid applause. "I thank you, yet ask that you share plaudits with Lucius Baebius. In a short span his leadership made our colony prosper."

"Pigshit!" Marius exclaimed, coming to stand next to me. "Baebius hasn't dropped enough sweat here to fill an inkpot."

Agrippa swept an arm toward the marketplace. "This beautiful portico. A magnificent basilica that will be complete before snow falls. The foundations of a temple to the Divine Three, and a shrine I shall finish *at my expense* after I am elected with my associate, Sextius."

Sextius rose unsteadily to a scattering of applause. "An' I promish you a theater."

At the slurred words, Agrippa motioned him to sit down. "Citizens, so long as I am a Senator, *Colonia Munatia* will never become the orphan of a tribune's veto!"

Marius fumed, "There's not much here to concern a tribune at Roma! We have only the promise of spectacular buildings to take a citizen's mind off dark forests across the river and the Germani in them!"

Someone shouted from the arcade for opposition candidates to speak. The unexpected request took Agrippa by surprise. Several veterans in the crowd took up the call.

I grinned at Marius. "I took Dividiac's advice and brought a few 'milk stools' for Agrippa to stumble over."

The senator leaned back to consult with Baebius, then faced the crowd with an affected smile—Vitruvius might report election irregularities to senators. Dusk was approaching so there was little time for long speeches. Filled with his food and wine, awed by promises, the half-drunk crowd would pay scant attention to the clerks and uneducated centurions who filed for office.

"Of, course, of course," Agrippa agreed. "It is the way of the Republic to listen to all viewpoints. I welcome them."

I nudged Puleio out of the portico, toward the rostrum. Nervous, he glanced around before speaking. "I'm used to givin' military orders, not fancy words. It's true that I sided with Pompeius when I thought the Republic was in danger, but Caesar gave us a pardon and land. I signed up here so's my family could make a livin'." He shuffled his feet and tried to think of a closing. "So, like I said, I'm used to givin' orders and pretty honest. I...I'd make a furcin' good *duovir*!"

Red-faced, Puleio returned to the portico amid sparse applause that broadened Agrippa's smirk. Other candidates came forward to tell of their experience and qualifications for the civic posts—and gained similar bland receptions from the crowd.

When my turn came, the sun had slipped below the arcade roof. I avoided the rostrum and stood at the edge of the platform. Wearing a holiday tunic like men in the audience, I was taller than any of the candidates. My blond hair and blue eyes unmistakably marked me as a northern Celt.

Sextius leaned toward the senator to hiss, "Can't you stop him? Why give this *brachatus* free publicity?"

"Fool!" Agrippa retorted. "Don't you read graffiti on the walls? He's had plenty and now will only prove what the insults say."

Vitruvius said, "Let Alberix speak. Marcus Marius thinks very highly of him." He called to me, "Celt, tell us why you wish to be a magistrate."

Agrippa feigned interest. "By all means, 'Celt', entertain us."

I identified myself. "Not only Celt, but Raurici. This territory along the river is my tribe's. The land on which we stand is my father's."

"Tell them more, you ass," Agrippa murmured aloud. "You've just lost half your votes by telling them you're barbarian."

I went on, "In my father's time a *sword* was the 'law' by which land was won and lost. I mean only to use the *law* as a 'sword' that will establish my inheritance."

"*Praefect*, I like him," Vitruvius whispered to Baebius. "He is truthful and evidently learned something about rhetoric by listening to Caesar."

"Today these lands are Romani," I continued. "I am an adopted son granted citizenship by our late Imperator. My father, Alrix, was a clan chieftain. In a vision he saw peace between Celts and Germani. One of my uncles was a craftsperson and I used skills learned from him to help build this colony. Another uncle was a druid who taught me truth in the heart and honesty in speech."

Marius clapped hands, starting a round of applause. Favorable shouts came from onlookers. I motioned to Apsa, standing nearby with Ger and Salia. When she came up on the platform with the children, women in the audience murmured approval. I held her around the shoulders. "My wife was a slave when I found her. I freed Apsa and now she also is a citizen."

Baebius snorted, "That won't get him elected. Every man here will fear his slaves will be freed by marrying locals."

One of Agrippa's clients shouted, "Fine words, Celt, but what do you know about governing?"

I told him, "Caesar backed my position as *vergobret* at *Benn Belenos* of our Sequani allies and I was reelected."

Agrippa felt intuitive alarm. *The Celt is better speaker than I anticipated. He hasn't promised the crowd a sestercius and yet they lean toward his words.* He abruptly stood up with a stiff smile. "Citizens, night birds appear. This speech-making goes on too long. The wine will sour—"

Calls for "Let him finish" and "Light torches" countered the senator's suggestion.

I signaled for quiet. "Senator Agrippa is correct. I have only a few more words. I believe *Colonia Rauricorum* will become a great town for you and your children. For *our* children. I wish to help make it so. I promise you no temples or arenas that fair taxation cannot construct. I do pledge that your *sesterces* will go toward developments here and not fatten other contractors' purses."

A few veterans bolted up to clap. Others whistled approval as if they had witnessed a deft parrying maneuver in the arena. Some came forward to reach for my hand.

Apsa handed me a papyrus. I unrolled and held it up. "A *centurio* befriended me and explained Romani concepts of justice and laws. These attracted me. Years ago, a Greek friend and I traveled into Gallia. Inside caves we saw evidence of tribes that lived long ago, but were no more. Perhaps one day this forum, this basilica, even this *colonia* will be known only by the remains of its walls and paving. If that time comes I believe that this statement by Marcus Cicero will be as true as it is today. 'The Law is the ligament binding that dignity which we enjoy in the republic, the foundation of liberty, the source of equity. The mind, and spirit, and judgment, and determination of the State are placed in its laws. Like our own body without its mind, which is muscle, blood and limbs, so the State without laws cannot best utilize its parts. Magistrates who administer the law, jurors who interpret the law, in fact all of us, therefore, obey the law that we may be free'."

I feared that renewed cheering would aggravate the uneasiness I was sure that Baebius and Agrippa felt.

Marius came to congratulate me. "Agrippa might as well realize that he'll be sharing the magistracy with a rustic rooster!"

Baebius, muttered slurred words. "These Galli are clever. If Roma isn't careful, they'll get more than old Brennus ever did!"

Vitruvius came to grip my hand. "Alberix, the crowds are on your side. Let them sleep with Cicero tonight."

I returned his grip, put an arm around Apsa, and went down to carry Salia home.

✌◈✍

The day after the *Neptunalia* was *nefastus*, a day prohibiting certain kinds of public business. I decided to take Apsa and the children on a wagon ride along the river to a backwater pool. Ger and Salia could splash in the shallows and have a light mid-day meal on its banks.

As the children played together, Apsa and I talked about the kind of life the colony would provide for a combined Romani and Celtic population.

"Husband, you're finally in a position to make your father's dream a reality."

"Apsa, it's been a long, hard road of almost twenty years. War, a prisoner of Vercingetorix...abducted into Germania—"

"Where you meet that Suebi girl. What was her name again?"

"Ah...Frieda."

"Tell me more of this Frieda. Did you like her?"

"I...I didn't know her long, but she was a remarkable woman. Resourceful... her own person."

"Alberix, did you come to love her?"

"It was a long time ago. An alien place—"

"Husband, I'm teasing you..." Apsa laughed and turned to look toward the children. "Ger and Salia are tired. We should go back."

As I drove the mules along the rutted trail, an axle linchpin abruptly sheared and caused a rear wheel to wobble off its hub. The jolt angled the wagon bed toward the ground. This frightened Salia, but she laughed when I convinced her that the accident was a new adventure. Having spent many days embroiled in vicious politics, the need to replace a linchpin only mildly annoyed me.

I used a barrel and plank to lever the bed high enough for piled stones to level the axle. While I prepared to slide the wheel back on, Apsa took Ger and Salia across the road to watch a lark and listen to the bird's trilling. When I lifted the wheel by two spokes, I unconsciously murmured the names of Caesar and Vercingetorix. Apsa heard and called to ask what I had said.

"*Cara*, as I held onto these spokes the names of Julius Caesar and Vercingetorix came to me."

"How strange."

"This wheel had gotten me to think about the Wheel of Life that Dividiac always mentioned. Those two men most affected my destiny." I slid the hub onto the axle and gave it a spin, then stopped the turns by grasping two other spokes. "These are Cluvios and Lucius. They showed me the best of Celtic and Romani beliefs."

Caught up in the analogies, Apsa came across to me. "What of Dividiac and Ollam Fodla?"

"They're here too...the spiritual leader and the dark corrupter."

"Alberix, there are eight spokes. What of the other two?"

I thought a moment. "Simonides and Marius? They weren't Celts yet became true friends. Taranis! My whole life is here in my hands!"

With a sudden burst of song, the lark flew off along the river, toward *Munatia Rauricorum*. Ger and Salia raced each other back to be first to reach us.

As Apsa hugged the children she remarked, "Husband, you have no more spokes. Where, exactly, do *we* fit in?"

I grinned as I hammered a new linchpin into place, and patted the hub. "You are here, Apsa, at the center of my life. You know that everything I do revolves around my family."

Apsa retorted with a half-cynical laugh. "Spoken like a true Celtic man. Quick-tongued and flirting a bit with the truth!"

I lifted Ger and Salia into the wagon bed and helped Apsa onto the seat beside me. I kissed her and clucked the mules into motion along the trail back to the colony.

Lying on straw laid in the wagon's bed, Salia giggled while her brother tried to imitate the exuberant call of the now-vanished lark.

Indeed, the long icy winter had passed.

EPILOGUE

In the elections of the following month Alberix was elected one of the *duoviri* that would serve with Agrippa. Citizens had been shrewdly aware—or persistently hopeful—that the mutual checks of the Roman two-consul system would work to their advantage by electing opposing magistrates that might balance each other. Agrippa's wealth was not a hindrance.

In that same month, legions backing Octavianus occupied Roma. Julius Caesar's young heir was elected consul along with Quintus Pedius, the late dictator's nephew. Marcus Tullius Cicero was murdered on the orders of Marcus Antonius; subsequently, the orator's severed head and hands were displayed on the Forum rostrum.

Thirteen years of a new civil war followed, in which the conspirators against Caesar were killed. Antonius and Cleopatra committed suicide.

A temple to the Divine Caesar was dedicated on the site where his body was cremated. Senatorial legislation quickly elevated him to the pantheon of Roman gods with the name *Divus Julivs*.

While Octavianus consolidated his power during the second civil war, Munatius Plancus's colony languished. After the Roman Assembly and Senate voted a new emperor Supreme Imperium, a surge of building activity completed the town. Renamed *Augusta Rauricorum*, after Octavianus adopted the title of Augustus—an honor proposed in the Senate by Plancus—the frontier town flourished during two centuries. Legion camps secured both ends of a bridge into Germania. Garrison legionaries protected the area against raids by a Germanic Alemanni tribe. Legio I Martius was stationed there and later, I Aduitrix and VII Gemina. The settlement's nadir came when Alemanni warriors pillaged and burned the city, some four hundred years after its founding.

Author's Notes

The Alberix novels are partly based on Julius Caesar's written account of his successful Gallic war, yet are not a translation or summary of his writings. Rather, the reader is taken back to a village in the year before the war began, and encounters the cultural, religious, and political life of the era through the first person account of Alberix, a Celtic youth, whose family is caught up in the war. The author's motivation for writing the novels was to investigate his family background of Swiss origin, following reading a volume about Celtic history by Gerhard Herm and viewing the television miniseries *Roots* by Alex Haley.

Today in Augst, Switzerland, which sits east of Basel on the Rhine River, visitors can tour the reconstruction of a Roman villa attached to an interpretive museum. The extensive site has the ruins of a theater and arena set among the foundations of temples and a partly reconstructed basilica. Dozens of other ruins and reconstructions testify to the Roman presence in Switzerland. Gallic sites in France can be toured "in the footsteps of Caesar."

The fictional village of Wermaros is today's St. Ursanne, on the Doubs River in the Jura Mountains. Residents of French-speaking Swiss Cantons still refer to themselves as "*Suisse Romande*." This western region is where speakers of Latin settled. Swiss postage stamps bear the ancient name HELVETIA.

Alberix the Celt Discussion Guide

This guide provides further exploration of the First Century B.C.E historical setting of the Alberix novels in Celtic and Roman culture and history.

Alberix the Celt Book 1: Weep the Long Sorrow

1. After his clan-chief father is killed in a raid across the Rhine River, by German warriors, Alberix, his mother, and crafter and druid uncles flee to Wermaros, a different tribe's village, where his aunt is married to the chieftain. Although highly placed in their tribe, the refugees have little standing in this village. In our own day, thousands of people have been displaced by wars. Has this been your experience or of someone you know? Were they resettled without prejudice?

2. Anticipating her husband's death, Briga takes charge of the refugees, cancelling their debts and enlisting skills of survivors that would be needed in a new future. What does this say of the status of women in Celtic society?

3. The training of a druid priest took twenty years of memorizing rituals to multiple gods and learning to write Celtic in the Greek alphabet. When Dividiac tries to make sense of little Klega's death, we learn that re-incarnation is a tenet of a Celtic afterlife. Does this suggest a distant connection with India? Since Celtic is an Indo-European language, The American Heritage Dictionary of the English Language has an Appendix of Indo-European Roots connecting the various languages.

4. An unexpected raid on Wermaros by Suebi warriors highlights the unstable Gallic peace, where their Germanic king has conquered part of Sequani lands and intends to bring in more tribesmen. Is this "ancient 'history" or does it happen in modern times?

5. When a treaty delegation arrives at Wermaros, the Roman Republic had been established 450 years earlier. Alberix is intrigued by concepts of law that Lucius describes and are in line with his father's dream of conciliation rather than combat in settling disputes. Roman offices evolved into many legal and legislative structures that are still observed by the world's democracies. How does the arrival of the "Shorthairs" impact Alberix's world view?

6. Harassed by raids from Germania, the Helvetii tribe votes to migrate west across Gaul. Two routes were open to them: north from their capital, Aventia, then west through Sequani territory, or seeking Julius Caesar's permission to follow the Rhone River at the northern tip of a province he governed. Orgetorix, an Helvetian nobleman, had a further goal. What was it?

7. Simonides meets Alberix on page 228. What function does the Greek historian have in the novel?

8. Psen-Ammon, the Egyptian surgeon attached to Legion X, oversees a Roman "M.A.S. H." unit, and practices both Roman and Egyptian surgical and healing techniques. Are you surprised that the ancients had such skills? Alberix had gathered medicinal and healing plants with Dividiac, and Psen-Ammon also uses them. How widespread is today's interest in natural plant remedies? What are some you might use?

9. Briga enters Lucius's life as a love interest, but she must follow Celtic tradition and marry her deceased husband's dying brother. Alberix sees Apsa in a possible relationship, yet circumstances leave her a damaged, suicidal woman. Frieda is an attractive free spirit. Is Alberix's lone escape justified by fearing he soon will be killed by Ogerth, or is he rationalizing when thinking that Frieda will not fit into Celtic village life?

10. Both of Alberix's uncles want him to "find a Caesar among your own people." While he ponders Lucius's idealism against legionary revenges against Gallic enemies, he hears of Vercingetorix and wonders if he could be the chieftain that might unite Gaul. Have you been faced with a somewhat less drastic choice in planning a career?

Alberix the Celt Book 2: Hear Again the Lark

1. Birth of an equinox child from a virgin druidess: in the absence of systematic information about the natural world, petitions to gods, sacrifices, auguries, and contrived "magic," were substituted. Hallucinatory drugs induced prophetic visions (Kannabis was well-known.) Sacred forest clearings, springs, dolmens, cairns, and menhirs are found throughout Gaul. Druids were mediators between the Now-world and Other-world, whose rituals kept the two realms in balance. Today, many people read astrological magazines, consult psychics, or attend séances. Have you had occult experiences?

2. Arvos re-appears, ridiculed by villagers as a charcoal maker "an occupation in which Celtic gods took little pride." In Antiquity slaves did the bulk of all menial work, a status that lasted until slavery was abolished in the 19th century of our era, yet endures today in parts of the Third World. Until then, guilds and benevolent societies had provided benefits to workers and soldiers. Today's argument is over minimum wage rates and so-called "right to work" laws. Do you know people involved in this dispute?

3. Alberix witnesses Vercingetorix expelled from his tribe's capital of Gergovia. When captured, he and Simonides are able to see boisterous warriors haphazardly recruited for a rebellion. What might Vercingetorix have done differently to build a reliable army?

4. After the Roman setback at Gergovia, Caesar bolsters the morale of his legionaries with a stirring speech that predicts their final victory. Can you recall morale-building wartime speeches during our 20th century?

5. Vercingetorix fails to follow up his victory at Gergovia and takes his army to the fortress of Alesia. If his intention is to lure Caesar into another frontal attack, the plan fails. What incredible task does the commander give his legionaries to complete, in about a month? Where did similar successful or failed battles occur in 20th century wars?

6. Vecingetorix's surrender is briefly described in Caesar's Commentaries, but later writers and artists greatly elaborated on the ceremony. Many readers can compare this with the end of WWI, the Fall of France, and ceremonies after the German and Japanese capitulations, especially the latter. How did Caesar treat most of the defeated Gauls?

7. After Simonides dies, Artemidoros tries to explain his death to Alberix in terms of an "atomic" theory circulating at the time. Compare this with the druids' reincarnation in a "Land of the Young, and current sectarian beliefs in an afterlife.

8. A previous Celtic marriage between Alberix and Aspa involved her slave manumission and the requirement that she choose Alberix. Then there was the quasi-Roman ceremony of Lucius and Briga. What elements of those remain in many modern marriage ceremonies?

9. The "Forest demons" in Chapter 18 are still constructed as a part of German-Swiss winter festivals—especially at Appenzell. The closest we may come is Halloween, the eve of the terrifying Samain New Year. What costumed events do you celebrate?

10. Alberix finally realizes his father's dream by helping to build and govern a Roman town on the Rhine, today known as Augst. His Wheel of Life has turned full circle. Do you believe everything happens randomly, or for reasons we may not yet know? Could you cite examples from your experiences?

Additional Illustrated Reference Books

Check used books sites for these titles.
The Celts by Gerard Herm. St Martin's Press, Inc.
The Celtic Realms by Miles Dillon & Nora Chadwick. Castle Books.
Julius Caesar / The Battle for Gaul by David R. Godine, Publisher.
Caesar Against the Celts by Ramon L. Jimenez. Castle Books.
Roman Gaul and Germany by Anthony King. U. of California Press.
The Army of the Caesars by Michael Grant. M. Evans and Company, Inc.
Roman Medicine by Audrey Cruse. Tempus Publishing, Ltd.
Ancient Egyptian Medicine by John F. Nunn. U. of Oklahoma Press.

About the Author

An artist and writer, Albert Noyer was born in Switzerland but raised in Detroit, Michigan. After Army service, he pursued degrees in art, art education, and teaching humanities, at Wayne State University. He subsequently worked as a commercial artist, taught art in a Detroit Public Schools technical/vocational program, and art history at a private college. Noyer retired to New Mexico with his wife, Jennifer, where he exhibits watercolor paintings and woodcut prints in galleries and regional exhibits. His artwork has been featured New Mexico Magazine and the Mature Life in New Mexico supplement of Albuquerque's Sunday Journal. He is a member of the New Mexico Watercolor Society, SouthWest Writers, Sisters in Crime, Croak & Dagger, and New Mexico Veteran's Art.

Noyer first published A.D. fifth century novels, the *Getorius* and *Arcadia* mysteries, set in an era now seen as critical in creating the political, religious, and cultural institutions that survive into modern times. Published by Plain View Press, his contemporary Fr. Jake Mysteries, *The Ghosts of Glorieta* and *One for the Money, Two for the Sluice*, are set in Michigan and New Mexico. *Alberix the Celt* is the retelling in two volumes of Julius Caesar's conquest of Gaul, but from the viewpoint of a Celtic youth caught up in the Romanization of the country now called France.